A DOUBLE-BARREL BLAST
OF WESTERN ACTION BY NELSON NYE—
TWO-TIME WINNER OF
THE GOLDEN SPUR AWARD!
A $7.98 VALUE FOR ONLY $4.99!

PISTOLS FOR HIRE

"The Kid said to tell you next time he's going to feed your guts to the buzzards."

Now everyone in the room was waiting for Evan's reaction. What he did surprised nearly all of us. He threw back his head and gave out with an ugly laugh.

"So that little bunch quitter is saying he'll get me, is he? All right, we'll see. We'll see who feeds the buzzards."

"He won't fight fair," warned Old Man Pierce.

Evans didn't answer, but his mouth showed tight, and there was a blue-steel gleam to his eyes....

TOUGH COMPANY

The gun went off, gouting flame past Walt's face, hammering the night with its tumultuous thunder; and then Walt was over him, pinning the man's middle with the weight of his body while muzzle light cut its streaks of yellow and purple against the black shapes of the shaggy pines. The man writhed like a snake, snarling curses and panting, as lead from those rifles beat against the shack wall, but Bender wouldn't let go. He rode the man's struggles as he'd ride a bad bronc, piling pressure as he forced that arm upward behind the man's twisted head until he heard bone grate....

D0731580

NELSON NYE

PISTOLS FOR HIRE/ TOUGH COMPANY

LEISURE BOOKS **NEW YORK CITY**

For
John L. Sinclair—
the Omar Khayyam of Lincoln

A LEISURE BOOK®

January 1996

Published by special arrangement with Golden West Literary Agency.

Dorchester Publishing Co., Inc.
276 Fifth Avenue
New York, NY 10001

PISTOLS FOR HIRE Copyright © 1941 by Nelson Nye

TOUGH COMPANY Copyright © 1952 by Nelson Nye

The name "Leisure Books" and the stylized "L" with design are trademarks of Dorchester Publishing Co., Inc.

Printed in the United States of America.

PISTOLS FOR HIRE

Although this is a story of the Lincoln County range war, it is purely fiction and is not intended to represent either the sequence of events or the exact history of those events, as the public has come to know them. Concerning such historical characters as must of necessity intrude upon this yarn, some endeavor has been made to reveal them as history actually has portrayed them, and no intentional liberties have been taken in this regard.

Nelson C. Nye

Lincoln,
New Mexico
1941

WARRANT FOR JESSE EVANS

SURE, I said, I would just as lief shoot Billy the Kid as any the rest of that polecat crowd that was stringing its bets with McSween.

It was one of them things you let slip on the spur of the moment. Likely, I wasn't the first who had said things that way after sampling the Major's rotgut. But I hadn't meant it—really.

The gaming room of the Murphy-Dolan store went utterly still. It was a hush undisturbed by even the slap of a pasteboard, yet the turning of men's heads caused a definite feeling. It made my guts turn cold and crawl. I guessed every eye was on me.

I was right.

There was a pleased, kind of pussycat look far back in the Major's stare. Interest brightened up the faces of his partners. Major Murphy chuckled. "Hear that, Johnny? Here's one buck ain't afraid of him."

John H. Riley aired his famous smile, and Jimmy Dolan, leaning forward, grabbed my hand and pumped it like I was leaving him my will. "Mister Farsom," he said, "I'm powerful glad to know you. If I'd half your nerve—"

I didn't want his compliments nor the attention they would bring me. I didn't want to be known as any gun-slapping bravo, either. Fact is, I wasn't brave. I was just a brash young fool who had shot off his jaw once too frequent.

"The guy you want to do business with," I scowled, "is Jesse Evans."

3

Riley's smile went a little tight, and the Major's brows started climbing up his forehead. "Don't believe I know the man— In the cattle business, is he? What grade of stuff's he peddling?"

That was funny. But I didn't do any laughing. Jesse Evans was one of those bucks who had cleared out of Texas a quarter-jump front of the Rangers. If he was peddling any cattle somebody else had raised them.

I let it ride. I'd gassed enough already; all the words in Webster's Dictionary couldn't talk me out of this thing now. There were seventeen men in the room, three of them officers from the Fort who would be only too happy to see that the word got around.

I scowled down into my glass and thought what it might be like to face that hell-bending Kid across pistols. It was no salubrious prospect; but I'd stuck my horns out now. I had made the brag public property, and it would soon be a damned sight more so.

I asked Major Murphy what he wanted. "Who—*me?*" He looked surprised. "Why, not a thing, Flick. Here, have another drink—"

I shoved the bottle away. I said, "Thought mebbe you was wantin' me to gun Alexander McSween."

The place had been still before, but it got a whole heap stiller.

Major Murphy, looking thoughtful-like, considered me a moment. And suddenly he laughed; rollicking, infectious laughter that made you want to laugh with him. He said with the mirth still shaking his voice: "Shoot old Alex— Listen at him, John! Why, hell's fire, if it wasn't for Alex McSween we'd have nothing to do in this pocket—no reason for living, eh, Jimmy? You heard about our big sale, didn't you? He like to bust a gut! Hauled twelve wagonloads of 'taters clear from the railhead to undersell us, an' I gave 'em away with every purchase!"

When their elegant laughter had cooled I said, "I was thinkin' about insurance . . . insurance an' that will—"

"God *damn* it, sir!"

I thought for a second the Major would strike me, but he kept his hands on the table. "Why, in God's name," he snarled, "won't people learn to let sleeping dogs alone? It's the loose talk rampin' round that's causing half the trouble! Look here, Farsom!" The Major leaned abruptly forward. "Alex McSween was hired to collect Emil Fritz's insurance money by Emil's brother and sister—by Charlie and Mrs. Scholland. I hadn't any part in it. If Alex got the money and kept it for himself— Well, it's none of my business and I can't see it's any of yours."

"It's none of mine," I said grimly. "But close as you've been to Charlie, an' Emil bein' a pardner of yours—"

"Yes?" said Murphy coldly.

"Well . . . I sort of figured—"

"You weren't asked to figure. Dammit!" he swore angrily. "Fritz and I wound up our connection before ever he went to Germany! I offered his share to Charlie, but Charlie didn't want it. In fact," Murphy added scowling, "he gave me to understand he could run his affairs without my help—"

"Sure," I said; "but things is different now—"

"Yeah," Riley murmured dryly. "The Fritz family and us is no longer feedin' off the same plate."

"In that case—"

"Just a minute." Murphy stared at me oddly. "They tell me you've quit Chisum . . ."

"They're a little premature," I said. "I told Chisum that I *would* quit him if he didn't catch up my pay check."

"And he did, eh?"

"He ain't yet."

The Major's chair squeaked back. "There ought to be something done about him. The old devil never pays for *any*thing— nor won't, long as he can keep hiring fellows like you to scare the collectors away."

"Oh, he'll pay right enough. There's a law in this land—"

Murphy gave me a slanchways look and snorted. "Come along," he said. "I want to talk to you."

I trailed him into the storeroom, where he nodded to the loungers, paused to slap one fellow on the back, and get off some barber-shop joke that left the bunch of them grinning. He had a way, all right.

We went up the stairs to the second floor, turned left, and went into a room he'd fixed up for an office. He locked the door with a thoughtful scowl, and put his back to the fireplace. He dragged a newspaper from his pocket. "Seen this?" He gave me a sharp look.

What he meant was right there, plastered on the rag's first page. I said, "I been hearin' plenty about it—"

"Read it!"

Headed *Lincoln County Affairs—A Full and Reliable Statement,* it purported to give the real McCoy on a number of much-argued subjects. Last summer Jesse Evans, Frank Baker, and others, it said, had lifted some mules and horses belonging to Brewer, McSween & Tunstall. Sheriff Brady had collected a posse, and after a brief exchange of shots had captured the loose-moraled gentry, near Seven Rivers on the Pecos, and had locked them in the Lincoln jail. Brewer and Tunstall, friends of McSween, had visited the prisoners frequently, and during said visits, the article claimed, had arranged to break them out on Baker's promise to return the stolen stock. A subsequent jail break had been carried through without a hitch.

Coming now, when feeling in the county was at fever pitch, this smart-alec article bade fair to start feud lead a-whining. But disclosure of this horse and jailbreak deal was mild as mothers' milk compared with the revelations that followed. The article said:

Dick Brewer, to avoid payment of a debt due L. G. Murphy & Co. [this was the closed-out Emil Fritz-Major Murphy combine], had placed all his property in the hands of Alexander McSween. McSween, as attorney for Charles Fritz, had gone to New York and collected ten thousand dollars, the amount of the policy on the life of Emil Fritz. McSween at first denied collecting the ten thousand dollars, and used it twelve months before Charles Fritz ob-

tained evidence sufficient to satisfy the probate judge to order Mc-
Sween to turn over the money to the administrators of Emil Fritz,
deceased. McSween, in open court, told the probate judge that he
had the money in his pocket and to get it, if he could, and, instead
of obeying the order of the probate judge, McSween made over all
his property, including that of Dick Brewer, to Tunstall. McSween
then started to the States, but was arrested at Las Vegas, and
brought back and placed under bond. Charles Fritz sued out an
attachment against the property of Alexander McSween. Tunstall
had this property in his possession on the Rio Felice. Tunstall and
McSween had armed and equipped a band of as mean men as they
could find, and informed every person that the sheriff could not
attach the property. They cut portholes in Tunstall's house; and
fortified it with sandbags.

When Deputy Sheriff Mathews and posse arrived at the Felice
ranch, Tunstall and party had been gone about two hours and a
half. Some of McSween's men had brought the word to Tunstall
that the sheriff was coming, and had the Pecos cowboys with him.
Brewer remarked, "If the Pecos cowboys are with the sheriff I am
not going to fight."

Jimmy Dolan and others of the sheriff's posse stopped at the
Felice with the cattle; the rest went in pursuit of Tunstall and
party to attach the horses. It was thirty miles from the Felice ranch
to where the posse caught up with Tunstall's crowd. A running fight
took place. How and by whom Tunstall was killed only the courts
can decide. If he was killed by thieves and murderers and escaped
convicts, as Brewer and party say, those thieves, murderers and
escaped convicts were turned loose upon the country by Brewer,
with the knowledge and consent of Tunstall and McSween.

There was more of the same, but that was aplenty. The anon-
ymous writer claimed himself willing to come forward with his
evidence any time the guilty parties were brought before a court.
But I could see right then this wasn't going to be any matter for
constituted law to do any passing on. Gun law loomed in the
offing, and there was something dark on the moon.

I eyed the Major curiously. McSween and Tunstall, with their
price-cutting mercantile business and their loan-and-foreclosure
bank, had knocked some pretty bad holes in the Murphy-Dolan
setup. Murphy was no saint, nor were his partners, Dolan and
Riley. Few men *were*, in the Lincoln of that day, though some
were trying to look like saints, and Tunstall, by the reported
manner of his killing, had gotten a halo gratis.

Murphy was a sharp and none too scrupulous trader, which was probably why Emil Fritz had finally quit him; he was a mighty cool article, but Alex McSween could give him cards and spades. A lot had been made of Tunstall's death, and nasty suggestions had been rumored concerning the manner of it; these had the effect of winning to McSween's side quite a number of men who had no use for Alex personally. Dick Brewer and his bunch of Texas owl hooters were making it mighty hard for Murphy-Dolan to fill its Government contracts; even Chisum, who had more cattle than he could keep tally of, was gobbling Murphy's beef. On top of these troubles a lot of the two-bit ranchers the Major had been counting on to help him get his quota had been scared off by the Kid, as young Bill Bonney was coming to be called. McSween's blight was on the land, and all who had reason to fear it were looking to Murphy for protection. The writing was on the wall, and those who weren't set to hum psalms with Alex had better start sprouting them wings. He was out to control the country, and it sure looked like he would do it.

But it looked to me like this article would be a big feather in Murphy's hat. I wondered why he scowled so. There was no satisfaction in his look, and when he spoke it was in a pretty sour tone of voice. "Do you believe that stuff?" he asked.

"Sure," I nodded. "Some parts of it I can swear to."

But he only shook his head. "It'll never come to court. If it does, this fellow won't show up—be signing his death warrant if he did. Brewer's gun-slicks would drop him quick as he opened his mouth. Flick—" he eyed me grimly. "Murphy-Dolan's got its back to the wall."

"That's tough," I said.

"By God, boy, I'm tellin' you serious! We'll fight because it ain't in us to take a beating lying down, but—"

"Put your cards on the table, an' quit beatin' round the bush!"

He almost grinned; but when he spoke his tone was solemn enough—sincere, too. "Flick, I need a gun fighter. McSween's got so many tough monkeys on his string my boys won't go out on the range—"

"Don't come to me!" I said. "What I was spoutin' about Bonney don't mean a goddam thing. I was just talkin' to hear my head rattle. Besides, you let on downstairs like you an' McSween was the greatest friends since Damon an' Pythias—"

"That was for those army knobs—"

"O.K. But I'm punchin' cattle for Ol' Man Chisum."

"And getting rich at it, eh? Salting away a fortune, are you?"

"I may not be gettin' rich," I said, "but I'm keeping my light above ground!"

He considered me awhile. You could see he was turning something over in his mind. He said softly, sort of reflectively: "You've got the rep of being a pretty cool cucumber—but we'll pass all that. You don't need to mix in this, but there's one favor you could do me; and I never forget a friend, Flick."

"Yeah?"

"You know this Billy the Kid guy—Bonney; and you know Jesse Evans. That's right, isn't it?"

I looked it over, but I couldn't see no traps. So I said: "Sure. Used to work with them. We all worked for Chisum last year— What about it?"

"Well, I'll tell you. What with Brewer, the Kid, Ike Stockton, Bowdre, an' a bunch of other guys all roughing the range for McSween, it's gettin' so I can't round up any cattle. I've got to get some hard eggs on my own string or get plumb out of the business. No two ways about it; you got to fight fire with fire. I want you to hunt up Evans, an' see will he work for me. It'll be worth his while to side with Murphy-Dolan; and I'll find jobs for any of his friends that want to string along."

I wasn't surprised, as I might have been. I knew Murphy never aimed to let McSween put the skids under him. But if he signed up Evans, Baker and company there'd be fireworks in a hurry—and plenty of it coming my way for playing go-between.

Murphy urged, "You can write your own ticket if you get Evans and his crowd to tie up with us."

I expect I know opportunity's knock about as well as the next guy; but what the hell good's the king's horses if you don't have no chance to get on them? I said: "No, thanks. You better hunt you up some other bird for that chore."

The Major's brows went up. "If you're scared—"

"You're goddam right I'm scared! I ain't hankerin' to do my reclinin' in no coffin!"

He gave me a hard look. Then a grin licked across his mouth that stopped me right in my tracks. "It ain't generally known," he said, "but it happens, Flick, you were in that posse—and I can prove it. You better think this over."

I knew what posse he was talking about. He didn't need to say another word. When they shoveled the dirt over Tunstall, Bill Bonney had snarled: "I'll get every son of a bitch who helped kill John if it's the last damn thing I do!"

All that ornery Kid would need would be the whisper of my name.

I took a long breath. "What if Evans ain't interested?"

"He will be—be pretty near interested as you are. Tell him McSween has got hold of Whisky-Keg Wilson, and bribed him into signing a bunch of fake warrants. Tell him Brewer's been appointed special deputy to serve them, and is larruping around the country with Billy the Kid, that Bowdre fellow, and a lot of other hard monkeys hunting any guy they can catch that was in Billy Mathews' posse!"

2

A BRUSH WITH BREWER

I HAD a pretty good idea where Evans, Baker and company had been doing their holing up. They had been lifting steers and horseflesh from Murphy-Dolan, McSween, and Chisum whenever handy, and without showing a deal of preference unless it were for Old John's Long Rail stuff. But Chisum could stand it; he claimed as his personal stamping ground more than fifty miles up and down the Pecos River, north of Seven Rivers, and had this country stocked with over sixty thousand cattle. He seldom could say how many steers he did own, but most of his stuff had come out of Texas one way or another, and had been gathered in by us boys on his famous "powers of attorney." He never worried much about the stuff other outfits stole from him. "They can't keep up with me," he used to say, "I steal a whole herd at once!" And that was no lie; two or three years ago, being short on his contract with Good night, he'd sent the outfit into Texas to make up what he was missing. "Never mind whose they are," he told us. "Grab up the first eleven hundred you can get your ropes on."

Jesse Evans had been his foreman then, and there were fifty warriors on his pay roll. We got the cattle; if a man wasn't tough Chisum had no use for him. Evans was plenty cultus, but he sure knew cattle, and four years at Washington & Lee had given him a way that was considerably blander than peach fuzz. He had more damn guts than you could hang on a fence post, and when he quit Chisum last year, Bonney, Baker, and eight of the other top hands quit with him. For a while these had hung and rattled in the Sacramentos, but that rendezvous had been getting a little public since the episode with Brewer. I had a notion that they'd come in closer to Lincoln—they were boys who liked amusement—and I kind of expected I might

11

find them up around Pajarito Peak, Pajarito being on the Reservation, and sort of handy for quick trades. Beef was just beef to the Apaches; they never asked where it came from.

It was getting along toward the shank of the afternoon when my roan stepped out of the hot sun's smash into the shadow of the Peak. We hadn't gone another half-mile when a blue whistler sang down from the rimrock. That shot had a meaning plain as a fellow's shirttail on a stick, and I whoaed pronto. I yanked my neckerchief off and waved it. Fixing myself more comfortable in the saddle, I got out the makings and rolled me up a smoke. Durham's memory wasn't half gone when three fellows rode out of the brush.

I said: "Hello, Jess. How's the cattle business goin'?"

He grinned, and pulled in his horse. Baker and Jim Mc-Daniels were with him. They said howdy, and Evans asked, "What's new in Lincoln, Farsom?"

I told him "Plenty! McSween has bribed that tequila-barrel, Wilson, to slap his John Henry on a bunch of hot warrants, and Dick Brewer's been appointed special constable to serve 'em. Them papers is labeled 'Murder,' an' Brewer's crowd is huntin' all the boys that rode in Mathews' posse." I said, "Will that do you for a starter?"

Evans turned the air blue, and Baker whacked it up some on his own hook. McDaniels scowled. "You figurin' to load us, Flick?"

"Load hell!" I said. "All you got to do is wait if you reckon I been ridin' all these miles to fun you. Brewer's gang's in the hills right now, an' the Kid an' Middleton's with 'em. So's that pot-shootin' greaser, Herrera."

"By Gawd," Frank Baker said, "that's shovin' things pretty far."

I grinned at him. "McSween wants to get this over quick, before the country gets wind of what he's up to."

Evans nodded thoughtfully. "He knows damn well he could never make that stick. Why, my boys are aces high at the county seat— If it wasn't for us, half these two-bit ranchers would have been sold down the river long ago." He scowled at Baker. "You see what he's up to?"

"Sure." Baker ran a hand around the moist inside of his collar. "He's told Brewer to rub us out— He's scared we'll cut in on his takings."

McDaniel slapped a fly off his horse's rump. "That little bastard, Bonney, wouldn't like nothin' better'n to see us under the grass roots."

I said, "He's carvin' notches now."

"Does Brewer know where we are?" Evans asked. "You think he's aimin' to find us?"

"Well," I said, "you did a couple of favors for Murphy once. McSween aims to plow Murphy-Dolan under; don't look like he'd be passin' up Murphy-Dolan's friends."

"By Gawd, that's right!" Frank Baker scowled. "I think we better swing with Murphy-Dolan. Our lives won't be worth a plugged nickel if McSween comes out on top. Did you know," he said to me, "your boss got away with six hundred head of Murphy's cattle last night?"

I shook my head. But it didn't surprise me. Before Chisum had cleared out of Texas he had talked a bunch of his feeble-minded neighbors into giving him powers of attorney. These let him cut herds any place, cloaking his steals with legality, and he lifted every Texas steer he could find. According to agreement, he was to get half of all cattle thus recovered. A slick stunt on his part, it had, with his policy of rousting settlers and of grabbing land and water rights, built him to such proportions that he was becoming known as the "Cattle King of America." No Texas cattleman had ever received so much as the tail off a one of these critters, and whenever any of them wrote him about it he passed the letters on to his men, and every one had a good laugh.

In the course of business, Murphy-Dolan had had occasion to take in a good many steers packing Texas brands, and it was these, I guessed, that Chisum had lifted. You could go to law about it if you wanted—and plenty of people had—but Chisum still had the cattle. His tough crew turned back all comers and, when things got too hot, Honest John took a vacation.

Evans was eying me thoughtfully. "Do you think Murphy would make a place for us?"

I said: "If you quit high-gradin' his herds he might. You boys would have to turn over a new leaf, though. Dolan won't stand for any monkey business."

Evans was pale, as compared to most men in this country; he had a skin that defied New Mexico's fiery suns. He had the appearance of a gentleman and, when he chose, could show a gentleman's graces. He was gray-eyed, intelligent, amiable. He was the only man I had ever met who could make John Chisum "take water." As he looked at me now he showed a kind of hurt expression; but I could see his keen eyes twinkling. "Don't you know, Flick," he said, "that I turned over a new leaf when I quit working for the Fence Rail? It's true—so help me! I put all those ornery tricks John Chisum taught me clear out of mind. To put it frankly, the only reason us boys have been hanging out up here in the mountains is because there are people down in Lincoln that would hate poison-bad to see a man cut loose of his past. Shucks! You don't think a fine upstanding man like Billy Mathews would have sworn us in on that posse if he hadn't believed we were reformed characters, do you?"

"If our good intentions, an' the wish to do things law-an'-order fashion hadn't shoved us in that posse," Baker grumbled, "McSween's assassins wouldn't be houndin' us."

I kept my mouth shut. The best course, I figured, was to let them argue it out. It could be that they'd talk themselves into it; but if they ever guessed Murphy-Dolan had a need for them they'd have seen the outfit in hell before ever turning a finger to help it.

"Did that lyin' Brewer," McDaniels asked, "tell you I had a hand in killin' Tunstall?"

"Brewer an' me ain't talkin'. All I know is what's round town. Wilson's signed them warrants, and Brewer's been appointed special deputy to see they're served. Like enough, McSween's behind it— Nobody else, unless you count Bonney, would give a damn what happened to that Britisher. Tunstall was askin' for what he got. I can tell you this much," I said grimly, "Brewer ain't hangin' around town any more. Nor Bowdre, McNab, nor Hendry Brown. An' yesterday Doc Scurlock, that Texas wildcat, Middleton, an' that half-breed Wayte, went larrupin' off towards the Pecos."

They thought it over, Baker kind of fiddling round with his rifle, and McDaniels looking hot and mean. Evans said: "You were with us, Flick. Can you honestly say which one of us killed Tunstall?"

"No," I said, "nor anybody else. All of us was firin'. Tunstall, too; though Brewer's claimin' he didn't have no gun. I can tell you one thing, Jess: my conscience ain't botherin' *me* none! If Tunstall an' McSween hadn't been playin' fast an' loose, Tunstall never would have got shot at in the first place. You seen the way he had his house fixed up. Would an honest man, that never had nothing to fear, go an' make a goddam fort out of his place? Another thing: There's been a lot of talk about him putting his money into that store and banking business with McSween, about him buyin' that place on the Felice, an' sendin' up to Colorado for the horses an' cattle to stock it. Any one with a lick of sense knows the money to start that store an' bank come out of the Fritz insurance policy— As for Tunstall's ranch, he never owned a foot of ground along the Felice! Charlie Fritz is the only man that's filed his ground any place in the whole damn country! You know that well as I do; an' I guess you know where Tunstall got his horses an' cattle likewise."

McDaniels grinned, and Baker snickered. Evans said, "But

that isn't stopping Dick Brewer and his bunch from slinging lead if they spot us."

"No," I told him. "Long as you run loose in these hills you're takin' a chance gettin' ambushed. Bonney has sworn he'll get every man in that posse, an' Wilson's papers will give him excuse. An' you know Dick Brewer."

Evans considered. "If we were to throw in with Murphy-Dolan what do you reckon he'd be wanting us to do?"

I didn't know. I didn't even want to know. I mentioned that Murphy-Dolan's ranch on the Rio Pecos was pretty shorthanded account of the Kid threatening to shoot any man that tried rounding up Murphy's cattle. "Like enough," I said, "Murphy'd take it as a kindness if you boys'd go out there, an' see that the work got done. He's short on his contract with the Fort and if—"

"Hell," Evans said. "We'll go out there."

I shacked up with them on the Peak that night and first thing next morning, we set out for the Pecos ranch. It was a bright clear day with the sun promising to boil its juice clear over before it got much older. But we were used to heat, and the "creature comforts" were things that hadn't been included in the itinerary of boys who had twirled their ropes for Chisum. I recall last year, when John was building his new house at South Spring. We were making ready for a drive to Dodge, and Chisum told us: "Just wait till you get back, boys. I'll have a place all furnished to suit you." When we got back he led us over to a little adobe he'd put up, and with a wink threw open the door. The place was bare as the palm of your hand, but in each corner there was a quart bottle of brand-new whisky, and in the middle of the dirt floor was a pint of gin.

There were five of us. Evans and Baker and McDaniels, Billy Morton and myself. We were all in pretty good spirits except Frank Baker; he was acting kind of daunsy, and every little while would start muttering under his breath, till at last

Evans said: "What the hell's got into you, Frank? If you don't want to work for Murphy-Dolan, say so."

"Oh, I'd just as lief work for them," Baker muttered. "Looks like it's either that or get rubbed out prowlin' round by your lonesome. But I tell you, Jess, I'd a heap rather not go out to that ranch this mornin'. I got a feelin' in my bones if I go out there I ain't never comin' back."

Evans gave him a long, hard look, and grinned. "Hell's fire," he said, "what you're needing is a change of diet. You've been playing round with those squaws too much."

We all laughed, and Baker took the ribbing in good part, but his outlook didn't take any upbound. He rode a little behind the rest of us, and didn't get into the conversation much, but kept squinting round like every draw was like to belch out a batch of redskins. And he kept his rifle across his knees.

But everything stayed quiet, and the up-slanting sun got hotter and hotter, till along about ten o'clock we were approaching the lower crossing of the Rio Penasco, some six miles short of the Pecos. That was when hell kicked the lid off.

We were riding along like we'd been all morning, Baker still lagging back of us, and the rest of us taking in a tall one Morton was telling about an Apache wench and Geronimo, when suddenly Baker yells.

He was pointing off across the bench towards where the bluffs come down for a drink. We took one look. It was an eyeful. A bunch of horsebackers over there was bulging out of a gully. Brewer and the Kid was in the lead, and every son was waving a rifle!

"Good Christ!" Morton howls. "We can't stand off no bunch like that!"

Evans was cool as a cucumber. "Don't have to," he grinned. "The Pecos ranch ain't over ten, twelve miles from here—maybe closer—Stick together; we'll make a run for it."

Right on the heels of his words, Brewer's crowd opened up with their rifles. Morton and Baker lost their heads, slammed their broncs around, and went larruping off towards the hills. Evans swore. Then him, McDaniels, and myself dug in our hooks, and fogged for the river. We crossed it in nothing flat, and quirted for the Pecos ranch with lead pelting round us like hailstones. "What'll we do about Baker an' Morton?" I yelled.

"They can take care of themselves," Jesse said, and led us into a draw, where all we could hear was our horses' hoofs. It led out into a dry wash, and we pushed the broncs along it for three or four miles, then Evans called a halt.

"It's getting damned hot," he said. "We better breathe these horses a little." He scowled off over the back trail. We were below the general surface of the range, and so couldn't make out much of anything, and when I suggested climbing the cut bank for a look, McDaniels snarled: "What do you want to do— Tell 'em where we are?"

Evans said, "I wish those boys had stuck together—I mean stuck with us like I asked them."

McDaniels spat. "They'll be all right. Ain't the first scrape Billy an' Frank been into. Let's get goin'—we'll see 'em at the ranch. They'll come draggin' in—you watch." He mopped his face. "Come we stick around here long enough them lobos'll be liftin' *our* hair!"

Still with that thoughtful frown on his face, Evans nodded. "I suppose they'll make it all right," he said.

And McDaniels argued: "Ain't nothin' we could do about it anyways. There's too many guys with Brewer."

We rode on. But nobody did much talking. I guess we were all kind of busy with our thoughts.

When we reached the Pecos I said, "Here's where I leave you, boys. Be seein' you at the ranch in a couple days. I—"

"Where you fixin' to go?" growled McDaniels suspiciously.

But Evans grinned. "He's got to say good-by to Sally."

I said, "You go to hell!" and left them.

3

AS PER USUAL

IT WAS midafternoon and hot as hell's backlog when I swung down before the cluttered shack John Chisum used for an office. He was there and, as luck would have it, alone. He sat humped over his battered desk, putting figures in a tally book. Some guys I have worked for would have raised plenty sand if a hand came back who had crawled the fence for a two-and-a-half-days' leave; but not Old John. He had the hardest outfit in the Territory, yet never packed a gun. To rule men of the caliber of the Kid and Jesse Evans a man had to be a diplomat, and Chisum was a master hand. I couldn't recall but once that I had ever seen him mad or scared; that had been when Evans left him, and even then he'd rounded things off with a laugh. There was a frosty twinkle in his eyes as he stared up at me.

"So you're back, eh?" he said gruffly. "Wasn't the grub there up to your likin'?" He snorted then and, turning back to his figures, said: "Ride over toward Horsehead Crossing. Boys are roundin' up calves, and I want a man over there that's got a little savvy—"

"Glad you've woke up to my possibilities," I said, "but the truth is, Mr. Chisum, I've rode in to ask for my time."

"Your time, eh?" He rasped a hand across his chin. "Well— You ain't worth it, but I'll give you ten dollars more on the month. I'm a little short-handed right now an'—"

"Forty dollars," I said, "ain't no better'n thirty if a fella can't never get his hands on it."

He looked me over from head to foot. "What would you do with all that money, if I give it to you? Blow it away, like the rest, on women an' likker! Tell you what I'll do: I'll put it into cattle for you, an' when you get to be old as me you'll have somethin' to fall back on."

"Thanks kindly, but I might not live that long. I'll take my money now."

"Well, it might be best at that. I understand the Kid's kind of looking round for you . . . I wouldn't want no ructions. But look— You'll have to see me Thursday, Flick. I ain't got my checkbook handy—"

"You better get it handy."

Chisum grinned. "You know I never pack a gun. Besides, I'm old enough to be your father. You wouldn't shoot an old man like me."

"No, by God, I wouldn't," I said, "but somebody ought to do it! You can take my money and stick it up your adenoids—but don't never call on me for anything again!"

"You don't mean that, Flick. You're all excited. All lathered up—"

"You'll be some lathered up yourself," I said, "when Murphy finds out about that six hundred head you stole off him! There's a limit to what this country'll stand for, Chisum, an' I reckon you've about reached it!"

He made me so goddam mad I could have chewed myself. If I was tough as Jesse Evans, mebbe, I might have collected what he owed me. But Jesse was in a class by himself, and nobody yet ever found out how he done it. For dishing out chicanery, Chisum made McSween and Murphy look like a couple of warts. "Some day," I thought, "the old bastard'll be getting what he's askin' for."

He did—but that has no place in this story.

I was climbing into the saddle, still muttering to myself, when a yonder flash of color stopped me. It came from the house veranda, and nobody had to spell me out the cause. It was Sally— I could tell by the way my ticker started thumping. She was beckoning.

I sent the blue roan over.

She held a hand out to me, smiling. I shook it carefully. "Where you been keeping yourself?"

"Oh, I been around," I said. "Spring work, you know, ma'am, keeps a fella sort of humpin'—"

"Ma'am? What do you mean by ma'aming me, Flick Farsom?"

I felt my ears getting hot. "Sally . . ." I said uncomfortably.

"That's better. Where you off to now?"

I scowled around, and kind of twirled my hat a little. She sure put me up against it. She wasn't John's daughter, but she sure thought a heap of the old reprobate—never would listen to a word against him. I hated to tell her I was quitting.

She seemed to guess it. "You're not quitting Uncle John?" The way she said it was an accusation. "Now? With all this trouble in the air? Flick—you can't really mean it?"

" 'Fraid I do."

"But you *can't!* Flick— Look at me! You're funning me, aren't you?"

I snuck a quick squint in her direction. She sure looked mighty fetching, with her face all sober, and her back against the post that way. Made me halfway start to reconsider— I might of done it, too. Only just then I thought of how dear Uncle John had used me, and how that notch-cutting Kid was out to carve my gullet—or would be, quick as ever he found out I'd been connected with that posse.

I told her: "Shucks! Reckon you know I'd do most anything to please you. Some things, though, a fella just can't do. I have to go by the cards, ma'—Sally. An' anyways," I said, scowling, "I can't go on workin' forever for a guy that won't pay off."

Like a flash she caught me up. "Flick Farsom! That's not so! You know very well Uncle John intends to pay you. It's only that he's kind of funny about things like that. You have to be a little patient—"

"I been eighteen months patient now."

But she affected not to hear me. She said, with one of those quick, bright smiles: "They're having a dance over at Hondo Saturday night— You're taking me, aren't you?"

"I . . . er. . . . Well, I—" Looking down into them sparkly eyes of hers that way I floundered like a bogged-down steer.

She didn't seem to notice. "That's fine," she said. "So, of course, you'll go on working for Uncle John till after that. By the way, Flick, which do you like best—sweet-potato pie or mincemeat?"

What the hell could I say? Girls like Sally didn't blow in with every tumbleweed. Young and sweet she was, and pretty as a speckled pup under a red wagon. Just looking at her was enough to make the Heavenly Host cut loose of their halos. "I reckon I can stay that long," I said, "but I ain't stayin' any longer. There's things I got to do, girl, an' gettin' away from this here spread is one of 'em."

4

APPEARANCE OF A POSSE

I should of gone right then. I never had any extra bells in my steeple, and those I did have quit their chatter every time I got around Sally. But knowing like I did what was in the wind I should have took off for the timber—girl or no durn girl!

But, of course, I didn't.

I hung and rattled on the Fence Rail. I went out and bossed the calf round-up, and Chisum grinned every time he saw me. I could of pushed his face in if it hadn't been for his whiskers. The cook was laid up with a sprained back end, and Sally was rolling the dough; so I got to see considerable of her, but didn't often get her alone. When I did she talked of the Kid, or Jesse Evans, or some other baboon-faced young polecat, and plain wouldn't listen to any of the fancy jaw-shoving I'd been practicing up to tickle her.

Sometimes I get to thinking I don't know women at all.

We was back at South Spring one night, where Sally had gone after some fool thing or other, when a party of riders came loping in. It was going on ten and dark as a stovepipe, but we could see there was quite a bunch of them. I made out something then that started my hair to crawling: One of those guys was that damn Bill Bonney, and two of the others was prisoners.

I felt Sally's grip on my arm. "Pull in," she said. "Keep your mouth shut, Flick. I'll do the talking—you keep out of it."

I didn't have much chance to argue. There was a lamp lit in the cook shack (Sally'd been over to see how Cookie was making out), and before I could speak the Kid and Dick Brewer came stamping up into the light.

"Howdy, boys," Sally said, and Brewer pulled off his hat. "Have you eaten?"

"No," he said, "but we'd just as lief."

"I'll rustle up something right away. Not looking for Uncle John, are you?"

"Not special. We was figurin' to hole up for the night." Brewer stuck out his chest. "This here's my posse, Sally. I'm special deputy now. We're takin' a couple pris'ners in to Lincoln." He looked at me. "Two of them hired guns that murdered Tunstall."

I could feel my belly muscles tightening. "Tunstall wasn't murdered," I said. "He was shot while resisting duly authorized officers of the law. Don't twist things round like that."

He said, "You're the one that's twisting things."

But I didn't pay much attention. I was wondering if Bonney'd hooked me up with them yet. I said to him, "How are you, Kid?"

"So you're the son of a bitch," he said, "that would just as lief gun me, are you? Why don't you try it on?"

Sally said desperately: "Come along, Flick. I need some help."

The Kid sneered. "I guess that was a joke." When I didn't say anything he growled: "If you ever drop another that hits the ground that close to me I'm goin' to crack your crust. Hear me?"

I said: "Don't parade your toughness, Bonney. You ain't scaring any one with a bone in his spinal column—not while they're looking at you, anyway."

He regarded me with a surly stare. Sally called again: "Come on, Flick. I'll need some help with this."

"You go ahead," I said, keeping my eyes on Bonney. "I'll be along in a minute."

Brewer said, "I'll help you, Sally," and was fixing to go after her when I shoved in front of him.

"I expect we can make out to manage, Brewer. You better stick with your prisoners."

The rest of his crowd came drifting up then. He said, "I guess we can spend the night here—"

"Sure. Spread your blankets in the bullpen."

He turned away. "Put a little bear sign on my saucer," he called after Sally.

I got a look at the prisoners then. They were Billy Morton and Frank Baker. I said, "What the hell have you boys done?"

"They claim we helped kill Tunstall—"

"What of it? Tunstall was outside the law when he got killed. Besides, the whole damn crowd was shooting— Why pick on you? If it comes to that, Tunstall was shoving plenty lead himself—"

"That's a lie!" snarled Brewer. "He never had no gun!"

"No gun?" I said. "What are you tryin' to pull off here? He had that—"

"What do *you* know about it?" Bonney barked.

I didn't even look at him. I said: "Don't you worry, Frank. When this comes up for trial we'll damn well see whether he had a gun or not—"

"Mebbe it won't get to trial," Bonney muttered.

Looked like I wasn't helping things much. I let it drop.

Morton said: "Mind ridin' in to Roswell tomorrow, Flick? I got a letter I wish you'd post."

"We're goin' through Roswell," Brewer scowled. "You can post the letter yourself."

"Got a new girl, have you, Billy?"

"It ain't to no girl," Morton told me. "I'm writin' my cousin at Richmond, case anything happens to me 'fore we get to Lincoln."

"You ain't figurin' on nothing happenin', are you?" I said with a hard look at the Kid.

"No. Brewer has guaranteed to deliver us safe to the sheriff at Lincoln. But you can't never tell. If he goes back on his word I'd like for my cousin to be informed."

McClosky, one of Brewer's men, said, "If anything happens to you, Morton, it'll be over my dead body."

I saw the Kid scowl at him venomously, but I didn't pay much attention. The Kid was used to scowling. He scowled at pretty near everything that didn't suit him. Not that he wasn't dangerous. He was—plenty! But he liked backs best for his targets. Long as you kept him in sight you were fairly safe. And I was damned well sure he wasn't going to get behind *my* back.

I went off to hunt up Sally.

5

WHAT A MAN HAS TO DO

Two days later I had occasion to go to Roswell. Among other things, Sally wanted me to get some yard goods, of which she had a sample. She was going to make a new dress for the

Saturday night dance at Hondo. I was glad to make the trip. Hanging around the Fence Rail, after having made up my mind to quit it, had not been putting any weight on me, and I'd been jumpy ever since the departure of Brewer's posse, if one cared to dignify such a collection of rowdies by that name.

It was midmorning when my blue roan's hoofs struck dust from the town's main street. Roswell was a bustling place where most folks had enough to do without worrying overmuch about the private concerns of their neighbors. But on this morning I found things a little different. The dust of a passing stage hung heavy on the air. The false fronts of the sand-scoured buildings held the same, remembered look—yet there was a difference.

The entire population, it seemed to me, had taken to standing out-of-doors. In the shade of wooden awnings the east walk was cluttered with men. A lot of them were talking, sailing quips at one another, gesticulating, laughing. Quite a few of them were grinning across the dust to where, in the sun's bright light, still other men were standing. These latter showed a lesser number, and mostly they were moveless, somber-eyed and silent, though a few of them were muttering. This was Chisum's town, and these were men who took little profit from his Fence Rail, and so were able to view things somewhat clearer than the grinners across the street.

Looping my reins about a snorting post, I went into the store where we did business, and gave my orders. Coming out, I nodded to several of the loungers, headed a couple of Fence-Rail hands back onto the road for home, and plowed through the hock-deep dust to where Ed Galton, a fellow I'd often played cards with, was propping up a porch post. "Ed," I said, "who's dead?"

His thin lips quirked expressively. He said: "I got my money on Frank Baker. But I reckon you wouldn't be takin' much risk was you to put two-bits on Billy Morton."

"Are you loadin' me?"

He didn't grin. He didn't answer, either.

I said, "Where'd you get that hunch?" I expect I spoke much sharper than a man with good sense would have. Some of that bunch across the way quit grinning; several muttered among themselves.

Galton said: "Martin Chavez of Picacho dropped by here yesterday evenin'. He allowed Brewer's party quit the Lincoln road, an' headed off towards Agua Negra after leavin' South Spring yesterday."

I stared at him. You could get to Lincoln by the Black Water trail all right, if you had a deal of time, and got a big kick out of riding. It was pretty desolate country and, mostly, people shied clear of it.

I could feel the goose bumps crawling. "Did he say how come?"

"Chavez an' me ain't speakin'. I got it from Frisco Charley—the big wart over there with the toothy map."

The bunch across the street were looking me over, some of them scowling. I guess I was doing myself no good swapping gas this way with a known partisan of Murphy-Dolan. But somehow that didn't seem to mean as much as it might have meant to me once. I was thinking of Billy Morton's letter, and of what the Kid had said the day we buried John Tunstall.

I guess a guy with sense would have cut his stick, but sense was never my strong point. And there were some things I couldn't stomach.

"We've had considerable fun together, Flick, but I reckon right here is where the road forks," Galton was saying. "If you're bent on loungin', you better do it across the street."

I gave him a look. "Don't be placin' your bets too hasty."

I went to the post office after the mail. Old Walchy gave me a fistful of stuff for Chisum's hands, two mailorder catalogues, and a big important-looking envelope addressed to Chisum from the Capital. Nobody had to tell me what that was! Murphy-Dolan, with one war on their hands already, were siccing Thomas B. Catron, United States District Attorney for the Territory, onto Chisum to recover the six hundred Murphy steers Chisum had lifted the other night. I guessed Old John would be hopping. He hated Catron like poison, account of the packing-house judgments against him that Catron also was trying to collect. When he left Texas, Chisum had figured to be shut of those Round Rock suits. He should of known them as dance got to pay the piper some day. But Old John's trouble was he never could believe he wasn't bigger than the law.

Several fellows were chewing the rag around the window, and I guess probably, being so busy thinking about Chisum's letter, I'd of gone out of there without never noticing, only suddenly, like some one had said "Boo!" at them, the whole damn bunch quit talking.

I looked up to catch them watching me.

And then I got it.

Frank McNab, one of Brewer's posse, was standing front of the window. "Howdy, McNab," Ash Upson was saying, "I thought you were in Lincoln by this time. Any news?"

"Yeah." McNab scowled. "Morton killed McClosky, one of our men, an' made a break. We had to kill them."

"You slat-faced snake," I snarled. "That's a made-up, goddam lie!"

He wheeled back against the counter, and his face got white as wood ash.

"Where'd Morton get the gun— You took his iron away from him!"

"He grabbed McClosky's, killed him with it an' ran, firin' back as he went—"

"Yeah— I can see him doin' it!"

"Well, it's true!" he snapped. But he didn't look at me, and he kept his hands well away from his sides. He was so scared he shook all over, but he stuck to his lies. "It's Gawd's own truth," he said. "We had to kill them or some of us would have been hurt. You don't have to take my word for it," he whined. "Ask Brewer—ask any of the boys."

"That bunch of border scum? I wouldn't believe that bunch on a stack of Bibles ten feet high! Nor will any one else that's got a lick of sense!"

They were staring at me, fascinated. That regard should have warned me to watch my step, and I guess it did; but I was too damn mad to give a rap. McNab had tried to wriggle in among the others, but they wouldn't have him. He was left to stand alone, pale eyes scared and body shaking, in the middle of the floor.

"A fine collection of scalawags," I said, "to serve the law! Good old Dicky Brewer—as good a two-bit cattle thief as ever run a iron—a gent carved with the same broad stripe that marks McSween an' Chisum; a great upstandin' cheater who turns all his belongin's over to some other guy to get out of payin' his debts! I wish the hell he was here, so I could tell him to his face! But he ain't much worse than the rest of you— Johnny Middleton's wanted all over Texas for bank-robbery, cattle theft, an' murder; everybody knows that halfbreed, Wayte, is a fugitive from justice. An' I guess most folks know Scurlock would sell his closest relative if he could get an ounce of profit. As for Bowdre, he'll work his gun for the highest bidder and five cents difference will buy him. I expect you all know Bonney, the little notch-cutter who was arrested last year for liftin' Cal Hunter's horses, and has sworn to *git* every mother's son that rode in Mathews' posse. Shucks, a finer bunch of deputies a guy could hardly find!"

No one felt impelled to speak—they didn't so much as bat an eyelash. Still filled with that brashness, born of anger, I walked up to McNab and cuffed him hard across the face. I said: "Come on, you cold-footed bad man! Let's hear the howl of your wolf!"

The marks of my hand stood plain against his livid cheeks. He wanted terribly to reach for his iron—you could read it in his gleaming eyes. But he hadn't enough beans in the bottle. He was scared he couldn't cut it, and he hadn't the guts to try.

I turned my back on the lot of them, and strode still mad through the door.

All the way to South Spring Ranch I tried to think what I would say to Sally. But the devil had my mind that day and all that I could focus it on was the murder of Baker and Morton. I knew it was murder, well as if I'd seen it done. It wasn't in that back-shooting crew to give a man a chance. McClosky, I was sure, had been dropped by one of his own companions— either by the Kid or by Frank McNab. And the reason wasn't far to seek. I'd heard McClosky tell Morton at Chisum's: "If anything happens to you it'll be over my dead body." It looked like he'd sure called the turn.

McNab was a Chisum hand, and would be coming back to the ranch. But not, I was pretty sure, till he was certain I had left it. And I was leaving pronto. Much as I thought of Sally, and bad as I wanted to make that dance, I'd no intention of letting either keep me longer on Chisum's spread. Events were shaping for a showdown, and Murphy-Dolan would be needing every man that could be had. But it wasn't so much for Murphy I was getting in this thing, as for the principles involved. Every guy packs some code to live by, and mine couldn't stomach what had happened to Baker and Morton. It looked like justice was bidding fair to get stomped plumb out of existence.

I'd been in this country long as most, and had seen this thing stacking up. I've heard most of the lies that have been told since, and a lot when they first was ladled. The plain truth of the business is this: After the Government had rounded up the Mescalero Apaches and put in its army post, Fort Stanton, to teach them the Golden Rule, there weren't many traders in the country—no stores at all. Emil Fritz and Major Lawrence G. Murphy saw the possibilities, left the service, and formed a partnership; a bang-up general store that carried everything

from top hats down the line to toothpicks. The Colonel seldom
came around, content to leave its management in Murphy's
hands. Some people have shook their heads at this—there's been
a lot of winking; but the Colonel was nobody's monkey on a
stick. He trusted Major Murphy because he knew him for a man
who *could* be trusted; for a man whose word, once given, would
neither be taken back nor broken.

Fritz made up his mind one day to retire. The firm was
solvent, the parting friendly. The Colonel had a little debt outstanding, but Murphy waved the matter aside. "Forget it, Emil.
If you're paying the old country a visit you'll probably be needing all your cash. Let it ride; I'll collect from your estate." They
had a good laugh at this, for Fritz looked good for a long while
yet. Soon after this Major Murphy moved to Lincoln, and
opened up a new firm with Jimmy Dolan and John H. Riley
for partners.

Alexander McSween, an asthmatic lawyer from Kansas, arrived. The event was most notable for the exceeding good-looks
of the lady he helped out of his rig, though a deal of speculation got itself afoot when it was learned this angular outlander
was to be attorney for the Murphy-Dolan Store Co. There was a
jump-or-be-damned kind of look in his eye, but he did all right
for himself, and for the company, until one, John H. Tunstall,
an English adventurer, sloshed onto the scene with his bulldog
pipe and funny pants in 1877. Brash as a brace of March hares,
he was, just the same, a handsome buck who could throw words
around with the best of them. He got along famous with Alex—
even better with Alex's wife who, by this time no doubt, knew
her Bible from cover to cover, and had sung all the nap off the
hymns.

But sanctimonious as Alex was, he had a mighty sharp eye
for the main chance; as was proved when Colonel Fritz died,
and he was asked to collect the leavings. By Emil Fritz's will, the
administrators were his brother Charlie, and his sister Emelia—
who had ought to've been bored for the simples. They hired

Alex McSween to take a trip East, and collect the insurance benefits. Alex did, but forgot to hand them over. He deposited them in a St. Louis bank, and used the account as the basis of a mercantile and banking business he opened with Tunstall and Chisum, and with which same he began a systematic campaign, directed at bankrupting the Murphy-Dolan Store Co.

Meantime, Dick Brewer, a fellow no more reliable than a woman's watch, had, by foolish spending and a lust for appearing important, become indebted to Murphy-Dolan. Thinking to pull a fast one, he turned all his property over to McSween. McSween, threatened by the Fritz interests for embezzlement of their brother's insurance money, in turn deeded all *his* property—and Brewer's as well, except for the much-mentioned house and lot he gave to the wife of Shields—over to partner John H. Tunstall, who had acquired a ranch of sorts on the Rio Felice. Aiming to let things cool a bit, McSween packed his grip for greener pastures, but was arrested at Las Vegas, and brought back and placed under bond.

Charlie Fritz, a little warm under the collar, sued out an attachment against the property of McSween; but everything Alex owned of value was with Tunstall on the Felice. Backed by McSween and a bunch of hired guns, he announced his intention of never giving up a nickel's worth. It was this brash stand on Tunstall's part that finally caused his death. Fortifying his buildings, he filled them with tough monkeys, and defied all and sundry to start something. When it came to the showdown though, his brass kind of petered out; he got cold feet and run for it. He was still on the run, with a gun in his hands, when posse lead had dropped him.

Shorn of its lies, that is Tunstall's story. You can judge for yourself who was right.

I had made up my mind what I had to do, but telling Sally wasn't easy. I said, "The dance is off."

Her eyes showed wide and stirred, grew suddenly dark and

gravely thoughtful. She moved a little back, under the porch roof's shadow. "But why, Flick—why?"

I fiddled with the reins. The sun was bending down towards supper, and the strengthening wind coming off the desert was whipping through the dampness of my hair, and playing a tune in the cottonwoods. Yet it was very still, and somehow the wind didn't cool me much. This was going to be some harder than I'd figured.

"Well," I said, "to tell you the truth—"

She nodded. "Yes, the truth is always best, Flick."

"It's this goddam war!" I blurted.

"What about it?"

"It's got me on the wrong side of the fence—I got to get back where I belong."

"What do you mean?"

"I mean I got to quit the Fence Rail. I can't go on workin' for John Chisum when everything he does—everything he stands for—goes against the grain."

"What does he do? What's he stand for that's suddenly so obnoxious to you?"

"Yeah . . . I guess it does kind of look that way. I been workin' for him three years now— But times is changin', Sally. The old ways don't fit in good now. These warriors—"

"You know Uncle John couldn't run cows in this country without—"

"He didn't hire tough rannies to run cows! He hired 'em— Hell! don't let's start quarrelin', Sally. A man's got to stick by his friends—"

"Oh!" Breath made a startled sound between her teeth. "Your friends are on the Murphy-Dolan side—is that it?"

I didn't know myself. I had friends on both sides. But I couldn't get Baker and Billy Morton out of mind. The cold-blooded murder of those two boys had got to working on me— it was like a fever in my blood. I couldn't separate my thoughts; there was no room in my head for calm or for reasoning. I told her so. I told her about Morton and Baker—about what McNab had said. I said, "I got to do something about those boys!"

"That's work for the sheriff—"

"What can he do—"

"What can *you?*"

"I don't know—but I can't stick around here brandin' calves while other boys are murdered. I—"

"You didn't get such a lather up when your fine friends murdered Tunstall!"

"Tunstall wasn't murdered! That's just another of these goddam lies! Tunstall had his chance—he was wrong from the start, but we gave it to him. I was in that posse, Sally; what they're tellin' round is lies. John Tunstall died with a gun in his hands. There was three other fellas with him; we called on them to stop, to surrender the horses. I dunno; mebbe they lost their heads. Anyways, they started firin'. They had no call to do that. The horses wasn't Tunstall's anyway; he didn't stand to lose a thing. If he hadn't been helping McSween do Murphy and the Fritz family out of—"

"Now, that's a lie! Alec McSween never stooped to a dishonest act in his life! He's an upright, God-fearing man—"

"He's a goddam hypocrite!" I snarled.

We glared at one another like a couple of fighting roosters. "The trouble with you," I said, "is you ain't never heard but one side of this business. All you hear is Chisum lies." I checked the drive of my lifting temper. "Damn it, Sally, let's not fight about this thing. You see things one way; I see 'em another. Let it go like that."

"But you're going to quit the Fence Rail?"

"I got to."

She said: "And—what about us?"

"What about *us?*"

"What about that little house we planned—the little herd of cattle—the roses you said we'd plant and—" She said almost hysterically: "Flick— Flick! You *can't!*"

I said, "I got to! Damn it, Sally, a man's got to live accordin' to his lights. I couldn't look myself in the face if I went on workin' for Chisum, feelin' like I do. You ought to see that. A man's got to have a little pride."

"But—but—"

"It's no use, Sally. I know what I got to do."

"If you quit Uncle John, you got to quit me too—"

My rope-hard fingers caught her wrist. "Listen!" I begged.

She shivered. She looked at me like I was a stranger, and her voice was flat as the prairie miles. "I mean it, Flick. If you quit Uncle John we're through."

I stared bleakly off at the sand hills, and the silence piled up like a wall between us. I wanted to say something; to tell her— But I could not speak. All I could think of was what had happened to Baker and Morton, and the sneering face of that gun-notching Kid. No words could change these things; and there was no argument in my mind that could make her see this as I saw it.

She had come closer; was leaning toward me, voice tender and softly coaxing.

She was everything I'd ever wanted; everything I'd worked for, saved for, planned for. For three years every thought I'd had of the future had been tied up with this girl. She spelled completion, and since coming to the Fence Rail I hadn't stopped to think what life could be without her. I thought about it then.

But I shook my head.

"I'm sorry you can't see this my way. But some day," I said, "all this trouble will be past and settled—it can't go on forever. When this feud has burnt itself out—when the smoke has cleared away—mebbe we can pick up the pieces an' . . ."

She was more pale than I'd ever seen her. "You've made up your mind?"

I didn't answer. What use to go through all that talk again?

Suddenly she cursed. "Go on then—do it!" There was flame in her voice, and her eyes were blazing. "Go ahead! Be a damn fool if you got to! But don't come back—don't come back here ever!"

In that brittle stillness I heard a ridden horse come into the yard. But I didn't care if it was Old Man Chisum himself. I reached, got an arm behind her head, and kissed her hard. "Mebbe I'll lose you," I growled, "but if I do there won't be no other guy get you. You're mine, by God, an' you got my brand on your lips!" And I kissed her again, like I'd leave a mark there really.

She tore herself loose and sprang back, disheveled and panting. She leveled a shaking hand at the gate. "Get out!" She said huskily: "Get—" and stopped abruptly, eyes springing wide, all her anger dissolved into fear.

I'd lived too long with Chisum's tough hands to pull a fool move like turning. I hurled myself to the left, lit on my shoulder, and rolled over twice. I came up on my knees.

I'd clean forgotten Frank McNab.

But he hadn't forgotten me. He was crouched by his horse not twenty feet off. There was a gun in his fist, and his eyes gleamed murder.

They gleamed something else when he dropped.

6

BLAZER'S MILL

THE look in Sally's eyes when Frank McNab pitched forward will stick with me forever, I guess. Like a curse it was—like her voice. "You're bad as that killing Kid!" she said, and ran away from me into the house.

I expect I never will understand the way of a woman's mind. McNab had been set to kill me and would have done it in another second. It was God's own luck I beat him; we fired together, and only a surer aim had been the means of my salvation.

Feeling sort of fed up with my luck, and with this whole damn business, I was in a mood to quit the country and rode halfway to Texas before I recollected what a long arm gossip had. "Flick Farsom?" folks would say. "You mean that fella what sold his saddle, an' cut a shuck fer the Rio?" Or maybe they'd say, "Oh—*Farsom!*" and kind of laugh a little. "Yeah, Flick used to live round here. Punched cows fer Ol' Man Chisum, an' was figured to be a up-an'-comer till it got out what he'd been packin' round fer guts was on'y fiddlestrings."

I reckoned I'd better stay. I had to live with myself, and it didn't seem like I could do it if I had to lug around such thoughts as them. I was pretty proud, I reckon. But pride was about all I *did* have, and I allowed to hang right onto it.

I did a pile of thinking in the next few days. I didn't rush about it either. I was reckoned to be right handy with a gun, and the way things looked I was going to have to prove it if I hung around the Pecos. Bad medicine was in the making, and before things got to the boiling point I allowed I'd better be making up my mind which side I was going to be for. I'd been working for the Fence Rail and, while I could put up with Chisum if I had to, I hadn't ever cottoned much to his partners in the banking business. Maybe I saw through Alex a little quicker than most. But I take no credit for it. My insight come of overhearing some chin music Chisum, McSween, and Tunstall had been putting out one day back of Alex's store.

But I wasn't too sold on Murphy, either. He was no guy to get in a trade with, and I wasn't up to his talking talents. His graft didn't bother me any— Everybody was out to do the Government; if he was counting his Indians twice, and feedin' them animated skeletons for cattle, that was *their* lookout. Old

Rutherford B. wasn't slated for any halo for his treatment of the red man, either.

One thing you had to admit: Murphy-Dolan had got here first. They'd taken the greatest risks. They'd worked up the market, talked up the country, brought a lot of settlers in, and helped plenty small guys get their start—kept Chisum off their ears. If there was any right in this feud, looked like it belonged to them. McSween and Tunstall weren't nothing but downright freebooters, no matter what's been said of them since. Murphy's sarcasm the other night on the matter of Alec's potatoes had been right to the point; only the boot was on the other foot. From the very start McSween & Tunstall had inaugurated a price-cutting policy designed to ruin their competitors. All right, that was business. I guess it was good business, too, when McSween exposed the Major's graft to the Washington investigator for the Department of Indian Affairs; and when, after John Riley had left his fireside circle one night, McSween had slipped Sam Corbett a cold-deck notebook, which Corbett pretended to pick up off the floor, saying: "Looks like Riley dropped something." Upon examination, McSween's guests discovered the notebook to contain the names of a score of known cattle thieves. Set down opposite each name was an amount of cattle, and a price computed at five bucks per head.

It was good business on McSween's part, I suppose. But it was no good way to make friends of your neighbors. Murphy, like Chisum, had never been particular where his cattle had come from, so long as he had them in time to fill Government contracts. But no one with a lick of sense could believe John Riley such a fool as to walk about with proof like that on his person. But it served McSween's ends, since at that time he was working hammer and tongs to discredit the Murphy-Dolan outfit any way he could, and was endeavoring to pile up evidence that could be used against them in court in case the Big Store crowd brought suit.

He would have been smarter to have kept on that way. But

the bulk of the country's business was still going to Murphy-Dolan, and Murphy-Dolan's teams were still raising dust on the trails. Murphy's wagons were hauling in supplies from Las Vegas, from Santa Fe, and from the far-off railhead at Trinidad; and the country's increasing population still liked to trade at his store. This was gall and wormwood to McSween, who was selling so cheap the stuff his men took from Murphy wagons. Lincoln was a hard-boiled town, and he decided that only equally hard-boiled tactics would ever insure him the lion's share of its spending.

He put a lot of talk in circulation concerning the need for a cleanup. He began quoting the Bible with a greater energy, and invited a Dr. and Mrs. Ealy to visit him, with the hint that Lincoln offered a lot of room for an up-and-coming missionary, there being "such an abundance of material," to work on. He suggested also the need for a Protestant meetinghouse. Behind this paraded virtue he got ready to speed up Murphy-Dolan's finish.

The killing of Tunstall, being without witnesses other than interested parties, offered considerable opportunity for a man of McSween's accomplishments. He made all that could be made of it. Brewer came forward to swear that Tunstall had been unarmed. The lie was circulated that one of the posse under Morton, Pantilon Gallegos, after Tunstall's death, had hammered the Britisher's head in with a stone. Both Brewer and the Kid, claiming they had seen the fight from a distance, swore to this. The Mexicans sent out that night by McSween to bring in the body reported that they had found Tunstall lying with his head on his hat, and with both hands folded across his breast, and that alongside, Tunstall's horse had lain with its head comfortably pillowed on the Englishman's folded coat. Much was made of these "facts," and they were bruited far and wide. Then, going to that drunken fool of a Wilson, who was local J. P. and already under considerable obligation to McSween & Tunstall, McSween got Brewer made special constable and, equipping him with a batch of Wilson warrants, sent him out to start the clean up. That Brewer's crowd could be depended on to carry out this work had been amply proved already by the fate of Morton and Baker.

It was the murder of those two boys, I guess, that decided my future course.

It was after dark one night when I rode up to the Pecos ranch. Most of the hands were out on the range, but Evans and Jim McDaniels were there to welcome me. "Where the hell you been?" McDaniels demanded. Evans said: "We thought you'd quit the country."

"I'm here, ain't I?" I said tartly. "Anything left from supper? I could eat a folded tarp."

McDaniels wanted to say some more, but Evans shut him up and led the way to the cook shack. They drank several cups of coffee with me while I padded out my belly.

When I shoved back my chair, Evans said, "Heard any news?"

"Yes," I said, and told them about Baker and Morton. They were all for taking the warpath at once, but I said: "Sit down, an' think it over. We don't want to do nothin' hasty. Remember you birds are workin' for Murphy-Dolan now, and the outfit's been painted black enough already. We got to think this out."

"You got anything in mind?" said Evans finally.

McDaniels was still pulling new ones from his can of private cuss words but I paid him no attention. I said, "I think I better go to town, an' talk this over with Murphy—"

"I think we all better go to town," said Evans grimly.

Well, we had it back and forth, but it was finally decided I should go alone to sound Murphy out. Evans and McDaniels to hold down the ranch meantime. I set out first thing the next morning.

About eleven o'clock—I'd got into the Reservation and the sun had got its dander up—I began to get hungry. I debated with myself for half a mile whether to get the grub from my saddlebags, and eat right now, or wait till I got to Doc Blazer's Mill, and maybe get asked to dinner. But the likelihood of no one being home decided me not to postpone my nooning in the hope of better fixings. If it stuck in my throat I could wash it down later with water from Blazer's spring.

So I crawled from the saddle, got out my grub and, in getting it, came across Sally's glasses. A good powerful set they were, and I guessed she'd be plenty mad when she found out I'd rode off with them. In the press of events I'd plumb forgotten she'd given them to me the other day to take in to Roswell. One of the lenses was a little loose, and she'd told me to git it fixed.

I screwed them out, and took a look around. They seemed to work all right, even if the lens was not as tight as it might be. I put them away, and hunkered down with my grub in the cool of a scrub oak thicket.

After I ate I smoked a couple of cigarettes, wondering what Murphy was going to do, if anything, about the murder of Baker and Morton. It was almost twelve when I got into the saddle again, and rode on.

I mention all this to show on what small things a man's life may hinge. One other small thing helped cost a man's life that day, but I'll be coming to that in a minute.

In due course I crested a hill from which, in the distance, I could see Blazer's Mill, and the Tularosa flowing in front of it. It was a long way off, as the trail goes, but I caught a flash of movement and, thinking at once of Apaches, I reached for Sally's glasses. They brought things up into focus. The Mill looked but a stone's throw off. The flash of movement had been made by a man—by a rider. Old Buckshot Bill Roberts was splashing across the river on his gaunt bay mule.

I lost interest.

Bill Roberts had come by his monicker from the lead twenty-five Texas Rangers had one day pumped into him to make sure their arresting took. He was a shiftless sort of hombre. Ran a haywire spread in the Ruidoso, and never had much truck with his neighbors. Which, perhaps, was just as well, they said; he wasn't any parlor ornament, being a kind of chunky, homely little runt without book learning, and all-fired slack in his habits. He'd been an old army man and, before his trouble with them, had seen considerable service with the Rangers. I'd stopped off to grub with him the day before my session with Murphy. When the talk hung up in politics, I asked, "Which side you backin' these days, Bill?" He scowled at his knife a minute, then looked up at me kind of grimlike. "Hell, Flick," he said, "I don't aim to git in this here war at all. I've had a bellyful of fightin'— All I ask is to be let alone." He shook his head. "My fightin' days is over."

They will tell you now he was one of Murphy's "scalp hunters." But that's a lie, made out of the same whole cloth as that yarn about an earlier and strangely uneventful lead-swapping he had with the Kid and Bowdre. How three such gun-slammers could stand and pump lead at each other, and never score a scratch is more than any one's been able to tell me; but there's people still stick to the tale. Those three never had such a brush. As for Bill being a Murphy scalp hunter—where in hell, let me ask, are the scalps? Where's the men he took them off, and what did he do with the money? Let McSween answer that if he's able.

I noticed just then that my roan was having trouble with his walking. Swinging out of the saddle, I picked up his off-front hoof. A sharp piece of rock was firmly wedged in the frog, and I sweat plenty before I got it loose. It had gone in pretty deep, and even after I'd got it out he limped some.

It looked like I was going to have to stop at Blazer's place, after all. Which meant I'd be held up for a little bull-swapping with old Bill Roberts. But, limping like he was, I knew damn well I'd never make Lincoln tonight on the roan, and if I tried it would probably ruin him. I guessed I could get a bronc from Blazer.

So thinking, I got out the makings and rolled a smoke.

I got out the glasses, and took another look at the Mill. Roberts wasn't in sight, but I got a slant at something I hadn't seen before. There was a bunch of anchored horses in a scrub oak thicket off to one side. That struck me as kind of odd, because from here it looked like they'd been cached that way deliberate.

I didn't get much chance to think about it though, because just then Bill Roberts, carrying his rifle, came around the corner of the house; and, like it was a signal, all hell shook loose on the instant. The front door bulged open, and a bunch of men came sloshing out. It was Dick Brewer's rub-'em-out posse. Bowdre was in the lead, and quick as a flash he went for his gun.

Roberts' rifle jumped to his hip.

It looked like both of them fired together, but Bowdre must have shot a fraction quicker. I could see the dust jump from old Bill's chest, and more dust jump from his back. How he kept his feet was a wonder, but he kept them. His shot had cut Bowdre's gun belt off him like a Bowie, and it fell to the ground as he ducked back around a corner.

It was like that show I saw from the front row over at Santa Fe. Sally's glasses brought it up that close.

The whole bunch were in it now, but Roberts held his ground. It was the bravest thing I ever saw, that one old man standing up to Brewer's killers like an army. Thirteen to one, and every man of Brewer's bunch a professional leather-slapper—several of them notorious killers, and front-page news in any man's paper. With Sally's glasses, I could make out every face. Brewer, the Kid, John Middleton, Bowdre, Jim French, Hendry Brown, Scroggins, the Coe boys, Stephen Stevens, a new guy that was a friend of the Kid's (a wild young sprout called O'Folliard), and a couple of other hired guns that were pulling down pay from McSween.

The lead poured into him by the Rangers had so badly crippled old Bill that he couldn't get a gun up to his shoulder.

But he had trained himself to shoot from the hip, and he was shooting now.

Sprawled against the wall he kept his rifle smoking. I saw that Texas buck John Middleton go reeling back, stumble around the corner, and pitch forward on his face. I saw George Coe let out a yowl, drop his pistol and go scuttling off, his gun hand shaking like a bellringer. Inside three seconds Roberts had that front yard empty as a gutted steer.

Shoving the glasses in my saddlebags, I piled into the saddle and sent the roan down the pitch at a larrup. I was a long way from that fracas, but if any man ever needed help old Bill Roberts was the man and I aimed that he should have some.

I have said that a man's life may hinge on a pretty small thing, and it hinged on one that day. If I'd not stopped to eat, but had decided to take my grub with Blazer, I might have saved Bill's life. It don't seem too likely, but at any rate the chance was there. If my bronc hadn't picked up a stone I still might have played some part in what folks since have called the Battle of Blazer's Mill. Two small things, but they cost a man his life.

I'd clean forgot about my horse being lame. But the roan sure hadn't forgot it, and neither had fate. I sent him down that ridge a-pelting. I guess he tried to favor his hurt. He took ten jumps, broke stride, lurching suddenly, and went down in a rolling fall.

I lit on my shoulder, and got up cursing. I cursed more and louder when I saw the roan. Standing on three legs he was watching me with a brute appeal, and whinnying softly.

His off-front leg was broken.

I had to shoot him.

The day was older by an hour and a half when I splashed across the Tularosa, and came tramping up to Blazer's Mill. I'd heard no shooting for some time and the yard was empty. But signs were plenty of what had happened. I headed for the front door bitterly, and was almost to it when Doc Blazer come out with a scowl.

"For Christ's sake! Where'd you come from?"

I told him. I said: "Where've they gone to? What happened? Where's Bill Roberts?"

"Bill's inside. He dead. Goddlemighty, what a fight!" He swabbed a handkerchief across his face. "They got him, but—"

"*Where are they?*"

"Put your shirttail in. They're gone. Take my advice, Farsom, an' don't never let on you saw it. Those—"

I grabbed him by the throat. I snarled: "*Where are they?*"

"They've cleared out—left here over an hour ago." He rubbed his throat as I stood back and mechanically straightened his tie. "Don't be a goddam fool! There's nothing you can do about it now. Bill's dead. I sent Patten to the Fort for the surgeon, but it's too late. Bill kicked off about ten minutes ago. God, he sure gave them something to remember him by. Brewer's on the ground over there by the window. Bill dragged himself inside the house, and Brewer, figuring to make sure doubly certain, sneaked over there to polish him off. Dick got most of the polish . . ." Doc Blazer wiped his face again. "Bill damn near tore his head off."

The Kid, he said, had taken command of the posse and, bundling Middleton, Coe and Bowdre in the ambulance, had gone tearing off to Roswell. Bill had shot Middleton just above the heart, and the Texan had been unconscious when they left. George Coe had got a finger shot off, and Bowdre had a pretty bad side where Bill's bullet had cut his belt off."

He finally let me have a horse, but only after he'd made me swear I wasn't going to try and catch the posse. I'd cooled off some by that time, and had no intention of trying to overtake that crowd of sidewinders. I headed straight for Lincoln.

It was good and dark when I got there.

7

BOB OLLINGER

Hell, I figured, was like to get a chunk shoved under it when Murphy heard my story. Long before the local cartridge supply had been bought up, the Major and Roberts had been friends and, though Bill had refused to back either side, it seemed altogether probable Murphy considered him an ally. He would not like what had happened to him. Nor would a lot of McSween's supporters. A deal of them were like to sing their anthems with less fervor, and some, I guessed, would climb clean over the fence.

There were two kinds of men in this country: those who'd come to rough it up, and those who'd come to ranch it. Old Bill Roberts was of the final kind, and had never harmed so much as a mangy cat since his bay mule had packed him in here. I was curious to know what sort of charge they'd trumped up to provide Brewer with a warrant. Brewer had had one, Blazer said. I'd asked to see it, but the Kid, Blazer said, had gone off with it.

Lanterns, flares, and plain wood torches dropped their pools of flickering light across the town, painting its baked-mud structures and hosts of milling faces with a pinkish complexion that was not at all out of keeping. Every public place was jammed, and the brothels were doing a counting-house business, with lines of impatient customers bulging noisily into the street. Every hotel was packed to the loft, and the chatter of crap and chuck-a-luck games, the purr of wheels, and the stamp of feet vied with the scrape of fiddles and women's laughter in swelling the boisterous din. Its mile-long street was athrob with life. Freight wagons and vehicles of every description crawled through its hock-deep dust cheek by jowl with riders and walkers, and the

frequent hails of reunited friends rang across its steady uproar
like bugles blown in a battle. A·lusty, raucous and tough young
place was this county-seat town, but its red-blooded denizens
found the life to their liking, and no one much kicked at the
price.

Cuffing the dust from my clothes I shoved a way through
Murphy-Dolan's crowded store, and on into the even more
jammed gambling room, where the thick tobacco haze put halos
round each lamp, and sound was a steady drone that pushed
against you like a hand. In the usual corner I spotted Murphy,
Riley, two officers from the fort, and a hard-case deputy marshal
named Ollinger. They had their heads together over a table that
was garbed with a brace of bottles and a sufficient number of
glasses. Riley and one of the officers were puffing on cigars.

They were talking of cattle, and of the time Murphy-Dolan
was having in getting hold of enough to fill its beef contract.
The Kid, Riley was complaining, had scared off a number of
small raisers on whom the Major had been depending for
rounding out his count. The Kid, Riley said, had threatened to
plant any man— That far he got when Murphy looked up,
and saw me. Talk sloughed off.

"Glad to see you back, Flick," Murphy told me heartily.
"Pull up a chair. You know these gentlemen, don't you? This
here's Bob Ollinger; he's looking into these cattle thefts. Says
he might make out to stop 'em."

I nodded, but made no move to take Mr. Ollinger's hand,
having well in mind what had happened to Juan Chavez, who
had made the mistake at Seven Rivers. "How are you,
Ollinger?" I said, and poured myself a drink.

I didn't like the fellow's rep, and I didn't much care for his
looks. He had his hair brushed back on his shoulders, like he
was Bridger or Wild Bill Hickok, and wore a buckskin shirt,
with a lot of fringe and bead work. He had his pants tucked in a
brace of fifty-dollar boots, and on one hip packed a Bowie,
and on the other a shiny sixgun. His hat was cuffed in a go-to-

hell slant that made me itch to smack it. But ignoring his mitt, I figured, was a big enough bite to chew on for the present. He used the hand to get out his makings. His grin was pleasant enough.

"What did you find out Flick?"

I hesitated.

Murphy said: "That's all right. Speak out. We're all friends here."

Well, he was boss. If I got any pay at all, I would have to get it from him. So I said, "Evans and McDaniels will hire out to you. They're at the Pecos ranch."

"Nice work. What about the others?"

"There wasn't any others with 'em but Baker and Morton. I guess you know where they are. If Evans gets treated right I guess the rest of his friends will back us. I've quit Chisum."

Ollinger said, "Looks like the Fence Rail will be going out of business," and grinned across at Riley.

For two cents I would have smacked his kisser. I guess Murphy saw the way it was with me because, "That's fine," he put in smoothly. "You fixed to go to work for us now? Good! I sure can use you, boy."

"Look!" I said. "I got more news for you, an' you ain't much apt to like it. You want I should spill it here"—I ran the edge of my glance across the deputy marshal's beefy red face—"or shall we hunt some place more private?"

"Why, this is all right, Flick. What's happened?"

"Brewer got a Wilson warrant for old Bill Roberts. They caught him at Blazer's Mill, an' gunned him like a snake. He's dead," I said to the question in Murphy's eyes.

John Riley swore. Ollinger screwed his face up, and allowed it was nigh time someone was putting Dick Brewer to rest. I told him someone had. "Bill Roberts," I said, "damn near blowed Brewer's head off. He got him a George Coe finger, give Bowdre a right good bellyache, an' if that Texas polecat, Middleton, don't kick the bucket it'll be because hell's full up already." I told them what I'd seen, and what Doc Blazer had told me. "What you figure we ought to do?"

"We don't have to do a thing," said Riley quickly. "Sit pat, an' let this business work for us. Jumping old Roberts is the worst thing McSween could have done. Hang an' rattle for another week an'—"

"This is terrible," said one of the officers, a bluecheeked captain. "Terrible! What can McSween be thinking of? What charge was brought forward to get that warrant?"

"I don't know," I said. "But it's something they've cooked up all right. Old Bill never harmed a fly."

"Almost puts him in your class, don't it?" Ollinger smiled. "I hear you tangled with Frank McNab the other day, an' shot him." His smile got toothy as he looked me over from the height of his growing rep. He shook his head. "You'll never quit bein' a amateur pullin' parlor tricks like that. Let me give you some advice, son: Never yank your cutter till you're set to blow the lid off; never do no shootin' less'n you aim to kill. Leavin' crippled sidewinders on your back trail—"

I said, "Ollinger, when I start takin' advice from you they'll be coolin' beer with the ice cut off 'n hell."

Riley's chair scraped back. The captain ducked below the table.

Bob Ollinger threw back his head, and laughed—a little loud, I thought. "Shucks, boy," he said, "I got to remember that . . . 'coolin' beer with the ice cut off 'n hell,'" and he laughed again.

I said nothing. He might have fooled those others, but he wasn't loading me. I had him pegged.

8

HATS IN THE DUST

Much has been said about the Kid's good qualities in the years that have passed since his death. Hardly a decade goes by that some new eulogist, inspired by the public hunger for hero-worship, or perhaps by rosy visions of pecuniary reward, does not finger a few dusty records, hark to the oft-stretched legends and, with a watery paste of fact, brew a steamy broth of fiction.

The Kid was neither a martyr nor a hero. He was the Dillinger of 1879. There is as much truth in these romantic yarns of him as there was in the tale of Mrs. McSween's famous piano which, we are told, she played all during the fight that led up to her husband's death. She neither played the piano nor owned it. The truth of the matter is that this oft-mentioned instrument was the property of Mrs. Scholland (the Fritz family's Aunt Emelia), who had sent it in to Lincoln for safe storage until she could get it shipped to Las Cruces. Had she guessed at the time how Alex was figuring to flimflam her and Charlie out of that insurance money, she never would have left it with him. But I guess Alex's Bible-tract front took her in like the rest.

There was some good in the Kid, I guess. But in his time Bill Bonney's bad points far outweighed anything to be described as a virtue. We are told that he "was brimming over with light-hearted gayety and good humor," that "moroseness and sullenness were foreign to him," that "one chance in a million" was all he asked, and that he took that chance "with the debonair courage of a cavalier."

One thinks immediately of Robin Hood, and imagines Bonney to have been cut from the same bold pattern—one could almost wish he had been, so far a cry is this conception from the truth. Where was this famous courage while the Kid, with twelve tough helpers, was whittling down Bill Roberts?—when from behind an adobe wall, aided again by at least seven powder-burners, he waylaid and killed Sheriff Brady? His sweating biographers, I reckon, weren't around when he stretched Jim Carlyle in the snow.

Carlyle's killing puts the brand of wishful thinking on every compliment that's been paid Bill Bonney; it tears the tinsel of his glamour into doll rags.

Billy the Kid was a murderer and a thief. He would drive a bullet through a fellow's heart as lustful as he'd rape a woman; and times beyond count did both. He was a man without remorse—without regret or pity. Yet they tell you he was of a generous, sympathetic nature; that the steadfast loyalty of his friendships was proverbial, and that "his courage was beyond question."

Do these descriptions fit the facts of Carlyle's death?

Jim Carlyle was a friend of the Kid's; he also was a deputy sheriff. When White Oaks sent Will Hudgens after Bonney, where the Kid and his crew were forted up at the Greathouse ranch, Jim Carlyle, because he was a friend, offered to go in and talk to the Kid, and see if he could persuade him to surrender without violence. He did go in, but talk proved useless. "I'll just kill you," said the Kid, "while I've got a good chance," and yanked his pistol. Carlyle was unarmed, having left his weapons with the posse. "Drink," jeered Bonney; "it's the last you'll ever take on earth!" Carlyle made a dive for the window—crashed through. Bonney shot him before he touched the ground. Bad wounded, but thoroughly cognizant now of the deadliness of the Kid's intentions, Carlyle tried to get out of range. He clawed to hands and knees, and was that way, groaning, when Bonney's second shot knocked him face down, dead, in the snow.

A curious fact emerges from a study of the records—none of

these whitewashing fables of the Kid ever saw the influence of print until the last important principal of the opposing faction had been laid to rest. Not until Murphy, Dolan, Fritz, Riley, Dad Peppin, and all the others were gone did Billy the Kid emerge from the past's red mists a hero, the swashbuckling Robin Hood of Lincoln County.

Several days passed uneventfully while folks at the county seat took stock of the situation, and laid their bets as to the outcome. Sheriff Brady cursed out Wilson for putting his damned John Henry on those murderous Brewer warrants. McSween's hired killers, he snarled, were ranging the country like a plague. The law was being travestied; order was become an obsolete word. Wilson snapped back at Brady for doing nothing to apprehend the killers of Tunstall. Tunstall, Brady thundered, had got just what he'd been asking for—and as for that crazy yarn about Mathews' posse being drunk, about its members bashing in the rancher's head, and arranging his corpse beside the carcass of his bullet-killed horse as though the two had bedded down together . . . Well, he could find no words that could fittingly describe the mentality of "any goddam nitwit" who'd believe a yarn like that! Brewer and the Kid had witnessed it, Wilson shouted. "Yes, fine upstandin' characters!" Brady scoffed. "Murphy's the only man in the country who'd ever trust Brewer—and *he'll* not do it again! And as for that sneak-thief Kid— Why didn't they stop it if they saw it?"

Wilson said: "They ain't the only ones saw it. Those Mexicans McSween hired to go out after the body—"

"Sure—" jeered Brady, "a couple of greasers! You ain't named a fella yet I'd believe quick's I would the men that were in that posse. In fact, you ain't named anybody yet that a person of sense would believe *at all*. Let me give you some plain advice, John P.— If you expect to live the rest of your days out here, don't sign no more of those warrants. Brewer's dead, and the

Kid's an outlaw; if this thing gets much worse the Gover'ment'll be steppin' in."

I guess Wilson took the advice because no further warrants were issued McSween's pet killers. But the town was in a ferment. The news of Bill Roberts' fate, coming so close on the heels of the slaughter of Baker and Morton, gave people premonitions of what might happen to them if they didn't cut loose of Murphy-Dolan, and go sing hymns with McSween. A lot of them switched their allegiance; they had families and property, and breaking with Murphy-Dolan seemed a damn wise thing to do. The vindictiveness of Murphy's enemies was paralyzing.

Brady, determined to stop this war if it cost his last vote, named every man in Brewer's posse an outlaw, charged with the murder of his deputies, and put a bounty on Bonney's scalp, to be paid whether alive or dead. It has been said Brady "hounded" the Kid because of the murder of Baker and of Morton. This was not so. Brady had little time left in which to hound anyone.

I'd been spending most of my time in the last few days hanging around the Big Store, waiting for orders that it seemed would never come. What the hell, I argued, was the good of Murphy-Dolan taking on guys like me and Evans if they didn't figure on getting some use out of them? And if they did so figure, why wait till all the smoke had cleared, and the victory was in McSween's capacious pocket?

But the Major only grinned. "Just keep your pants on, Flick. This here isn't rightly the kind of thing a fellow had ought to rush. We want to think this business out careful. No sense going off half-cocked. I got to be sure McSween's really behind these killings before I— Oh . . . Good morning, Miz Chisum."

With a green-apple feeling at the pit of my stomach, I turned to see Sally Chisum walking her big-chested bay down the road toward the McSween end of town. I didn't stop to wonder how it happened she was riding in from this end. She nodded civilly enough to the Major's greeting, but she did not speak and her eyes were bright with scorn.

I said, "Excuse me, Major—" and hurried after her. She walked the bay another half-dozen paces, as though intending to ignore me; then stopping him with a sudden flexure of her knees, stony-hard she said, "Aren't you making a mistake, sir?"

Sitting her saddle that way, with her big hat dangling behind her shoulders from its chin strap, the morning sun made a kind of halo of her hair, and lighted up the contour of her canted cheeks like something in a picture. She looked mighty fetching in her man's blue woolen shirt, and divided leather riding skirt, her beaded vest and gauntlets. Any other time and place my heart would've beat a tumult. But it didn't beat one then. Every word I'd meant to say hung choked in my throat. It wasn't what she'd said. It was the way she'd said it—the look that was in her eyes. It was like I was some kind of strange bug that had landed on her skirt.

"Sally—"

"Miss Chisum, if you please, sir. I reserve that other name for friends."

I expect I stood there like a ninny. I forgot there was other people in the street. I was conscious only of that tall, proud figure in the saddle. The cold disdain of her regard was like a whip's bite.

I thought, "If she would curse me I'd feel better."

But she wasn't cursing. Calm as cactus, she said, "Do I have the pleasure of your acquaintance, sir?"

"My God!" I said. "Sally—don't talk like that!" I hardly recognized my voice; it had that tight, scared sound I'd caught in Fred White's voice just before Bill Graham had dropped him. "After all we've been—"

"Really?" Scorn brightened in Sally's eyes. "Are you trying to tell me that a Chisum and a Murphy gunfighter could have anything in common?" Dropping her pose, she said abruptly, hotly: "You had your chance, Flick Farsom! You quit me with your eyes open—quit me cold, an' of your own free will! I told you at the Fence Rail before you shot poor Frank McNab, that if you walked out on Uncle John you could say good-by to me! It's God's own mercy you're not a full-fledged murderer, like the rest of that conniving Murphy outfit— But I suppose you will be, quick as you get the chance!"

"What's the matter over there? Sounds like you two're squabblin'."

It was Billy Mathews. He was standing with Dad Peppin, Sheriff Brady, and George Hindman (one of Brady's deputies) on the porch of Murphy's store. Murphy was standing where I'd left him. Mathews grinned at us.

He might as well have been in Roswell, for all the attention Sally gave him. I didn't say anything either. Sally's shoulders moved impatiently. She said bitterly: "Don't ever stop me like this again. We're all through— Hear me? It's past and done with, every bit of it. Now stand aside and let me pass—"

"Sally—"

She said almost hysterically: "Those fools are staring at us, Flick—let me go! Get your hand off my horse's bridle!"

I guess I didn't move quick enough. She was so wrought up she didn't half-know what she was doing. With a kind of sob she snatched up her reins, and brought forward her quirt in a whistling arc whose song stopped short in my face. It drove me back, but she struck again. She was gone in a clatter of hoofs.

I picked up my hat in an utter quiet.

The group before the porch stood like they'd frozen.

I shot one look at their wooden faces, and slammed my eyes straight front. I started for the store. I expect I walked like a man gone blind. I don't believe I saw another thing until I'd got inside, and didn't see nothing then until I saw John Riley lounging by a window. There was a big grin on his face.

I saw red then.

"What's so goddam funny?" I said, walking up to him, and looking him hard in the eye.

"Why, nothing much, Flick," he said mildly. "I was just thinking what a fit McSween's crowd'll have when they find court's been postponed."

I gave him another hard look. "What do you mean—*postponed?*"

"That's straight. Alex's crew's been making some brags about what'll be done if the judge don't talk to suit 'em. But Judge Bristol's sent up word he ain't goin' to hold no court this term," Riley chuckled. "Thinks Lincoln's too 'unsettled'. He's give Brady orders to open up court, an' then adjourn it."

"What's Brady hangin' around out front for then?"

"Been waiting for Billy Mathews—Billy's Circuit Court Clerk, you know—and Dad Peppin. He don't aim to open no court in this town without a couple deputies handy. The word's around the Kid has sworn to nail Brady's hide account of that reward Brady got out for him."

I said, "I guess I'll just go along with them in case." I was feeling a little less ornery now, but was still plenty on the prod. I thought if any of McSween's tough bucks came around to cut a few shines, or maybe make good on their brags, I'd work off my temper on them.

But when I got outside, Brady and his three Fridays were way on down the road. Otherwise the street was empty—even Murphy had gone off some place. It was a warm bright day, drowsy and peaceful looking as two pups in a basket. A couple of Mexicans were loafing in the shadow of the church. Across the way another fellow, plowing up a field, was lazily swearing at his horses. Everything was bright as a pin, and I could almost smell the flowers in Mrs. McSween's little garden. I thought, "What the hell!" and sat down on the steps. The courthouse was most a quarter of a mile away, and I had just had my boots cleaned, and thought of the lather I'd work up plowing through all that dust decided me to stay right where I was. It was pretty comfortable here, and I'd got a lot of things to think about. Looked like Bob Ollinger had ought to have wanted to go along to that court opening, him being in such a lather to get a rep built. But I hadn't noticed him any place around. I've often wondered since if he wasn't one of them cagey souls that can gauge to the split second when the better part of valor is to be doing something else.

As for Sally Chisum, to hell with her. Any dame who could hold a man in such low esteem, as to swing a whip at him, wasn't much worth wasting thought on. Which was damn good as a theory, but not much force any other way. When your every waking thought for three whole years has been focused on a girl, when everything you've done or hope to do has been tied up with her, you don't get her out of mind in any baker's-dozen of minutes. Specially after she's just done cracking your face with a quirt. I reached a cautious hand up; gingerly felt the welts. I said, "God damn her anyway!" and then scowled round to see had anyone heard me.

I could see her horse down there, where she'd hitched it to the tie rail fronting the McSween & Tunstall store. Buying something for Chisum, I guessed, or maybe come in to bring Alex a message. Funny, I mused, how folks had got to calling him Alex—"Alec" was the way he put it on his paper. Not that it made any difference. He'd been called a lot of things since hooking up with Tunstall. I wondered if he really was bad as we thought him, or if he was just a weak sister that Tunstall had taken advantage of. That didn't make much difference, either. He was bossing things now, and would have to pay the piper for the things his men were doing. The chances were, however, that they were carrying out his orders. He had certainly got all the benefit from old man Fritz's insurance. He had got Wilson to sign them warrants, too, and had got Brewer made special deputy. I ain't the sort to judge a man too harshly. But the facts were pretty plain.

Well, they'd soon be opening up court. Brady and the others

had pretty near reached McSween's store. I saw them wave to Saturnino Baca who was sitting on his porch. He waved back, and went on smoking. They nodded to several loungers loafing in front of the store. One of them called some quip, to which Brady laughed good-naturedly. The dinky building being used for a courthouse wasn't much over a stone's throw ahead of them now, and I guessed McSween's hired guns, if they were really planning trouble, would be getting fixed to go over—or were maybe there already, waiting for the judge. Judge Bristol's stunt, in my opinion, was damn poor strategy; give those crooks an inch, and they'd take a mile. The only way to deal with guys of that caliber was to show them you couldn't be buffaloed —and if they got too gay, bat 'em down.

I've said quite a lot about the Kid. Maybe I've given you the wrong impression. He was a tough little monkey, right enough; but I don't reckon he was such a hell of a sight tougher than a lot of other guys hanging round Lincoln. This was damn hard country; and, at the time, most folks looked on him as just another fresh young squirt who had ought to get his ears batted down. He wasn't considered a heap important; more folks called him "that damn little horse thief" than called him the Kid. He was rightly considered to be "feeling his oats"—trouble was, none of us guessed how far those oats would take him. Since the killing of Baker and Morton nobody wanted him behind their backs, and there's no denying a kind of fear of him was getting round. But up to now he was "just another wild gun fighter," and he still had an amateur standing.

It was ironic that today was picked by fate to alter all this. April 1st it was, and it seemed like everyone was playing pranks. Judge Bristol had refused to hold his court. Sally had struck me with a quirt. And the Kid, by the caliber of *his* prank, was slated to be snatched from the obscurity of frontier rowdyism into the searing spotlight of front-page news.

A crash of rifles broke the quiet. It jerked my head up quick enough to see Bill Brady throw his arms up wildly, drop his rifle, spin, and stagger. I saw him crumple in the dust. Saw those with him take to their heels.

I jumped to my feet with an oath.

Ambush! A dry-gulching!

I knew it the minute I saw that line of rifles across the wall. Remembrance of the Kid's bruited threats was in my mind on the instant. Forgetful of the danger, I started running toward them. There was nothing in my head then but a burning, white-hot desire to come to grips with Brady's assassins. I don't guess the risk I was foolhardily taking ever entered my mind. I was too damned mad to think. I jerked my pistol, and put all the steam I could into getting there before those bastards got away.

Mathews, Peppin, and Hindman weren't stopping to do any shooting. They were too almighty close to a dead man. They were jumping for cover like frightened rabbits—all but Hindman. He seemed to have lost his head completely, and was running straight down the road. Dad Peppin and Mathews were sprinting for the house of a Mex across the street. The firing was all one-sided; it was coming across that wall like a broadside from a ship. I saw George Hindman stagger. It was like some one had hit him in the back with an axe. He took three lurching strides, and plowed up the dirt with his face.

Through a curtain of rage I saw French and the Kid vault over the wall. They scuttled toward the sheriff's body. And then another figure came into the road— Ike Stockton; but he didn't do any lingering. He said something quicklike, from the side of his mouth at Bonney, and then beat a hurried retreat. A woman came panting into the road with a hatful of water for Hindman. It was Mrs. Captain Baca. Her look should have withered Bonney.

But he didn't pay her any attention. With a whoop, French snatched up Brady's rifle. Bonney stooped. Squatted above the sheriff's body, he was fixing to peel off Brady's gun belt when Billy Mathews, from the doorway of the place across the street, opened up with his rifle. The Kid jumped like a snake had bit him. French let out a yowl, and spun clear round with both hands clapped to his hip.

I was damn near up to them—up to pistol range, I mean. I started shooting. Even if I'd got closer, running the way I was, I guess I wouldn't have hit much. But I was making plenty noise, and Peppin and Billy Mathews still were adding to the racket. The Kid flicked one more wishful look at Brady's shell belt; then crouched low, he ran for the wall. Wayte was just getting over, wanting in on the loot, I guess. Bonney's shoulder knocked him back again. French, hanging onto his hip and still lugging Brady's rifle, limped up to the wall, and was yanked over.

Mrs. Captain Baca crouched before the church with Hindman's head in her lap. Otherwise, and except for Brady's body, the street was empty.

And it stayed that way.

I charged the wall. But there wasn't nothing back of it but the wind-whipped fields stretching away to the river, and on the ground some empty shells.

The dry-gulchers had got away.

9

STARS FOR HIRE

A STORY is told that Alex read the scriptures to young Bonney next time he saw him. I don't know anything about that, but if he did, the wait he was forced to undergo before the preaching of this sermon was a mighty short one, because it was found out within the next half-hour that the Kid and his back-shooting compadres after the killing of Sheriff Brady had gone directly, via back lots, to McSween's home.

It has been said that Alex told his gun chief: "Your crime, Billy, was not only cold-blooded, but foolish. You could have done nothing more serious against my interests if you had tried deliberately to injure me. I cannot afford to appear to uphold you in the perpetration of such outrages. I propose to have you indicted and brought to trial for this assassination. This is a duty I owe to my conscience and to the public."

I ain't got much doubt but what, some time or other, Mc-Sween really made that speech. It was entirely in keeping with his character. Regardless, however, of the amount of sincerity one might consider to have been behind these fine upstanding words, the fact remains that actually McSween did nothing whatever in this direction. The Kid not only remained at large, but set about the immediate inauguration of a reign of terror that, backed as it was by his growing and ever more bloody rep, was to assure him a place for all time in the annals of his state.

For the next few weeks no name was so constantly on the country's tongue. Brady's death had robbed the county of its last slim pretensions to law and orthodox order. Gun law ruled the land, and no gun talked one-half as loud as Bill Bonney's lightning-quick six.

No matter what McSween actually thought about the Kid's broad-daylight murders, he was swift enough in seizing every advantage he could wring from them. Erstwhile supporters were dropping his banner in wholesale lots; but if he felt dismay, chagrin or anger at these desertions, at least he lost no time in consolidating his position. He engineered an election that was a farce from start to finish. With the Kid and his swaggering pistol-pushers quartering the town like martial law, he put John Copeland, a weak-kneed old bell mare with an oversized opinion of his own importance, in the sheriff's saddle, and made haste to barn what hay he could while Copeland's star spread its thin veneer of legality over whatever he wanted done. Copeland bunked at McSween's place, got out a lot of hand-bills describing Jesse Evans, Billy Mathews, Dad Peppin, Kip McKinney, Old Man Pierce, Andy Boyle, myself, and several lesser lights as outlaws, and showed himself around like he was the greatest lawgiver since Moses. Most of us that had our names on his posters kept off the street in daylight, but Kip McKinney said he'd be damned if he would and, with Old Man Pierce, proceeded to go about his business as though John Copeland hadn't existed. Old Man Pierce even went so far as to take a couple shots at Bowdre, but nothing ever came of it. Nor of the attempt they talked John Copeland into, of trying to arrest Jesse Evans one night when he and myself, on a tip the Kid might show up there, were downing a couple at Patron's.

Jim French and Stephen Stevens were with Copeland when he entered, and all three had their mitts wrapped round their pistols. Evans looked them over and grinned. "By God," he said, "just look, Flick— Peace, Good Will, an' Mercy Mild! Aren't you three sports getting careless?"

French growled, but Copeland let go his gun like it had burnt him. Putting the best face he could on the matter he grabbed hold of his companions, saying: "C'mon, boys. Reckon we got a bum steer some way. He ain't aroun' yere no place."

By this time echoes of our feuding had spread clean out of the Territory. Emigrants from the Eastern states had been swarming westward like a bunch of grasshoppers. Home seekers, gold seekers, seekers after everything but trouble—they were giving New Mexico a wide berth, and the Territorial authorities, anxious to get the country settled up, were on the verge of chewing their toenails.

Murphy, desperate, went straight to Governor Axtell. He put his cards right down on the table; gave him the situation in a few well chosen phrases, covered Copeland's election, and offered the names of fifty witnesses, many of them prominent citizens. The country, he declared, was well on its way to the dogs.

Axtell heartily agreed.

"An' it'll never be no better," Murphy said, "till you've got rid of that killin' Kid. God damn it, half the people are so blankety-blank scared they won't even come out of their houses—you got to deliver food to 'em like they was under a quarantine! A hell of a situation!"

There wasn't much doubt of that; not even Axtell doubted it. He promised to do something.

And did. He yanked John Copeland out of office within the week, and appointed George W. Peppin to fill out the term. The same Dad Peppin who'd been deputy under Brady—one of the three men who'd been with Brady when the Kid and his crowd gulched him.

Peppin was a good and upright citizen—a square shooter if I ever knew one. He was five-foot-nine; a typical Westerner who'd always been content to mind his own business, and let other gents do the same. He'd been farming the Bonito bottoms for quite a spell, and doing pretty good at it, too. He was a family man, had four or five kids, and the stuff he raised took care of them. He had a big fruit orchard he'd set out by himself; and sometimes when he'd be wanting ready cash for something, he'd sell a little hay, or grain, or maybe a wagonload of apples—he grew the best apples in the country.

He was a fair-looking man, clean-shaven usually, with a deep bronze skin beset by wrinkles the wind had ripped into him. You knew by his look he belonged in the country, even if he wasn't any cowman. He'd been pretty well liked by all and sundry, and had had a lot of friends; guys that knew he liked kids, and brought their own along with them when they'd ride over sometimes for a spend-day. But the badge Axtell pinned to his shirt made considerable change in his standing. By that same time next day the news had skinned clean round the country, and Peppin could count all his friends on one hand. That's what a range war'll do for you, and authority—even that little. But he didn't let it fret him. He'd an honest regard for the solemnity of his oath, and he got busy right away.

Ike Stockton was pretty well considered by Murphy's Texas men to be trimming his sails for a McSween-Chisum victory; these claimed to have it on good authority that he was an undercover ally of the Kid. In support of this, they pointed out how his presence had drawn no fire from the Kid's crowd that day they had rubbed out Brady.

"That don't mean anything," I objected. "They wasn't throwin' no lead around me none, either."

But that made Evans laugh. "Hell," he said, "they was so busy strippin' corpses they never even saw you."

Anyway, it seemed to me that Ike was doing his best to plow a course of amity between the two belligerent factions. While most of the county was working itself into a lather, shouting like Gabriel for one side or the other, Ike kept calm, and kept his mind on his business. I, for one, kept trading with him. Like I said one time to Dolan, "If Ike *is* carryin' tales, there's just a chance we can get some change out of 'em if we got the sense to keep our ears clean."

I asked Ike once where it all would end. He shrugged, and grinned at me cautious. "I can tell you one thing, though," he said. "There won't be a heap of folks left to see if she keeps on way she's goin' now." Them was my own sentiments, too. He said: "I'd never opened here at all 'f I'd seen this business comin'. Take that damn Kid— Glass he's breakin' buildin' up his rep 'll put me in the poorhouse!"

He grinned wryly when I laughed. "It's the truth," he said. "When he don't break it personal, one of his gang does. They ain't got no more regard fer my expenses than like they'd never drunk here. Hell— They got no regard fer anything!" He eyed me thoughtful. "Did you hear about Rip Farness' girl—*Pssst!*

Here's a couple of your friends." He turned away, swiping his rag across the bar.

It was Evans and Kip McKinney come to say the Major wanted me. He did. He had Bob Ollinger with him, and a scar-faced White Oaks fellow named Bell was lounging just outside the door. "Your name Farsom?" I said it was, and he followed me in. He stood against a wall, and got his teeth in shape by chewing on a match stick.

Murphy said, "Howdy, Flick— You know Bob Ollinger, don't you?"

"We been introduced. Evans said you wanted to see me—"

"Right." He put away the knife he had been using to prune his fingernails, and eyed me hard a minute. "Weren't you the fellow told me once he wasn't afraid of the Kid?"

There it was, coming home to roost. "What I meant was—"

"Yes. Quite so. Well—" he grinned, "we got a little job for you. Course, we could have given it to somebody else, but it needs a cool hand, and a fellow that knows how to shoot. Happened to recollect what you said and . . ."

In the pause Bob Ollinger smiled.

I shifted my weight around. "What the hell," I said, "are you gettin' at?"

"Guess you've noticed the Kid ain't been seen much since we got a new sheriff appointed? He's been busy though, and Bob here has just found out where he's—"

"Why tell me about it? I ain't interested in his whereabouts. Go talk to Peppin—"

"Unfortunately, Peppin's out of town—"

"He left a deputy here!" I told them. "Get him to swear in a posse—"

"No," Murphy said, "it ain't that easy. Anyway, Flick, I don't put a deal of stock in that deputy. He's been hangin' round Ike's bar too much. I want a man we can depend on—"

"What's the matter with Ollinger?"

"Nothing," Ollinger said. "Only it happens I'm a deputy

marshal. I can't get mixed in things like that," he told me smugly.

I didn't like it—I didn't like it a little bit. It wasn't so much that I was afraid of Bonney, but I knew what his rep was built on. I wasn't craving to see any cartridge with my name on it. I scowled. "What about Evans?"

Murphy shook his head. "Won't touch it—Says anything else he don't mind doing; but the Kid is out. Been too close, he says. Claims he's slept with him, fought the same Indians, bucked the same towns, et with him. Says it would be like going after his brother."

I let go an oath. I had et with him, too, if it came to that. But I had shot my goddam mouth off, also. It looked like I would have to make good.

"If he's scared . . ." began Ollinger, grinning.

"Another crack out of you," I said, "an' you'll see how scared I am!" I glared at Murphy. "Get it off your chest! What is it you're wantin' me to do?"

"I want the Kid got out of this county—"

"Oh," I said. "Is *that* all?"

"It ought to keep you busy for a little while," guessed Ollinger, happily.

"The kid," said Murphy, "is holed up over on the Ruidoso. He's at San Patricio. There's only a few fellows with him. Brown, O'Folliard, Scurlock, Bowdre, an' Middleton—"

"Jeez," I said, "he's in one hell of a fix, now ain't he? Must feel plumb deserted." Those five were the toughest bucks in McSween's whole outfit. But the Major ignored my sarcasm.

"They're at my beef again," he said, "an' I want it stopped. Axtell's promised to do something. But you know how it is with the Government—be months before he gets the red tape chopped off. Meantime, I'll be a pauper sure as hell, if Chisum and that Kid keep on. We got to stop that stealin'—"

"I might do somethin' about the Chisum angle . . ."

"Catron's taking care of him." Murphy's fingers drummed

the table. "Your job's to bother the Kid. Upset his plans, an' make life miserable for him till I can get those cattle out of there. I don't care what you do, nor how you do it, so long's you keep him off my beef herd. I'm leavin' it with your conscience, Flick— But keep in mind that crowd's all outlaws, anyway. If you happen to knock any over you'll probably be a national hero—"

"You may even get to be President," Bob Ollinger tucked in.

I was fed up with his goddam riding. Balling my fists, I walked over and stuck my jaw in his face. "What was that?" I said.

His slaughterhouse look got a little dim. "I was only funnin'—"

"Take care," I said grimlike, "your fun don't explode. If it does, all you'll be is a memory!"

"Quit wranglin', you two," Murphy growled. "Bell, go down an' help Flick round him up a posse—"

"Keep your posse!" I snapped back at him. "I can do what needs doin' without one!"

San Pat was but a couple of whoops and a holler off, if you went by mountain trail—which was how I aimed to go. A fellow on a good stout bronc could make it in an hour. I wasn't in no tearing rush. Boot Hill loomed plenty close, without any speed on my part. I figured it likely that Bonney'd have word before I even got near the place. If the Kid was to be got, or bothered, it would have to be by strategy. And while me and strategy wasn't even shooting compadres, I figured to do my best.

First thing, as I saw it, was to get in a chunk of shut-eye. Jumpy nerves were no kind of thing to take on a hunt for the Kid.

I went over to Stockton's bar, and took a couple snorts with the sports that were bellying his long place. Some white-collared whippoorwill was unwinding one of them long-drawn-out kind of stories about some farmer's daughter, but I couldn't see much

to laugh at. After a minute I caught Stockton's eye, and beckoned him off to a corner.

"Look," I said, "you got any place where a guy could grab
forty winks without gettin' rolled, or wakin' up with the
angels?"

"Not right now I ain't." Ike winked. "I don't know what's
come over folks, but all my beds are full up. I'm sure sorry,
Flick—"

"Sure. I'll make out, I reckon. Ain't much point to sleepin'
anyhow these days. I expect," I said, thinking grimly of the
Kid, "I'll be havin' all the shut-eye I can handle pretty quick."

I got my horse, and hit the trail.

A collection of mud huts sprawled along the river; San Pat
had little enough to commend it to a stranger, I thought sourly,
squinting round. Nobody but Mexicans lived there, and it was
God's own wonder how they made a living.

The Kid wasn't around, but Bowdre was. He said, "What
brings you over this way, Flick?" He eyed my rifle. "Goin'
hunting?"

I nodded.

"Not huntin' trouble, are you?"

"That depends," I said. "Murphy don't like what's been
happening to his cattle."

"No?"

"No. You fellows better lay off awhile."

He grinned. "I'll speak to the Kid about it—"

"I'll speak to him myself," I said. "Where is he?"

"Why, I reckon he's roundin' up some of Chisum's horses.
We got word your friend Evans was figurin' to jump 'em."

We looked each other over. Charlie seemed kind of restless;
kept itching his back against a post. Then I got what he was
up to. "Keep junin' around," I said, "and you'll have something
besides that itch to worry with."

He grinned at me slanchways, but stopped his fiddling. "You got a suspicious mind."

"I sure have. I got a pronto way with a pistol, too, in case you ain't been informed. When you expectin' Bonney back?"

"Hell, you can't never tell about him. He might be back most any time. Get down an' rest your saddle."

"No, thanks." I looked around good as I could, with one eye still on his gun hand. I expected we were being watched, but there wasn't anyone in sight, so I said, "Whereabouts is your horse at, Charlie?"

"Figurin' to steal him, are you?"

"You an' me," I said, "is goin' to take a little trip. We're—"

"Not so you could notice it!"

He was reaching for his smoke-wagon when I gave him a look at my gun bore. "Better not," I said, "unless you're huntin' a good long rest."

He managed a sour kind of grin, and let go his gun. "I ain't huntin' one *that* long."

There was a corral across the street with three horses in it. There was two saddles on the fence. Charlie took the hint. But he didn't hurry any, and without forcing the issue I didn't see no way to make him.

But we got there finally. He reached for one of the saddles. I said: "Be careful how you handle that. I'd hate to have to shoot you, Charlie."

"Yeah—wouldn't you?" But he was careful all the same. He unfastened his rope, and with it in his left hand was preparing to slide through the bars, when I said: "Just a minute, hombre; you won't be needin' no iron in there. Leave it out here, where I can see it."

He gave me a horsey look, but put his pistol in a pepper tree crotch before he crawled through the bars. The broncs were watching him distrustfully.

So was I. "You don't have to put it on by hand," I told him.

He said something I didn't catch, shook out his loop, and let it ravel. It missed a roan's arched head by inches. The three broncs spun on a dime; cut the dust for the pen's far side. There they huddled, fiddled nervously while Charlie hauled in his rope, each one trying to hide behind the other. Charlie missed again.

I said, "Your next throw better cut it."

He gave me a look and spat. "If you don't like my style get down an' try it yourself."

"I got a better way than that," I said. Charlie's next throw did the work.

With a sour look on his pan, he led the bronc outside. He slammed the gate. Reaching for his saddle, he suddenly straightened. "Bets are off, boy," he said grinning. Staring past me down the road he chuckled "Here's the boss a-comin'—"

"Sure," I said. "That one was packin' whiskers when Aesop swam the Styx. You get on with that saddlin' before I knock your ears down to where they'll do for snowshoes. I wish," I said, "your damn boss *would* come round; it's gettin' on towards supper, an' while he might be a little tough I reckon I could wash him down."

"You're sure goin'—" The rest was lost in the Kid's wild yell. I reckon my guts turned over three times before the noise of it finished. The wind had been making such a racket I hadn't heard any hoof-pound—but I heard it then. I guessed the whole damn bunch was coming.

One thing was sure. I'd made a bad mistake fooling round with Bowdre—a mistake that was like to cost Major Murphy another hand. Some guys would have run for it, maybe; but I knew running wouldn't do me any good. Hindman had tried running. I had cut my string too short, and I would have to face the music.

I didn't dare risk a look around even. Bowdre was too close to the tree where he'd put his sixgun and would like nothing better, his expression said, than to make a grab for it. He had the sand to cut it, too.

With the goose-bumps crawling up my spine, I waited.

10

THE FENCE-CRAWLER

IT WAS not so much a question of courage, my waiting, as it was a choice I hoped might prove less fatal than the other choice that was left me. I didn't have any chances—all the bets were coppered. If I ran they'd turn me into a sieve before my bronc got ten paces. I stood my ground as foundation for a bluff.

The Kid's crowd batted the dust hat-high as they hauled up in a circle round me. Those hungry stares in that brittle quiet were like the terrors of nightmare. I could almost taste the powder smoke a started cough, a slanchwise look, or careless move would break loose.

But it was bluff or else. I gave Bowdre a quick, tight grin. "This ain't helpin' you any, Charlie."

The Kid shoved Scurlock out of the way. He put his horse up against me. "You talk pretty brash," he said, "for a guy that's just about run his rope out." He gave me a disapproving stare that went from boots to headgear. "Who you think you're imitatin'—*me?*"

"Hell, no," I said with a laugh. "I wouldn't be in your boots for all the gold in Chisum's safe."

He thought that over, and snorted. "What you up to, puttin' that gun on Bowdre?"

"Why, haven't you heard? Charlie's been proclaimed a outlaw. They've put a bounty on his scalp, an' I'm takin' him in to collect it."

A couple of the others snickered. The Kid grinned a little, too, but it wasn't pleasant. We sat there for perhaps a minute on our restive horses, the Kid with his hands resting on the pommel, me with a sixgun trained on Bowdre. Neither of us let our eyes stray for a second from the other's face.

Then Bonney said: "Mebbe I might have somethin' to say about that. If Charlie's an outlaw, so are all of us. Why don't you take the whole bunch in?"

I said, "I'm workin' up to that."

The Kid's eyes narrowed. They got smoky like gray sage, and then of a sudden he laughed. But I'd seen that trick pulled, too. I kept my gaze hard on him. I said, "What for do you want to come bustin' in like this on a private party?"

"You sure got a gall," he muttered. "I've a damn good notion to blast your mortal tintype."

"Go ahead—you got plenty of help here, ain't you?"

"Why damn you,' he said leaning forward, a hand spread over his gun. "Are you hintin'—"

"If the boot fits, pull it on," I said. "I've always heard since you took to cuttin' notches you didn't give a damn how you got 'em." I shoved my gun back into its scabbard. "Go ahead—turn loose your lightnin'."

He was surprised all right. Looked for a minute like I had him stumped. But I'd banked a deal too strong on his humor, away too short on his temper. With a snarl he grabbed out his gun.

I heard the hammer go back.

"Blow his face off!" Middleton shouted.

It looked plumb like he aimed to. He was mad as a peeling rattler. "Another of your goddam jokes—"

"I wouldn't waste my time," I said, "tryin' to joke a buck with no more humor than you got!"

His eyes was like hot coals. I figured my goose was cooked anyhow, so while I was at it I told him plenty.

"By God," he said, "I believe you mean it."

"Sure, I mean it— You're nothin' but a two-bit fence-crawler that's gone hog-wild with a gun! Go ahead! Shoot an' get it over!"

I braced myself. I damn near fell off the horse when I saw he was putting his gun up. I couldn't believe my eyes.

His crowd seemed surprised as I was. "Go on," he growled, "hop it. When you get back, tell Evans he better sing low or I'll be feedin' his guts to the buzzards."

I'm brave, I guess, as the next guy. But I ain't no total knot-head. Six of their kind to one of me spelled something I wasn't hankering for. I was wheeling my horse when I heard a grunt, the scuffle of boots—a panted oath. I flung a look back.

Bowdre and the Kid were struggling. One of Bowdre's hands was clamped to the Kid's, the Kid's was wrapped round a gun. Backward, forward they swayed; Bowdre's face looked white with strain, the Kid's long-jawed one murderous. "Git!" yelled Bowdre. "Clear outa here, you fool!"

I did. I got out of there like a shot.

11

"WE'LL SEE WHO FEEDS THE BUZZARDS!"

A. A. McSween was a man of culture, brains, and training, And he had ambition—which is all right in its place, but not in the place he brought it. Too many gents there held similar cravings already; Chisum and Murphy, to mention the most outstanding. But that didn't bother Alex. He was a shrewd and able lawyer; and because a lawyer was a new thing in that country, and because this one had a right pert piece of calico besides, Lincoln County took to litigation like a bunch of ducks to water.

These facts, I reckon, are known to all and sundry. What folks seem to have forgot, however, is that when Alex and wife first arrived in Lincoln in their fall-apart two-wheel oxcart, they couldn't have scraped up a dime between them. All they had between them and starvation was a letter of introduction to Murphy from Otero, Seller & Co., Trinidad merchants. You've heard a lot about McSween's fine home, but has any one said where it come from? Well, it came from Murphy and Dolan; same as their grub, their money, and the clothes they put on their backs.

Under Murphy's patronage Alex's business grew like the beans that fellow planted. But it didn't keep up with his druthers. He craved to be a brass-collar dog, and Murphy and Chisum had liens on all them collars available. But, as luck would have it, he didn't have to wait for more than a mustache before the main chance up and smacked him in the eye. Charlie Fritz and Mrs. Scholland come and give it to him on a platter.

Now, I wouldn't claim Alex McSween and Alex Hamilton came out of the same box of sand, but both of them was sure plain hell when it come to writing letters. McSween wrote more letters than a guy could shake a stick at. Every day he wrote them. While he was away in the East he must have wrote Charlie every five minutes—same kind of stuff old Hamilton wrote in that letter before Burr killed him. Real high and noble stuff, you sabe. Yes, sir! Alex sure could make a pen talk; but none of his grand flourishes quite managed to rub out the fact he put the Fritz insurance money into a St. Louis bank under his own John Henry and the Fritz crowd never got a smell of it.

It was this same slick insurance business tossed the spark into Lincoln County's powder keg; but the only part in the fracas Charlie Fritz had, was to feed all the outlaws who come along. And they came frequent. They made his place a stop for grub and shut-eye every time they got run out of Lincoln. Charlie's opinion of McSween ain't never been put on record—I expect they couldn't find paper stout enough.

As for Murphy, I knew his family oak pretty well, as did most of the crowd round Lincoln. For years he'd been the country's leading citizen, one of the most influential men in the whole Southwest, and a friend to every guy in need. His life was an open book. Born in County Wexford, Ireland, his folks had christened him Lawrence Gustave. He'd got his learning straight from the Old Sod—some place called Maynooth College. But the role of father-confessor, which was what his Ma had hoped he'd have, hadn't much appealed to his kind of red-blooded fellow and, quick's he'd graduated, he hopped a ship for America, where he'd heard things was a bit unsettled.

He got into the army over here—got to be a sergeant-major. When the Civil War broke out, he signed up with the First New Mexico volunteers, and was made a lieutenant under Ceran St. Vrain. I reckon he was wasted on a looey's stripes. They made him regimental quartermaster, and he held that job until '62, when the Volunteers was reorganized. Every one was mustered out. But that didn't suit Murphy nohow, and before the year was out he was back in again, wearing his lieutenant's gadgets. Two months later he'd been made regimental adjutant. Next year they made him a captain, and a bit later brevetted him a major for "gallant service." Many's the time I've seen his commission, and his honorable discharge, where he keeps them in that funny little Irish-wood frame above his desk.

He was a great Mason—not your ordinary kind, but 32nd degree. He was damned well liked, I guess, because when he died in Santa Fe a resolution was passed to drape the lodge for thirty days, and they had a—

But I'm getting ahead of the story. Murphy didn't cash his chips till along in October—the twentieth. Right now it was only June, and nobody so much as dreamed his luck would buck out that quick.

First thing I did after making town was to hunt me up the sheriff. But Peppin was still away some place, and nobody could say how to reach him. Let the Kid get wind all the Law was out of Lincoln and *Good Night!* Something had· to be done. I scouted out Murphy.

He was in his office. And alone, as well—which wasn't usual. There was smudges under his eyes, and in the lamplight he looked pale and drawn as a quartered beef. "What's wrong?" I said. "Ain't you feelin' good?"

"I'm all right," he grunted. Yet you could tell by the way he sat he wasn't. But he wouldn't give in. "You get any line on the Kid? It's him that's lifting those cattle, isn't it?"

"It's him, I guess." I told him what had happened. He whistled softly in surprise, then scowled. "You were lucky. I wonder why Bowdre did it?"

"It's got me beat. I've known him sort of casual ever since he come here, but I ain't never had no truck with him. Mebbe," I said, "he figured the time wasn't right. I can tell you this much —he's for the Kid one hundred per cent."

"Well, he saved your life. I should have insisted on you taking some men along. Nobody else must go after Bonney without he takes a posse—"

"The trouble," I said, "with posses is they make too damn much noise. What I figured was to sneak up close, where I could get a line on things, and mebbe drop a few slugs around for warnin'."

The Major shook his head. "You better tell Evans what the Kid said. We don't want him taken unawares. And if Bonney ever finds out Peppin's away from town he'll bring his bunch in here quicker than you could down a drink."

"Speakin' of drinks, if you ain't got no further orders for the moment I reckon I'll go down and get one, an' mebbe," I said, "a couple of hours of shut-eye."

Jesse Evans was whooping it up in the Murphy-Dolan bar.

McDaniels, Andy Boyle, and Old Man Pierce was with him. They was singing their empty heads off. I say singing, but it sounded more like a bunch of coyotes giving the death rattle.

Jawbone the Loose-Mouth was thinlike an' slatted,
  His ribs was as sharp an' as plain as plowed ground—
Face matted with whiskers, his boots shone like mirrors;
  His pleasure the ladies it was to astound.

He forked a wild mustang, a flea-bitten bronco,
  A bundle of sin that was wrapped in sho't hair—
Nose curved like a compass, his teeth was like shovels;
  His neigh was a blast like the snort of a bear.

A schemin', connivin', obstreperous rascal—

I stood it long as I could, then interrupted the racket by pouring somebody's whisky down the back of McDaniels' pants. He didn't like it. He let out a squawk that could've been heard clear down to the Torreon. He was all for yanking out his gun, and working me over, but Jesse let fly a left-handed wind-letter that folded him up like an empty purse. While he was bent like that, and gasping, Evans took the gun from his hand, and tapped him on the head. Jim lost interest suddenlike.

Jesse grinned. "What's on your mind, Flick, besides your hair?" he asked, tucking McDaniels' sixgun in his belt.

"Mebbe we better talk this over outside—"

"Hell, tell it here. I haven't any secrets from these boys. They all savvy the dames can't leave me be. Which one's figuring to throw herself in the river this time?"

"It ain't no dame," I said. "It's Bonney." You could see the grins fall off like wormy apples. After a minute I told them how I'd run into the Kid. "He said to tell you next time your trail crosses his he's going to feed your guts to the buzzards."

Crack rider, sure shot, gambler, and an all-around tough monkey, Jesse Evans was headed as straight for hell as a fellow could go to get there, but he was a man to command respect by reason of his prowess and, like the Kid, could be downright entertaining when he cared to. Though it wasn't generally known, Evans and the Kid had been great friends a couple of years back, had raised all kinds of devilment together down through the border country, and at Mesilla had joined up with Frank Baker, Billy Morton, and McDaniels. It was McDaniels who had first called Bonney "Billy the Kid." A tough crew, all of them, but it was Bonney who had proved himself the renegade. Already he had killed Baker and Morton, and here he was, a bare two months afterwards, threatening Jesse Evans.

Maybe Evans was considering this. He looked like he was remembering things in this hush that had grabbed the room. Everyone was watching him, wondering what he'd do. What he did do, I reckon, surprised nearly all of us. He threw back his head, and laughed. Then, abruptly, the laugh turned ugly.

"So that little bunch-quitter is saying he'll get me, is he? All right, we'll see. First time any of you boys hear of him being in town just tell him where I'm at, and come let me know he's here. We'll see who feeds the buzzards."

"He won't fight fair," warned Old Man Pierce.

Evans didn't answer, but his mouth showed tight, and there was a blued-steel gleam to his eyes.

12

STRANGE INTERLUDE

MURPHY was sick, down flat on his back in a bed. Dolan, with sleeves rolled up, was wading through the mass of contradictory report and rumor brought in by Riley's scouts. "The Kid," he scowled, "has shot three more of Murphy's backers . . .

He's been seen at Seven Rivers, and— Yes, here's another one, claiming they've identified him at Tularosa. . . . This guy says he's headed for the Border. Got away from Peppin, and is forted up on the Pecos. Damn it," he said irritably, "does anybody *know* what's going on?"

I knew how it was; I felt that way myself. This kind of thing was Murphy's specialty. Riley was the scout and news-getter; Dolan was our trouble-shooter, the fighter, the man of action. Murphy was the man who made decisions—the shaper of company policy. With Murphy down, Dolan and Riley had to double up a bit, and neither of them liked it. They were like two steers in a soap hole. Dame Rumor was working overtime, and every gent who rode into town packed in a different story. Dolan flung me a look, and cursed. Riley, pounding a rut in the floor, was muttering to himself and, every so often, would snap a glance at the clock, and mutter a little harder.

"For Christ's sake," Dolan snarled at last, "shut up, an' go sit down!"

Riley gave him a surly stare, and kept right on with his tramping. He had got the wind up bad, looked like. But not without plenty of reason. With Peppin gone off with his posse the town was left short-handed, and most of Murphy's fighters— what weren't out at the Pecos ranch—were off with the company wagons that were bringing in goods from the railroad. Our side was in a jackpot if the Kid's crowd came in now.

"Well, you boys don't need me," I yawned. "I'm goin' to catch some shut-eye."

"Send Evans up here when you go down," said Riley.

Dolan swore. "Who's running this damn show anyway?"

"You want to get our whole crowd planted? Jesus Christ, man—use your head! If the Kid ever learns the way we're fixed—"

"How's he goin' to learn, when he's holed up out in the brush?"

"Any of these Mexicans crippled? I ain't seen none hobblin'

on crutches. All McSween's got to do is to send a few scouting
—Salazar'd go in a minute! But who says he's holed up in the
brush? You're only guessin' he is— Didn't Flick see him out on
the river? You know what he said last week about comin' in
after Evans—"

"Bluff!" Dolan jeered.

"Well, bluff or not, I'll cover anything you bet he's on his
way in right now!"

"If he was coming in," Dolan said, "he'd be here! San Pat—"

"He's probably been out rounding up recruits. When he
plops a shot between your eyes don't say I didn't warn you—"

"When he plops a shot between *my* eyes you can hand him
one of your medals!"

I got up. "Well, save a few sticks of the furniture. I'm goin'
to try an' get some sleep."

"Send Evans—"

"God damn it," Dolan glared. "Have we got to go over that
again?"

"No," Riley said. "You can send for Peppin, or I'm goin' to
take a vacation."

Riley's fidgets was catching.

But Dolan wasn't the sort to give an inch without he put up
a battle. "We're short-handed now. If we send anyone after
Peppin we'll be that many less to defend this place in case the
Kid *does* come in—and if we send anyone, it sure ain't goin'
to be Evans."

"If you won't send him, don't send anyone. Nobody else
could get through."

Dolan's breath coming through his teeth made a noisy, exasperated sound. He looked at him. "What do you think, Flick?"

"Hell," I said, "don't ask me to put in my oar. Whatever
you do is O.K. by me—"

"Send him, then," Riley growled.

"Not on your tintype!" Dolan had an exaggerated opinion
of my ability as a warrior, classing me even above Evans, the

best fighting man he had. "Flick," he said, "is the only guy in this camp that's got the nerve—"

I said: "Let's skip all that. If you want somebody to go after the sheriff—"

"How about Bob Ollinger?" Dolan asked.

"We couldn't ask him," said Riley. "His marshal's duties—"

"Send McDaniels then."

Riley scowled. "Send Evans *and* McDaniels, and we'll mebbe get results."

And that was what they finally did. They sent Evans and McDaniels. The next day Bill Bonney moved in with a dozen tough bucks at his back.

Hemmed by lofty crags and pinnacles, guarded on all sides by the frowning jowls of crouching mountains, Lincoln County was a cowman's paradise, greater than many an Eastern state—two hundred miles square of wind-swept hills and waving grasses; a booted and belted empire ruled by the fastest draw.

When the Kid took over the town, Murphy-Dolan had but three fighting men in Lincoln—Old Man Pierce, George Davis, and myself. We didn't do much advertising, being in somewhat of a lather lest the slightest overt move on our part would bring about some form of ghastly reprisal on the part of McSween's hired killers. Pierce, Davis, and me weren't doing the worrying; it was Riley. He was still scattering gloomy predictions, like a wet dog shaking water, and had talked Dolan into giving us strict, if reluctant, orders. On no condition were we to bring about a clash between the factions. Regardless of the magnitude of insult, we were to swallow our pride and take no issue. "You'll have all you want of that," Dolan told us, "when the sheriff gets back."

"When Peppin gits back," said Old Man Pierce, "you won't catch a McSween leather-slapper inside twenty miles of this place."

"Maybe not," admitted Dolan, "but we can't afford any fight here now. You keep in mind what I told you."

So a kind of armed neutrality settled for a time on Lincoln. There was little business done, however, for mostly people kept indoors, and did not venture out unless the need were urgent. The Kid's swashbuckling gun-packers swaggered round the town, swearing, sneering, making their windy brags, and keeping the night hours noisy with their brawls and wild carousals. We kept ourselves out of their way as much as possible, having little stomach for their cat-calls, quips, and sallies. The Kid filled in his time with drinking, wenching, and shooting off his jaw about what he'd do when he got his hands on Evans. I was fortunate enough not to bump into him until a couple days before his crowd pulled out.

During their stay, John Riley's smile was conspicuous for its absence. He was like a goddam raven, with his croaking, always getting off some gloomy prediction, and pretty generally making himself obnoxious until finally Dolan, with a black scowl, told him where to head in at.

We were under constant expectation of an attack on the company's property; and once the Kid, O'Folliard, and half-a-dozen other bucks started for the store with rifles. Davis grabbed a gun up, and crouched beneath a window; I rushed upstairs and manned another; Old Man Pierce, with a box of cartridges, hunkered down in the crotch of the stair well, while Dolan stepped out on the porch with a shotgun to find out what they wanted.

"We're goin' to take this place apart, by God!" the Kid shouted up at him, grinning.

They were fixed to try, all right, and I guess they would have, only just then Sally Chisum, white of cheek and breathless, came galloping up on her big bay horse, and finally argued them out of it. She wasn't any more scared of Bonney than a kid would be of a lollypop.

"You ought to be ashamed," she told him hotly. "Aren't you

in enough trouble now without stirring up any more? If you don't care for your own sake, you might have some regard for the light you're putting Uncle John in! Do you expect him to countenance things like this?"

"I expect him to pay what he promised!" he snapped. "He said, after Tunstall got killed, he would pay us fightin' wages if we'd take up for him an' McSween. He ain't paid a goddam cent so far—but you can tell him for me he's goin' to, or I'm a-comin' in after his scalp!"

An ironic week, that first one the Kid and his crew held Lincoln. While friends of both factions stayed home behind barred doors, the Kid and his gang held fiesta. Night and day, the town rang to the plunk of guitars, and the squeal of fiddles. It was holiday and how! Every corner echoed to the giggles of excited Mex girls. They wore their best, and swung it round like bullfighters. And Patron and José Montana did a land-office business, and flashed their broadest smiles every time the outlaws came round. It was Old Home Week for the Mexicans, and baile followed baile in their honor. The best was none too good for *El Chivato*.

Not least of these ironies was the Bonney clan's attendance at church. Doc and Mrs. Ealy—the missionaries McSween had sent for—had opened, in a part of the McSween house, a mission school for kids. On Sundays this became a meeting house, and Doc Ealy preached the Gospel. The Kid and his bunch were right on tap, as solemn as righteous citizens. They attended— boots, belts, sixguns, and all; and when it came hymn-singing time you could hear them damn near to Hondo.

The Kid was strong on music. Sometimes during the afternoons Mrs. Ealy would feel like playing, mostly old hymns and Bible songs, and some of us took the habit of drifting over. I was there listening on one such occasion with Davis, when the Kid, O'Folliard, and Bowdre came trooping in. The Kid slid on a scowl when he seen us standing there, but Bowdre winked, so I said: "Hello, Charlie. Bringin' the Kid to confession?"

Charlie laughed. "Shucks," he said kind of sheepish, "I reckon we was aimin' to sort of brush up some on our music. You ought to hear Billy sing."

"I've heard him," I said dryly, and would have made my meaning plainer, only just then Davis nudged me with his elbow, and I remembered Dolan's orders. Bonney kind of scowled, and rubbed a hand across his holster, and Mrs. Ealy said real hastylike, "Won't you boys come join us?"

So Bonney dragged off his hat, Bowdre and O'Folliard dragged off theirs, and the three of them came clanking up and draped themselves on one side, while Davis and me held down the other. Mrs. Ealy played *Nearer My God to Thee*, and I guessed some of us was near as we'd ever get.

Bonney cocked his head to one side and, with his eyes like a dying calf's, let go all holds. He sure had a lusty voice. Every time one of us come near getting up to it you could feel him start to fidget, and see them eyes of his take on a frosty glitter, till the guy kicked off the peddle. Seemed like Mrs. Ealy didn't know them hymns real well, or might be she was absentminded, like they say professors is, 'cause every little while she'd pop a note that didn't seem much force beside the one the Kid had reached for. Maybe she was nervous.

After getting as near to God as good stout lungs could take us, Bonney says kind of shylike, "I wonder—I wonder could you play that one about Sweet Alice?"

"You mean *Sweet Alice Ben Bolt*?"

Bonney nodded. He was kind of pink and sweaty, like his collar had got too tight (which I wished it had); but I guess it wasn't, because it didn't seem to cramp his style none and he still had plenty volume. After we'd wore *Sweet Alice* out—him saying "Again!" every time she figured to stop—I suggested maybe *Blessed Assurance* would sound pretty good. But Bonney said, real impatient. "Hell—we sung that yesterday. Let's have *When Israel Out Of*."

So we had it. And afterwards, when Bowdre was fixing to

ask for something, Bonney, giving him a hard stare, says: "Let's try *Redeemed*, Miz' Ealy— Don't look like nobody ever wrote a better piece than that one. Makes me feel all bumpylike inside."

She give him a smile, like he'd named her favorite number. Then she struck a few chords and the bunch of us waded in:

> Redeemed, how I love to proclaim it,
> Redeemed by the blood of the Lamb;
> Redeemed through His infinite mercy,
> His child and forever I am.
>
> I think of my blessed Redeemer,
> I think of Him all the day long;
> I sing, for I cannot be silent,
> His love is the theme of my song.
>
> I know there's a crown that is waiting,
> In yonder bright mansion for me;
> And soon with the spirits made perfect,
> At home with the Lord I shall be.
>
> Re - deem'd, Re - deem'd,
> Redeem'd by the blood of the Lamb;
> Re - deem'd, Re - deem'd,
> His child and forever I am!

We sure knocked the props from under that one, and if carrying-distance had anything to do with it, I reckon crowns was dusted off for every one of us.

We bellowed with Mrs. Ealy most of the afternoon, and when it got time for supper I was hungry enough to eat a horse with the hide on. I don't know if it was on account of the Kid or not, but when we was fixing to go, Mrs. Ealy said: "We don't have anything fancy, but wouldn't you boys like to stay and eat with us—I'm sure the doctor would be real pleased to have you."

The Kid scratched his flaxen curls and looked at Tom O'Folliard. O'Folliard says, "Sure—I'll set in, if the Kid will." Bowdre didn't look too keen about it, but he said: "We're obliged to you, ma'am. We'd like to." Then she looked at us.

I said: "Thank you very kindly, ma'am, but I reckon we better not. Me an' Davis here has got to catch up them horses—"

"Humph!" says the Kid real nasty. "Murphy's sure gettin' mighty careless, trustin' his broncs with guys like you.

It sure did get my hackles up; but Davis got a tight grip on my arm and steered me out the door. And just as well, no doubt, in view of Dolan's orders. Elsewise, I'd probably taken a poke at him, and got myself shot up.

It was four hours later, with the stars blinking down like sleepy mockers, when I finally got my chores done up, and decided to get a drink. As I reckon I've already mentioned, I liked to wet my whistle at Stockton's place, and that was where I headed. I hadn't talked to Ike much lately, account of the Kid and his bunch making the place their hangout when they wasn't at Montana's, or kidding the dames at Patron's. I was still feeling ringy over that crack about horses, or I reckon I wouldn't have gone there.

I was just reaching out to push open the doors when a guy swung down at the rack. There was something kind of familiar about him, and I paused for a second look. A feather would have pushed me over.

It was Evans—Jesse Evans—and mad enough to eat the devil with his horns on.

13

THE TENDER SPROUT

"HOLD ON!" I said. "Thought you was huntin' Peppin?" He might have been hunting daisies. for all he said to the contrary. His mouth was folded ominous, and there was something about his eyes that was like a Yukon moon on ice.

I made a grab for him. "Listen—" I said. "The Kid's—"

I ain't figured yet just what happened, but suddenlike I was spinning across the walk, exerting every faculty to keep from piling up. My jaw felt like a mule had kicked it, and Jesse's broad, black-shirted back was shoving through the batwings.

When he'd swung down beside the tie rail the street had been deserted. Now, ten seconds later, it seemed like a fellow was mighty lucky if he could even find him gasping room. The news had spread like magic: *"Jess Evans is back! He's goin' into Stockton's bar!"*

I seen a fellow stoop, and come up with a hat. He cuffed it off, and handed it to me. It was mine—but damn if I know how it got there. Then it come to me what was toward, and lamming guys right and left I started, cursing, for the batwings—made them. Crushed my way inside.

The only sound in that tight-packed room was the clank of Evans' spurs.

Against a sea of scared white faces I saw the Kid backed up by the bar. Doc Scurlock was backed up with him. And Middleton, with his outlaw's eyes like pin-points.

It's sure too bad there wasn't no tripod expert handy to get a picture of that scene. The barkeep was gone clean out of sight. Stockton, with a look hacked out of wood, was frozen by the faro bank, and off to the side there was Ollinger's eyes standing out like two bugs on a stick.

Like most Texans, Evans was used to fixing the bulk of his

works up with swagger. But he wasn't swaggering now. He was coldly, deadly in earnest. He was walking up to Bonney with no look I'd want turned on me.

I didn't like the way John Middleton was standing—a kind of slanchways crouch it was. He had a hand draped along the bar edge within two inches of a bottle. Scurlock was shifting weight with a solemn care.

But these things didn't stop Evans. He brought up in front of Bonney and, without a word, smashed him full in the face.

Hurtling backward, the Kid struck the bar and hung there, spread-eagled, while the place got cold and wicked with the vibrance of men's desires.

Thick with rage and repression, Evans' voice was like a butcher's maul. "Get up on your feet, an' start makin' good on them brags!"

Scurlock's eyes rolled wildly. Middleton stared with a shocked amaze. But the Kid never moved an eyelash. He cowered where Evans' blow had sprawled him; fear bright and naked in his eyes.

Contempt rolled Evans' lips back. "Get up, you whining cur, and take your medicine like a man."

Bonney's cheeks got mottled, went suddenly gray and clammy. He tried to speak, but it stuck in his throat.

A commotion broke out back of me—near the doors, I guess, by the sound. I could hear men grunt, growl protests; but I didn't turn, nor did Evans. A kind of change had come over Bonney, nothing a guy could lay hands on . . . but it was there. And he'd got his voice back.

I saw him straighten a little, careful. "Why, Jess—" he said. "I—I thought that we was friends. Have you forgot—"

"I haven't forgotten anything. I haven't forgotten Baker or Billy Morton, or the way you got Bill Brady."

Some unknown thinking laid its bitter mark across Evans' high roan face. "If you know any prayers you better be sayin' 'em," he declared grimly, "because whether you drag that iron or not I'm goin' to drop you soon's I count ten. One, two—"

"*Evans!*" Dolan's voice slammed the name in sharp command.

Middleton saw his chance. His hand grabbed up the bottle, had it halfway set to throw, when flame burst whitely from the region of Evans' waist.

Scurlock's face was gray as wood-ash. Middleton stood there, staring stupidly, with the bottle neck clutched in his hand. Bonney, hard against the bar, abruptly shook as Jesse shoved his gun in leather.

Evans said, "Go on, you bastard—*flash it.*"

He waited stiffly. But the Kid had forgot his "chance-in-a-million" motto. It was an even break Jesse offered him; we looked for him to take it. But, licking a tongue across dry lips, he muttered: "God, Jesse! Don't shoot—You know I'm nothing but a little boy!"

"The time to've considered that," Evans said, "was before you got into this business. Some sidewinders is little too, I notice, but they bite just as bad as the big ones."

"I give you my word—"

Evans laughed.

Bonney threw up his shaking hands, begged like a cane-threatened school kid; but like doom through his sniveled pleas on rolled the sound of Jesse's count: ". . . five . . . six . . . seven—"

"*Stop!*"

It was Dolan that saved the Kid's life, though little thanks he got for it. Why he did it will probably never be known; but he came plowing through that crowd with a sawed-off shotgun held at ready, and with a look in his eye that said he'd use it if he didn't get his way.

He had both barrels cocked, and the way he handled it whitened more than one of the hard-case watchers' faces. "Clear out!" he told young Bonney, "an' take your playmates with you. And remember this: if you ever come back you're goin' to stay here permanent!"

14

"—IF I HAVE TO ROB A BANK!"

I T LOOKS like I ain't much force at telling this kind of a story. Seems like a pretty mild affair, you'll say, compared to the things you've heard of it; more like a Maypole dance than the tale of a bloody range feud. I expect probably you are right. I ought to be painting it a sight more creepy, put corpses on every corner and have a shoot-out every chapter. But it wasn't that way. I'm telling you like I saw it. There was plenty blood spilled before it got done but the actual shootings was a heap sporadic, and pitched battles was fought mighty seldom.

Bush-whackings was a deal more popular than the kind of fights you read about. It wasn't so much we was scared, I guess, as it was that victory got that way was surer. And a whole lot less expensive. I could go on for pages, telling you of fellows riding solo which got themselves chased up gulches, run down into man-trap pockets or into some 'Pache's scalping knife. A real writer I guess would tell it that way; and likely you'd be tickled, and buy his book—maybe tell your friends to buy it.

But I ain't no kind of writer. Just Flick Farsom, a puncher whose talent with a .44 got him a front place seat in a range war. I have to tell this thing the way I saw it. I didn't see them chases. I only took part in one of them, and in that was the guy they took after. But quite a lot of it went on; in the five months Doc Ealy was with us he took care of thirty funerals, and only one of them come about natural.

Telling a story, I reckon, is a lot like punching cattle. Plenty of fellows punch cattle, but only a few ever get to be top hands. I expect it's that way with story telling; I expect you got to be born for it—like Bonney was born for killing.

What I'm trying to say is that a range war ain't all bloodletting. Anyone that tells you different has been a heap busy filling up gaps. We spilled considerable blood in Lincoln County, but we did other things besides. Most of the time we did other things. There was lines to be rode, and gear to fix, and all the forty other things that has got to be done round a cow spread that expects to make any money. What little time most of us had to ourselves we didn't spend hunting trouble.

It didn't need any hunting.

After his scare, and Dolan's Scripture, the Kid shoved his crowd out of town. Peppin's posse was still out, too, so things took a lull for a spell.

I didn't hear no one complaining.

Then one afternoon an event come to town that started tongues wagging again.

I was lounging in the cool blue shadows of Murphy-Dolan's store porch when it happened. I was chawing a cud and, kind of lazylike, watching Old Man Pierce whittle a basket out of a peach stone, and listening off and on to Evans and his brother, George Davis, arguing the relative merits of a pinto and a buckskin, when up the road we spied a dust and, pretty soon, out of it rode some soldiers.

"Batch of buff'lo troopers from the Fort," observed Pierce, and spat. "Now what in thunderation you reckon *they* want?"

"I expect we'll learn," I said, "if we keep our shirt-tails in."

Evans scowled darkly. "Some of McSween's antics, like enough. Probably sworn out a charge against us for scaring Little Boy Bonney."

Pierce snorted. "Ought to be a charge swore out ag'in' you, mismanagin' that affair like you done! You ought—"

"By God, boys," I cut in, "this looks like company! Look! There's Nanny-Goat Dudley an'—"

"Who's that hombre with him?" Davis wondered.

Pierce said, "Looks like a dad-burned carpetbagger!"

"Look at that hat!" cried Evans. "Bet you he's a parson, or a gambler—"

"No parson," objected Davis, "would want to be found buried in a coat like that sport's got. He's—"

"Mebbe he's a 'vangelist."

"Those clothes," I said, "case you don't know it, is the latest rage at the Capital. All the men is wearin' rigs like that. Go to the theater in 'em—"

"Do they do their gallin' in 'em?" Davis wanted to know.

"Hell!" Pierce said. "A man wouldn't stand no more chance in a rig like that than a stump-tailed bull at flytime!"

"Shh!" Evans winked. "You mustn't say such things in front of Flick—he's still kind of tender in his feelings."

They all started grinning, but I made like I didn't notice. Squinting up the road, I said: "That hombre looks important. You reckon he's a U.S. marshal?"

Davis shook his head. "Ain't likely. If they was figurin' to send a new fella, Bob Ollinger would of heard of it."

The troopers had stopped in the road out front. The wind was blowing towards us, and the dust them roosters made was like to clog our gullets. "Com-pany dis*mount!*" the lieutenant snapped, and the soldiers piled off their horses, and stood at sloppy ease.

The dust we got from that maneuver was worse than the original sample. "Damn!" muttered Davis scowling and, puffing the adobe from his mustache, he started cuffing off his clothes. Evans said, "Hell's fire!" and spat. "I never seen a horse soldier yet that didn't pack his brains in his britches," he declared loudly, looking at Dudley.

But the colonel affected not to hear. He was fussily herding the stranger toward the porch and, as they started up the steps, Evans changed the slant of his position, hooking his thumbs in his gun belt.

The stranger, an urbane, pleasant looking gent whose graying hair, of an inclination to curl, framed a cared-for face somewhat out of keeping with the kind of country ours was, looked us over like we was something got loose from a cage. "Are these some of them?"

Dudley gave us a fish-eyed stare, and said:

"Yes."

After they'd gone inside the store, "Who's his nibs?" Davis asked the soldiers. But none of them answered. The lieutenant scowled down his nose.

"You'll get pop-eyed doing that," Evans warned him earnestly.

Old Man Pierce got up, put his knife away, and started for the door. Deciding my curiosity needed satisfying too, I followed him. Evans and Davis drifted in after us. Every one was staring toward the stairs that led up to the company office. Dudley and the stranger wasn't any place around. But Ygenio Salazar was lounging happily by one of the windows—happily, that is, to judge by outward indications. He was grinning like a chessycat. He was one of McSween's staunchest partisans, and I could not figure how he came to be in Murphy's store—nor how he dared be.

Evans eyed him with a scowl. "What the hell's that bastard doing here?"

It was plain that Salazar heard him. But, far from showing resentment, he actually grinned a bit broader, as though whatever it was he found funny was the funniest thing in years.

Old Man Pierce hitched an angered hand toward his holster. But, nothing daunted, Ygenio put the flat of a hand to the side of his grin, and called in a loud stage whisper: "Did you see His Excellency?"

"Excellency . . ." Davis muttered. "What Excellency?" he and Evans demanded together.

"Why—" Salazar looked shocked, "the *Governor*, senors!"

"Was that ol' buck the Governor?"

"But certainly!"

It was apparent now what lay behind Ygenio's impudence. He knew very well nobody'd pull any rough stuff with him while the Governor was around, and had been smart enough to take no chances on our being ignorant of the man's identity. He leaned back against the wall now with folded arms, and regarded us with considerable humor. He had his share of sand, all right. Suddenly chuckling, I grinned back at him.

"Now what in the devil is Axtell comin' down here for?" Davis wondered. Salazar told him, "To arrest El Señor Murphy, of course— What else?"

Pierce let out a snort, and looked at Salazar nastily. "Mebbe you've forgot what I said to you the other day—"

"It was the good joke, eh?" said Ygenio grinning. He seemed not at all abashed by the ugly looks directed at him. I thought of Daniel in the lion's den and, mentally, took my hat off. Just the same Salazar was showing a deal more guts than sense. John Kinney, leaning against the counter across the room, was staring at him unpleasantly. Several of the others were, too. Old Man Pierce picked up a rifle from the corner, and started fiddling with its mechanism in a highly suggestive manner.

"Mebbe you better drift," I said. "You'll find the climate healthier across the street."

But the damn fool wouldn't budge. With a great show of unconcern, he got the makings out of a pocket and rolled him up a corn husk smoke. Struck a match on the wall, and lit it. With the smoke purling out his nostrils, he hummed a Spanish ditty that made Old Man Pierce see red.

Up came the muzzle of his rifle. Evans knocked the weapon from his grip just in time. Luckily, it didn't go off; but it made a hell of a clatter when it struck the floor. "For Christ's sake," Evans said loudly, "look where you're going, will you?" and stooped to retrieve the rifle.

It was quick thinking, because half-a-second later Axtell and Colonel Dudley stepped into the store from the stairs. The Governor looked around keenly. But he didn't say anything— Dudley didn't give him time. Keeping up a flow of garrulous chatter, he steered him across the room, and out the door. I looked round just in time to see Salazar departing by way of the window.

I went out myself, and so did Evans. Dudley and the Governor were getting into their saddles—the troopers were already mounted—and immediately afterwards the whole works walked their horses down the road toward the lower part of town, Salazar sauntering after them.

"Give him his due," I said; "he's a damn brave hombre—"

"He's a goddam fool!" Evans growled, and went stamping back into the store.

The Governor and Dudley called at McSween's—though I didn't find this out till later. McSween and his wife were out of town, however, having pulled out right after the Kid left, so I guess Axtell didn't linger there much longer than he'd stayed with us, which was only a handful of minutes. It is said he talked with Dr. and Mrs. Ealy. If he did, I reckon they gave him an earful. They were ardent McSween partisans, and usually referred to our side as "those drunken desperadoes." I don't know what Axtell came to see Murphy about—I suppose it had to do with the feud. But that night—and I didn't find this out till later, either—Murphy left Lincoln for Santa Fe, and remained there until his death. Financially bankrupt by the war, by McSween & Tunstall's ruinous mercantile competition, and by the wholesale looting of his cattle, harried and hounded by the bilious fever which was to bring about his death, L. G. Murphy was a broken man. Active direction of the Murphy faction passed to Dolan, and it was a summons from Dolan three minutes later that took me back into the store.

I found Dolan in the gun room, and he got immediately to business.

"I have a letter here from Chisum," he said, extending it. "Read it through, and tell me what you think."

It was addressed to the Murphy-Dolan Store Co., and was characteristically brief.

Gentlemen:

Regarding Governor Axtell's wish that hostilities should cease, the writer is willing to go halfway. In proof of his good faith, and having heard how short you are of contract count, he would be agreeable to selling you 600-head prime beef at current price provided you can take delivery at his South Spring Ranch and have the cash in hand.

CHISUM.

"What about them strings?" I said. "Can you get around them?"

"We can take delivery at South Spring all right . . ."

"But can you get the cash?"

Dolan scowled. "That ain't going to be so easy." He took a turn or two about the room. "What do you think of the proposition? You know Chisum better'n I do."

"I know him," I said, thinking about them wages he'd got out of paying me. "You better keep your eyes skinned if you plan to do any business with him. Governor or no Governor, it don't sound good to me."

"But we've got to meet those contracts! God damn it," Dolan scowled, "what could he do? We've got this letter—"

"Lot of Texans got his letters too," I said, "and it's all they *have* got. I tell you that old buck would skin a flea for its hide an' tallow."

"I thought you was sweet on that niece of his?"

"What's that got to do with it? Anyway, that's all off. She threw me over when I signed on with you. But I ain't beefin'," I said hastily. "Any dame that would throw a man down just because—"

"I've half a mind to chance it," he muttered.

I don't guess he'd even been listening to me. I could see his mind was made up so I said: "Go ahead. What you do with your money's no skin off my nose, just so you hold enough back for my pay check. Kind of odd, though, him askin' for cash when folks round here always writes a check if they only want a postage stamp."

"But dammit," he said, "he wouldn't have the nerve—"

"John Chisum would charge hell with a bucket of water."

Dolan wheeled with a scowl, jammed his fists in his pockets, and started tramping the floor again. I said, "Well, what does Murphy think about it?"

"Murphy's in no condition to think. He's a damn sick man—out of his head, in fact." He made the fireplace twice again, then stopped, and slammed a fist down hard on the table. "By God, I'm goin' to risk it! We got to have them cows or Murphy-Dolan's finished. Go round up some hands. I'll see what I can—No, by God! I'll have that money for you in the morning if I have to rob a bank!"

15

SPITE

I WASN'T much worried about him having to rob a bank. The Murphy-Dolan Store Co. had been taking an awful beating, but I reckoned they could scrape up the price between them. Murphy, I thought, still had his hotel and cattle ranch. Even if they'd been heavily mortgaged—as some claimed—to pay his fighting men, the partners, I figured, could still slap another mortgage on the store. It was Chisum that had me worried. What kind of deal had that slick old devil got cached up his sleeve for us this time? All this fine-sounding talk of burying the hatchet was just so much damn chin music. I was convinced that, in his anti-godlin way, Chisum was fixing to pull a fast one. He had no more love for Murphy-Dolan than McSween had—probably less, because it was Murphy that had sicced Tom

Catron onto him again, and it was because of Tom Catron that Chisum right now was languishing where he was. It was my knowledge of where he was that made me so damn uneasy. It had also brought to mind the number of cattle he had offered in that letter to Murphy-Dolan. *Six hundred.* I wondered it hadn't rung a bell in Dolan's head. It had sure rung one in mine, because six hundred was the exact amount of steers he'd lifted from Murphy's beef herd at the start of this fandango. And the more I thought about it the darker my suspicions got. But Dolan was the boss, and if he felt like shoving his horns out I didn't see I had any call to shoot off my mouth about it.

Chisum's strange lack of activity in the Lincoln County War has been laid to many things, but never to the right one. The plain truth is that the only reason he wasn't seen in the powder smoke is because he was where he couldn't get in. He was in jail. And that was where Dolan's letter had come from—I'd taken pains to notice the postmark.

Murphy had hired Tom Catron to get back those six hundred cattle old John had lifted; but when the business came up for hearing, Chisum had laughed, and thumbed his nose. He enumerated the brands on those six hundred critters, hauled out his powers-of-attorney, and got the case thrown out of court.

I reckon he felt pretty cute. But he underestimated Catron. Tom got on his tail, and stuck there for the rest of Chisum's life. He still was trying to collect his judgments on Chisum's old packing-house didos and now, being made fool of by Chisum's powers-of-attorney, Tom Catron got fighting mad. He was a first-rate lawyer, and he had his wits about him.

New Mexican law permitted jailing a man for debt, and Catron kept his eyes peeled. About the time our war got going full steam, Chisum decided he had to take a trip to St. Louis. So he packed his things and started. But he had to go through Las Vegas, and when he got there Catron grabbed him. "Now, my buck, you'll pay or else!" said Catron grimly. But Chisum didn't. So Catron had him arrested, and they put him in the

Las Vegas jail. Chisum could have paid his debts and walked out of there any time he wanted—could have paid them twenty times over. But it was his most cherished maxim never to pay for anything, so he spent his time in Las Vegas' jail till the Lincoln War was ended.

I rounded me up six fair-to-average hands, who could regard the prospective visit to South Spring Ranch as being somewhat in the nature of a lark, and bright and early the following morning dropped in to see Jimmy Dolan. As I'd more than half expected, he had managed to scrape up the money. He had it all done up and waiting in a little leather bag.

"Did you get the men?"

"I got half-dozen—"

"Half-dozen! Christ sake," he howled, "you could of handled them cattle with three! You tryin' to put me in the poorhouse—"

"I'm tryin' to make sure you get your cattle," I told him flatly.

He let off a string of cussing that would have warmed a bull-whacker's gullet; but when he paused to fetch another breath, I said, "You got any idea where that note of Chisum's come from?"

But he waved the matter aside. "You damn leather-slappers must think Murphy-Dolan's *made* of money. I tell you, by God, it's taken every resource I can command to scrape up the dinero for these scrubs Chisum's figurin' to palm off on us. Three men's plenty, besides yourself, to handle this—you tell them other three they better go roll their hoops."

I gave him a good hard look, and unloaded my jowls at the fireplace. I picked up the bag, and dumped his money on the table. "Got a sack?"

"What the hell you want a sack for?"

"I don't want it to put no apples in!"

"You think," he demanded scowling, "somebody's goin' to stick you up?"

"I ain't layin' no bets they won't," I said. "If you got a sack, let's have it."

He rummaged around and fetched one out, and I scraped the cattle price into it. He tramped with me far as the door. "Keep your eyes skinned," he warned me, pulling it open. "An' if you see anything looks suspicious, do your shootin' first, an' chew it over after—If you lose that money Murphy-Dolan's done for."

My men was waiting front of Stockton's bar. Dolan had said to lop off three; but he'd said a lot of things besides his prayers, and the way I looked at it six was going to be none too many. A part of my job was to see that money got to South Spring Ranch, and I aimed for it to get there.

It did. And the first guy I saw when we pulled into the yard was that pot-shooting Frank McNab, who was rodding things now for Chisum. I said: "Hello, Sunshine. Are they still lettin' you run loose?"

He gave me an ugly scowl, and bunched his fists like he was minded to speak the truth for a change. But whatever he'd been going to say, he must of changed his mind. He took a look at the guys I had with me, spat, and said gruffly, "I guess you've come for them cattle. We been holdin' 'em—"

"Keep right on holding 'em then," I said, "because we ain't takin' no delivery tonight."

He didn't like it, but I didn't give a damn what he liked. I wasn't trailing no six hundred head of half-wild steers out into the brakes with a tired crew. I'd cut my eye-teeth on this spread, and knew enough about the tough bucks working it not to make any play like that. "We'll spend the night," I said, "and take delivery in the morning. Where-at's Miss Sally?"

I could tell by the look in his eye that McNab had been counting heavy on our taking delivery immediate. He closed his face hard enough to bust his nutcrackers, jammed his fists in his pockets, and went stamping off in the dark.

"Well," I said to the boys, "put up your broncs, an' throw

your gear in the bullpen. You'll find the cook shack off there
yonder. I'll be seein' you subsequent."

I got off my horse in front of the house. Unfastening the sack
of money, I threw it over my shoulder, stepped up on the porch,
and knocked.

It was not without some misgivings that I stood there waiting
for Sally. A lot of things had happened since she'd struck me
with her quirt, and memory of that little exercise was not con-
ducive to any great amount of equanimity on my part. I
wouldn't have been a heap surprised if she'd refused to come
to the door.

But she came. I knew that firm quick step of hers like I
knew the face of my horse. The sound of it set my heart to
knocking like one of them Injun war drums. I felt some
ashamed to think I could still get that way about a woman
what had took a quirt to me.

And then I saw her there in the shadows, staring through the
screen at me. Seemed like we stood a mighty long while without speaking. I dragged off my hat, feeling flustered as a kid
caught stealing a melon.

"So it's you again, is it?"

There didn't seem much point in answering that one. I
couldn't make out her expression because she was standing
with her back to what light came out of the parlor. But I didn't
have to see her face to know she hadn't changed much. What
she thought of me was in her voice. I wished the hell I was back
in Lincoln.

She said coldly, "I thought I made it plain that day in town
that I wanted nothing more to do with you—"

"You needn't think I came out here to intrude myself on
you," I said. "I come because Dolan sent me—elsewise wild
horses couldn't of drug me out here! I got more respect for
myself—"

"Yes," she said, "you ought to have a lot of respect—"

"Where you want me to dump this money?" I gritted, furious.

"What money?"

"The money for them cattle your uncle's sellin'."

"Oh!" She seemed to be looking me over more careful. "I can't think what's come over him— If it was me, I'd see Murphy-Dolan roast in hell before *I*'d sell them any cattle! Uncle John's too easy, too willing to turn the other cheek. If any one had dared throw *me* in jail—"

I said, "Where do you want this money?"

"Why do you bring it here? Why didn't you turn it over to Frank McNab? He's—"

"He sure is," I said. "I wouldn't trust that sneakin' dry-gulch artist any farther'n I could throw a bull by the tail! If you want this money you better take it. Elsewise I'll be packin' it back."

She gave me a scornful look, but she pushed open the door. "Very well, then. Bring it in if you're so suspicious. I suppose," she said, following me into the parlor, "a person gets that way working for a man like Murphy."

I let it ride. There was no use trying to make Murphy sound good to her. She believed everything McSween and her uncle told her. I put the sack down by the table.

I turned to find her looking at me curiously. "You haven't eaten, have you?"

I said: "Don't bother. I've got some stuff in my saddlebags."

She glared. "You sit down in that chair, and stay there! You can drink a cup of coffee anyway— You'll drink it if I have to pour it down your throat. I'll not have it said Uncle John let *anyone* go away from here hungry—"

I said, "I'm not goin' away from here till morning," and started for the door.

She flung herself in my path, stood with her back hard-jammed against the door.

I looked at her. Finally with a grunt I dropped into the chair. I didn't want her bawling. But it wasn't much fun sitting there, listening to her bustling around in the kitchen, and thinking that but for a difference of opinion—and for this damn feud, that had brought that difference round—we might have had a kitchen of our own for her to fool in.

After awhile she called me, and I went out and sat down at the table. Sally was a damn good cook, and she had done herself up proud, but I can't tell you what I et now. All I know is that I hope I never have another time as miserable as I had that night eating Chisum's grub.

All the time I was shoveling food I could feel her sitting there, watching me. I didn't look at her. I was having bad enough time as it was.

When I got done, and shoved back my chair, she said: "Don't you want some more coffee?"

"No thanks," I said. "I better be gettin' back to the boys before they get themselves—"

"We been hearing about you," Sally said. "You're becoming quite a character."

I didn't say nothing.

"They say Murphy has signed up all the riffraff in the country—every back-trail rider he can find, every border renegade—that he's got together the worst collection of warriors that ever came out of Texas. Men who'll bank their luck on the turn of a card, who don't care what kind of crime they commit just so they're paid what they ask for."

She was watching me oddly, sort of studying me, I reckon, her look at once half-speculative, half-contemptuous. "You must feel real proud of yourself to be counted among that number."

I let it ride. If she wanted to see things that way, no words of mine could change her. No words of mine had ever changed her. She was like her uncle that way—stubborn.

It got still as hell, uncomfortable. I scowled at the crumbs of sourdough biscuit I had dropped around my plate, and thought of what we'd planned to do come grass; of the house I'd aimed to build, and of the roses she'd been going to plant about the door—them kind that climb up sticks with a little yellow center.

Well, the grass had come, but not the house—nor the goddam roses, neither. All we had was a swell big feud, and we never would get to build that house. Sally and me had took different trails. I could of had her if I'd done like Chisum wanted. But I hadn't. So I was done with her—pitched out like an empty sack.

I got to feeling like I had the day she'd used that quirt on me in front of all of Lincoln. The silence grew, and nothing got through it but the solemn tick of the great tall clock that stood in Chisum's parlor. It was just like sitting with a dead man. And the thought wasn't half farfetched at that, because death sat in that room with us. The ghost of what might have been.

Then Sally said, abruptly: "Is it true Murphy pays his men by bounty? Pays so much for each one of us they bring down?"

I was sore. In a mood for revenge, I said, "He'll pay five thousand dollars to the man who gets McSween." She winced, and I felt better; built a new lie. "He's promised another five," I said, "to the guy that gets your uncle."

Every bit of color left her cheeks.

I noticed of a sudden how tired she looked—the dark circles under her eyes. It gave me a malicious satisfaction. I decided to improve the lie a little. "They're exceptions, of course," I said. "He only pays a hundred bucks for guys like McNab and the Kid."

She shivered, and her stare looked glassy.

I felt pretty good. She'd set out to hurt me, to rub salt in my wounds. I had wound the business up by rubbing a bit in hers. I'd shown her two could play at that game, and had given her something to think about.

She sat there like a statue, with her hands laying limp in her lap. The glassy shine was still in her eyes, and I'd about decided she'd forgot me, when she said, "You'd better go."

She didn't say it really. The words were kind of a whisper that crept out of her stiffened lips. I couldn't see them move at all. I felt more satisfied than ever. But I'd one last ace that I meant to play.

I got to my feet, and played it. "Sure," I said, "I'm fixin' to go. But I'll take a receipt for that money first. Write one out, an' put your name to it."

It was quite a while before she moved. Then she turned her head in my direction. But she wasn't looking at me. I could tell by the funny look of her eyes that she wasn't seeing anything.

I felt a little sorry then. After all, I'd talked to her pretty mean. And there wasn't a bit of it true. I started to say so, then changed my mind. She hadn't cared how *I* felt. Let her take a few shocks for herself!

She got up sort of stiff and, like she was on a lass-rope, walked into the other room. I followed. Watched her go to a desk in the corner, pull out a little book, and make a few scrawls with a pencil.

She dropped the pencil on the floor. I don't guess she even knew it. She left the paper she had wrote on where it was and, still moving like she was in her sleep, walked out of the room, and left me.

I went over to the desk. It was a receipt all right. I put it in my pocket.

I didn't do much sleeping that night. I had ought to of felt pretty good, I guess. But I didn't. I kept remembering the way she'd looked when I'd told her them lies about bounties. Murphy had put no price on any one's scalp, not even the Kid's, though he'd wanted him bad enough. I'd just told her that to give her a scare, to give her a taste of what I felt.

It was a dirty trick that reflected little credit on either myself or Murphy. I'd been an ornery so-and-so. No matter what she's done to me, I thought. I'd had no call to act that way.

I felt a little better then.

In the morning I would tell her the truth.

16

GIT ALONG, DOGIES

Bᴜᴛ when morning came round I got no chance. She didn't come near the cook shack. We ate the grub Chisum's surly cook planked down on the table in silence. At least, without no talk; I expect we made plenty noise. While the boys was saddling I went up to the house. I knocked on the door five or six times. Loud enough to wake a deaf man. I guess she heard me all right, but she wouldn't come to the door. Finally, I said: "Come out here a minute. I got somethin' I want to tell you—something that'll make you feel better."

But she didn't come. She didn't want nothing to do with me, and I couldn't blame her much. I'd been a goddam fool talking to her that way.

I called myself some mule-skinner names, and stamped off down to the corral. Somebody was displaying his talking talents. Getting closer, I seen it was Tip Jones, one of the trail drivers I had hired. He was plastering the air with a lot of labels no man would ordinarily take without they came from his wife. I couldn't make out who he was talking at; but four or five Chisum hands was hunkered down by the kakpole, and he seemed to be doing his looking in their direction.

Last night I had made considerable of a fool of myself, and didn't aim to repeat the process. I came up with a diamond hitch on my temper and, with a brief nod to the squatting Fence Railers, stopped in front of Jones. "What's wrong?" I said. "Why ain't you got your horse cinched up?"

"Why, is right!" he snarled with another burst of profanity.

"What do you mean? He's in the corral there, ain't he?"

"Not unless he's hid behind a knothole!"

I looked the horses over. Jones was right. There wasn't any sign of his animal. "Where do you reckon he's gone?"

"I don't have to reckon," he said loudly. "I know goddam well where he's gone to! One of them bastards stole 'im!"

I knew well enough who he meant. But I didn't want no trouble. I had come over here to get a herd of cattle. "All things considered," I said mildly, "that's a pretty brash statement. Like enough someone forgot to put up the bars and—"

"And Blacky come out, an' saddled himself, an' strolled off to pick a few posies, eh?" Jones snorted. Cuffing his hat down over his eyes, he started for the Fence Railers.

I grabbed him, spun him round. "None of that," I said. "I'll tend to this. You stay right where you are."

Chisum's hands considered me warily through their Bull smoke. I said: "Where's McNab?"

One of them jerked his head toward the house. McNab had just come off the porch, and was headed towards us. While waiting, I gave myself a sermon on the evils of hasty action, threw another hitch on my temper, and prepared to be polite.

He gave me a surly stare. "Ready to take delivery on them cattle?"

"I will be in a minute." I said: "First off, though, there's a little matter about a horse that needs adjusting. One of my men is shy his nag; it seems to have got out of the corral some way—"

"Tough," McNab said. "He ought to have been more careful —can't hardly expect nothing different though of a guy that would ride for Murphy."

I let that go. "The point," I said, "is that he can't very well work without no mount. Have you got a spare one that—"

"Sorry," he said. "All our broncs is busy."

I looked at the corral. There was eighteen horses in that pen if there was one. "That's our rough string," he said, taking time out to spit. "Besides, they're just off the range. I've had 'em brought in for a graining."

"Little late in the season for that, ain't it?"

He shrugged; gave some orders to his men.

I could read the jeer in his eyes. But I managed to hang onto my patience. "Couldn't one of your boys make out to lend him a mount?"

" 'Fraid not. They're keepin' all their strings busy."

"O. K.," I said. "Those skates in the corral may be just off the range, but they're better than going afoot. I'll buy one off—"

"Sorry," McNab said again. "Hate to seem unobligin' but . . . No horses for sale—Chisum's orders."

I stared at him.

Spleen was taking him quite a way.

"All right," I said, and started for the house.

"Hey, wait! Hold on! No use you goin' up there."

I wheeled. "Why not?"

"Because she ain't there. She's gone to town—fogged off while we was eatin'." The mockery in his eyes was bright and plain. He grinned, a kind of gloating look that made me itch to paste him. I expect he was enjoying this more than anything he'd ever done, unless maybe it was the time he murdered McClosky, or the part he'd played in the killing of Hindman and Brady.

I walked across to my trail crew. "All right, boys," I said. "Get up behind O'Connor, Jones."

McNab came trotting over. "You takin' delivery now?"

"I'm takin' off for town."

"Town! Say, listen! If you think I'm goin' to hold that herd while—"

"I don't give a damn," I said, "what you do with that herd! The deal is off!"

"Off!"

His air leaked out like a mule had kicked him. He hadn't figured on nothing like that, I reckon. It was good to see the shocked surprise that tugged at his shaved-hog features. Then he got mad. A half-scared kind of anger that would have been laughable if things hadn't been so serious. "Now looky here—"

"You heard me," I said. "Off! Either you give this fella a bronc to ride, or you can stick that herd up your pants-leg!"

"Murphy'll—"

"What Murphy'll do ain't goin' to hold a patch to what *Chisum* will do to *you* if you don't unload those steers on us!" I told him. What I figured was that if Chisum aimed to pull any kind of monkeyshine, that monkeyshine pretty near had to be based on the assumption that the money was paid, and the herd belonged to Murphy. And it looked like I was right.

McNab paused with his mouth open, paused right in the middle of his bluster. He stood there stiff, and stared at me, his face wrinkled up like a caught fence-crawler. Then he grinned like a fellow will who has just been the butt of some horseplay.

I grinned, too; quick and hard and ominous. I'd had enough of his goddam smartness. It was plain as paint this business of Tip Jones' vanishing horse was a little improvement McNab had thought up, and not a thing included in Chisum's original scheme.

I was glad to know there was a scheme. My hunch had been right. Skullduggery lurked behind the bushes.

All right. Forewarned was forearmed. They might get away with this but, by God, someone would rue it!

The grin was gone off the Chisum boss' face. "He can take my horse," he growled at last. "Now let's see the color of your money."

But I wasn't that dumb. Once let him know that the money was paid, and we'd have tough luck aplenty. "Not so fast," I said. "Whereabouts are you holdin' these critters?"

"Down on the flats. I been keepin' the bunch close-herded—"

"Your tally show six hundred?"

"Say! What the hell is this? You buyin' cattle or conductin' a inquisition?"

"I reckon," I said grinning, "we'll just run a count on them cattle. I used to ride for this outfit myself. Murphy reckons to get what he pays for. Send one of your hands for that horse, and we'll go and look them over."

He didn't like it. He didn't like it at all. His face got red and ugly, and he half-bunched up his fists like he was minded to start the jamboree right then. His hard-case crew scowled too. Their still, intent attention held a cold and wicked look.

But I'd played poker myself. "Have it any way you like," I said. "Take it or leave it. If you want to sell them cattle we're goin' to have a count."

I fished out the makings, and rolled a smoke like I didn't give a damn what he did. He was fit to be tied. I reckon he hated me so bad he could taste it. But he had his orders, and a couple growled words sent one of his Fence Railers off to the stable. Pretty soon this fellow came back with a bayo coyote in tow. "This your bronc?" he said with a scowl at Jones.

Jones gave back as good as was sent. "You're goddam right it is!"

"Where did you find him?" I said mildly.

Another puncher came up, leading a horse for McNab. Jones threw his gear on the buckskin, shoved his foot against its barrel, and yanked the trunk straps tight. Gritting his teeth like he could eat the sights off a six-gun, McNab slammed into the saddle, and went larruping off toward the holding spot, the rest of us stringing out after him.

There was no six hundred head in the bunch Chisum's hands were holding. I saw that much right off. It was lucky I was hep to King John's ways, or they'd have hooked us right at the start. I had a hard time holding my temper, and had to keep reminding myself that what we had come for was cattle. If Dolan's need hadn't been so urgent . . .

I came up to where McNab sat waiting and, swallowing some more of my pride, dug out Murphy-Dolan's beef book.

"Drift 'em over to the chute," I said. "We're going to have this count right."

"We'll stretch a rope—"

"You'll drift 'em over to the chute, or the deal is off. And it'll be off permanent *this* time."

He took a good hard look, and changed his mind. "Over to the pens!" he bellowed. "We're going to haze 'em through the chute!"

With half-a-gut more he'd have yanked his gun. He was wanting to bad enough.

When the count was done it showed an even six hundred, not a damned steer turning up missing. "I don't know how you done it, but that was pretty slick work," I said thinly. "One of these days you'll cut it too fine, and they'll chisel your name on a headstone."

He let it ride. He said with a sour look, "I'll be takin' that money now, mister."

"Not today you won't." With his whole crew looking on, I got out the paper Sally had signed, and stuck it under his nose. "You can read, I guess? Read that then."

It was a pretty late start, but it couldn't be helped, and I didn't dare waste any more time. If we could of headed that herd towards the Pecos ranch I reckon I'd have felt some better. But we couldn't. Murphy-Dolan had a contract to meet, and there was only three days left to meet it. It would have been better on their weight-and-market price if we could have eased them along, allowing them to graze as they moved, but I couldn't afford to do that either. Not only was it necessary to get them into Dolan's possession, but the farther and quicker we got off Chisum's range the greater the chance of Dolan's getting to see them. I wasn't putting any money on his chance of seeing them anyway, but if didos was going to be pulled, I figured they'd be pulled the first night out.

We shoved them fast as they could hoof it.

Being trail boss, I rode ahead. Sometimes I'd get a mile or two off from the rest of them in my search for usable water, in my hunt for graze that would let us keep the herd bunched.

It was not my intention to let them cattle spread much; they could get out of hand too quick and easy. Way I looked at it, the boys would have trouble enough getting them trail-broke, and I wasn't forgetting the large possibility that tonight would see blood on the moon.

But I never let more than two miles get between myself and the outfit, having well in mind the part distance had played the day Buckshot Roberts got killed. And every half-hour or so, I'd crest a rise for a good look back to make sure the herd was still coming.

It was a stirring sight to watch that marching column of cattle with the yellow dust boiling up about it, now obscuring it, now blown clear by the vagaries of the wind; to hear the sullen rumble of hoofs, the clack of horns, the cries of the sweating riders. The constant bawling of the herd was a familiar sound, for I'd been with two herds twice this size clean up the trail into Kansas.

They were longhorns, descendants of the cattle brought over from Andalusia in the days of the Spanish Conquest—the only kind the Southwest knew. Lean, lively, and full of protest they were, ornery as a corn-drunk squaw. Trailing them was a risky, soul-trying business.

Riding close to the head of the herd, one to either side, and acting the role of pilots, were the point men, Jones and Harris. They were the most reliable hands I had, which was why I had give them the honor. Riding point was considerable responsibility with a wild bunch of steers like these were, for on Jones and Harris depended the guidance of the herd, the task of setting and keeping direction.

About a third the way back came the three men I'd given the job of riding swing and flank. Theirs was the chore of keeping the line strung outright, or turning back the bunch-quitters; and they rode up and down the whole column. Their horses got the toughest work. It was lucky they were good ones. Each man, of course, should have had a string, but without advertis-

ing our intention it would have been impossible for us to have
got out of Lincoln with that many extra horses. And, times
being what they were, we hadn't dared to risk it.

Riding drag, was young Tim Buckner, a kid scarce turned
fourteen. He had the most disagreeable job of all, having to
prod along the laggers, and what was worse, eat the dust of
the entire herd. But it was the least dangerous post I could give
him, and he held his end up well.

We choused them steers along clean up and into the evening.
But with the sun's glare fading off the highest hills, I began to
look round for a bed-ground. A stampede was what I feared the
most, and we'd been herding them cattle like dollars.

When I found the place I wanted I rode back to have a talk
with Jones. He had plenty of cow savvy, and I wanted to get
his notions on a thing I had in mind.

Riding up, I said, "I've found a pretty fair bed-ground, Tip,
but I ain't sure it's wise to stop."

"These critters is pretty tired, boss."

"I know they are; that's what I been mullin' over. Tired like
this, they ain't a heap apt to stampede, and if we keep on goin'
we ought to make the Fort by tomorrow noon—"

"If we don't run into no trouble."

"Yeah."

"They're pretty tired," he said again.

"Think we ought to stop, eh?"

He rasped a hand across his chin, squinted off towards the
mountains. "Well, it's up to you," he muttered finally. "But
if you're askin' me, I'd stop."

I turned it over. "Say we bed 'em down. They get rested up.
They're goin' to be pretty damn spooky along towards morning
case some one starts wavin' a tarp."

"Sure. On the other hand, this way we'll have picked our
ground. The other way if trouble breaks we'll have our ground
picked for us."

We eyed each other, thoughtful. "Besides," he said, "if you

keep 'em goin', by the time we hit Fort Stanton they won't have enough beef on 'em to wad a shotgun with."

"To hell with that," I said. "What I want is to *get* 'em there."

Jones spit out his chew, bit off another, and waited for orders.

It was a buck of a choice I had to make. Damned if I did, and damned if I didn't. But what he'd said about location was sense. "All right," I said. "Bed 'em down."

17

MELODY IN LEAD

WHILE dusk was corraling night's shadows, the herd was thrown. Riding them down, we gradually eased the point and drag steers closer and closer together. Bedding down a straight steer herd of longhorns was no kind of chore for any but the most seasoned of veteran cow hands. It was touchy work, and the day's hard drive, with its many exasperations to tempers already short, did not tend to make it easier. Start in crowding cattle, or allow them too much territory, and you're bound to pick up grief.

It was dark when we got them settled.

I named two men to sing to them. The rest of us hunkered down to what cold fixings could be dug from our chaps pockets.

The solace of an aftersupper smoke was denied us, for we dared not show a light. Not only was there danger of attracting unwelcome attention to our whereabouts, but the cattle, despite the long stiff drive, were nervous. The mere striking of a match might serve to touch them off.

The tenseness of the men themselves may have contributed

to this condition. We expected trouble, and cattle are a heap sensitive to atmospheres. We kept the horses under saddle, and slept by fits and starts. As Tip Jones truly put it, "You'd have to ride a mile to spit."

The moon came up with ghostly brilliance. It put a gown of deceit on distance, and the night wind shouldered off the mountains did little to make our lot more cheerful. Bodies stiff with saddle cramp, we huddled in our blankets, listening to the hymns of the circling riders. Religious tunes, whose profane words were drearily punctuated by the plaintive lowing of the restless herd.

The night seemed endless.

The changing of the guard marked the only interruption to the dragging march of minutes. They rode in two-hour shifts, and each hour seemed an entire night in passing.

I dared not sleep; the responsibility of the herd was mine, and mine would be the blame if anything happened. It was not a pleasant thought, for Dolan had said with bitter earnestness that the company was done for if it couldn't meet its contract, and its ability to meet it was dependent on this herd. I wondered if we lost it would Dolan, desperate, do as Chisum once had done in Texas: order his riders to get another?

For the first two shifts I doggedly fought off slumber, fought the jerks of my jagged nerves. I watched the far, pale glitter of the stars that gleamed in the heavens, and thought of the sermon Doc Ealy had preached last Sunday about the pearls the guy threw to the hogs.

I got to thinking then of Sally, of the things we'd told each other last night at Chisum's ranch. If a man could see ahead a bit . . . But no, that wasn't what this country needed to improve it. We needed a better hitch on our passions, a more tolerant view of our neighbors' works and attitudes. I considered the attitude I'd held last night toward Sally. An example in point, a good one.

It was hard to get Sally out of mind. I knew too well

each familiar gesture, could recall too easy the toss of her head, the curve of her lips when they smiled, the merry tinkle of her laugh. She hadn't laughed much lately.

A coyote howled from a hilltop. Made the country seem more lonesome somehow, increasing the desolation of our lot. A drop of sound in the vastness of forgotten space.

A girl in ten million, Sally; a girl discovered, and as swiftly lost. I was in no doubt about that last part. I had lost her, right enough. A man, if he moved, went forward. There wasn't any going back.

I must have dozed.

I came awake to a tense awareness. The call of an owl came softly from a thicket of squatting cedar three or four hundred yards to the right. The place was a blob of shadow, black as a stack of stove lids. Snatches of night-guard singing drifted vaguely from the herd. I never did care much for owls, and this one's continued *whoing* scraped my nerves like a file.

It called to mind the redskins, that our camp was in redskin country.

I watched the thicket till my eyes ached. Half-a-dozen times I seemed to catch a changing of its pattern, some small altering of its shape, only to conclude at last, disgustedly, that this had been some prank of the wind. That owl hoot, I decided, was a heap too real for a redskin. I wished the damn bird would choke.

Maybe it did.

I woke to a sudden touch. A man who has followed the trail of cattle through the 70's don't do his rise-and-shine act with a yawn. He comes up like thunder. So did I. Gun in hand, eyes slashing at the dark.

"Hold it!" Harris' voice turned thin, turned jerky with fright.

"What's up?" He hadn't woke me to ride my trick. His shape was too rigid. I tried to see his face, but the moon was gone behind a cloud.

And it was very still.

"It's Jones," he said, "an' Buckner—"

"What about 'em?"

"They took the graveyard shift. They ain't been singin' an'—*they ain't come back!*"

I listened. The hair crawled along my scalp. He was right. No singing. And the herd was up, was stamping in nervous excitement.

I said bitterly: "Why in—" and stopped, with the breath hung up in my throat.

Something was flapping in the cedars.

A wild Apache yell rang out, and split the night wide open.

I stood, for one stark and awful instant, frozen.

Came a rattle of hocks and horns, a bellow of fear from the half-crazed cattle, another yell. The ground shook with the thunder of hoofs.

All about me men were coming up out of their blankets as, with a muttered curse, I sprang for my horse. I wasn't stopping to give orders—they knew what to do.

We could scarce see the ears of our ponies. All we knew was that some place ahead the Fence Rails was crowding a hole through the night. We didn't think of the danger then. The herd must be headed, be headed and turned. It was up to us—there was just us two. Just me and Harris. The rest was lost in the murk behind.

Bent low, we drove our broncs with quirt and spur. Neck and neck, we raced with the crazed brutes jamming our flank. Their breath and the night wind fanned our faces, our ears were filled with their bawling, and through it all drummed the ominous rumble of churning hoofs.

Dust had us in its smothering clutch, but we were gaining. Little by little we were clawing ahead. Nearer and nearer, we crept toward the front. We had almost cut it, when a muzzle flame blossomed from the fog on our left. I heard no shots, no scream of lead, but a look found Harris gone out of his saddle.

18

THE CARPETBAGGERS

I DON'T know how long the stampede lasted. I quit working with it three jumps later—I had to. Something happened to my horse. I felt him shake. With a squeal of terror, he climbed straight up for a fall-back. I blew both stirrups. Before I could settle myself to go limp and land rolling, I was on my way, flying low, and using my face for a rough-lock. I remembered to roll, but it was about all I did remember till I opened my eyes on an empty range with the cold gray light of dawn just beginning to crack the eastern sky.

I say an empty range, but it wasn't really that. You couldn't call a place empty that had as many bits of gear and carcasses strewed round as lay in the hoof-scored dust of Dolan's vanished herd. There were ten dead steers in sight, three horses, a handful of feathers, somebody's rope, a spur that had belonged to Buckner, a hoof-battered rifle, and the mangled, almost unrecognizable remains of Harris.

I didn't discover these things at once. They were the results of prowling later. My first thought when I come to, was to make sure I was still in one piece. I was. I hadn't broke nothing, but all the hinges and bolts was loosened.

I got shakily to my feet. Three large birds took a running start, flapped their black wings, and departed with sullen croakings. I looked after them a moment, and shivered. It was then that I saw Harris. He wouldn't never be no deader.

Well, they'd cut it. My hunch had been right. They had got our money, and scattered the herd. I wasn't in no doubt as to where to put the responsibility for this little dido. Sight of those scattered feathers only curled my lips back. I stooped and, with a black scowl, picked a headband from the dust. Apaches wore them, but no damned redskin had lost this one. Nor those feathers.

With a bitter oath, I put the thing in my pocket.

We hadn't vented the brands on Chisum's cattle. There hadn't been time. I should, I suppose, have got a bill of sale for them. But I'd been too intent, at the time, trying to deal a hurt to Sally —not that it mattered. No bill of sale or anything else was going to get them cattle back, nor the money. Chisum had driven the final nail into Murphy-Dolan's coffin.

I stared out over the range, wondering what had become of the others. Would some of them turn up again, or had they met the fate of Harris? For a long time I stood there looking, but could find no sign of movement. I might as well have been on the *Jornada*.

If I'd thought about it I expect I'd have been glad that I was any place at all. It is cause for considerable wonder that I was.

I shall never forget my experience coming off that horse, the things that crowded my mind.

I limped to where the bronc had thrown me. Nothing now to show I'd been there, nothing but my memories. All sign was gone, plain vanished—gouged from sight, and torn away by the scarring havoc of countless hoofs.

Only my speed in rolling saved me. That, and Providence. I would never miss death much closer.

Crossing to a live oak thicket, I dropped exhausted in its shadow.

The sound of voices woke me.

I have said that a man of my experience, a cow hand of the 70's, jumps from sleep to reality with a sixgun gripped and ready. That wasn't the way I woke up then.

I was more used up than I'd allowed for. A kind of laziness was on me. I lay there with my eyes closed, hearing the drone of voice-talk, but not trying to make it out. I wondered idly where I was, and how I'd come to be there.

Suddenly then, events came back in a rush.

I reached for my gun, and sweat broke out on me. Gone! Jarred loose, like as not, when I'd taken that spill. I hadn't even got my rifle; it was out there on my bronc—on what the cattle and birds had left of him.

The voices had grown much louder.

I scanned my chances. If those comers should beat the thicket—

I guessed I'd better have a look.

It was part of my trail crew; three of them.

I came out of the brush.

"Farsom!"

They sat in their saddles eying me. "What's the matter with your map—"

"Never mind my face," I said. "What's happened to them cattle?"

They shook their heads. Brace said: "They're scattered clear to hell-an'-gone. Leastways, most of 'em. We found some piled in a— Gawd! Is that thing *Harris?*"

I said presently, "See Jones or Buckner any place?"

"We seen Jones." Brace squinted across the range. Charlie Rudolph busied his hands with rolling a smoke. "Mescaleros," the other guy said. "Looked like a goddam pincushion."

"Dead?"

"Well," Brace said, "he's planted. I didn't hear no protest."

I asked if they'd seen any horses. They hadn't. "What you figure to do," asked Rudolph, "try roundin' up them cattle?"

"We're goin' to town."

I caught their glances, quick as they were. I didn't say anything. I climbed up back of Rudolph, him being the lightest of the bunch.

We were a pretty dismal crowd. We didn't get very far before we come across young Buckner. He was laying half buried in the dust, and was no nice sight to look at. I located four or five goodish-sized rocks, and rolled them over on top of him. They might help to keep the coyotes out.

Nobody said very much, and afterwards I seen them eying each other again. They took quite a while about mounting. I got up back of Rudolph. "Well," I said, "what's holdin' us?"

"Say you're headin' back to town?"

"That's what I said."

Brace scowled. He sat there eying his saddle horn like some way it had done him dirt. Rudolph batted a fly off his horse. The other guy cleared his throat.

"All right," I said, "let's have it."

Brace's scowl turned mean, uneasy. He fiddled round, untying this and tying up that—cuffing trail dust out of his Levis. Then, suddenlike, he blurted: "We ain't goin' back!"

So that was it.

There wouldn't nobody meet my eye.

"What good would our goin' back there do?" Brace argued. "Wouldn't be no help to Murphy an'—Hell! the Big Store crowd is busted. Busted flatter than a last year's leaf!"

"McSween's too much for 'em," muttered Rudolph.

I kept my mouth shut. What could I say? Looked like they was right. Murphy-Dolan was headed for the rocks, no two ways about it. Each passing day saw more of their gun hands drifting, saw the company deeper plunged in debt. Dolan had said himself that if they didn't get the Jingle-Bobs through, their rope would be plumb wound up. And Peppin was off in the hills some place—didn't nobody know where he was.

McSween had half-a-hundred riders out, rampaging through the hills. Regulators, they called themselves, but what they regulated besides plain hell I hadn't yet found out. McSween himself might be refugeeing on the Pecos, like some folks claimed, but wasn't putting no pot-lid on the medicine his bunch was brewing. Raiding, burning, killing, they'd reduced Murphy-Dolan partisans to a pitiful handful of desperate, bad-scared men. All you had to do was mention Bonney's name, to see their knees start knocking. As for the homesteaders, Chisum's crew had done for them.

"Time to pull for the tules," Donner muttered.

"Throw in with us," Charlie Rudolph urged, "an' pull out while you're able."

I just looked at them.

Brace finally shrugged. "O.K. We'll take you to your funeral —we'll take you far's the edge of town—"

"Not me," I said. "Don't bother. I wouldn't want none of you gettin' hurt."

I got off Rudolph's horse then, went over, and got my rifle.

"You can't walk—"

"Fella can do a heap of things if he's got to."

They felt mean, I guess, as new-sheared sheep. But their determination hadn't slipped none.

I started walking.

"Hell," growled Rudolph suddenly. "You take my bronc, Flick. I'll make out to ride with the others."

It was that way that I left them.

19

TWENTY-FIVE CHISUM PUNCHERS

DAD PEPPIN was back, and the town was full of riders. There was a lot of talk going round, but Peppin wasn't making it. For a mild-mannered man he was looking pretty proddy. He didn't look no better when he heard about Chisum's cattle. But he kept his thoughts to himself.

I found Dolan in Murphy's office.

"Bad news," I said. "Your cattle took a ramblin' jag. Lot got killed. Rest of 'em's scattered from hell to breakfast." I gave him the details. He took it standing up. Never asked no questions, never said a word. "Three men cashed, an' three men quit. Here's a little keepsake—" I gave him the Apache headband. "Better hang onto it. It's like to be all you'll get for the price of that herd."

He was standing there, turning it over in his fingers, eying it kind of slanchylike, but never opening his mouth, when Andy Boyle tramped in. Crotchety old devil, Boyle, touchy as a teething snake. If it was me, I wouldn't of had him round for piling kindling. But he got on all right with Dolan. They was like two six-shooters in the same belt.

He took one squint at that headband, and right away puffed out his cheeks. "Well!" he said, kind of windy. Then he flapped his hands on his hips, and said the same thing over. After which he teetered on his boot heels, and looked real hard at Dolan.

They knew something I didn't, them two. Dolan tossed the headband on the desk, and Boyle grunted, looking me over, "Where'd you get that, boy?"

"I'm of half-a-mind not to tell you, gran'paw!" But Dolan nodded, so I did. Then Boyle said: "Very nice. Very nice, indeed."

"Lovely!" I said, furious. "Who in hell would've guessed it?"

But Boyle just grinned at me, chucked a wink at Dolan.

"If you know whose it is, whyn't you say so?"

Boyle's grin got sly. "What give you that idee, boy?"

"To hell with you!" I said, and left them, angrily slamming the door.

Peppin had been fruitlessly scouring the Pecos, when Mc-Daniels finally reached him with Dolan's message. By Mc-Daniels' way of it, Peppin hadn't been impressed much. "That's tough," he said, "but I been appointed to this office to do a job of work, not to warm the seat of my britches on a bench in Lincoln plaza. When I'm satisfied the Kid an' his crowd ain't down here I'll go elsewhere—an' not until, by grab!"

McDaniels' arguments had failed to sway him in the slightest. But when, two evenings later, a small-spread rancher, who was siding Murphy, rode into camp with word the Kid was at Lincoln, Peppin had thrown gear on his horse, and lit a shuck for the county seat. He arrived too late because the Kid had left ere news of his presence had ever reached the posse.

A fellow would almost think by then he'd had all the riding he wanted. But when a puncher from a down-state outfit rode into Lincoln, the day after my return, with news that members of Bonney's gang had been seen in lower Bonito Canyon, Peppin swore in another posse, and took off south like a twister.

I was with them. There was twelve of us altogether. It was late when we got started, but we lost no time on the way and stopped at Fritz's Spring Ranch for supper. Hardly had we got to eating when Bill Campbell, a lawyer who'd been left outside to watch the horses, came tearing in with word that McNab, Frank Coe, and Saunders was getting a drink from the spring out by the road.

For a mild-mannered man, Peppin's eyes held a lot of frost when he looked around at Fritz. "It's a good spring," Charlie said defensively. "Don't blame me. Everybody stops there— you'd think my place was a Harvey House. I got to feed an' water every squirt that comes along!"

Some of us laughed, but not Dad Peppin. Wiping his mouth on the back of a hand, he grabbed up a rifle and lit for his horse. "C'mon," his voice drifted back at us. "This here's posse business—you can do your eatin' later."

Piling up into our saddles, we went dusting for the spring. Sure they saw us coming. They went larruping off down the canyon like a bunch of Neuches steers. Hell emigrating on cart wheels never made more noise.

Saunders, maybe thinking to slow us up some, twisted round in his hull, and started sounding off with his Winchester. "Goin' to make it a corpse an' cartridge occasion, eh?" snarled Peppin, bristling. "By grab, we'll give you a bellyful!"

Everybody opened up. The way artillery got unlimbered you'd of thought it was the Civil War all over.

I jerked my neckerchief up over my mouth and nose. Seemed like half the dirt between there and Hondo had took to flying through the air. I looked up just as Saunders' saddle slipped and pitched him into the cactus. In that same split second somebody slugged McNab's horse, I guess, because it went straight up like a rocket. I counted three complete summersaults, and when the dust had cleared enough to see anything there went McNab and Saunders, both afoot and streaking it for the side hills. Coe, still aboard his bronc, was whamming down the canyon like he had a scorpion up his pants-leg. He was a good ways off, and wasn't pausing for no kissing.

I let the others have McNab and Saunders. Hoisting my boots from the stirrups, riding sharpshooter fashion, I drove three shots at Coe fast as I could work the trigger. I might as well of whistled! Twelve hundred yards ain't nobody's biscuit.

I jumped from my horse, lit rolling, and came up spitting grit. Mister Coe wasn't doing no pony express, if I could help it. Down on a knee I dropped. Took careful aim, cheek against the carbine stock, and—

Wham!

Coe's bronc went down like a pole-axed steer.

It was pretty good shooting, if I do say it. But I didn't stop to say it then. I started running.

But I hadn't took three jumps when young Johnnie Patton, a sixteen-year-old button, went past me like the hammers of hell. He should of been one of them jockeys like I hear they got in Kentucky—he sure was a riding fool. He reached Saunders just as Jim wriggled loose of his saddle.

Patton leaped from his horse. Both men emptied their six-shooters. It was about the poorest shooting I've ever seen. Neither one scored. I saw Coe dash for a gully.

Saunders was down and groaning. Three or four fellows had their guns on him. McNab wasn't anywhere in sight. I guessed he was being took care of. So I hotfooted it for my horse, swung into the saddle, and took out after the others who were shoving towards where Patton, crouched back of Coe's dead horse, was stuffing fresh shells in his sixgun.

We fanned out to cover the gully.

"Better call calf rope, Coe, an' come on out of there," Peppin called. "I'll see you get fair treatment. Guess my word's good, ain't it?"

Coe didn't answer very quicklike. Bob Ollinger growled: "Why fool with him? Blow the bastard's guts out!"

"None o' that!" Peppin said curtly. "If that's what wearin' a star does for you, you can hand mine back right pronto."

"Yeah? Well take your goddam star!" snarled Ollinger, and ripping it from his shirt he slammed it into the dust front of Peppin's horse. "Happens I'm a deputy marshal, an' I'm goin' to blast—"

"Not while I'm around here," Peppin told him. "You rode out of town with my posse, an' you'll take my orders, star or no star! Now put up that gun before I lose my temper."

And, surprising us all, Ollinger did just that—put his gun up, though with considerable scowling and muttering. He enjoyed being known as a real double-action engine and, if things was right, was not averse to demonstrating. Reckon he figured we'd have all lined up with Peppin and, like enough, most of us would have. We hadn't anything much against Coe.

"How about it, Frank?" Peppin called again. "Comin' out, or have we got to come after you?"

"I reckon I'll come out," Coe said.

McNab was dead, gone to his just deserts for the murder of McClosky, and his part in the killing of Hindman and Brady.

We hauled him out of the brush, and buried him. Saunders we put to bed at Fritz's place. He'd broke his ankle, and had a wound in his hip. With Coe under guard, we camped that night at the edge of town, never dreaming that others of McSween's outfit had come in while we were gone, and garrisoned the Ellis house.

There must have been a good dozen of them, and first thing we knew of their presence was when, just after the sun shoved a leg out of bed, somebody opened up with a rifle and Campbell, scouting along the Bonito, gave a yell, and crashed down in the brush.

The battle was on, and it lasted till afternoon. With lead from McSween's crowd kicking up dust all around us, we raced for the cover of outlying buildings.

Frank Coe was none too pleased finding his light in danger of getting blown out by a bullet from some friend's rifle. He hinted as much to Walt Ollinger, Bob's brother—different as night from day. "Might be I could sneak you across the river," Walt said, and looked at Peppin. Peppin nodded. "Try it if you want to, Walt. If you make it, put him upstairs in Murphy's store."

Along towards noon the firing, which up till then had been pretty general, took a lull. I guessed McSween's crew was running low on gun fodder. We had sure used up aplenty. And, far as I could see, without doing any damage—unless you count the damage to Ellis' adobe.

Pretty soon the shooting quit altogether. Peppin and two or three of the others hunkered down to talk things over. The upshot of it was that Peppin, hoisting a hunk of shirttail on his rifle, walked out to make palaver.

No one took a shot at him. And nobody answered his call. Beckoning Bob Ollinger and me to join him, he started for the house. It was pretty well marked by rifle lead. We found a couple of dead horses piled up by the back door but, except for them, the place was empty as a burned-out lantern.

McSween's brave gunies had slipped away.

Fighting took a slump for awhile. But nothing was like normal. It was a kind of trigger-finger peace that needed but a sneer or cockeyed look to start lead flying. A peace, moreover, that did not extend beyond town limits. Bushwhacking went on as usual, and McSween stayed hid out on the Pecos. Murphy-Dolan had gone to the wall, and there was word that any day now Tom Catron and the other big creditors would be sending reps to look things over.

But the war was far from finished. We all sensed, I reckon, that the feud would be going on long as either side had one guy left that could squeeze a trigger.

Campbell hadn't been hurt much, just a busted leg was all. We sent him up to Fort Stanton, to the hospital, to get him off our hands. And afterwards we sent the ambulance after Saunders, and had him took up there, too. After getting Frank Coe to Murphy's, Ollinger had given him a pistol, and slipped back to join the fight. The loungers decorating Murphy's nail kegs came along to join it likewise. Left thus alone, Frank Coe had lost no time in moving to better graze.

There wasn't no reason for McSween hiding out; no reason that I know of. No warrants had been issued for him, not yet, at any rate. But he'd little sand in his craw, for all he was heading one side of the war, and I expect he felt more comfortable hid out. Dolan declared Peppin better watch out, or Alex would skin clean out of the country. But it looked like Peppin wasn't much afraid. "He's tried that once," he reminded us. "He's still under bond for that Fritz insurance business, and it'll go hard with him if he tries to jump his hobbles."

You'll think it's queer, maybe, that with most of his side known outlaws, with prices tacked up for their pelts, we hadn't got nothing on Alex. But we hadn't—nothing, leastways, but the bonds Charlie Fritz had slapped on him for making off with the Colonel's insurance money. He was nominal head of the McSween-Chisum-Tunstall combine, but he'd taken mighty good care not to mix in the fracas personal. Until his trial came up he was free as the air, long as he stayed in Lincoln County. And his trial, the way things stood, was a long way off because Judge Bristol refused to hold court.

And then one day came a fellow along, who had word to relate that sure changed things. McSween, he said, was holed up with his bunch at Chisum's South Spring Ranch.

"Mebbe so, an' mebbe not," remarked the sheriff shrewdly. "Marion," he told Turner, one of his deputies, "get yourself together a posse, an' go down there and see about it. Take these warrants and, if they're there, you serve 'em. I want the Kid, Doc Scurlock, Bowdre, Middleton, O'Folliard, and French. If there's any others bring them in too. Guess that'll do for a starter."

It was plain from the way he talked he didn't believe overmuch they was down there. But I decided to go with the posse, and Turner seemed glad to have me.

They was there all right. We surrounded the place, and bottled them tight, but not before some guy grabbed a bronc and departed. Turner read off the names of the men he wanted, and called on them to surrender. All we got was catcalls, and three, four pieces of lead. Fortunately, none of them hit us.

We took cover, and sent some lead back.

It wasn't rightly what you'd call a battle. There was a powerful lot of shooting but nobody felt called on to show off much of his anatomy. There wasn't no bullets collected. It got pretty tedious finally, and a bunch of us got to speculating about that hombre what had ridden off. We wondered where he had went to.

We had a pretty good notion some four hours later when a big dust showed along the river. Didn't hardly look like it would be any help for us. It wasn't. It was twenty-five Chisum punchers.

The posse rattled its hocks.

20

SPRINTING SPACE FOR ALL

THE store was empty as I'd ever seen it. A half-ass clerk dozed behind the counter. Two one-time customers, draping kegs before it, stared owlishly as I picked my way among the sacks and barrels in the wake of Turner, with Andy Boyle, still lugging his sawed-off Greener, rowdily bringing up the rear.

So many things we take for granted . . . what few we miss until they've gone. Yet what great holes some leave behind them. Like the stopping of a clock.

It was that way with Murphy's gambling room, the place where I'd got into this. Its roar of business was departed—gone like a gutted candle. Forlorn as a banquet hall after the last stuffed guest has been carried out, Boyle's ribald quip echoed drearily among the scattered cards and cigar butts that strewed its unswept floor.

We found Dolan in Murphy's office Seven Up-ing with Old Man Pierce. Dad Peppin was in a corner with hands jammed into his pockets, and his chin upon his chest. He regarded us without much interest. "No prisoners, eh?" he said.

"No prisoners," Turner grunted. "But here's news—the Kid's in town—"

"Young Bonney?" Peppin got up with an oath. "Were is he?"

"McSween's—Alex's house. Bowdre, Brown, Scurlock, O'Folliard, French, Morris, Middleton, an' a bunch of others is with him. There's somethin' up. We had a brush with them at Chisum's—"

"Let me get this straight. The Kid's at McSween's place *now?*"

"You bet!"

Boyle was shoving in his oar, but Peppin hushed him. "How many's with him?"

"Must be upwards of a dozen."

The sheriff thought awhile, staring off into the haze of cigar smoke. "By Hannah," he declared at last, "I believe we've got him this time. I don't see how he can get away—"

"You're goddam right we got him!" Boyle cried. "We'll nail his hide to the fence!"

"Ain't dismissed your posse have you?" Peppin looked at Turner. "Good! Countin' them we ought to have close to fifty men. Mostly Mexes, drat the luck—but fighters anyhow, and fellows that'll do their part. Let's see . . . Reckon the Kid don't know how well we're fixed. An' yet— Don't look like he'd walk into a trap this way . . ."

"Well, he has," growled Boyle with bluster. "He's jumped plumb into it, an' this time we'll spring it on him!"

"Never mind this trap stuff," Dolan, leaning forward, remarked. "We got enough to rush the place—"

"Now, wait a minute," said Turner, holding his hand up. "We got him dead to rights, and we don't want him slipping out. We better play this safe—"

A clatter on the stairs checked Turner in mid-sentence. We all whirled a look at the door. It shoved open, Kinney back of it. He came in breathing heavy like. "Your posse," he gasped at Turner, "has yanked its picket pin an' melted."

"The hell!" swore Boyle, and started cursing.

Turner stared like he thought the man was batty.

"By God, it's true!" Kinney thumped the table. "Go look for yourself! There ain't three fellas stayed!"

Turner shoved him out of the way, took the stairway like a cyclone. He was back five minutes later, and his face was confirmation of Kinney's words.

We looked at each other gloomily. "What we going to do about it?"

"Well, I'll tell you, Mr. Dolan," Turner muttered. "I got an idee. Mebbe it'll work, an' mebbe not; but we ought to try it. The Kid ain't got no way of knowin' how short of hands we are—ain't been here long enough to learn. If he hears my voice he'll sure be figurin' I've got back here with my posse. He won't know they've gone. Mebbe I can talk him into givin' up his guns."

Nobody thought much of the likelihood, but nobody thought up anything better. Peppin said, "Might's well try it." So Turner, with Kinney, and me, an' Dolan, grabbed up our guns, and went downstairs.

"Back door," Dolan said, and Turner nodded.

Working our way—*feeling* our way, for the night was dark as a wolf's mouth—through the bottoms along the river, we came up behind McSween's big barn. We crouched down low and carefullike, and Turner set up a shouting.

Just when it looked like he wasn't going to be answered we heard the kitchen door squeak open. "No," Bonney's voice reached out to us, "that wasn't no jack in a tin shack you was hearin', Bowdre—it was that floppy-eared coyote, Turner, givin' the death rattle. Choked hisself on his spleen. I reckon, an'—"

"All right, Kid, we got you surrounded," Turner growled, cutting short Bonney's pleasantry. "You better come out of there humble, and come quick. Make a fight of this an' we'll gun every so-an'-so in there. But if you want to save us a little trouble I'll guarantee you won't be hurt."

We heard Bonney's jeering laughter.

"This ain't no foolin', Kid. You better give up now, while you got the chance."

"Humph!" You could hear him snorting. "I'd last about as long as a wax cat would in hell! What kind of a fool do you take me for?"

"I'm guaranteein' you protection—"

"Never mind. I'll stay where I am, an' protect myself! If you want me so all-fired bad come get me. Tell your gang to come a-smokin'. By grab, we'll give you a bellyful!"

Well, that was that.

There wasn't two ways around it. Bonney had us. If Turner's

posse hadn't dug for the tules— But it had! Not once since the damn feud started had we been so short of hands. The word had gotten out: "Murphy-Dolan's busted!" The rats had left the ship.

A rumble of horse sound rolled from the east. A chorus of yells. Sharp, flatly, wicked, the crashing of rifles. "By Judas!" Kinney shouted. "I'm gittin' out o' here!"

Turner, too—off like a pot leg.

Dolan looked at me, and swore.

"Guess some one stuck a chunk in the trap. What'll you bet," I said, "that ain't more help for Bonney?"

"Hell, I like a few odds when I bet," Dolan grunted. "C'mon; let's get moving. This ain't no place for Horatio."

"It sure ain't! Nor for me neither, if it comes to that," I said. "No dead hero stuff for mine!"

21

MESSAGE TO DUDLEY

Peppin had more deputies than that bunch which had slid out on Turner, but they were all up around San Pat, keeping their eyes skinned out for Bill Bonney. That was seven miles off by mountain trail. He sent a man to fetch them.

The horsebackers, like we'd expected, was sure enough more help for Bonney. Thirty-five fighting Mexes and McSween had rode in with them. Looked like they was out to blast us this time. They had forted up in the town's four thickest buildings, with McSween's own house for headquarters. Chavez, bossing the Mexes, took over the stores of Montana and Patron. This we learned by the sweat of our spying, and by the same way found out McSween had holed up at home, where he could feel reassured by the company of such great pot-shooters as O'Folliard, French, Scurlock, the Kid, Morris, Frank Semora, and several other Mexes, including that shining light, young Salazar, who was patterning poses off Alex. For most of these fellows the sheriff held warrants—had been several times ordered to serve them.

From all indications McSween's warriors were in high spirits, feeling uncommon happy about the whole bloody prospect. They were laying bets with each other how quick they could whittle us down to where we would beg for their mercy. McSween was making a lot of talk about God, and righteousness, and the faith he had of divine interference before any blood could be spilled, and a lot of other like foolishness, just as if all the time he hadn't ridden in with them Mexicans for the particular purpose of wiping us out.

Peppin had but six fighting men to work with, counting myself and Dolan. We had Dolan's clerks; but they was so shaking scared they couldn't of poured a slug of whisky into a barrel with the head out. There was three or four townsmen, and a small-spread rancher trapped in the village who was likewise endeavoring to lend us aid, but thought of the Kid gave them the willies so bad they hardly knew one end of their guns from the other, and more often were underfoot than where they might do any good. Most of the town crowd had sloped in a hurry to find them some holes to crawl into.

The night dragged through to daylight, punctuated only by such scattered shots as were gleefully let off by the celebrating owl hooters, cocksure of the coming pay-off.

They'd little reason to doubt success, the odds being what they were. Unless the San Pat posse arrived before a rush came, there didn't look like there could be but one grim outcome.

The next morning was Monday, July 15th. The firing started shortly after eight o'clock. I place that time because Doc Ealy, who'd been holding a school in his end of McSween's, was outside opening the shutters. It was a kind of rite with him and, rain or shine, he run it off prompt as ditchwater. I seen one of Shields' kids dash around and grab him by the coattails. Ealy jumped like he was shot, lammed a quick, scared look around, grabbed up little Pearl, his eldest, and went hellity-larrup inside. The shooting started right then.

But, though it kept up most all day, it was no more battle than that fiasco we'd had at Chisum's. A rattle of shots went off every time a guy stepped out on the street. Otherwise it was pretty quiet. A stranger driving through would likely have thought the town deserted.

It was getting along toward the shank of the afternoon, when a cheer went up from the Torreon, the old Indian watchtower, where Peppin with four of his men were barricaded. I was with Dolan and his "Oh-God-ain't-this-terrible" clerks in Murphy's store. Looking out across the sill of a window, I saw the cheer was for the arrival of the San Pat posse we had sent for the night before. I suggested they ought to be voted a medal to memorialize their speed.

Accompanied by Charlie Crawford and Turner, each waggling a shirttail on his rifle, Peppin came out, and gingerly stopped before McSween's. "Open up!" he shouted, and Alex did, Bible under arm, eyeing the sheriff warily.

"Alex McSween," said Peppin sternly, "you are giving aid and succor to wanted outlaws for whom I got United States warrants. What have you to say about why I shouldn't consider you part an' parcel of 'em?"

"I refuse to commit myself," McSween said loudly. "God is my refuge and my strength. Though you do your worst He will care for me."

Peppin eyed him a moment, shook his head. "I ain't come down here to discuss your convictions. I came to warn you that the harboring of known criminals is a serious offense, one that'll jeopardize— Hell! You're a lawyer, I guess you know all that.

I ask you as a law-abiding citizen to refuse these outlaws the shelter of your roof."

McSween's controlled face reflected pain. "But—but these men are—" It looked like he had been going to call them friends, but at the last moment he changed his mind. He began again. "Surely—"

"Those men are known and badly wanted outlaws! You show a damn poor taste consorting with them, Alex," Peppin said. "My advice to you is that you put them out of doors without delay."

McSween's white face showed strain. The shine of sweat was on it. He looked undecided, bewildered, helpless, torn by conflicting wishes. Then suddenly: "I *can't!*" He made a wail of it.

"Afraid to? All right. That's reasonable; the men are desperate. You can show your good intentions," Peppin suggested slyly, "by staying away awhile, by keeping out of your house while they're in there, by withdrawing the authority of your sanction."

He looked at Alex, waiting.

It was an honest invitation by a forthright sheriff. By accepting it, McSween could establish himself on the side of law-and-order, put an end to faction warfare. But that was the joker.

Alex, as all of us knew, had no intention, no least wish, to end the feuding until he got the upper hand. He thought he had that hand right then, was determined to wring reward from it. We were badly outnumbered, and he was sure he had us licked. But he was much too slick to show that notion public. He did not want, if things broke wrong, to have to stand the consequences. He must have the rôle of fortune's scapegoat, plaything of destiny. He must appear to have been the victim of a malign conspiracy.

"But Peppin— I *can't!* My wife—"

"Nothing to stop her coming out, is there?"

I didn't catch what McSween said then because Andy Boyle was beside me, overbusy with comments. But I could see, and

I saw a sudden backward step put Alex's shoulders against the door. He muttered something, harriedlike, but the wind that twisted at his mustache fluttered the words away.

"If you persist in this attitude, Alex—"

The rest of Peppin's talk was lost, too.

McSween's bony shoulders rose. Stiff and erect 'his black-frocked figure showed an arrogant, sneering defiance. Once again Boyle spoke at the wrong time, but I could see Peppin's neck flame red. "You'll hang with 'em then!" he snapped hotly.

We all heard what McSween said to that. Clasping his Bible firmly, "I'll rest my case with God," he said.

Beside me, Boyle cursed loudly. "Missed his callin'!" Kinney jeered.

It was my own conviction. No wonder people were fooled. I've seen all kinds of bunko steerers, but none that could stack with Alex. He had the kind of tongue-oil could talk a gopher into climbing a tree.

He went in the house, and closed the door, but Peppin stuck in the dooryard till he'd read his list—asked the specified gents to surrender. All he got was a roar of booing.

He stamped into the store mad as hops.

"Told you it was a waste of time," Dolan muttered.

Peppin ignored him. He said, grimly white, "I've a duty to do, an' come hell or highwater, by God, I propose to do it!"

Murphy's Hotel, across the street, was catty-cornered to the store, and some fifty yards this side of Alex's place. Peppin sent Turner and a couple of other men to man it, with orders to pour in a hot fire soon as Bonney's outlaws opened up again. Leaving the men in the Torreon where they were, he posted the rest of us back of windows in Murphy's store. There was a little more shooting, but night came on with most of the damage confined to the outsides of the adobe buildings. They were getting to look a little dilapidated. No casualties were reported.

That night, though men were kept on guard in shifts, passed

off without attack. McSween's crowd must have thought they had forever. Bonney's carousing saddle crew filled the darkness with crazy shoutings; kept their hell-bending up almost till dawn. You'd guess this whole business was some kind of lark, to hear their carryings-on.

But Tuesday dawned at last and, with the sun's first light, the shooting took up again. More violent now, and much increased in volume, as though they'd gotten more cartridges, or were done with fooling, and getting down in earnest to the task of polishing us off. Half-a-dozen guys with rifles got up on the roof of Montana's store, and proceeded to make our lives miserable. From behind its parapet their skill and eternal vigilance made a mighty risk for such of us as were brash enough to venture out for water.

As the sun climbed higher it got hotter than the hinges inside Murphy's store. Powder stink and the lead-thumped dust from the walls like to have clogged our gullets. Dust got so thick you couldn't hardly breathe, and sweat made dirty streaks of our faces, till we looked like something from a circus.

Seemed like the morning would never pass.

Montana's store was like a fort house. Slugs from the powerfulest of our rifles failed to break its thick, baked walls. Wasting shells on Bonney and company was about as useless as trying to scratch your ear with your elbow, long as they was smart enough not to come out in the open. If we was to get any place in this fandango, looked like somebody had got to figure out some scheme for teasing them out where we could hit them.

"We could keep this up till Christmas," Kinney said, "—if our lead would hold out that long. Anybody spare the makin's? I got a mouth like a butcher's foot."

Montoya tossed him his Durham. "*Amor de dios!*" he growled disgustedly. "These damn' dust she's plug my whistle."

"How about a drink?" someone hollered from the other room. "It's hotter'n hell's backlog in here."

"Gimme them buckets," Turk Grobney, a squatter from the Ruidoso, grunted. "I'll get some of that water for you."

He ducked through a window at the back, and Evans, levering a fresh shell into his barrel, stepped out after him. I started that way too, figuring maybe I could give them a hand. Just as I reached the window, a surprised curse came from Grobney, the clatter of dropped pails. With both hands grabbed to his middle he jackknifed forward onto his face.

"Christ!" said Evans fervently, and knocked me sprawling in his haste to get inside. Three slugs tore splinters from the sill behind him. Teeth bared, he whirled and crouched below it, emptied his carbine up at the hills.

"They've got sharpshooters up in the rimrocks!"

"We got to do something," Peppin muttered.

"Mebbe we could dance a jig!" snapped Old Man Pierce sarcastically.

The sheriff scowled. "Pierce, you and Andy see can you blast them fellows out of there. We got to have help!" He flung a badgered look around. "I guess I'll send a note to Dudley—anybody volunteer to ride it?"

Some fellow I didn't know spoke up to say he'd tackle it. I watched while Peppin scrawled his note. It said:

General:

I have the honor to respectfully state that mostly all the men for whom I have United States warrants are in town, and are being protected by A. A. McSween and a large party of his followers. They are in the houses of A. A. McSween, Ellis' sons, J. B. Patron and Jose Montana. They are resisting, and it is impossible for me to serve the warrants. If it is in your power to loan me one of your howitzers, I am of the opinion the parties for whom I have said warrants would surrender without a shot being fired. Should it be in your power to do this in favor of the law, you would confer a great pleasure on a majority of the people of this town, who are being persecuted by a lawless mob.

GEO. W. PEPPIN
Sheriff, Acting-Deputy
U. S. Marshal.

Handing the man the message, he eyed us grimly. "That Chavez outfit has got to be driven off the roof of Montana's store. I want four or five of you to get into the hills south of town, and blast them fellows out of there. Any volunteers?"

"Count on me," drawled Charlie Crawford, ejecting the empties from his rifle.

"Me, too," Montoya grunted.

I said I'd go, and McDaniels allowed he'd take a crack at it likewise.

We stuffed our pockets with cartridges. We hadn't much choice about how to go. Straight across the road was shortest, and we'd get plenty lead thrown our way anyhow.

McDaniels elected to go through a window. Montoya thought the door would be best, because a guy could get plumb riddled while he was getting himself over the sill.

"Go any way you want to, only get started," Peppin told us. "We'll cover you best we can." He raised his voice. "Everybody over this side for a minute! . . . Now give 'em hell!"

22

A HARP AND A HALO

WE MADE it.

Getting into the rocks and brush on top of that hill was something of a chore, I tell you. It was dusty, broiling, hazardous work, and took us well over an hour. The sun flayed our backs, and we had to go careful so Chavez's bunch wouldn't guess where we were headed for. We were glad that it was windy; that helped some after we got there. Below us, spraddled out like a painted picture, was the deserted town—leastways it looked deserted, till you noticed the puffs of smoke that showed at sundry windows. Alex's house showed up first-rate; Montana's was like staring in a pool of water, almost straight down. There was nobody on the street, no sign of movement any place. But the parapets of Montana's roof was still a nuisance; we could see past them, but not too good. We could see about three-quarters of the roof, and the same way with Patron's. I saw a guy's leg, and was fixing to pot it when:

"*Mira—look!*" Montoya whispered.

We did. A man had slipped out of Patron's, was hurrying across to Montana's. "Martin Chavez!" Crawford muttered. We fired together, Crawford, me, and Montoya.

The shots knocked dust against Chavez's boots. He started running. Crouching forward, McDaniels drove three slugs screaming after him, but Chavez made it. The slamming of the door made a tiny burst of sound heard even through the echoes of our rifles.

"God damn." Crawford's tone was exasperated. "For such shootin' we should ought to get medals—"

"The pennies off a dead man's eyes!" McDaniels jeered.

"It was purty far," Montoya mentioned.

The fellow's leg I had been aiming to shoot at wasn't there now. He had drawn it back, being minded to keep it the way it was, I reckon. I hunted something else to shoot at. But three rifles got to talking down there some place before I saw anything. After that I was too busy saving my own hide. When the firing quit, Crawford poked his head out for a look. "All clear."

We all got into it then. We wasted shells for half-an-hour while the sun climbed higher and hotter. Even the snakes started looking for cover. After a bit I said, "We better shift around a little—"

Too late! Even as I spoke there came a screech of lead on metal. Crawford's scream drowned the clatter of his rifle. He rose straight up, rigid hands clawed out to either side, head thrown back, and bared teeth gleaming. Then he was crumpling, was falling forward across the rock, was sliding—rolling. He must have struck every goddam bump on that hill before he fetched up at the bottom.

I felt pretty sick. Watching McDaniels heave his breakfast didn't help my stomach any. Even Lucio Montoya looked a little pale. I saw him cross himself, mutter something about *Dios!* and start edging forward with his carbine.

"Hey, wait!" I yelled. "Don't stick your cabeza round that side!"

Might's well saved my breath. He was too hell-bent on vengeance to leave room for any thinking. He stooped, leaned outward, peered narrowly round the rock. He crouched with a wicked grimace, thrust a flexing knee ahead of him. I saw his rifle lifting, lower. He put an elbow on the knee to steady him. Again the rifle lifted. I could see the white place where the stock squeezed against his cheek.

He was bent like that when the bullet took him. Shattering his leg, it smashed the knee from under him; flung him backward in a groaning agony. His hat fell off, and rolled until a bit of catclaw stopped it.

I ducked forward—dragged him back behind the safety of the rock. Looking round, I saw McDaniels with his knees ashake. He struggled to get hold of himself, clenched his Winchester fiercely to stop the tremble of his hands. But it was no go—the hands shook anyway. He cursed, and hurled the rifle from him.

"I'm goin' to git—"

I grabbed him, spun him around. "Pick up that rifle. You come up here to do a job of work— Get at it!"

He glared, and I glared back at him. The desperateness, all the wild malignance of a cornered beast, stared out of those red-rimmed eyes. A clawed hand dropped, hung poised above his pistol.

But I held his eyes. "You better stay where you are," I said, "or you'll be finding it's one thing getting up here, an' something entirely else gettin' down. We're stuck here till dark comes anyway. Make the best of it. Even if we could get away, we'd never make it with Lucio—"

"Hell with him! I ain't riskin' my neck for a goddam greaser nohow!" He whipped his gun out, started bácking, slitted eyes as watchful as a cat's.

"All right, bunch-quitter," I said thinly. "But just remember this: Next time I cross your track—"

"In that case—" he said, the hard-bitten lines of his features reshaping themselves to a new, more malignant pattern, "in that case, mebbe I better make goddam sure—"

That was far as he got. With his mind wrapped up in ideas for getting shut of me he had forgotten the immediate danger —the thing that had brought up this business. He had backed himself into the open.

I saw the dust bulge out of his shirt; heard his gasp, heard the crack of a rifle. Twisted face a fish-belly white, he went staggering slanchways. He dropped, with his mouth stretched open, in a screéch that never came.

23

DEAD WITH THEIR BOOTS ON

IT WAS close on to nine o'clock when I rejoined the bunch at Murphy's. The trip from the hills was a nightmare. It would have been enough of a chore had I been doing it solo; packing Montoyo I like to never made it. The man was helpless, burning up with fever. Expecting like I was any moment to be confronted by some of the scouts or pickets McSween was certain to have out, Montoya's ravings, shouts, and curses kept my nerves honed raw. Time and again, I sucked my breath in, knowing I was done for, yet determined to sack my saddle dear as possible.

But we made the trip unchallenged. Bonney and his owl hooters must of been too busy emptying snakewater bottles and chasing skirts around the post to think of putting guards out. Yet even when convinced of this I wasn't kissing good-by to danger. The bullets of your friends will kill you just as dead as any.

But it looked like Peppin, too, had plumb forgot his bylaws. When I came in the whole shebang whirled round like seeing Peter. "My God!" said Evans staring. "Aren't they playing cards in Heaven?"

Dolan swore.

I put Montoya in a corner, and mopped off some of the sweat. "Where's Dudley's cannon?"

"He was afraid we might nick the paint on 'em," Old Man Pierce growled, plumb disgusted.

"McSween's crowd shot the messenger, so we don't know *what* he said," the sheriff told me. "I've sent another man—"

"Might's well look for hair on a frog, as expect any help from Dudley!"

Andy Boyle, of course. He had to put his oar in.

I told them what had happened. "Anybody buck out here?" Evans shook his head. "I think we got Ben Ellis . . ."

It was nearly noon when the boys playing spy back of upstairs windows yelled down to say a dust was coming from off towards Double Crossing. Peppin snatched for his glasses, and went hotfooting up to look. The silence in his wake was suddenly broken by a shout. "Soldiers! Dudley an' his buff'lo troops! An', *Yep!* He's brung a couple gatlin's!"

We piled for the windows. Sure enough! Pretty soon we

heard the clatter, and round a bend of the road came Nanny-Goat's whiskers riding high and proud as ever. I damn near choked. Never had I seen a sight more welcome than that long double column of blue-clad Negro cavalry, and the stuff they was fetching with them; four-mule wagons piled high with tents and camp duffle and, rolling right in the middle, sleek as cougars' teeth, the two big guns.

Just as well we didn't know the kind of reed we was putting weight on.

Setting up a lusty cheer, we eyed each other joyous when they stopped out front of McSween's. Evans sailed his hat away. Boyle's shout like to deafened me. "C'mon," I said, shoving clear of him. "Let's get over there an'—"

"Not so fast!" called Peppin. "Don't you know those—"

"Hell's fire!" I said. "They won't be takin' no shots at us while Uncle Sam's around!" and ducked on out.

I looked back to see Peppin shrug. The others were shoving past him.

We reached McSween's as a red-haired officer was hammering Alex's door. We got comfortable. The fight was over, we could afford to feel expansive. Pierce winked at Boyle.

Out came Alex, solemn as Moses. He had his dog-eared Bible tucked under an arm. The rest of his bunch came sidling after him. Some grinned, three or four scowled, but every man of them packed his rifle. They made as tough an ornery-looking outfit as you'd find in ten days' ride. They stood around on their carbines, grinning, wisecracking, and generally flaunting their brass right under the colonel's nose. The Kid stood back of Alex, hard eyes bright and restless.

Dudley stayed in his saddle. Pulling himself straight up as a ramrod, he scowled down grim at Alex. "Mr. McSween"—you could hear the rattle of ice in his voice— "Mr. McSween, I'd like the meaning of this demonstration!"

Alex waved his Bible, glared at Dudley, self-righteous with indignation. "Demonstration"—his voice quavered with emotion—"is the word for it! Demonstration of a crew of lawless blackguards hiding behind the guise of a shrieval emblem in their spiteful persecution of a defenseless citizen whose only crime—"

"Is stealin' the Fritz insurance money!" piped up Andy Boyle.

Dudley ignored the interruption. I doubt if he even heard it. I don't reckon he'd even been listening to Alex. He was too wrapped up in his own act. This was *his* show, and he didn't aim for anyone to hook it.

"McSween," he admonished sternly, "this fighting must terminate at once!"

"I am in hearty concurrence with that sentiment, sir. But"— Alex dug out his martyr look—"I am powerless to end it."

"You must cease firing."

"I shall be only too happy to cease firing if [he glared at us] these Murphy scalp-hunters can be likewise made to quit. They're the ones that started this! You see in me but a pawn to fate, the victim of dark conspiracies, a man besieged in his own home by forces of lawlessness and chaos. We are fighting for our lives, for our very *lives!*" he cried, waggling his arms around. "End this wanton attack upon us, and you will end the battle."

The colonel drew himself stiffly. "You have my orders, Mr. McSween. Defy them at your peril. Stop this shooting at once or suffer the—"

I felt a touch upon my arm. I saw the broad, big-shouldered back of Jimmy Dolan departing like he wasn't going no place, and had all day to get there. Kind of curious, I followed. It was plain as paint Dudley's hot-air campaign wasn't going to oil no sixguns. Nor wouldn't unload any, either.

Drifting behind the screen of halted troopers, I found Dolan waiting on the porch of Murphy's hotel. Boyle and Old Man Pierce were with him.

"What's up?"

"You'll see. Step lively now, and keep your head on your shoulders. No point listening to that windbag any longer."

I followed them inside. Dolan had a cup and a can of kerosene.

"Hold on—" I was getting suspicious and if I read signs right—

But Dolan held his hand up. "Not now. I'll tend to all that later, Flick. This here's the time for action, and we've got to work damn fast. Out back," he said. "Grab up those baskets, boys."

In the back yard was a chopping block. The ground was littered with chips and shavings. My suspicions had been right. "Pull up a second— This kind of stunt ain't goin' to help us! Dudley—"

"You just leave me be the judge of that, Flick," Dolan grunted. "Fill them right up full," he bade the others.

"Listen!"—I said. "Dudley—"

"You want to see them killers rampin' loose again?" Dolan thrust his jaw within an inch of mine, eyes hot and angry. "I made one mistake when I saved that damn' Kid's life that time. I don't aim to make another! The way to stop this fight is to put McSween and Bonney out of commission. And that's the *only* way!"

"But the women—?"

"We'll give them a chance to get out, don't worry. But I'm going to fix things so those owl hooters got to surrender. Maybe then we'll get to have some peace around this place!"

It was plain Dudley's talk wouldn't get it for us. And, after all, the house was Murphy's and Dolan's. If Dolan wanted to burn it, who was I to stop him? McSween had never let scruples stand in *his* way!

"C'mon!" growled Boyle. "What we waitin' on?"

"O.K.," I said, and began heaving chips in the basket.

It might be a good idea, Dolan mentioned, if we was to get

back into the crowd without attracting too much notice. I thought that a heap like locking the barn after the horse was took. Mrs. Ealy having seen us—she had seen *me,* anyhow. "Are you going to burn us out?" she asked. I told her that depended. "If Bonney's crowd's in there I reckon, ma'am, we'll just about have to." She said they wasn't, but the way she got all red and flustered even a kid would of known she was lying. However, Dolan was the boss.

I angled back to the front of McSween's like I'd been to visit the privy. But like it was a signal, no sooner had I got there than a trooper raised hell with a bugle. There was a rattle of arms. The soldiers dressed ranks, or whatever they call it in the cavalry, and the long blue column got under way like some huge snake stretching out in the sun.

The crowd split up. There was plenty of slander back and forth, but we managed to get parted without any guns going off. A few of our bunch went over to the hotel. No one went back to the Torreon . . . it was a heap too lonesome for safety. Most of us went into the store, and Peppin, not wise to the stunt we had pulled, called a council of war. "That so-an'-so Dudley," he exclaimed, speaking plain, "had ought to be slapped in the lock-up! What good's he think this stop-firing stuff'll amount to? He can't camp his soldiers here forever. Soon's he goes it'll be the same dang thing all over!"

"If for any reason," Dolan said, "them birds should make a break for it, I move we better drop 'em—Dudley or no damn Dudley."

Peppin's glance was sharp, suspicious. "Why should they? They've nothin' to gain makin' a run for it. They've got it over us like a tent, as long as they stay holed up where they are." He said, grim and bitter, "They'll be stayin' there."

A chuckle came from Old Man Pierce. A grin licked across Boyle's map. Peppin, looking hard at Dolan, said, "You got any reason for thinkin' different?"

Dolan shrugged. "Lot of things might decide 'em to get out of there—"

"Such as . . ."

"How do I know?" Dolan grunted. "But if they *do* come rampin' out, I say we better not fool around none. Drop 'em while we got the chance."

For a mild-mannered man, Peppin could sometimes look pretty ominous. "Dudley's give orders—"

"Hell with 'em!" Boyle said loudly.

"You might keep in mind he's reppin' for Uncle Sam—"

"Ahr-r—what can he *do?* He can shoot off his mouth till kingdom comes, but it won't bring those bastards to life again once we pot 'em!"

"God damn right it won't!" Pierce chimed grimly.

Peppin said, real quiet: "We'll decide on that when, and *if,* the time comes."

It was going to come. Peppin swore when he saw the smoke come curling out of McSween's. "You're a damn good prophet," he jerked at Dolan, "but some of the best have been hanged! By God," he said, and he seldom swore, "I've a notion to put you in irons!"

Dolan grinned. We all grinned with him.

"There comes Nanny-Goat," Kinney, by the window, mentioned.

We all looked out. Sure enough, there come Dudley up the road, squawking like a hen with its eggs took. He had two officers with him. McSween wouldn't come to the door.

After pulling the soldiers away from McSween's, Dudley'd gone into camp across from the church, with his guns trained square on Montana's and Patron's. Martin Chavez had been in charge of the McSween men there, and Dudley had called him over. "You see these guns?"

Chavez nodded. "If they should happen to go off," the

Colonel said, "they'd blow down those houses, and kill every man you've got in them."

Chavez frowned, "Per'aps I do not onderstan', *señor*. You 'ave bring your soldiers for protec' the life an' property, no?"

"Exactly! If your men fire another shot I'll blow those houses plumb apart." Dudley eyed him sternly. "I suggest you withdraw from Lincoln. Take your men, and clear out. I'll see that you're not fired upon. But see that you get clear away. Otherwise I shall send a troop of cavalry after you, and take you up to the Fort."

Chavez shrugged. A short time later we saw his whole crowd get their horses from the stables at the Ellis place, and leave.

Unable to get McSween to come to the door for a parley now, Dudley and his officers went over and knocked upon the Ealys' door. There was no shooting going on. We could hear everything they said, enough anyway to understand the gist of it. "This is most distressing!" Dudley muttered. "A terrible state of affairs!"

I looked to see him wring his hands, but he didn't. Doc Ealy said the Government had ought to stop this business, and give the citizens a chance—I guess he meant the outlawed citizens. It seemed to get Dudley's mad up; he said he'd no authority to interfere. "I can assume charge only in the event the situation gets out of hand—"

"Out of hand!" screamed Mrs. Ealy. "Do you—"

"I mean," supplemented the colonel, "beyond the control of the local authorities. Of Sheriff Peppin and his duly authorized deputies."

"The man is a Murphy partisan," Doc Ealy told him loudly. "He is directing this attack on us!"

"The outlaws in McSween's employ refused to surrender when called upon."

"Where would they have been now if they'd done so? *Murdered!*"

"I doubt it," said Dudley. "They'd have been safely lodged in jail."

Mrs. Ealy caught him by the coat sleeve. "Save us!" she wailed. "Oh, save us! If you don't do something those terrible Murphy ruffians will murder us all! If you won't do anything else, at least arrest the men Sheriff Peppin claims to have warrants for, and give them the protection of your troopers—"

"My soldiers are United States troops," answered Dudley stiffly. "This is a civil matter and—"

"Do you call it a civil matter," she cried, "for those Murphy blackguards to fire the house? You know it *is* afire, don't you?"

"I have . . . ah . . . seen some smoke," replied the colonel.

For a second I thought the Doc would have a stroke. Then, "Lord, grant us mercy!" he said gustily and, still purple round the gills, pulled his wife inside, and slammed the door.

Andy Boyle heaved out a guffaw, the colonel looked so furious. But Dolan said: "Flick, I'm askin' Nanny-Goat to find some kind of place where those women an' kids will be safe from gunfire. Take this over to him, will you?"

I took the folded paper and, without doing any shouting, slipped out by the back. There was nobody shooting at the moment, but I knew some fool might let off a gun most anytime. I reached Dudley's encampment in front of Patron's, and Montana's places, and gave Dolan's message to an aide. With a scowl, he hurried off to find the colonel. I wondered how such an old hen as Nanny-Goat had ever got so far in the army, but I had to credit him for one thing: his evacuation of Chavez's sharpshooters had given us a break. Peppin might not yet be bossing the situation, but at least McSween no longer had the edge. I could see the chance was coming for us to weed out some of his owl hooters. The place was really burning now. It was adobe, and the walls were thick, but it had finally caught and a gusty wind was driving huge billows of smoke across the road, and the sound of flames was like the Pecos in spring flood.

I went back to the Murphy store.

Dusk was thickening rapidly but the flare of the burning building knifed the shadows like light from a fluttered candle, and for yards around the trampled dust was bright as day. The west wing was gone, the front a mass of ruins, from which the smoke still curled and spurted like pale steam from a gypsy's pot. Of all that great fine house the Major and Jimmy Dolan had given McSween, only the east wing kept its shape. And that was burning—was burning fast.

Alert for any sign of a rush we saw Dudley drive up in a wagon, saw an orderly jump down, and run to thump a summons on the door. We saw it open; saw inside, limned black against the fire-glow, the Kid's slim gun-hung figure, crouched and catlike, set to pounce. Saw it back away, give place to shapes less desperate. The colonel was come for the kids and women.

We watched them out. Watched them climb resignedly into the wagon. We counted nine. Little Pearl, silent and abashed for once; Doc Ealy; Mrs. Ealy, with the baby; Mrs. Shields, and her brood of four. There was a pause, some kind of hubbub. We could hear the orderly arguing—Mrs. McSween's sullen voice, no longer throaty, but gone sharp, and shrill, and shrewish. We saw her plain in the firelight. She was consigning the irate Colonel for all eternity to a much warmer place than her home was. Dudley snapped: "Then stay there, dammit!"

But she didn't. I guess some one talked her out of it. She came out like a cat with its back up, shrieking, swearing, sobbing, calling down curses on all and sundry. She leveled a shaking arm at Dudley. "As long as I live," she shrilled, "I'll not leave a stone unturned to fasten on you the guilt of this criminal outrage!"

The orderly bundled her into the wagon, but he could not stop her tongue. "I'll sue you through every court in the land!"

"On what?" Boyle winked.

"On what's left of the Fritz insurance money!" came Old Man Pierce's high cackle.

Night closed down like the jaws of a wolf. The wind-lashed flames tore through the house, while the roar and cackle, the thud of falling timbers, were like crazy echoes to the barks of heated rifles. Almost, I could feel sorry for the men trapped in that final room. Almost—until I recollected the reason for their being there. A crew of killers, ruthless, implacable, athirst for blood as any vulture. Hired guns to McSween's ambition and avarice. A wild bunch, bought by promises never intended to be kept. Mad dogs.

Only the kitchen was left, and it was ten o'clock.

"We better get up closer," Peppin said. He had quit ragging Dolan about the fire after the remarks passed between the Ealys and Colonel Dudley. But he had not forgiven him. It was a good many days before he so much as spoke to him again. But right now his mind was fixed on doing his duty. The outlaws were going to have to run for it, and he meant to grab them if he could.

We closed in. Slipping from the store, clinging always to the deepest shadows, by roundabout ways we crept up closer to the kitchen where McSween's owl hooters must make their final stand. Silently, we took places in the gloom that flanked the stable, crouched beneath the wall that divided the stable pasture from McSween's backyard. Each man crouched, with rifle ready. The kitchen roof was blazing; they could not hold out much longer.

Peppin gave final orders, the word was passed. "Shoot to stop, but not to kill." Boyle grinned when he said it. Beckwith chuckled. The distance between myself and the kitchen door was not very great, about fourteen yards.

Suddenly the door bulged open, black with shapes against the flames. To the Kid's wild cry they came out running, pistols belching their leaden blasts. It was like some scene snatched out of hell. The scream of lead, the shouts, gun thunder, running men, the black shapes falling and, over all, the fitful play of the dancing flames like light from a witch's kettle.

Among the runners I saw Romero, face twisted, ghastly— saw him fall. Sound was blotted by a crash of rifles, out of which came Beckwith's shout. *"I got him! By God, I got McSween!"*

It was to have been expected some one would get him. It had been the declared intention of more than half the posse. But some way, with that cry in my ears, I felt a little shocked. A crazy thing to say, God knows; but that was how I felt. I'd no cause to regret his passing, no reason to condemn his fate, yet strangely I felt suddenly isolated from the rest, the bond that bound us gone.

Perhaps some of the other boys felt that way. The shots dimmed out. There was a lull. There were blotches on the dusty ground. Firelight licked their rumpled clothing, threw dark stains of shadow round them. Toward these Beckwith suddenly sprang, with a wave of his rifle went charging forward.

A shout welled up: "Here somes the Kid! Get him, boys— Don't let the varmint git away!"

Out they spewed from the kitchen door. O'Folliard, French, Doc Scurlock, others. I saw the Kid's lean bucktoothed face. He had a gun in each of his hands. One raised—a white flame leaped to Beckwith's chest, and he staggered backward, clawed hands flailing. It pulled my attention away from Bonney.

When I looked again the Kid was gone.

The yard was empty . . . empty of all but six still shapes. These were the fallen. Dead with their boots on.

The war was finished.

I went into Stockton's bar for a bracer.

Two soldiers had just finished planting McSween out back of his store, by the side of Tunstall.

Six men had dropped in that yard last night, but only five

had been there this morning: Beckwith, Alex McSween, Morris, Romero, Semora. The sixth had gone, crept away in the night—Ygenio Salazar, poser to the last. I said, "Good luck to him."

Stockton nodded. "The Kid got away, too, didn't he?"

"Yeah. O'Folliard, French an' Scurlock likewise. We'll be hearin' of 'em," I growled morosely. "But the Lincoln County War is done with. Folded like an empty tent."

Ike sighed. "A wild, tough crowd—but boys to ride the river with. God rest them," he said shaking his head.

We downed our drinks in silence.

Sight of my bronc, when I went outside, brought round my thoughts to Sally. She'd said, "If you quit Uncle John you quit me too." I knew damn well she'd meant it.

But it's ever been a woman's way to change her mind, and it might be, I hoped fervently, that Sally had again changed hers.

With the thought I climbed into my saddle.

Postscript

Billy the Kid did not die until some two years later when, so the story goes, Pat Garrett on the night of July 13, 1881, caught and killed him in a bedroom of the Maxwell House at old Fort Sumner.

For the background and raw material of this book, acknowledgment is due to many published sources; and, in particular, to Mr. Henry F. Fritz, of Capitan, for all his kindly help, advice and reminiscences, and to his daughter, Mrs. Wallace Ferguson, for her good offices. I am also indebted to Mr. C. W. Hyde, one-time sheriff of Lincoln County, for reminiscences and aid in arriving at a just conception of Sheriff Dad Peppin and his work; and to Mr. John Sinclair, of the Lincoln County Museum, for worthwhile aid in other research.   N.C.N.

TOUGH COMPANY

1 | BLUE ROAN RUNNING

OBSCURITY was what Walt Bender was hunting when he climbed up out of the desert's white glare and found this wild tangle of greenery before him. There was a dilapidated shack half buried in the pines where he could rest for awhile and get the saddle kinks out of him and a heap of new grass to pad out the ribs of that stout-hearted horse which had moved him eighty miles on a hatful of water.

They were travel worn and weary and there was no real reason, so far as he could see, why they shouldn't hole up here. This was a homesteader's claim and long abandoned by the look of it, the warped door hanging open, the rusted stovepipe drunkenly canted and the cleared land before it grown to crab grass and jimson. It made a picture of futility not many would have cared for, but Bender was in a mood to find any place suitable which had no star-packers cluttering the scenery.

He was a bleak-eyed man with sun-blackened cheeks and a mass of yellow hair sweatily plastered across his forehead. This was how the reward bills showed him, and if you didn't want trouble you had better sheer away because he was all done with running. Six solid months he'd been pushed by tin badges, driven from his ranch, turned away from jobs and people—and all because of a whittle whanging sidewinder who didn't care no more about dropping a politician than he would about finding worms in his biscuits.

Naturally the dodgers said nothing of that. They said WANTED FOR MURDER in boldfaced caps; that was how Lasham had framed him for being too damned fond of his grass. Had it been anyone less than old Toby Bronsen the fat slob couldn't have cut it, but Toby had been a state's senator and no one could see how the sheep crowd could profit by killing the goose which had laid all their eggs—no one, that is, but Walt Bender. And who was going to listen to a fool caught red-handed with a gun in his fist while Lasham bellowed "Grab him!" at the top of his lungs?

He'd got away from that crowd by the skin of his teeth and was still on the dodge, Lasham managing that adroitly.

"Sheep killer" was what Lasham called him, and "cold turkey" was another of the vinegarroon's pet names which the sheep pool took up and hung onto him. If there was any one man in that West Texas country Walt Bender would sure like to blast into dollrags, that feller was Lasham. Deef Lasham who had tossed Walt aside like he wasn't no more than a chunk of waste paper. Lasham who, loud in front of the packed mob attending that rally, had called him "a damn exterminatin' son of a bitch!"

And the hell of it was Bender hadn't killed anyone—he'd been just a white chip in a no-limit game. But a thing like that can work on a man.

It had been working on Bender.

Every time he had run into another of those handbills Lasham's hirelings had scattered from Grandfalls to Canutillo the crazy tightness in his head had got tighter, the volcanic rage inside him a little nearer to tearing loose.

Oh, they'd been cute, all right—they'd been slicker than slobbers with never a sign of a broadsheet before him so long as he'd kept his horse pointing west. But let him turn north, let him lope awhile south or try to cut back east, and there were those handbills flaunting his likeness from tree, post and outhouse.

And that was how he'd been closed out of Texas.

The line was forty miles behind him, across the damn blow holes and that white hell of desert, beyond the green spikes of the sentinel yuccas. Ahead lay the West Potrillos, their upthrust peaks showing over the pines in a high ragged sweep of broken blues and purples against the bright rim of the dying sun. Not exactly a promised land perhaps, but one at least not, likely to be overrun with lawmen.

Manyanner land, the Texicans called it, a place where one day was much the same as another and nobody cared where the hell a man came from so long as he did not upset cherished customs. A land permeated with the hush of past centuries, where traditions were honored and the nights were made gay with guitars and laughing lips and only mission bells told the careless passage of time.

And so to hell with Texas—let the damned sheep have it!

NIGHT was crowding the shank of evening when Bender's roan crossed the level and moved in toward the shack. He was almost abreast the swaybacked roof of the porch when a shot ripped a startling hole through the stillness.

Bender's eyes turned narrow and he held the horse quiet, hearing the echoes of that report strike and shatter against stone. It had come, he decided, from somewhere beyond and to the left of the building. And then he heard brush break beneath a fast traveling body and maneuvered the gelding around the shack very quietly, again sitting motionless with hand outstretched to choke off at once any sound from the animal.

Now he heard horses move with a rush to the right, their hoofs soft-drumming through the ¬isles of the pines, coming steadily nearer; and he moved again.

Full dark came suddenly and, with an equal abruptness, very shortly thereafter three horsemen burst from the pines and tore past, traveling south.

Bender felt the call of this night, of this wilderness, not wanting the smallest part in this business but not wanting, either, to go off with the thought of somebody dying because he hadn't had guts enough to go to their aid.

He listened to the three who had passed roar away in the darkness and he put the roan into movement, thinking to go through the pines and perhaps find what the score was. Certainly the shot had come from over there someplace, from some ravine or gulch.

He found it black, black almost as ink, drifting through

the aisles of these lofty pines. He kept thinking about the report of that shot, about the way it had sounded, the suddenness and the finality of it, and the uncaring rush of that later departure. Almost it had sounded like a bushwhacking.

Because the gelding's hoofs were making very little sound on this matted covering Bender had thought several times to catch the rumor of something. Now he heard it distinctly, the strike of iron on stone, and his mind translated this into an approaching rider, his analysis of the sound convincing him the man was coming off a rim. Now a rim to Bender meant a gulch or canyon and this tied in nicely with his earlier thought that the shot he had heard might have come from such a place. Was this the one who had fired it or the one who'd been fired at?

It might be just as well, he decided, to let the fellow work past without realizing his presence. Accordingly he stopped. But the man didn't seem to be in any great hurry. It was his mount, by the sound, who was picking the footing. He did a considerable amount of stopping which could indicate, of course, the cropping of grass. Except that grass didn't usually grow well on stone. Bender reckoned he could chalk those pauses up to nerves on the part of the rider. The guy was feeling edgy and was doing a lot of listening.

He was, Bender figured, perhaps a hundred yards ahead of him, a little over on the right and still traveling in rock. When the hoofs stopped again there was sound on Bender's left, also ahead of him, though more nearly on a level. It was horse sound, it was closer and it was also moving nearer.

Cursing under his breath, Bender wished he'd had the wit to have stayed out of these trees. There were others moving up behind him now and to move at all would be to court discovery.

The man off the wall abruptly raised his voice. "See anything?"

"Nothin' round the shack," one of the group behind Bender said. "Think we better try combin' that canyon, Art?"

The man to the left and ahead of Bender said, "Who fired?"

Bender was beginning to feel acutely his lack of knowledge of this region.

When no one answered Art's question about the shot, Art said, "Did anyone get hit?"

But no one answered that, either. The group behind Bender now began to move up and, perforce, Bender also moved, but much more slowly, much more carefully. Somebody said, "If he come this far he must have gone into the canyon unless he struck for the desert."

"He wouldn't do that," Art said, "if he could help it. We'd have him cut off if he went into the desert."

"I ain't so sure about that," one of the others objected. "He's bound to know we mean business. He may have decided this deal ain't worth dyin' for."

Another said impatiently: "If he went into the canyon he may slip out the other end—"

"No danger of that," Art said. "I've got Curly and Beans and Spuds Moran over there just waitin' for him to show his damn face."

Those behind him were getting nearer Bender now; the first man wasn't more than a horse length away. His rifle, like Bender's, was laying across his saddle. Bender now swung left to go around a tree and was sorely tempted to keep right on going only he knew he'd never make it. Riding with the group was one thing, riding away from it something else. He took only long enough to let that first man get ahead of him, then he came around the tree and paired off with another who was just a black shape in this gloom beneath the pines.

They came out of the trees in the next twenty feet and it was too late then for him to drop aside. The dark maw of the canyon opened directly ahead of them and he caught a vague look at the man who'd come off the wall.

Another dimseen shape trotted up from the left and this was Art, Bender guessed, checking his mount with the rest. This bunch was all about him now, choking the canyon's mouth with their horses, milling around in restless movement yet too close in their jingling and creaking to suit him. He tugged his hatbrim lower and bent forward in the saddle, reaching down as though to take the slack out of the roan's front girth.

"I keep thinkin'," Art said, "about that shot. Uncommon odd, I call it, with the whole crew scourin' round here that none of you'll admit to knowin' anything about it. That damn gun never fired itself!"

A man three horses away said, "What the hell? That stinkin' tomale prob'ly let off his pistol. He's been jumpy enough or he'd not have cut over this way in the first place."

"Would a *mozo* risk givin' himself away like that?" Art's voice turned rougher, the violence of his thinking getting into it now. "Forty-five hundred's a big chunk of money, more than some of you gents'll ever make in a lifetime."

All the horsemen around Bender sat still now. The head of his roan was against a dun's shoulder. A yard away on his right a pair of riders faced toward him and a man on his left had his knee against Bender's. If one of this bunch should decide to strike a match . . .

"You know what I think?" Art abruptly demanded. "I think one of you brush poppers come up with that feller. I think one of you slick sons got the bright notion of gettin' hands on that dough an' then rollin' your cotton."

"That," cried the man on Bender's left, "is a hell of a thing to say, Art!"

"I'm sayin' it. And I'll tell you something else. I better not come onto that pepper-gut's body and not find no damn dough in his pockets." He let them digest that and then he said quietly. "Chuck, I want you up on that north rim again. I'll take the south and the rest of you rannies spread out and comb all the brush in that canyon—and what I mean, *work* at it. If this peckerneck gets back to the ranch with that dinero it's goin' to be too damn bad for somebody. Now get at it!"

A lean gap in their ranks showed now just behind Bender and he backed the roan into it, swerving him then to round the man on his right. His leg brushed roughly against that one's leg and the man growled sharply, "For Christ's sake Joe, have you got your damn eyes shut?" And a man up ahead of him wheeled, saying, "What?" And the first one's head twisted round to look at Bender. He said, "Wait a minute, bucko," but Bender kept going, sliding the roan in between two passing others and cutting back of them to edge around a third and stay with this man awhile.

Glancing back across his shoulder Bender saw the one he'd locked knees with yank his horse out of line and sit there blackly waiting for the three last riders to pass him. In a minute, Bender knew, this one was going to be coming after him, and he tried to make his mind up. He wanted like hell to run but knew very well that the instant he did he'd have this whole damn push piling after him.

Just then the two men directly before him passed into the canyon's black obscurity, the heavier darkness swallowing them; and, with one quick look at that man coming up, Bender sent his own mount into this murk, shortening the length of the gelding's stride until the man who'd been siding him pulled ahead. Then he went with cocked muscles across the front of the drag, letting the roan drift a further ten paces till he had the low face of the south wall before him, there stopping.

Slipping his Winchester back in its scabbard, he pulled the blue neckerchief up to his eyes and again turned the roan till it was pointed as the others, holding the animal there without motion. His intention was to wait till the rest of this outfit moved deeper into the gulch, but the man who'd been hunting him was still plainly at it and now this one's voice, climbing over the riding sounds, cried: "Chuck! There's—"

"Button your lip!" Chuck slammed back at him wickedly. "If you ain't got no more sense than to go shoutin' names—"

"Hold on," Art called. "What's the matter down there?"

Bender, against the wall, was now unable to see any of them, but he could hear the low grumble of exchanged comments, the restless milling of horses, spur sound and bit sound.

Through the felted blackness the hunter's dissatisfied voice rose again. "There's a stray down here someplace. I think that spik's with us—"

"I think you're crazy," Art said, "but we'll damn quick find out. Don't any of you move from his tracks till I tell you. Chuck, move your horse up that wall twenty paces."

The sound of Chuck's horse came down plainly to Bender. If they were fixing to count noses he didn't think it would tell them much, now that he had got himself out of their way. He thought a light might do it if they could get a light strong enough, but if he'd judged this bunch right they weren't going to be wanting to have their mugs seen.

"Okey," Chuck called.

"One at a time now," Art said, "you rannies down there step your broncs up ten paces. As each man moves forward he will give his name clearly, then hold his horse quiet till he gets recognition, thereafter settin' still till we get this thing done with. You in the lead now—move up."

Bender grinned in the dark, hearing the first man go forward. "Jid," this one said, and Chuck called for another. There was horse sound again and a different voice: "Ed." A third rider moved up but before he could speak there came a sudden wild clatter of metal on rock. It seemed to come from beyond them, deeper into the gulch, both okeyed men firing instantly. Sound battered monstrously against the stone cliffs, clattering down and around them in shattering fragments. Through this came curses, shouted questions, more sound piled on sound as saddle guns drove unseen lead through the uproar. One man's yell went racketing above it and a sudden concerted rushing of riders flung hoof thunder into the tumult.

Bender whirled his roan and, clinging flattened against its side, sent it streaking in the direction of the pines he had so recently come out of. The barrel-toned roar of Art's angry orders was almost submerged in the bedlam behind him and somewhere a horse gave one scream of great agony.

What it was which had startled that bunch into firing Bender did not know, nor did he give it much thought. He was directing all his attention toward getting out of this gulch with his scalp still in place if there was any chance of doing it. He might have got clear right then except that all of this bunch hadn't lost their heads.

He had the roan gelding pushed to its limit when they crashed head-on into the rump of another which appeared to be bound in the same direction. A girl's frightened cry came out of the blackness and was instantly lost in the scream of her pony as the force of collision hurled it onto its knees. Bender's own horse managed to stay on its feet but was flung half around, throwing Bender's masked face full into the glare of an exploding pistol. He felt the heat of that blast and tossed away in that moment of lifting temper the caution which thus far had kept these guns off him.

He lifted the Winchester out of its scabbard and struck with it, club like, the brought-around barrel beating breath from a man who fell off his horse backwards. Gripping hard with his knees Bender pulled himself upright, sliding the saddlegun back in its sheath and reaching—sheer reflex—for the butt of his pistol.

It was lucky he did, for another dark rider was driving straight at him, already so close Walt could see the pale blob of his face in the starlight. Gigging the roan to one side as the fellow lashed past Bender hammered the back of his head with the beltgun.

Then he flung the roan forward. "Where are you—where are you?"

"Here!" cried the girl, and she sprang from the shadows.

Kicking a boot from the stirrup he gave her his hand. She came up sure and swift, being dressed like a man, settling lightly behind him with a *"Madre de Dios!"* He felt her hands clutch his belt. He felt her lips at his ear. "Through the trees," she cried softly, "and be quick or we'll die here."

He spurred the roan toward the pines while behind them a gun laid flat crashes of sound through the canyon. Yet loud as this was Bender heard Art bellow. "Drop them, you fools! Cut them down—cut them down!" Almost instantly then the voice of a rifle began to break up the night with its crack-crack-crack chatter.

Bender crouched just as low as he could get in the saddle, feeling the girl's body crowding ever tighter against him, raking the gelding's wet flanks with his spurs. But the horse didn't have the reach he'd had that morning. Those grueling hours in the desert had taken their toll and this girl's added weight was not helping. The horse was doing its best but its wind was a racking in-and-out rush of sound and it was moving stiff-legged in what was almost a stagger.

Bender heard those blue whistlers singing closer and closer but he still thought they'd make it and get into the pines when something went *thwut* and the gelding broke stride. He didn't quit, he kept going but he was losing momentum.

Bender groaned when the horse began to fall apart under them.

"We're goin' to have to get off."

"Yes," the girl said. She took her hands off his belt and was gone on the instant. Bender felt like a deserter pulling his boots from the stirrups. He hauled up one leg, patted the gelding and jumped.

2 | THE SUDDEN TURN

THEY plunged into the trees, Bender striving to follow the elusive shape of the girl, wondering how she'd got into this trap, wondering if she were the one with the money. He could smell the dry mold being kicked up by bullets and he could hear other bullets droning viciously around him, ripping bark off the pines and squealing in ricochet. He'd grabbed the rifle off the roan when he had jumped, and still had it; but he didn't feel at all inclined to stop right now and use it.

That lead-slinging bunch had been looking for a man, but the girl's clothes might have fooled them—not, Bender thought, that it was like to make much difference if she were the one who was packing that dinero. He didn't have to see faces to know these men's kind. He'd met gun-hung drifters of their stripe before and understood very clearly how much mercy could be expected by a woman at their hands. It was the only reason he tagged after this girl against every impulse of experience and judgment.

He believed they would both have a much better chance of getting clear if they split up now, but he did not offer this thought to the girl. He was too curious, for one thing, and his pride would not permit him to put forward a suggestion which might seem, if later repeated, a disparagement of his manhood. But he could not help reflecting they weren't being very smart. Afoot they would be lucky even to get as far as that shack which at best, as Bender saw it, would be damned indifferent shelter.

The trees by now were beginning to make an effective screen against the guns. Panting, Bender called to the girl and she waited for him to come up with her. While he was still trying to catch enough breath for his question they heard a rush of horses and the girl caught his hand. "We must get to the house—"

"We can't stand them off there for—"

"Please!"

Bender shrugged. "All right," he said grimly, not seeing that it made much difference. If dying in that shack would make her feel happier it was okey with him because they'd sure as hell die if they remained in these pines. Art wouldn't make the same mistake twice; it was plain by their sound that he had spread his men out to where not even a rabbit would elude them this time.

They broke out of the trees and saw the shack's bulk before them. He followed the girl across the creaking porch and dragged the door shut behind them. He felt her hand on his arm guiding him over to a window. "There is where they will have to come out. Try to hold them off a little while with your rifle."

She moved away from him then, her spurred heels crossing the floor with a deal more confidence than Bender could feel. "You have a gun?" he asked.

"Not any more. I threw it away to distract their attention. Have you plenty of shells for your rifle?"

"About a dozen, I think—"

"Then you must make each one count."

She was the coolest dame he had ever bumped into.

Make them count. Bender grinned. You could trust him for that. He had no more desire to be killed than the next guy. "You better get down an' stay flat on the floor."

His eyes got blurry peering into the gloom and he closed them a moment, hearing her busily scraping at something with her foot. He wondered who she was, how she'd got into this business, and asked her if she had the money they were hunting.

She admitted she had. She said, "I'm going to try and hide it. Hold them off as long as you can and don't be afraid of killing them. They are Chesseldine's men—that was him they called 'Art'."

He heard her grunt, heard the squeak of strained boards, and then he dropped behind the window and cuddled the Winchester to his shoulder, thrusting its barrel across the sill. Where he heard the girl's breath there was a flat slap of sound as though of something heavy falling, and he twisted his head, calling out, "Are you all right?"

"Yes," she said, panting. "Let me worry with this. You watch out for those cow thieves and don't waste your cartridges."

At the edge of the pines Bender caught a blur of motion but he held his fire, waiting as she'd suggested till he could make his shots count. He said softly, "Who's Chesseldine?"

"He is suspected of being the leader of all the stock thieves around here. He calls himself a speculator in cattle and pretends to be a great friend of my father who is very simple about such things. He stopped by our ranch two weeks ago and told my father the government was throwing open two hundred thousand acres of—"

The report of Bender's rifle crashed through the shack, obscuring her words; and just in front of the place where the pines loomed blackest a running man threw up his hands and pitched headlong. "Down!" Bender cried, and dropped flat himself as the answering fire of Chesseldine's men hammered the boards of the wall with their bullets, some of these tearing all the way through the shack. The smell of dust rose up and mingled with the acrid stench of black powder.

When the men in the pines dropped back to reload Bender kicked out a short length of rotten board near the floor and, stretched prone, thrust the barrel of his rifle through this and waited. "You all right?" he called again to the girl.

"Yes. There's an old root cellar beneath a trap in the floor. I've hidden the money—"

"You stay down there," Bender said, and then, after a moment of closely watching the pines, "How'd they get onto this forty-five hundred?"

"Chesseldine said we could bid in the grass nearest us—about eight thousand acres—for that amount of money. My father said we didn't have that amount and Chesseldine said he knew a man who would lend it. He said this man knew my father's reputation and if we cared to fill out a paper he left with us we could see this man in Columbus on the twentieth and he would let us have the money."

"The twentieth was yesterday—"

"Yes. My father sent his foreman—"

"How did *you* get hold of the money?"

"When I read the small print on the paper we were to sign, I told my father the loan would be secured by a mortgage on Tres Pinos—that is the name of our ranch. He said no matter. But I did not like for him to sign this paper, even though I knew we had the need of more grass. My mother, of course, would say nothing; when I tried to tell a little of what I thought my father became very angry and signed it. So then he sent his foreman to Columbus for the money. But something," she said, putting a hand to her breast, "came to warn me against these Greeks bearing gifts—"

"Greeks? You mean," said Bender, startled, "this Chessy guy's—"

"Oh, no—a figure of speech only. They are Americans, of course—of a very low type. But I became extremely suspicious:

for, consider: this Chesseldine, who even among the gringos has a poor reputation, comes directly to my father to speak about this grass. I ask myself why this should be so; and, when my father says he does not have so much money, is it reasonable for this man who speaks of Mexicans as 'greasers' to know already of another generous *Norte Americano* who will advance my father the price of this grass? And the date! This so-generous man will be in Columbus only on the twentieth —could we be indeed so fortunate?"

"Yeah. I see what you mean," Bender nodded. "But I thought this bunch talked like they were expectin' a Mexican—"

"My father's foreman is Mexican. His name is Pedro Gonzales."

"So you went instead."

"No. It was all settled that Pedro should go for this money. Chesseldine said he would arrange for it to be given to no one but Pedro. After Pete left, I made the excuse to go and visit a friend who lives at Afton. Instead of the provisions that were placed in my saddlebags I took these clothes—a foolish thing."

"But the money?" Bender said, twisting around to try and see her.

"I waited along the *Camino Primativo*, about three hundred *metros* beyond the town's last house. When I saw my father's foreman I rode out of the brush and called him. He was very annoyed when he saw who I was. I thought at first the man had not given him the money, expecting to see a great sack on his saddle. But he said he had got it, that they'd given it in paper which he had in a belt underneath his shirt. I told him I would take it, that I felt sure he was going to be robbed of this money. He made a great deal of talk but in the end gave it over—"

A sudden thunder of hoofbeats cut into her words and Bender, cursing, whirled back to his peephole but they were already past where he could fire from the floor. "Git flat," he growled angrily, and was jumping toward the gray square of the window when that wall of the shack began to rattle like a drum. Something tore past his hip and went *chunk!* in the back wall, and Bender flung up his Winchester and fired where he was.

He heard the thin whine as a slug cuffed his hat-brim and the instant *thwut* of it striking the wall. The thunder of Chesseldine's riders swept past and was muted a little as they cut back toward the trees. Bullets still crashed into the boards of the shack and he could tell where they were by the side these were striking.

That rush had been to test him, to find out how well this shack would be defended. The next time they came they'd rush this place in real earnest. He told the girl: "You'd better run for it. Crawl out that back door and duck into the lean-to. While they're rushing this side try to make those east trees an' keep—"

"Ride right into it this time!"

A round blast of flame leaped out of the pines and someone commenced a high rebel yelling. As Bender flung himself flat to get away from that lead he heard a second rush of horses tear out of the timber. He came onto one knee and ripped a slug through that blackness, continuously firing until his rifle clicked empty. He heard the girl come crawling across to his side and she caught up the Winchester, saying, "Give me your cartridges."

He wanted to tell her to get back in that hole but there was no use in that once he'd used his last bullet; they'd come after her then and how the hell could he stop them? He gave her what he had and then crouched back on his haunches. He lifted his pistol, waiting till he saw the dark shapes of Art's riders swing hellity larrup across the front of the yard, laying his quick fire through a corner of the window. Lead ripped splinters of wood from the sill and other slugs batted the wall all around him. He fired again, putting two shots into that huddle of riders. A horse went down and the rest swept over him. Another rider reared up and went off his mount screaming.

Bender dropped his dry gun and took the reloaded Winchester. "You've got five shells, that's all," she said and, fumbling at his belt, began reloading the sixshooter.

Bender laid the barrel of the rifle across the sill. He took one quick look and crashed out four slugs as fast as he could trigger. One horse went up on its hind legs, pawing, toppling backwards square in the path of another. One was so close when Bender's slug struck, it smashed sideways into the corner of the building, flinging its rider clear across the porch, stopping with its head and one leg through the wall. Chesseldine's crew broke and scattered, Bender dropping one more as they raced for the trees.

"Close," he grunted, sleeving sweat from his eyes. "You should have gone when I told you. They won't try that again. They'll be coming for us afoot now, creepin' an' crawlin' from all sides at once."

He thought to see her shake her head but in this gloom he wasn't sure. "I think," she told him soberly, "the odds will be in favor of their going away—"

"Without that dough?" Bender stared at her pityingly. He thought anyone exhibiting that kind of faith must be either very young or in line for a string of spools. He'd been through some close shaves and had sometimes wondered what shape the end might take but had never imagined himself boxed in a shack getting ready to die with an unknown woman.

He thrust a hand across the loops of his brush-clawed shell belt, finding them entirely devoid of live cartridges. Art's gun throwers, he thought, were probably injuning up now. They'd be a little more careful on this trip he reckoned; and abruptly remembered the man who'd been flung across the porch. If he could get that guy's cartridges. . . .

The girl said through the darkness, "You probably think I'm a fool to believe they'll go without the money, but you're forgetting they expected to encounter little trouble. They planned this very carefully as Chesseldine plans everything. The man's a coyote, not a wolf—"

"But the stake," said Bender drily, "is forty-five hundred dollars and around this kind of country that's a hell of a lot of money."

"And little good to him if he's caught."

"But who's to catch him?" Bender asked skeptically, "out here forty miles from nowhere?"

"This house is on my father's ranch. It belonged to a man who was sick in his chest whom my father permitted to live here. This robber knows as well as I how near he is to my father's *casa*. He knew that when he planned this thing. He had to get close because three trails come together just above these pines and he had to wait there or risk missing his quarry. It was expected to be simple—one shot, one dead body and away with our money. But I did not keep to the trail and now he's done too much shooting. He will be afraid to wait longer."

"How far off is your house?"

"Hardly over two miles by the trail; actually nearer. Already our *vaqueros* will be mounted and riding."

"They could still be too late." Bender lifted his head and took a look through the window. He was not reassured. "What's to prove they would have heard—"

"How could they help? Sound does curious things around here. The gallery of my father's *casa* faces this place and picks up many rumors, but I have more proof than that. When this sick man would get bad he would always fire his pistol and my mother would fix the herb medicine for him—"

"This bunch might not know that." Bender was willing to admit. Art might be getting a little nervous after all that firing, but he didn't believe the man was ready to ride off and say goodbye to that dinero. He had already shown himself contemptuous of Mexicans and, from the girl's talk, it would seem the whole Three Pines crew was chile-eaters. They were the best damn cowboys in the world and Bender knew it, but there were plenty of so-called white men in this region who professed to believe Mexicans were a cowardly lot who had no rights at all. And, from what he'd seen and heard, he imagined Art was of this persuasion.

"Let's just figure for the moment that we ain't out of this yet. One of them horses I shot threw a guy across the porch. On the chance he's got some shells I'm goin' to slip out there."

"I'll go with you—"

"You'll stay right where you are," Bender said to her sharply. "You may be figurin' this right, and I sure hope you are, but you're not setting foot outside of this shack until I'm convinced that bunch has gone diggin' for the tules."

It never occurred to Bender she might ignore his orders. He paused a moment to unlatch his gut hooks and then commenced crawling across the littered floor. He had not heard the girl close the trap but he knew he was on it when he felt the boards give a little under his weight. He thought the root cellar a damn poor place for that money but, considering the girl's convictions, he reckoned that at a pinch it might perhaps serve her purpose. His main interest right now was in gaining replacements for the loads in his pistol.

He saw the black hole of the doorless rear exit as a more solid oblong of the darkness before him, and moved up to it cautiously, stopping when he reached it to listen intently. He heard nothing which alarmed him nor did he hear any sound of the Three Pines *vaqueros*. As he had supposed, this doorway opened directly into the lean-to. The lean-to's open side, he remembered, faced east and was about two yards from that corner of the shack. The thrown rider, as near as Bender could figure, should be about the same distance from the corner at the opposite side; and the end of the shack around which he'd have to crawl was the farthest removed from the bunch who were bent on stopping his clock. Which was no proof, of course, that they had not changed position.

He debated the advisability of drawing his pistol, well aware if it were needed it would be needed mighty quick. But he decided to leave it in its sheath on his belt; there was too much risk, in his hand, of the stars striking up a gleam which might betray him.

The deep gloom of the shed closed around him like the smothering folds of a pure-black blanket. To the left and before him this murk was complete. To his right, along the house wall, night made a patterned wedge of blue shadows. Still on all fours, Bender pointed himself toward this and moved forward.

Bit by cautious bit he worked nearer, muscles tight and pulses pounding. He kept his face geared down, trying to pick a quiet way through an accumulated litter of discarded junk, finally reaching the opening and moving out of the shed.

It seemed to him at once as though a thousand eyes were watching. He was, in that moment, a cold and wholly desperate man who had counted his chances and accepted the risk; and then a low wind drifted across his face from the pines and he jerked up his head with both ears cocked, suddenly stopping.

He'd have sworn he'd caught the close-by breaking of a stick, and the skin at the base of his scalp began to prickle as he plowed the shadows with a widened wicked stare.

For frozen moments time stood still; then Bender's hand came off his gun butt and his shape recommenced its crawling and came against the wall's east corner.

Here the bulked ragged black of the pines came within twenty yards of him and he heard the tumult of his heart as he paused there, briefly listening.

Expecting any moment to hear the crash and bang of gun-fire he dropped flat on his belly and commenced a forward wriggling meant to take him round the corner. He moved an arm, the opposite knee, and thought in that split second to catch the faroff sound of hurrying hoofs; in the next all thought was swept completely out of him as the fingers of his left extended forward-reaching hand, going round the building's angle, suddenly brushed and gripped another hand, gun-weighted, moving toward him.

3 | ONE FOR THE BOOK

SOME gents would do a world of thinking with their hand that way on another guy's wrist. Bender did not think at all. He flung all the weight he could get on that dewclaw, grinding it into the gravelly ground, banging it hard as he could against the house wall, then taking it with him as he rolled round the corner.

The gun went off, gouting flame past Walt's face, hammering the night with its tumultuous thunder; and then Walt was over him, pinning the man's middle with the weight of his body while muzzle light cut its streaks of yellow and purple against the black shapes of the shaggy pines. The man writhed like a snake, snarling curses and panting, as lead from those rifles beat against the shack wall, but Bender wouldn't let go. He rode the man's struggles as he'd ride a bad bronc, piling pressure on pressure as he forced that arm upward behind the man's twisted head until he heard bone grate.

The man screamed and went limp. Scooping up the dropped pistol, Bender unlatched the man's belt, buckling it about his own lean hips, half straightening then and hanging fire for a moment, not liking to leave this fellow so exposed. But he did, after all, because just then he heard the horses—heard them coming through the timber on a hard and lifting run.

Not caring to be trapped where he'd have no chance Bender dived around the corner, colliding with surprise against a crouched shape hurrying toward him. He damn near put a slug through the girl before he realized who this was he had hold of. He felt the strike of her heart against his ribs. Spurred then by anger, pushing her roughly into the shed, he said: "I thought I told you to stay inside—"

"But I was afraid you were hurt. I. . . ." He felt her shape stiffen. She cried, "Listen—the *vaqueros!* I told you they would come!" She would have gone running out there if Bender hadn't stopped her, forgetful of flying lead and everything else in her excitement.

But it was plain she had the right of it. Rifles were crashing all through the pines and there was a lot of wild yelling, the sound of the guns growing steadily more remote as the crew from the ranch strung out after the bushwhackers trying to fight clear through the black of that canyon.

"You're hurting me," she said, and he let go of her shoulder. He scowled in an embarrassed silence. Then he said to her gruffly, "Better get in there an' dig up your money while we're waitin'. When your crew gets back I'll be rockin' along."

He stepped out of the shed and went back around the corner, thinking to have a closer look at that fellow who he believed was the man that had been flung across the porch. But the man was no longer lying there.

Bender roved a hard glance through the roundabout shadows, then crouched and looked again. He couldn't believe any fellow with an out-of-whack shoulder was going to be able to get very far and, with this thought in his mind, carefully combed the whole clearing, still without finding him. Thoroughly unconvinced, he cruised into the pines but finally gave it up. The guy might not have spilled his guts anyway.

When he came back to the cabin the girl said, "I'm ready."

"For what?" Bender asked.

"Why, to go home, of course. Did you think I'd planned to camp here all night?"

"Your crew will be back—"

"I've had enough of this place.'"

She gave him that news as a queen might have spoken. Bender scrinched his eyes, scowling. "I ain't too partial about it myself, but we don't have no horses and trampin' two miles with a hull on each shoulder is more than I'm engagin' to care for right now."

"One of the crew will pick up your saddle when he comes after mine in the morning."

"Maybe I won't be around in the morning."

"Maybe you won't, but unless you like walking you'll have to come to Tres Pinos to get hold of a horse." She eyed him a moment. "You may as well come with me."

"I'll get a horse from your crew."

"If you wait for the crew you'll be more apt to get a bullet. They'll think you're one of that crowd they've been chasin—"

"I'll chance that."

"You've no need to. Why must you be so stubborn?" she asked angrily. "It would be different if you were bound somewhere else, but you're not. You're going to pass the ranch anyway—"

"Where'd you get that notion?"

"Didn't you come off the desert?"

"What's that got to do with it?"

"If you stay here awhile—"

"I'm not stayin'," he said impatiently; and he sure as hell wasn't. Not after that gun welcome he'd just gotten. The last thing he wanted was any more trouble.

She appeared to be trying to work out something. He could feel her eyes on him, saw the way she was canting her head as she watched him. "Perhaps not," she told him finally, "but I think you're mistaken."

"I'm leavin'," Bender said, "just as quick as I get a horse."

"Then you may as well see that I get home with this money. The nearest place you'll get a horse is at Tres Pinos. We raise nothing but the best. And if you should happen to admire one my father will insist on giving it to you."

Bender looked at her slanchways. "I'm scared that kind of horse would come too high," he told her drily.

She stood awhile not speaking but continuing to watch him, and then she remarked abruptly: "What you do with your life is, of course, your own business—but a man never got away from anything by running."

This girl's calm assumption of so cool an authority, quite as much as the way she'd pushed that last remark at him, stirred the cramped boil of temper that was smoldering in Bender; and he flung back at her sharply: "You're a sight too smart for your own good, missy."

Her small laugh was short and held an edge close to bitterness. "You are not the first Texican who has come up off that desert but you're cut to the pattern. 'Drifter' is what Cash Fentress would call you—meaning a man who is footloose and seeking new pastures. I am probably not as charitable as our estimable sheriff who came that way himself. I think you're a noose dodger. A man who's left Texas because he didn't dare stay."

Bender opened his mouth and clamped it wickedly shut while a wind off the peaks waved the tops of the pines.

"But don't let that bother you," she went on inexorably.

"My father's pride will not let him take advice from a woman. He'll welcome you as he has all the others who've come into these hills and now live off our cattle. To my father all strangers are brothers—especially gringos. He does not understand that only the no-good ones ever come to the Potrillos."

She quit talking to him then and moved a little way apart and Bender, bleak of eye, strode into the shack and put on his spurs. She did not speak as he passed her nor when he came out and went savagely tramping off into the pines.

He was back after a while with a saddle on his shoulder. "All right," he said in a curt tone of voice. "Which way?"

She led off without answering, moving into the timber. The stars were much brighter now and, over in the east beyond the tops of the mountains, the black sky showed a shining where the moon was coming up. Bender judged it was about ten.

They walked in a complete silence. She walked fast for a girl and, as the saddle got heavier, he would have been perfectly willing to have slowed down a bit, but he was damned if he would say so.

Presently he saw the lights of the ranch and reckoned her folks were waiting up for the outfit. The moon, now above the black shapes of the crags, threw a pattern of blue and silver across the steadily rising trail which made their travel much easier. Bender, at least, was able to quit stumbling although the pitch of the trail made a noise of his breathing which did little to improve the gravelled state of his mind.

Noose dodger!

He'd never been so set back in his life by a woman. Who the hell did she think she was, by godfreys!

They reached the top of the trail and came out on a table-land flat as a mesa. Tres Pinos looked huge in this bright flood of silver flung down by the moon. Typically Spanish, this layout was built like a fortress and looked near as vast, Bender thought with his glance taking in the great walls. There was a deep and dark gallery all across the part facing them, the posts supporting its roof big around as his waist.

Several *mozos* came hurrying out of the shadows, the girl quieting their hubbub with a few words in the lingo.

"We'll go in," she said, turning. "My father will wish to thank you—"

"He can keep his damn thanks. All I want is a horse."

"That can wait till the morning. My father would feel insulted were you to refuse to spend the night."

Swearing under his breath Bender followed her.

One of the *mozos* went hastening ahead of them and, as they stepped onto the gallery, flung open a great door. Lamplight, butter yellow, put a golden shine on the flagstones and, in this refracted glow, Bender saw that the girl was in the clothes of a charro. And then he'd followed her into the room and she was saying, "Papa mio, you are beholden to this man for the life of your so-disobedient daughter." And to Bender, "I would like for you to know my father, Don Leopoldo Jose Ramon Lopez y Gallardo, master of Tres Pinos."

Bender, looking across her shoulder, saw an old man stand, peer and start to come forward. He was tall for a Mexican and thick through the middle with a scraggle of whiskers curling out from his chin. He was dressed in a garb befitting a *ranchero* and there was gray in his hair and an air of unchallenged authority about him as his bright active eyes explored the stranger before him.

His voice, a rich baritone, was sincerity incarnate. "My house is yours," he said, smiling, and reached out a hand which the Texan took reluctantly.

"Mighty white of you," Bender said, "but a house ain't what I'm lookin' for. My name's Walt Bender. I'm fresh off the desert an'—like I told your fire-eatin' daughter—all I'm wantin' right now is a horse."

"You shall have the best one in my stables," declared Don Leo, at last releasing his hand. "But first will you not have a little coffee—some *frijoles* or, at least, a glass of wine with some cakes? The coffee was roasted by my wife herself, and the wine by a distinguished friend in Socorro. Eladio!"

He clapped his hands and at once a swarthy pock-marked

mozo came from an inner doorway and stood, hat in hand, awaiting his pleasure.

"Shall it be cakes and the *vino*," enquired the old man, "or *tortillas y frijoles?*"

"Whatever you say," grumbled Bender, impatiently, wanting nothing so much as to get the hell out of there. "I'm in a kind of a hurry, and if you'll sell me a horse—"

"Eh? But to be sure," smiled Don Leo. "Tomorrow you shall have the finest horse of my raising, but tonight you shall be my guest and sleep in the bed of my illustrious grandparent, who was man-at-arms to the Emperor Maximilian." He gave a few rapid orders in a kind of bastard Spanish and the *mozo* hurried off to attend them. "Will you wash, my friend?"

Looking round for the girl, Bender saw she was gone, so with a shrug he followed the old man into a large inner patio that was pleasant with shrubs and the sound of a fountain. There was an arcaded walk around the four sides of this and a kind of orange light was shed over the whole by eight wrought-iron lanterns hung from hooks placed at intervals in the logs which supported the walk's ramada-type roof. The whole center of this patio was open to the stars.

Bender followed Don Leo into a ten-by-twelve room whose dirt floor was freshly swept and recently sprinkled to keep the dust down. A gleaming mirror of hand-rolled glass framed by tin embossed with much workmanship hung above a chest of drawers on which were a wash basin and pitcher made of Indian-glazed pottery. The biggest share of the space was given over to a huge white four-poster with an image of the Virgin above it.

"Nice place," Bender said as he washed away the grime and combed his hair with his fingers. He picked up one of a stack of towels and dried himself, shook his shirt out the door and got into it again. He started to pick up his hat, caught the old man's expression and tossed it back in the chair.

"This will be your room for as long as you care to stay," pronounced the old man, smiling pleasantly. "We do not have too many strangers, but every man is welcome. Everything you see is at your disposal, and if there should be something which you want which is not at once apparent you have only to clap the hands and one of your servants will find it for you."

"I'm much obliged," Bender grunted, "but I must go in the morning. To tell you the truth, I'm in a sweat to reach . . . Deming," he said for lack of anything better.

Don Leo's eyes sharpened slightly but he was much too polite to make any remark which might be construed as a question. He led the way into a dining room and took a seat with his guest at the gleaming pine table where an old woman, her hair swathed in a *rebozo*, brought coffee, a tall stack of new-made tortillas and a giant-size olla of red beans cooked in chili. Bender attacked these with gusto for it was long since he'd eaten and the sight of this food made him ravenous.

When he had finished and was lifting his third cup of coffee, a man in a big hat stepped in off the patio, briefly scowled at the visitor and waited for Don Leo to notice him. He wore his big black sombrero on the back of his head and kept it in place by two straps of cured leather which passed under his chin and were secured by an engraved silver concha. He was incredibly thin and surprisingly redheaded with the skin of his face both florid and freckled.

Don Leo waited till Bender had put down his cup. "This is my foreman, Pedro Gonzales, who has grown from a boy at Tres Pinos," he explained. "Mr. Bender is spending the night with us, Pete, and tomorrow you will show him the best of our horses. He has business in Deming and will need a good mount."

Gonzales' face showed no interest. He said to the old man in Spanish: "I did not see Blanca but we found her dead horse and I have just been told she came home with this gringo. We followed those cow thieves through the canyon, not quitting till they got into the bad lands. Only four got away."

Also in Spanish the old man said, "I will talk of this tomorrow," and then, in English, "Let us go into the sala. Josefa will bring us the wine and little cakes."

They took chairs in the main room and, after they had been served by the old woman in the *rebozo*, Don Leo clapped his hands and told a servant to request the pleasure of his wife's and daughter's company.

Bender presently caught the tap-tap-tapping of a cane moving nearer along the flagged walk in the patio and the low murmur of feminine voices. He got to his feet when the ladies appeared, very conscious of the girl yet bowing gravely when Don Leo presented her mother. Dona Ruthena was small, a little angular and stooped, much fairer of complexion than her husband whose face was deeply bronzed from frequent contacts with the sun.

Bender noticed these things as he acknowledged her greeting, but mostly his attention was on the younger woman. He found it hard to reconcile his earlier conception with the extraordinary appearance of the girl now standing before them.

She wore a daring gown of bright red silk, but she wore it demurely and was amazingly proper, not speaking save when spoken to and revealing not the least sign of that bitterness with which she had called him a noose dodger or of that adamant spirit with which she'd advised him to make every one of his cartridges count.

Only by her voice would he have known her. It had the same husky cadence, the same precise inflection. The lamplight exhibited charms the night had hidden. She had a golden complexion that was in startling contrast to the appearance he had imagined. She had the narrow hips and astounding eyes of a creature stepped bodily from the best work of Villalbaso. She had hair that was black and black eyes, too, and a sultry, passionate look to her features that well matched the shape of her supple body. Grace seemed inherent in the least of her movements and, altogether, she was a great shock to Bender. He finally dragged his eyes off her and dropped into his chair where he did his best to ignore her.

It was not easy.

She moved with the lazy rhythm of a gypsy, with that slight sway of flank peculiar to women of Moorish blood. And, despite his intention, Bender found himself watching as she crossed to a couch and sat down beside her mother.

Don Leo said perplexedly, "I cannot think what we are to do with you, Blanca." He considered her with a worried frown plowing up the corrugations of his forehead. Then, turning to Bender, he asked apologetically if the Texan understood Spanish, smiling with real pleasure when Bender answered that he did. "Mostly, at Three Pines," he said, "it is our custom to speak the *Americano*, but sometimes it a little confuses me." He then asked in Spanish for his daughter to recount her experiences.

Blanca said, "First, papa mio, did you hear the sound of firing?"

When he said they had she did not look at Bender but he was not slow to get the point she was making. "Although he had just himself gotten home," said Don Leo, "Pete was certain you were in trouble and, although I did not believe any would offer you harm, when the firing became general at his insistence I allowed him to take the cowboys and look into it. And now, if you please, I would hear why you did this very foolish thing."

Blanca said she had been suspicious of Chesseldine's motives from the moment he had told Don Leo about the lease lands; that, after reading the paper which had to be signed to secure the loan, she had been more than ever convinced it was a plot of some kind designed to endanger her father's possession of Tres Pinos.

"But how could that be?" Don Leo protested.

"Have you not heard," she countered, "of such things happening to other ranches owned by Spanish-Americans? The Miraflores Ranch—"

"Is in the Burro Mountains," her father said testily, "where there is metal. There are no minerals at Tres Pinos. There is nothing here except land and cattle and too little grass at the moment for our own. The idea is fantastic!"

Bender did not say anything, although plainly the girl had been expecting his support. "Nevertheless," she said stubbornly, "I was convinced there was a plot and I am still of that opinion. I was chased. Men sought to rob me—"

"Of something Pedro shouldn't have given you," Don Leo

said, sternly eyeing his redheaded foreman. "If there was a plot it was against Pedro and not against you or myself or Tres Pinos. It is absurd to believe that a man who is kind enough to loan me money could possibly have any designs on this rancho—which he knows is not sufficient to support my own cattle."

"It is more unbelievable to *me*," she said half angrily, "that any drifter like Chesseldine should go out of his way to tell you of these grasslands and, when you say you haven't the money, to provide some man who will loan it. How did he know of this man? How, in the first place, did he learn that the American government would be throwing these Indian lands open to lease?"

"How can we know?" Don Leo said, plainly exasperated. "The *Norte Americanos* know many things about their government which a woman cannot understand. This does not make them any the less true. As for Mr. Chesseldine coming here and telling me about it, why indeed should he not? He is my friend. He knows I am short of grass. Surely the rest follows naturally."

"Too naturally for me," she said. "Art Chesseldine, if you want the truth, is a cattle thief and—"

"Blanca! I will not hear such words. I forbid you—"

"Furthermore," she cut through his talk, "he is the one who tried to take that money away from me—ask this man. He heard them talking."

"What!" cried Don Leo, surging up from his chair. And even Gonzales, the foreman, looked startled.

Bender recrossed his legs. "I can't say about that. I did hear some talk. The big wheel of this bunch was a fellow called 'Art' but—"

The girl said impatiently, "What other Art is there?"

Her father looked shaken. Gonzales, in English, asked, "How well could you see these man?"

"Not very well, though I might recognize his voice." A silence built up and Bender said at last, reluctantly, "I think the girl is right. They knew about the money. They were expecting a man from a ranch and it was plain from their talk they weren't hunting no gringo."

Don Leo, still frowning, abruptly pulled up his head. He looked briefly toward the couch then gave his guest a quizzical smile. "Because my daughter happens to be beautiful does not make her always right. How can I believe that a man who has sat at my table and given every assurance of being my friend—"

"Does a coyote have friends?" Blanca's eyes flashed round scornfully. "Does a lobo turn his back on a calf in a bog hole?"

"Enough!" her father shouted. "Are you the master of Tres Pinos? Am I then become so aged I must seek advice of a woman? *Chihuahua!* A buyer of cattle is not classed as a drifter and a man who has friends who can loan so much money is hardly the kind to become a robber."

"That depends," Bender said, "on things a man don't generally advertise—like the jams he gets into and how bad he needs cash." He considered the next thing he said quite awhile before saying it, finally speaking out anyway. "I understand there's been talk this fellow might be a rustler."

"Mother of God," exclaimed Don Leo, sinking into his chair, "must we credit the rumors given wing by our enemies? Anything can be heard if one stretches the ear enough and my daughter has not cared for this man from the first. She hears these wild stories and, because we lose a few cattle, she declares he has stolen them . . . whereas we will probably discover that our cows have merely strayed."

"Still it's queer," Bender said, "that he should be the one to speak to you about these leases, that he should understand your interest and be so certain you'd need money that in advance of speaking about it he should even arrange for the loan."

Don Leo frowned and tapped the arms of his chair. "I can hardly see a mountain where a molehill fails to exist."

"Well, it's none of my business," Bender shrugged, and Blanca said, "Would you like, papa mio, to hear the rest of our experiences?"

"*Carai!*" he said. "Is there more?"

"The first shot was mine. When I saw how they had me cut off from Tres Pinos I fired my pistol, hoping you would hear it. They came so fast and all about me I dared not make another sound. No one knew who fired the shot and this one they called Art became very excited. One was sure it was Pete but this man Art had other notions. He said it was a lot of money and that one of the others was trying to get it for himself and go away with it. The other men did not like this. There was a little more talk and then one man said. 'There is a stray down here somewhere,' and I supposed he had seen me. So, when this mysterious Art said each man should move forward and call out his name, I threw my pistol farther into the canyon. It struck a rock loudly and everyone commenced shooting."

Then she told about Bender knocking her horse down, about him picking her up and about his horse being shot out from under them. She really did quite a job, being very dramatic, and when she came to the fight at the cabin even the senora's mouth dropped open and her father said, *"Sangre de Cristo!"* She told of hiding the money, of digging it up again, and claimed the Texan had cut down some seven or eight men before the Tres Pinos cowboys had got there to help them.

"Ha, ha!" laughed Don Leo, abruptly recovering his good spirits. *"Muy hombre!"* he said, grinning, as though this were the best news he'd heard in a long while.

"Shucks," Bender scowled, "I probably didn't kill any of them—leastways not more'n a couple." But the old man wouldn't have him playing it down. It was plain he considered this traveling man from Texas a kind of second Billy the Kid. And there wasn't much doubt but that his foreman did, also. Gonzales did not look happy.

Bender took the occasion to ask the old rancher if he'd known of the man who had made him the loan. "No," smiled Don Leo, "but his *dinero* is *'sta bueno* and now we shall bid in those eight thousand acres and have grass *mucho mucho* for all of my cattle."

He had broken into English in his pleasure and excitement but Bender went on following the thought in his head. "You hadn't ever heard of him but still you were sure he would make you the loan?"

"But, of course. My good friend, Senor Chesseldine, had told me he would. Should one contemplate the teeth of a gift horse?"

"Sometimes," said Bender, "that can be a good idea. What's the name of this gent that chucks his dough around so easy? An old settler, is he, or one of these Johnny-Come-Latelys?"

"I think," Blanca said, "he was just there to lend the money."

The old don, with a look of long suffering, ignored her. "His name is Lasham," he answered politely. "Aaron Abijah Lasham."

4 | DELILAH OF
| THREE PINES

BENDER sat very still and felt the cold stiffness coming over his face. He became aware of Don Leo with his cheeks like fried parchment shrinking back in his chair, and only then did he realize he'd got out of his own. He took his hand off the old man's shoulder and swiveled his head till he could catch the bulging eyes of Pete Gonzales and the distended cigarette-yellowed fingers that were spread above the butt of the gun at his groin. "You saw the guy. Tell me, was he thin or fat? *Speak!*" Bender snarled in the voice of a cougar.

The edges of the foreman's hair gleamed raw red in the lampglow. He had to sponge his lips with his tongue three times before he could get any words out, and even then they were unintelligible.

"Speak out! Was he *fat?*" Bender's eyes blazed like hellfire and the Mexican, making the sign of the Cross, gulped noisily, jerkily nodding. "*Si . . . mucho mas . . .* like the hog," he said, blanching; and Bender cursed in a passion.

"Jesus and Mary!" exclaimed Don Leo, jumping up. "Must you talk in this way before women?"

Bender stared. "You may sound a little mixed up yourself, old man, when you understand whom you've to deal with. This fine friend of your friend is Deef Lasham, the sheep king, and if you can't add that up you'd better go back to school because you sold out the cows when you signed that skunk's paper."

"Sheep!" The old *ranchero* looked stunned. "You think he might bring these sheep into the Potrillos?"

Bender laughed harshly. "I don't *have* to think, damn it! Why do you suppose he loaned you that money?" He did not wait for an answer; he started cursing again. Up and down the great room he strode with his face black as thunder, and no one ventured a word until Blanca, with a shudder, said, "I was right, after all."

"Right?" Bender shouted. "You didn't guess the least half of it! This deal was so slick you're licked no matter what you do. All that guy needs is a foothold, the thinnest kind of excuse—and you've made him a partner in this Tres Pinos Rancho!"

Don Leo pulled his chin off his chest. "That is not so," he said stiffly. "I have given him a lien against the ranch and that is all. When I pay—"

"You'll never get the chance to pay him off," said Bender flatly. "He won't give you any chance—this ain't a game he plays for marbles. He don't handle his sheep like they do in the stories. This guy's *big business!* His crew's as different from the old-time sheepherders as wolves are from rabbits. In the old days the herders walked, like *peones.* Lasham's men don't walk, they ride like *caballeros.* He's got a bunch of Yaqui Indians and feeds them well on other folks' beef. He gives every *pelado* a .30-30 rifle and all he ever tells them is 'Feed my sheep.' What chance have you got against a bunch like that?"

Don Leo reared back his head and glared. "You shall see!"

he said sternly. "Those sheep will not come here—in the country, perhaps, but not on Tres Pinos. My *vaqueros* will see to that, I assure you."

Bender looked at him sadly. "Well, I hope you are right. But there was a guy thought like you do back home in West Texas; he was a plenty tough hombre and he went on the prod. He got together his men and established a deadline. It didn't keep Lasham from getting what he wanted. He warned him: 'Deadlines ain't legal,' but the guy kept his chin out. Then Lasham moved in. He lost a couple of Indians but they put the sheep all over this guy's place. Then the law took this fellow and put a rope around his neck for killing those two herders."

"That will not happen to me," declared the *ranchero* fiercely. "My people have fought *los Indios* for hundreds of years. This ranch is mine and I shall keep it. That man in Texas, if he had enough men, could have kept those sheep away from him. We have no laws around here which cause a man to be hanged for protecting his property. Let them try to bring sheep here—"

"Okey," Bender said, "but they'll do it. You've got two strikes against you already. This Chesseldine's had a good chance to look around. While he was eating at your table you can bet he sized this place up, and you can bet whatever he saw was passed right straight along to Lasham. He'll know exactly how you're fixed, how many men you've got and everything, including the way your land lays. On top of all that he owns a piece of your ranch—"

"What this man says," declared Gonzales in Spanish, "can apply just as well to himself as to another."

"Right as rain," Bender smiled, and got heavily out of his chair and stood up. The look he passed from range boss to owner showed plainly the hardness that had been ground into him by too much experience too swiftly acquired. "I'm just telling you," he said, "the way it stacks up to me."

"What do you think I should do?" asked Don Leo.

Bender shook his head, frowning. "Best thing you can do is dig a hole an' crawl into it. But if I was in your boots," he grumbled, sliding into English, "I'd make a blue streak gettin' that mazuma back to Lasham. I don't expect he would take it even if you could find him because that's probably the edge he's settin' up his plans on. But if I was you I think I'd try it. Failin' that, I'd say you better lay in some strychnine because, whenever he's ready, he's goin' to move in here just as sure as God builds them little green apples."

Gonzales said, sneering: "Too much you know about these man."

"Right again, Pedrocito. I know that guy like the back of my hand."

"Perhaps, papa mio," Blanca said without expression, "you might persuade Mr. Bender to stay on at Three Pines and sell you the advantage of his experience in this matter."

Bender's look turned stiff as frostbite. "Not me," he said curtly—"ain't no use of you askin'. I know when I'm well off."

Gonzales' laugh held an open contempt.

Bender read the same thought in the girl's climbing eyebrows but he'd had all of Deef Lasham that he was aiming to stomach. Let them think what they wanted. Only a fool tried to buck a stacked deck and he was all done with being a fool for Aaron Abijah Lasham.

Don Leo smiled brightly. "The very thing," he said. "A man of your parts would know how to deal with that one much better than my people. Every man on the place shall be at your disposal. Consider it, my friend. With such an army behind you this man would not dare to bring his sheep on Tres Pinos—but you are tired," he said contritely. "We will talk of this in the morning."

"In the morning," Bender said, "I'm gettin' out of this country."

HE had meant every word of that firm resolution, but he had not reckoned with Blanca. Don Leo was waiting in the patio for him when he came out of his room before the sun had got up. *"Buenos dias, senor.* Our breakfast is waiting. I hope you find our poor food to your liking."

Not a word about the horse or about leaving, Bender noticed. But if the old man wanted to swap small talk that was all right with him. When he got some hot grub stowed under his belt he was going to get out of here, horse or no horse. So he dragged up a smile and answered politely, following Don Leo into the *comedor*. There, to his disgust, he found Blanca already seated. She looked cool and breezy in a fresh gingham print and greeted his arrival with a very artful smile. "I hope you slept well in our poor bed, Mr. Bender. You weren't too cold, were you?"

"I slept all right," he answered, and slid into a chair without enlarging on the matter. The meal, a very good one, progressed pleasantly enough with the old man talking about conditions in the region, the price of beef and some horses he had seen during the racing at Silver City. He asked if Bender were acquainted with Herefords and, when he said he was, he asked some thoughtful questions about them, telling Bender afterwards he hoped some day to raise them. "I saw a few head last spring at El Paso—magnificent animals! Less stock and better quality would appear to be the answer on a range such as ours."

After the *moza* had fetched their coffee and they'd pushed back their chairs for a comfortable smoke, the old fox got around to what was filling his mind. "With less horns and more beef," he said, "my range, with the land I plan to lease from *los Indios*, will be able very well to accommodate two outfits. On Tres Pinos there are two spring-fed lakes, one of which is near these lease lands."

He must have read Bender's mind about then for, turning, he said abruptly, "My foreman, Pete, will be here in a moment to take you around to have a look at our horses. Should it be your wish to leave I will put nothing in your way; but, first, I have a small matter I should like to put before you."

"If the main thing behind it is to keep me around," Bender said, "I ain't interested."

"Frankly, that is true," the old man admitted. He took hold of his whiskers and chewed on his lip, finally saying, "This visit to Deming . . . you could not put it off?"

Bender gave the girl a hard look and said curtly, "I've already tangled with Lasham once and got myself sheeped plumb out of the cow business. I ain't hankerin' to have my ears pinned back again."

"But this is not Texas. We do things differently here. Tres Pinos is patented land, every acre, and the law gives a rancher the right to protect it. If you will stay here and help me against this *picaro*, I will give you one lake and a whole mile around it, in addition," he said grimly, "to the lease lands for which I have borrowed this money. All this I will give you plus one half of my cattle."

Bender's mouth fell wide open. He pulled it shut with a scowl and blackly stared at the girl, convinced in his own mind that she was behind this. He recalled what she had told him last night about the desert, about the men who came across it, and began to understand then how this kind of deal made sense. *You are not the first Texican who has come up off that desert, but you're cut to the pattern.* That was it, all right. That fight at the shack was the clincher.

But where else would he get such a chance to start over? It was a bonafide offer, Don Leo was dead serious.

He squirmed around in his chair and rasped his jowls with damp fingers. Eight thousand acres of grass and a lake, and half of the Tres Pinos cattle to stock it! A man would be a fool to turn his back on such an offer.

But then he remembered what was back of this philanthropy. Deef Lasham and his sheep and those kill-hungry Yaquis. Lasham's power and crooked influences. And behind these Lasham's marshal. For anyone else it was still a good offer for, as the old man said, this was New Mexico, not Texas. But it was no damn good for Walt Bender—not with that noose hanging over his head.

He stubbed out his smoke and got up, feeling ringy. "You're better off alone," he said, and picked up his hat.

The girl's eyes raked him scornfully. "Are you so frightened of this man that you would throw away a fortune?"

"Reckon that's about the size of it."

Don Leo sighed, not speaking. "What," Blanca said, "do you have to have to go with us?"

"Aren't you forgettin' what you told me last night?—that nothing ever comes off that desert but trouble? You better thank your stars I'm not stayin'."

Don Leo bowed to the inevitable. *"Dispensame, senor.* I will have my foreman bring you a horse."

Bender watched him step into the patio. Getting old, he thought, and hating to show it.

He felt the demand of the girl's eyes, resenting it. Even across the space of this table, not turning his head, he could feel the vibrant magnetism of her.

She got up. "Some kinds of trouble I can handle. I do not think I could handle your Mr. Deef Lasham."

"That's why I'm goin'. I don't think I could, either."

"But if we're willing to chance that?"

He stepped around the table and saw the pulse in her throat beat quick and hard. He saw her eyes dilate but she didn't back off, didn't try to get away from him even when his hand reached out and gripped her shoulder. The sun flung blue lights through the black of her hair and, twisted by his grip, the thin cotton of her dress was pulled tight across her breasts in a fashion that excited and then enraged him.

He let go of her shoulder as though it had burnt him but her eyes didn't change. He didn't step away, either. All the long hungers were fusing inside him, building up something which was stronger than judgment and made a roaring in his head through which he saw her as a magnificent animal— strong, cruel, tawny as a panther. A beautiful savage, primitive, flawless and entirely desirable. She was a strange wild melody that sang through his blood. And he remembered then one other thing she had told him, that a man never got away from anything by running.

It was the truth.

As from a long way off he heard himself saying, "And when do I get these things your father promised?"

He watched the way her red lips pulled away from bright teeth. "When Tres Pinos no longer finds danger in Lasham. Come—we must tell them you have changed your mind."

5 | A MAN OF THE OLD SCHOOL

He spent the bulk of that day in the saddle, riding over the place with Don Leo for guide, listening to the old man's stories, discovering the more important landmarks and familiarizing himself with the locations of lakes, trails and outside boundaries. On the south and east Three Pines came against the unbroken dun sea of the desert whose bright glare stretched away through the heat waves and dust devils to the Land of Manana and undiscernible Texas. It was plain enough to Bender then that, if the sheep came off the desert, they could only come onto Don Leo's ranch by way of the trail he himself had ridden. There was no other break in the long line of bluffs here dividing the low from the high lands.

At the cabin in the pines Pete had a crew burying horses but, answering the *patron's* questions, the boss of these swarthy shovelers said they had not come across any dead men. Bender had not been expecting them to, for if he'd actually killed any of that bunch last night, their leader would have been a whole lot too smart, if the man was Art Chesseldine, to leave them around to be identified later. Even the brands had been cut off their horses.

Don Leo had mounted him on an exceptionally fine dun with a brown dorsal stripe and zebra markings on the knees. The animal had been gelded, was very handy and quick and showed many signs of having considerable endurance. The *ranchero* rode another which looked amazingly like it and, when Bender complimented him on the quality of these horses, the girl's father said the strain had been in the family many years, having been started by his grandfather, a man

197

of many parts. The family had ranched near Durango in those days and done a little mining on the side when pressed for cash. Bender thought it was too bad they hadn't a mine to fall back on now.

Dusk was thickening fast when they returned that evening and two peons came running to care for their horses. Bender said he would see to his own, would then eat with the crew and sleep in the bunkhouse, but the old man would not hear of it. "No, *amigo*, you have a room already and a man in your position—"

"Yeah," Bender nodded, "suppose you tell me about that. If I'm to work with your crew won't they think it damn funny if I'm put up in the house?"

"You will not work with the crew—that is my foreman's concern. You are officially my guest and will so continue until I shall be rid of this accursed sheepman."

Bender had to admit that this would cause less friction though he didn't like the thought of being so much around Blanca. She was a deal too disturbing; and then, besides, there was Gonzales. Unless he'd misread completely the signs observed last night, the foreman was not going to like having them share adjoining rooms.

He'd been somewhat puzzled himself when he had first discovered they were doing so, for this seemed to him to be contrary to much that he had heard of Spanish-American customs, which were mostly rather astringent as regarded unmarried young women. Now, more familiar with the layout, he could see they had not had any great choice, the only other available room being the much larger one shared by her father and mother which they probably considered too near to the bunkhouse. Not that the breaking of any stuffy convention was likely to bother overmuch a girl as forthright as Blanca.

So, though he was far from being pleased with the arrangement, he said nothing more but, picking up Chucho's reins, led the horse around back and through the high gate which gave onto the *parada*, as the open ground was called between the stables and the quarters given over to the men. After caring for the horse and making sure he was properly fastened in for the night, Bender was about to head for the passage leading into the patio when he observed two shapes against the bunkhouse wall. Both men were watching him and one of them was Gonzales.

Three hanging lanterns had been lighted to illuminate the *parada* and, although it was still pretty much filled with shadows, he could see well enough not to care for the expression on the foreman's face.

As he was about to move along Gonzales stepped from the wall. "Hold on," he said in Spanish, and the other lounged forward and barred Bender's way.

"Well," Bender said, "what's on your mind, Pedrocito?"

"I want to know why you are staying here."

"Why don't you ask the *patron* if you're curious?"

"I'm asking you, Gringo."

Both men were armed and Gonzales looked ugly. The second man was heavier with a hairline that came almost down to his eyebrows, a burly ruffian with mismatched eyes and the mark of a knife across one cheekbone.

Bender, caught off balance and at the decided disadvantage of not wanting trouble in a place of their choosing, tried to swallow his outrage and said, thinking fast, "I am staying because I've been asked to stay. The *patron*—"

"Do not lie to me, Gringo"

"Why would I be lying? You heard the talk last night. You must have heard Don Leo—"

"He but agreed with his daughter. He did not ask you to stay—"

"He asked me this morning. At breakfast."

Gonzales stared at him, scowling. "I think you make this up. Even if it should be as you say about this sheepman, why would a gringo put himself out for a Mexican man old enough to be—"

"Well, you've got something there," Bender grumbled. "As a matter of fact, he made me a proposition. Because of what happened at that shack on the bluffs your boss has me pegged for a second Bill Bonney. He said, if I will stay and buck

Lasham and keep the sheep out of here he will make me a present of those lease lands, the upper lake and half of his cattle."

"What!" cried Gonzales. "Do you think I am a *fool?*"

With his face contorted by a terrible anger he caught the Texan's arm in a grip of steel and, before Bender quite realized what was happening, the scar-faced man had pulled open the *parada* gate and he was being shoved through. "There—" snarled Gonzales, pointing, "there is the road. Now go!"

Before Bender could speak there was a commotion behind them and a roar from Don Leo that made both men jump. "What is this?"

He flung Scar Face aside with the flap of a hand, catching Pedro's shirt at the throat with the other and slamming his shoulders hard against the adobe wall.

"Is a guest to be turned from my house like a beggar? *Sangre de Christo!* Ungrateful son of a goat! What is this you would do behind my back? *Habla! Pronto!*"

Gonzales quailed from his glare. His *compadre* took this chance to slink away in the shadows.

Don Leo shook Gonzales until the man's mouth fell open. "*Andale—habla!* What is this you would do, eh?"

The foreman caught up with his breath. "This man said—"

"And who are you to question the remarks of a guest? Since when have you become the master of Tres Pinos? Tell me that!"

"It was for your own good entirely. This *gringo* comes here with his lies and you swallow them—"

With a curse Don Leo struck Gonzales across the face. "Begone, ungrateful dog! Get back to your kennel. I will deal with you later."

AFTER supper, when he was walking with the *ranchero* in the patio, Bender said out of a thoughtful silence, "Don't believe I'd say any more to your foreman. He had your interests—"

"This is good of you, my friend." Don Leo stopped beside the fountain. "A forgiving spirit reflects much credit, but . . ."

He spread his hands with a shrug. "Let us talk of something better."

There was a barrel standing handy about two feet this side of the shrubbery and Bender, about to settle his hip, was astonished when the rancher plucked him unceremoniously away from it. *"Dispensame, senor,* but there is an unpleasant death in that barrel. A coral snake, you understand, that was trapped near the fountain by one of my *mozos."*

Bender, startled, thumbed a match to flame and saw the sinuous shape transversely banded in red, yellow and black, the lightning-swift flick of its darting red tongue, the black snout with its horrible eyes staring up at him; and he drew back, his flesh creeping. "You ought to kill that damn thing!"

"I have a friend at Santa Rosa who will be very pleased to get hold of that fellow. He is making a collection of poisonous reptiles."

"And he'll collect a quick grave if that bastard gets hold of him." Bender tossed the burnt matchstick into the fountain. "I'm pulling out in the morning."

Don Leo's face turned sober. He put a hand on Bender's shoulder. "I beg of you, *amigo,* do not say that you are leaving. Ask what you will but do not tell me that."

"All I could bring you by remaining is trouble. This business of Gonzales has shown me the truth—you'd be playing right into the sheep crowd's hands. If you're going to buck Lasham you don't want no man of straw."

"Straw man—you?" The old *ranchero* laughed. "You make joke . . . ees too fonny." Then he said, swinging back into Spanish again, "Stay, my friend. I will flog that dog of a Pedro. I will . . . eh?"

"Would you place a rotten apple in the crate with the good ones?" Bender's hard unhumorous smile crossed his lips. He cuffed the dust from his hat against the side of a leg. "You can't fight Lasham with gallows bait, pardner. Across the line, back in Texas, I'm wanted for murder."

"Carai! What is this?" Don Leo exclaimed, but he did not look in the least disconcerted. "In the heat of passion a man does many things he will spend the rest of his life regretting.

This I understand; but do not ask me to believe you'd kill a man without good reason."

"I didn't kill him," said Bender harshly, "but one day the law will catch up with me. And if it catches me here you'll be done for."

"Have no fear about that. My little Blanca has told me how you stood off those *ladrones;* how you saved her life and—what is more precious—her virtue from those *bandidos*. Do I forget that? Never! So be of good cheer. If you did not kill the man perhaps we can prove—"

"Not a chance," Bender growled. "It was Lasham who framed me because he wanted my grass. The fellow who was killed was a Texas state senator who was ready to put the skids under Lasham, but no one will believe that because he worked for the Pool. I can see it all now . . . why they kept shoving me this way . . . Lasham's aiming to use me to get his hooks on Tres Pinos."

"He will not get Tres Pinos!"

Don Leo rose from his chair and commenced pacing the grass, chin bowed in thought until at last, wheeling round, he snarled, "A curse on this man, this *hijo de diablo!* We are not beaten yet and, if you stay, we shall not be." He struck his fist into his hand and glared at Bender fiercely. "My people are fighters with much experience of *Indios;* they will not run away from this *Tejanno* and his *Yaquis*. You will find, my friend, that this is different than Texas. Here the laws will protect the cattle—"

Bender shook his head, sighing. "That's what they said in Grand Falls, too, until Lasham's fine friends and the sheep pool made new ones."

"No matter! They will not make new ones here, I can tell you. The Spanish Americans run the government here and they have no love for these *Texanos*. No, my friend, you have given me your word and I shall hold you to it. Here you shall stay till we are rid of this devil!"

"Well . . . if you feel that way about it, all right," Bender frowned, "but don't say I didn't warn you. Now, what about this Texican sheriff you've got—this Cash Fentress?"

Don Leo brushed Fentress aside with a smile. "If that one should get too big for his saddle, we shall call in my good friend Don Ramon Eusebio de Vega at Santa Fe. And tomorrow you shall go and make the bid on those lease lands. So be of good heart; we will show these dogs of *Texanos* that Spanish Americans know how to fight for their grass."

6 | AND NOW IT BEGINS

WITH his big-roweled spurs clawing sound from the board walk, Bender strode by the side of Pedro Gonzales who had not said one word since they had quitted the ranch. They'd got off to a good early start before daylight and, though it yet lacked three hours before the bids would be opened, already the town appeared crammed full to bursting. The street was a clutter of spring wagons and buckboards and hitched horses made an almost solid line at the tie racks.

Quite a place, this Deming; a lot larger than he'd imagined. It might be a railroad town like he'd heard, for there were the gleaming iron rails over yonder, but this morning the cow crowd had taken it over. Big hats and boots were the order of the day and everywhere men cried out greeting to Gonzales so that they were continually stopping while he swapped comments and badinage with people of his acquaintance. More than one of these *vaqueros* sent covert glances at Walt Bender, surprised no doubt to see their friend strolling cheek by jowl with a gringo. It must have graveled Gonzales plenty, yet not by a word or the edge of a look did the Three Pines foreman admit Bender existed.

Which was all right with Bender. He had enough on his mind without having to keep up with any double-faced talk. Somewhere in this mob of milling gun-hung riders there would be, he felt certain, at least one man representing Deef Lasham, and his interest at the moment centered in picking that one out. For it did not make sense that Lasham ever had intended to let any other bunch get hold of grass he wanted.

The bidding on these Indian lands was scheduled to take place in one of the railroad warehouses just across the tracks, and he found it no job at all to tell which one by the size of the crowd hanging round in front. The long plank platform already was thronged with jostling shapes in all manner of clothing and the street before it showed a lot of the overflow standing round in gesticulating groups, some talking vociferously, all boisterous, many laughing—all in a holiday mood by the look of them.

The biggest part of the crowds were solidly Mexican, the fat and portly Dons extremely gay in their colorful finery, their swaggering cigarette-smoking foremen looking very important with their groups of *vaqueros,* the only sour notes to be seen anywhere being made by the gringos.

It was these Bender paid most attention to. He didn't see any of them laughing. They stood apart by themselves in little knots of twos and threes looking surly and suspicious with their bleak, bony faces and hard-eyed stares. He did see three or four who looked both well fed and pompous, and his lips curled with scorn. They reminded him of Toby Bronsen and were obviously politicians.

Gonzales presently touched his sleeve, breaking abruptly his long front of silence. "We are going to eat. Over there," he pointed.

"Suits me," Bender nodded. "I could use some grub myself."

Dislike was a plain and undisguised scowl on the face of Don Leo's segundo. Outrage made his green eyes look like emeralds, but he swung away without answering, Bender following. When Gonzales sat down with his friends at a table Bender sat with them, not caring what they thought, caring less that they ignored him. He knew Deef Lasham's methods. Someone at Tres Pinos, he would have bet his last centavo, was in the sheepman's pay, and he did not propose to let Pedro get out of his sight for a moment.

THE auctioneer took his stand at one o'clock. He was a deputy commissioner and one of the politicians Bender previously had noticed, a burly blowsy-faced man in a top hat and tailcoat. "This federal auction," he intoned, "is to place by public bidding certain lands in the care of the Indian Department . . ."

He got through his preamble in less than two minutes, then explained how the land had been thrown into blocks, specifying by acres how much each contained; Block 10, much the smallest, was the one Tres Pinos wanted. "Now we'll open these bids at ten cents an acre and we'll start with Block 1—"

"Fifteen cents," called a Don in silver-braided sombrero.

"Seventeen!" cried another; and Block 1 was knocked down at nineteen to the first man when nobody else offered to go higher.

While the deputy commissioner was going through his legal description of Block 2, Bender took the opportunity to discover who stood round him, nowhere seeing any member of Lasham's crowd he was able to recognize. When the second block was bid in at twenty by the same man, Bender's narrowing stare looked him over with a closer interest. He gave his name as Esteban and was a short, rotund, very haughty looking hombre whose garb, although expensive, showed a considerable amount of wear about the seat and elbows. When he also acquired Block 3 at thirty-two Bender nudged Don Leo's foreman. "Who is this guy?" he asked under his breath.

Gonzales shrugged. "He is a small *ranchero* from the vicinity of Holy Cross."

"Holy Cross, eh? What's he want with all that land away to hell an' gone away from him?"

Gonzales shrugged. He turned around and became engrossed in a conversation with a man on the other side of him. When he again faced front he said without inflexion, "This man thinks Don Esteban is buying for some people who haven't appeared here."

This coincided with Bender's thought and, when the fellow bid in Block 4 at forty, Bender said to the deputy commissioner, "I understand these bids are in U. S. dollars."

"That's correct."

"Cash on the barrelhead?"

"Naturally the money must be put in my hands before these lands are disposed of—"

"Before this shindig is over?"

"Yes, of course—"

"I ain't seen you take any of that fellow's dough yet."

The deputy commissioner wiped his face with a handkerchief. A jabber of talk started up all around him while he peered at Bender with an irritable frown. "I can't see what difference that makes to you," he said at last. "I haven't heard anyone else here objecting and you're not making any bids that I've noticed—"

"I'll bid," Bender said, "when I want to buy something."

"Then what're you butting in now for?"

"I'm hankerin' to see the color of that guy's money."

There were half a dozen others who seemed to have the same feeling, and now these all commenced talking at once. The deputy commissioner got red in the face and banged with his gavel till he got enough quiet to make himself heard. But, before he could get his voice into action, a bleach-eyed cowman to the left of him cried: "B'Gawd, he's right—let's see this bird pay fer what he's got already!"

Don Esteban scornfully waddled over to the clerk, whipped out a well stuffed money belt and counted the purchase price into his hands. It came to slightly in excess of one hundred thousand dollars and many of those nearest, seeing that none of this currency was beneath a four-numbers figure shook their heads in awe. But when the corpulent Don, jamming the receipts in his pocket, got back to where he'd been doing his bidding, Bender saw him mutter to a tall beak-nosed Mexican who'd been standing beside him and, a little bit later, saw that man leave the building.

Bender bided his time and, when Esteban opened the next block at twenty, he said, "I'll bid fifty."

The fat Mexican glared. He finally said, "Fifty-five."

"Seventy," Bender said, and there was a sharp startled silence.

The deputy commissioner mopped off his face again. "You aim to let that bid stand?"

"Thought I told you I'd bid when I—"

"Eighty!" snarled Don Esteban.

The stillness grew brittle.

The deputy commissioner looked nervously at Bender. "Well!" he said, scowling. "You goin' to bid any more?"

"Not on that chunk. He's gone too high for me."

There were several cries of *"Ladron!"* and hard looks and grumbling all around the deputy commissioner; and several of the Mexicans who had come there to bid, but didn't have that kind of money, wheeled about in their tracks and, cursing, departed. One glowering Texan in a shirt stained with sweat told the clerk in a snarl to hurry up and take his money. "Some of us boys has got better things t' do than hang an' rattle in this bake oven watchin' that greaser lord it over white men."

Bender halfway looked for some of the other Dons to take umbrage, and he did see a couple of them drop their hands to knife hilts, but the most of the Spanish Americans on tap appeared too incensed with the man themselves to much care what a damned gringo called him.

Several of them crowded around to watch him count out the money, their own lips moving in unison as bill after bill fluttered down on the table. Block 5 had cost Esteban twenty thousand dollars.

It was while the legal description of Block 6 was being read that Bender became aware of Pete Gonzales' startled interest. The man was watching him like a hawk, the ugly suspicions churning back of his eyes telling all too plainly what direction his thoughts were taking.

"Don't let the tail wag the dog," Bender told him and, to the man with the gavel, "If you're ready on Block 6 I'll give forty cents an acre."

"Forty-five," grumbled Esteban.

"Forty-eight," said the Texan in the dusty, sweat-stained shirt.

Esteban growled without turning, "Fifty."

"Sixty-five," Bender muttered, and Esteban stared at him blackly.

"Seventy!"

Bender fished out the makings and twisted up a smoke. "Fifty-seven thousand acres," he told the deputy commissioner reflectively, "at seventy cents an acre comes to thirty-nine thousand, nine hundred dollars. Quite a parcel of money. Do you reckon he's got it?"

The government man looked at Esteban. The Mexican swore in three different dialects. Bender said, "I think you better make sure," and moved up to the table to see for himself.

Esteban jerked out his poke in a rage and commenced counting. He piled thirty-nine thousand dollar bills on the table and was beginning to sweat when Beak-Nose pushed up through the crowd with the rest of it.

Bender grinned sourly. "Okay. Let him have it."

HE went back and beckoned Gonzales to the door and stepped outside with him. "I've got five hundred smackers," he said without preamble. "That's Lasham's dough that's biddin' in these leases and I been tryin' to make the bastard whittle it down where he can't hurt us. But you saw that guy come in just then; he's fetched him another roll and now I don't know whether we'll cut it or not. When Don Leo gave you the money to bid with this mornin' did he give you anything over that forty-five hundred?"

Gonzales shook his head. He began to look worried.

"Well, there's nothin' we can do about it," Bender said, "but hope for the best. That roll he just got looked big enough to choke a horse, but it's handled dough that's been in circulation. There might not be any grand notes in it. If I can just make that clown bid enough on these next three. . . ." He let the rest trail off and they went back inside.

Block 7 had been bid in while they'd been talking outside. It had gone at forty-five to the sweaty-shirted Texan who was now counting his money onto the table in front of the clerk. There was a look of satisfaction on his harsh wind-roughened countenance as, folding the clerk's receipt, he buttoned it into

his shirt's left pocket. With a short ugly laugh he shouldered
Esteban out of his way, saying as he strode past Bender,
"There's *one* that range-hoggin' spik didn't git!"

Bender grunted, not at all sure he liked the sudden turn
this thing had taken. He opened Block 8 with a bid of twenty
cents.

Encouraged by the Texican's experience a dark slender man
with bells on his sombrero hesitantly called, "Twenty-five,"
and the crowd looked at Esteban. The portly Mexican stared
back at them, his gashlike mouth tightly folded across his
teeth.

The deputy commissioner looked at him unhappily, finally
mopping his cheeks with the limp piece of rag that still dangled
bedraggled from his pudgy left fist. "You care to bid on this
block, Mister Esteban?"

"No!"

One of the hard-faced crew against the back wall said,
"Twenty-six."

The man with the bells said, "Twenty-eight," and got it.

Bender saw the play now clearly. This was no spur-of-the-
moment affair but a plan that had been gone over and over,
a plan engineered with all someone's cunning. The pool never
had intended to bid in *all* of these lease lands; the farther-
most grass was what they had been after to cloak their stealing
of the rest with an appearance of legality. Bender had bothered
them in only one particular, forcing their agent to pay more
than had been counted on. The new roll just now hurried in
by Hook Nose was brought to secure Block 10, the grasslands
bordering the north of Don Leo's holdings.

Lasham, to get his sheep onto pasture in the grass he'd got
already, was going to have to cross Tres Pinos or go five
hundred miles out of his way. No court in the land would
expect a man to make a swing of that magnitude; and the
lien he had on Tres Pinos would go a long way toward estab-
lishing his right to cross it. Now, if, in addition he got hold of
Block 10 he would have any court fight licked before it started.

Tres Pinos had one chance left as Bender saw it. And this
had to hinge on how badly he'd strained their available cash

by running the cost of those earlier blocks up. They knew how much money Don Leo had but they may not have counted on aid coming from Bender. This, then, was their chance, the only one Walt could see.

For the pool wasn't dumb like this nump they had bidding; the moment they'd got word from Esteban's messenger they'd have known Bender'd run the cost up on a bluff.

BLOCK 9 went the way of the last two, with Esteban never even opening his mouth.

The stillness in this room became increasingly more intense as the deputy commissioner bucked his way through the abstracts of legal phraseology, preparatory to the throwing open of Block 10 for bidding. Whether anyone here—aside from Walt, Gonzales and, possibly, Esteban—fully understood Don Leo's situation, or had heard of the note he had given to raise money, more than a few must have realized his pressing need for additional range and sensed in this parcel a partial answer to his problems. This was implicit in the looks now flashed at his foreman.

A fine sweat broke out upon Gonzales' florid cheeks. He scrinched green eyes against the smoke from his cigarette and straightened bony shoulders.

A man across the room opened the bidding at fourteen cents. Another called "Fifteen"—Esteban raising it two. The original bidder went up one more cent and Gonzales then said twenty.

With a scornful sneer Esteban made it thirty and Gonzales hiked it another ten.

Grinning maliciously, Esteban said, "Fifty-five," like that settled it, and commenced pushing his way toward the clerk's writing table.

The man representing the Indian Department took a long hard look at Gonzales and let his breath out. He allowed his glance, through the smoke haze, to rummage a few other faces. "Fifty-five cents on eight thousand acres is forty-four hundred dollars. If there are no further bids on this parcel—"

"Fifty-six," Bender said.

It couldn't have caused more commotion if he had hauled out his sixgun. The commissioner's mouth dropped open. The clerk closed his eyes. Esteban whirled from the table with a bleating screak of outrage.

The deputy commissioner mopped his face and looked unduly perturbed.

"Is—is that a legitimate bid?"

Bender nodded.

The man from the Indian Department sent a fluttery look at Lasham's livid agent, who snatched up his money with a furious oath.

"How can these man do these thing?"

"Chew or spit," Bender said. "Do you want it?"

Esteban's face turned an unhealthy gray. He put a tongue across his lips. He finally groaned "Fifty-seven," and you could just about hear him.

Bender said, stony faced, "Sixty-two," and watched the fat Mexican stagger into the crowd.

Someone let out a yell and the three or four Texicans still in the building began whooping and pummeling each other's backs. The deputy commissioner banged with his gavel and a ripple of motion ran through a group round the doorway. "If there are no further bids, Block 10 goes to—What'd you say your name was?"

"Name's Bender, but—"

And that was where the breath got suddenly hung in Bender's throat.

A pair of men were shoving toward him, the crowd falling back around them. Both had leveled guns in their hands. Something winked coldly from the second man's shirt, but it was the first who caught and held Bender's stare.

The man had on a red hat. He was short, broad and burly, with a weather-blackened skin and a heavy cropped mustache that did not even begin to hide the arrogant curl of his gun fighter's lips. This was Syd Hazel, boss of Lasham's sheep.

He indicated Bender with a jerk of his gun snout. "There's

your turkey, Fentress. I'll arrange for extradition. You won't have no trouble collectin' the bounty."

The deputy commissioner peered around as in a daze, finally appealing bewilderedly to obvious authority. "What's—"

"Disregard that last bid," Hazel snapped at him. "This fellow's a criminal wanted for murder. As such, not entitled to bid on anything."

7 | DARK PURPOSE

BENDER sat on the jail cot's lumpy mattress and tried to think what chance he'd had for handling this different. He may have had such a chance but he was damned if he could find it. The one essential factor which had never entered his head was that Lasham could become so uncontrollably enraged that he would sacrifice everything, every plan he had laid, by sending out the order for his scapegoat's arrest.

For that was Bender's role, all right. From the very start, in the sheep king's plans, he'd been carefully built up and cleverly made over to serve as whipping boy for Deef Lasham's crimes. Every angle, every sequence—those long months of ducking and dodging, gave incontrovertible proof of this truth. There could be no other answer. Lasham's pet marshal had never attempted to come up with him; he'd been satisfied to loaf behind tacking up his damn dodgers.

And here was the essence of the sheep king's craft. Lasham had not wanted Bender caught—you couldn't escape it. Those hand bills had been printed and hung up to keep him moving, to fetch him on the scene of Lasham's next intended project at precisely the time when his arrival could be counted on to more confuse the issue and to strengthen Lasham's hand.

What other interpretation could be put upon the business?

The sheep king considered all cowmen fools and was totally contemptuous of Mexicans. So he would hardly have taken such pains with Bender just to wreck or steal Tres Pinos, even considering its strategic location. These must be the facets of a much larger purpose.

What *was* the man after? Bender asked himself.

He got up and stared out of the narrow barred window, eyes morosely prowling the unlovely view of rusted cans and broken bottles—by-products of the hash house on the one side and of the honkytonk on the other. Beyond these mounds of discarded trash the range ran bleak and brown to the footslopes of the Florida Mountains.

He gripped the bars with his hands and stared unseeingly between them for long uncounted moments while his still incredulous mind refused to believe Deef Lasham was done with him. It didn't anyplace make sense, which was one of the reasons they had taken him without gunplay when they'd come barging into that warehouse. It was much easier to think that Syd Hazel, without sufficient knowledge of his overlord's final objectives, had acted on his own in bringing off this coup.

For it had been a coup—there was no getting around that. With one quick swoop Lasham's gun boss had put Bender completely out of commission, grabbed the land he'd taken away from them and killed Three Pines' last hope of wriggling clear.

Bender, conceding these facts, remained dissatisfied. He was wholly unable to convince himself these were the ends for which Lasham had groomed him. Had he finished what he'd been going to say, that he'd bid in Block 10 for Tres Pinos, he would have understood this better, for then it might have been argued he had achieved the sheep king's intentions. But he hadn't had time to give more than his name; there'd been no public connection between himself and Don Leo.

The sun must have dropped behind Red Mountain. Mile-long shadows lay across the range, thickening fast in the gathering dusk. The Floridas, southeast, were all blues and purples; and Bender turned from the window thinking briefly of Blanca. He need not ask what she'd say when she heard of the outcome. A tenuous hope which had failed of its purpose, she would write him off as a casualty to the sheep crowd and cast about her for some better weapon.

He moved over to the door and idly scowled through the grating. The corridor was gray with the approach of night and no place in the building could he hear anything stirring. The muted clatter of kettles and hardware and crockery from the hash house next door stirred a faint core of hunger that had been growing in his belly.

He shook the bars and called: "Fentress!" but all he got for an answer were the echoes of his voice.

Shut up and gone off to celebrate, he reckoned; and wondered what would happen to the five hundred dollars the sheriff had taken from his pockets and chucked in the drawer along with his pistol. Not, he decided, that it would make much difference. Money right now was the least of his worries.

He went back and dropped down on the edge of his cot. In another couple hours Gonzales would get back and they would learn at Tres Pinos what had happened to their gun man. He could imagine the yarn the Three Pines ramrod would spin, the importance he would attach to Bender's tame surrender.

But he wasted no futile thoughts about that. What he wanted right now was to get the hell out of here; and he commenced looking round for something he could use.

He didn't find anything. There was the cot and the seatless flush toilet, and alongside the latter there was a damned filthy lavatory that didn't look to have been wiped off since the day it had been installed. The cot was made of iron and had been bolted to the floor. One of those bars covering the window would have made a good weapon, but they were set in solid and he couldn't budge a one of them.

So much for that.

He went back and sat down. He was not resigned to staying here but for the moment, at least, it looked as though he would have to. He stretched out on the lumpy mattress and tried to dream up some way by which he could get the best of whoever came in with his food. He thought of feigning sleep, of pretending to be sick; but when his jailor came at nine he hadn't hit on anything which even remotely looked like being of any use.

He heard the front door bang and then heard bootsteps in the corridor. "I've fetched you some grub," this unseen party said; and there followed a small racket as of a tray being placed on the floor.

"Have I got to eat it in the dark?" Bender growled.

"No. I been fishin' for a match but it looks like I ain't got any. You wait right there. I'll be back in a couple of minutes."

Bootsteps went off down the corridor again. The front door slammed and Bender dropped back on his cot, wondering if all jailors were as absent-minded as this one. Some old man, like as not, which the county was getting for little or nothing.

Still, it seemed a bit odd the sheriff would go off with so small a concern for the safety of his prisoner. He had not impressed Bender as the kind to let a fast buck slip away, and the five hundred dollars collectible in bounty looked a rather substantial nest egg for any such careless handling.

No jail was any stronger than the personnel in charge of keys. Even a fool should be bright enough to figure a man jailed for murder wasn't going to pass up any chances. It was possible, of course, that Fentress had made arrangements which were not yet apparent. And it was possible, too, that such an arrangement was under way. A lot depended, Bender realized, on whether or not the sheep crowd was done with him. If they were, the intention might very well be to engineer an escape which would put Walt Bender where the sheriff could blast him down without danger of repercussions.

The more he thought about that the more he was inclined to believe it was the answer. As things stood right now neither Three Pines nor its owner had been smeared by contact with Bender. If Lasham or Syd Hazel could make it appear that a notorious killer had been loosed by Tres Pinos. . . .

But how the hell could they when Bender, so far as the general public knew, had utterly no connection with Don Leo or his outfit? Was Hazel willing to take the gamble that Bender had been seen enough with Gonzales to establish a connection?

He shook his head, more puzzled than ever. It was not Lasham's style to let any plan go off half cocked. He liked to tie a package up neatly in fancy paper and pretty pink ribbons. Of course they might be in possession of information withheld from Bender which would make a jail break plausible, but he couldn't imagine what that would be.

Turned abruptly motionless, he crouched there, listening, thinking to have caught some furtive sound up yonder; but, if he had, it wasn't repeated, and his mind switched again to the problem he'd shelved earlier. Even in view of his more recent conjecture it still didn't make good sense, to his thinking, that Lasham would have gone to so much bother and now discard him with so little gain to show for it.

There was gain, all right, but it lacked considerable of being anywhere near proportionate to the amount of time and effort which had been expended on saddling Bender with a hired killer's rep.

Turned completely still he probed the corridor's blackness, convinced this time that he had caught a muffled cry. At once, upon its heels, he heard the thud of something falling, the scrape of something dragged. There was someone in the office.

It was the building's total lack of light which really put his teeth on edge. Whatever was being done out there was intended to be kept secret—any nump could figure that. But the question was—from whom?

There came a tiny metallic clatter and again booted feet . moved toward him. He said through the blackness: "Find your matches?" The boots came nearer but he didn't get any answer.

Bender's throat began to get dry. After all, he *could* be dry-gulched right here.

The dark silence suddenly exploded in a terrific tinpanny clatter as one of those approaching booted feet whammed into the tray holding Bender's supper. He caught the jolt of a staggering body, a smothered imprecation; and then a girl's scared voice cried tight and frantic: "Bender! Walt! Where are you?"

8 | "YOU'RE NOT RUNNING OUT!"

BLANCA!

Relief made the hinges of Bender's knees go wabbly but he got hold of himself, knowing well how little time they might have before somebody stuck his nose into this.

"Here," he called softly, shaking the door's grating. "How'd you manage to get here so quick? Did Gonzales—"

"I haven't seen Pete. I was with that bunch of *peones* on the platform when Fentress brought you out of the warehouse. I came as quick as I dared; I had to locate your horse—"

"Was that you out front? What'd you do with the jailor?"

"I hit him," she said with despair in her voice. "I hid back of the door and when he came in I tripped him. I got his gun away and—"

"All right," Bender said, his words sharp with impatience. "Hurry up and get this door open—"

"I can not find the *keys!*"

She must have caught the sound of his indrawn breath. She moved away from him a little. "I dropped them when that horrible clatter—" Frustration clawed through her desperate tone. He could hear her hands scrabbling round through the dark.

"We've got to work fast," he said. "Strike a light."

"I have no matches."

He listened to her knees thumping round on the floor, the slither and scrape of her searching fingers. Trap smell threatened to cut his breath off. Fright sunk its hooks deep into him and like a man gone berserk he flung his full weight against the steel of the grating. It did no good, of course— none whatever; but he saw now where what had happened here made sense. This girl was the segment which completed the circle. She furnished all they needed to hook him up with Tres Pinos.

She gave a sudden choked cry. He heard her scrambling upright. The blessed clatter of steel against steel as she turned the found key in the lock left him trembling. He felt the grating swing away and then a mutter of voices pulled the slack from his muscles.

"Quick." He caught her arm. He hurried her down the black corridor and into the sheriff's almost-as-black office. "Get the old man's gun—"

"I have it."

"Then get out on the street and walk toward the horses. Whatever you do, *don't run*."

She pulled open the door. Light from outside turned the gloom a vague gray. His hands found the desk. He heard her move down the steps. He yanked the drawer halfway out and got his gun, got his money. Fiddle scrape and hilarious voices came from the honkytonk to drown any sounds he might otherwise have heard. He thrust the bills in his pocket, the gun in his holster. Its weight did not give him the ease he'd expected. He thought: *Steady does it,* and moved through the door.

Across the way four still shapes were blackly limned against lampglow. The honkytonk fiddles sawed themselves into silence and in the midst of the clapping he pulled the door shut, moving his lips as though talking to someone. Though every sinew cringed he turned around then and tramped down the steps.

The four across the street continued silently to stand there, too far removed for him to make out their faces in that pattern of light and shadow. A rider was coming around the hash house with a led horse; he knew at once that this was Blanca and sensed the sudden interest of the motionless quartet.

If they spoke it was too low for him to hear but he could tell that they were watching by the stiffness of their postures, and again fear touched him. Seventy feet of space lay between himself and them but a .45 could kill at almost double that distance.

Sweat came out and lay cold against his neck but there was no help for it. He could not wave the girl back now. He could turn and move away from her but this he dared not do.

Unaccountably she stopped. He felt his muscles loosen; then she raised a hand and beckoned.

One of the four across the street half wheeled away from his companions. Bender did not wait to see what else the man might do. He was gathering himself to break into a run when the girl's voice called clearly: "Where will I find the sheriff?"

Bender felt a little giddy but his mind worked swift as hers. He threw a hand out. "There's his office but you won't find him there. I been waitin' half an hour. Nobody there but the old man and some feller they got in the cooler."

If those men across the street had any connection with Red Hat or Fentress he did not think this would fool them very long. But the girl was closer to him than they were and if he could keep them undecided just a few seconds longer. . . .

He walked toward the girl. "Anything I can do, ma'am?"

"It's about my brother. I was supposed—"

Another dance got started in the honkytonk. "I can't hear you," Bender shouted, and moved forward as an impatient man might have done. Of Blanca's reply all he caught was the one word *jail*, but a look flung over his shoulder disclosed the gist of it promptly. There were only three shapes on the far walk now; the other was mounting the sheriff's steps.

Bender let go of caution and broke into a run. A shout went up behind him. A gun kicked a hole through *Sally Gooden* and Bender, catching the reins of the led horse, vaulted into the saddle and they were off in a rush that was laced with screaming lead.

Bender kneed Chucho right, forcing the girl's horse to whirl and duck between two buildings. "Go ahead," he growled, "take the lead an' let's get rollin'. We've got to hit brush before that moon comes up."

She swung her horse ahead and he followed her up an alley and then between two more houses and onto another road and up it hellity larrup. They were heading west and, although he knew Tres Pinos lay somewhere to the south and east, he offered no objections. He glanced back from time to time but the night was too dark for him to make out anything against the lights of the town and the flogging rhythm of the horses' hoofs was too close and too loud for him to hear anything else.

Five minutes later the road forked ahead of them, the left branch turning south, but the girl ignored this and kept on straight ahead across a series of sand drifts and rode another ten minutes before pulling up. They both swung round in their saddles to listen. Then Bender got down and put an ear to the ground.

He climbed back on Chucho and shook his head. "Not a sign. We better cut south now and work around those damn mountains."

"Too long," Blanca answered. "We'll go through them."

BENDER felt none of the elation this escape should have given him. He was alone in the night with a beautiful woman and that didn't cut any ice with him either. He rode with grim face and an increasing feeling of bitter dissatisfaction. He was free for the moment and that was all. Things hadn't changed. This trip had not helped Don Leo. Lasham had got the land he'd been after even though he'd been forced to pay more than intended. Tres Pinos had gotten nothing and Syd Hazel's play, whatever its ultimate intention, made Bender realize very clearly that Lasham wasn't through with him. He'd got away from that jail too easily to be fooled into thinking Lasham's range boss had been caught napping.

After half an hour of riding he put a hand out and pulled up.

"No use in me goin' back there with you."

She pulled in a sharp breath and stared at him. "What do you suppose I got you out of there for?"

"I don't have to guess about that. But it's no good, I tell you. I'm no good to your father now. I've been exposed to your sheriff as a man wanted for murder—"

"If you're afraid," she began, but he cut her off curtly.

"What I'm tryin' to get through your head," he said, "is that all Tres Pinos means to Deef Lasham is a means to an end. As a piece of property he don't give two hoots in hell about your spread. The thing he's after is that two hundred thousand acres of Indian grass!"

She stared at him a moment. He caught the swell of her breasts. "Are you trying to tell me he isn't after our ranch?"

"Sure he's after it; but it's the situation, not the place, he wants. What you've got is a natural gateway, the closest one in reach. So he'll use it. He'll go through it—"

"If he can. That's what I got you out of there for. To stop him."

"I didn't think you did it for love," Bender snarled. "If you'd stayed to home where you belong this might have ironed itself out. Even if I managed to get him stopped now it wouldn't help your old man. We had a chance to beat Lasham but you threw it away—"

"*I* threw it away!"

"Hell. Can't you *see* it?"

"All I can see," she cried with eyes blazing, "is that broad stripe of yellow you've got running up your back!"

In that luminous half light peculiar to the desert he considered her without expression. Then he picked up his reins. "Tell your father I'm sorry about the way this had to end—"

"It hasn't ended," she said, "and you're not running out." In the stars' pallid gleam he caught the shine of her pistol. "You're going right back there with me. Now rattle your hocks."

9 | THE TASTE
OF SWEAT

THEY got in before daylight.

Though plagued by hunger and angered by the knowledge of the girl's continued vigilance, Bender had done a heap of thinking. It had been a cold ride and he climbed down bone weary, staggering a bit with saddle cramp, as he handed the reins to a sleepy-eyed *mozo*.

He followed the girl into the house without speaking and wolfed down the food she put before him in the kitchen, ignoring her silent regard as he ate it. He dippered a drink from the bucket that stood full on the sink, eyeing her across it. "You can go on to bed. I ain't fixin' to leave here."

"Keep your voice down," she said. "I want you to listen to me a minute."

They hadn't turned up any lamps but he could see her well enough by the moonlight flooding in off the patio. She must have been near as dragged out as he was but you'd never get next to that notion just seeing her. She was a hell of a lot of woman any way you wanted to figure it.

"Since we've lost that land we were going to give you I suppose it's about time to reach a new understanding." She watched for his reaction but his face remained like rock.

He didn't say anything. He put the dipper back in the bucket and fished his shirt for the makings, shaping up a smoke as though indifferent to her inspection.

"You'd probably like to get back in cows," she said with the edge of a smile on her lips. "After all, you must want to look forward to something. A man in your fix—"

'Never mind about me. You've got all you can handle lookin' out for your own fix."

"Yes . . . but I've something to bargain with. Would a halfway split in this ranch satisfy you?"

"I don't need any bribe to throw a fight at Deef Lasham!"

"But you'll fight a lot harder if you've got a stake in it."

He went over to the stove and found a match. When he looked at her again his eyes were like agate. "I don't know what kind of a jigger you're huntin' but it's damn plain—"

"Let's put it this way," she said, getting out of her chair. "We're an old and proud line, not the kind of a family which likes to accept favors. We'd sooner lose Tres Pinos—"

"You're goin' to lose it, all right! You can make up your mind to that. Nothin' short of an army will keep Deef Lasham from goin' through here just about as he pleases."

He blew smoke through his nose and made a black blob of the butt on his plate. "I'm going to tell you something. You don't have to hold no bait out to me. I'll buck these sheep, but I'll do it on my *own terms* or I ride straight out of this mess tonight."

She stood watching him a moment, the swell of her breasts squeezed tight against her shirtfront. It was hard for him to guess if she were frightened now or furious.

There was nothing but contempt in her voice when she said, "I thought we should get to this finally. Go ahead and make your pitch."

Glaring, Bender rammed big fists in his pockets as though half afraid he might take a swing at her. He started to go without speaking but the scorn of her red lips swung him around. "When I talk turkey," he snarled, "it won't be with no petticoat. Maybe you can make your old man jump through hoops but you ain't about to make no trained seal outa me!"

She didn't move aside, didn't appear to move at all, but suddenly he became uncomfortably conscious of her body. Something strong and unsettling ran vividly between them and he watched those jutting breasts in the lift and fall of her breathing.

He reached out and hauled her toward him. He could feel

her thighs hot against his own. Her lips flattened under his mouth and came apart and the tips of her fingers dug into his shoulders. Time stood still and then she shoved him away.

Against the whiteness of her cheeks her mouth made full and crimson contrast. She said in an outraged breath: "Are those your terms?"

Bender wheeled with a savage fury, too wild to trust his voice with an answer. He crossed the patio, spurs clanking angrily, and went through to the *parada*, jerking open the door to the bunkhouse and standing there a moment like some dark Nemesis, raggedly listening to the sounds of those within.

When he closed the door he had himself in hand again but his face was still turbulent with the violence of his thoughts. Finally he let his breath out and went back across the patio and into his room without a glance at Blanca's door.

HE woke up in the shank of the afternoon, feeling more like himself, and washed at the basin. He slicked back his hair with his fingers and gave some study to the face in his mirror, not particularly pleased with the visage that stared back at him. If he let his whiskers grow it might stall off for awhile those who didn't know him well, but saying "To hell with it!" he shaved. They would find him soon enough if they really made up their minds to.

He got into his shirt, cuffed the dust from his levis and put on his hat. He looked awhile at his shell belt and gun-weighted holster but left them where they hung on the chair-back.

The patio was patterned with sunlight and shadow and over by the coolness of a flowering *palo verde* he saw Don Leo watching the birds about the fountain. The old man smiled and waved him over, inquiring after his health in the gracious Mexican manner. He answered, asked how things were with his host, and then the *ranchero* said, "I was told you were back. I have been waiting for a word with you."

Avoiding the barrel, Bender said, "Too bad about that land."

Don Leo shrugged. "What is spilled cannot be returned to the bottle. All is not yet lost, however. I still have Tres Pinos and if you will see me through this trouble, *amigo*, one half of it and half of all my cattle will be your share when this thing has been finished."

"The picture's changed," Bender grunted. "We had a fifty-fifty chance when we started but Hazel's coup has knocked that in the head and Blanca, breaking me out of that jail, has put this spread right where Lasham wants it. Sure, I'm willing to admit they may not have got onto her, but they know from her voice if was a woman got me out. You better pull in your horns and let his sheep go through—"

"Never!" Don Leo cried fiercely.

"Well," Bender shrugged, "I guess you know what'll happen. He'll go through this spread with every sheep he can get hold of and when he gets done you won't have enough feed to chink the ribs of a locust. Let him pass without hindrance and you'll still have the land—"

"Of what good is land without honor?" Don Leo grumbled. "No, my friend, we may be whipped as you say, we may even lose everything, but we will fight to the end. We will fight, *senor*, till there is none left among us but no *Texano* shall ever say a Lopez was afraid!"

His curly beard bristled and he scowled like an angry eagle, but the spirit was stronger than the flesh it reposed in and, after a moment, he sank back in his chair, mumbling and muttering impotently in Spanish.

Bender glowered too but he nursed his hate in silence. And then the old man said, "Please understand, I wish you to stay here—"

"Look," Bender growled. "I've been publicly arrested—I'm a fugitive wanted for murder. You want them bastards to hang it on you? That's what they'll do if I stay here. They'll brand this spread—"

"No matter. I want you to stay and take charge of this fighting. Ask what you will—"

"All right, I'll stay. But on one condition. That I have complete charge. That what I say goes until we're done one way or the other with Lasham."

Don Leo, peering up at him anxiously, nodded. *"Seguro, si,"* he said, and gave Walt Bender his hand.

THEY sat a brief while in silence then, Bender pulling his notions together. There were still several things he didn't properly understand, but one thing he knew beyond question —he couldn't go at this with wraps on. In the bunkhouse, for instance, there'd be a heap of resentment. There would undoubtedly be times when the old man would wish he'd never heard of Walt Bender. This was a job for Simon Legree.

He got up, saying briskly, "The most of them ought to be in by now so we may as well get the ball to rolling. I want you to tell them I'm the new general manager."

Don Leo sighed and led the way to the *parada*. Several of the men were busy caring for the horses but he beckoned them away and called the rest from their quarters. In Spanish he told them about the threat of the sheep and introduced Bender as the new *majordomo*. "His word in all things will be final."

Bender, studying their faces, stepped forward as he finished. "Don Leo has told me he has fourteen cowboys. I count fourteen noses. Who, then, is watching the cattle?"

He threw the question at Gonzales and saw the man's eyes widen. In a tone barely bordering on civility the redheaded foreman said it wasn't their custom to watch the cattle at night.

"Then we'll change the custom," Bender told him. "Perhaps in the old days that style was okay; cattle weren't worth so much a man would mind losing a few off and on. But the price has gone up. There are gringos in the country now and we adopt gringo ways or we don't stay in business. You will divide the crew in relays and make sure that six men are with the cattle always. In the night they'll be close-herded and at the least sign of trouble one man will ride the fastest horse and come at once to report it. Is that clear, Pedrocito?"

Gonzales' eyes, turned narrow, swung a look at Don Leo and came sullenly back. He jerked his face in a nod. And then he scowled and spat disgustedly.

"Also," Bender said, ignoring this, "you will keep two men continually on watch at that shack above the bluffs. At the first appearance of sheep on the desert one will fetch the word while the other remains to keep an eye on developments. And mark this well: no stranger is to pass or be allowed to approach the *casa* without I have okayed him."

He looked them over again, beckoning one from the line, an old dark-faced fellow with a large bristling mustache and a neck criss-crossed with the creases of time and weather. Holding his hat in his hand he met Bender's eye without fear or favor.

"What's your name?" Bender asked.

"Jose Maria Roblero, *senor*."

"Well, Jose," Bender said, "do you think you could hitch up a team and drive a wagon?"

The old man's eyes crinkled with laughter. "I think I could do that, yes."

Bender nodded. "There are coyotes around these parts, Jose. I think we should lay in a large supply of strychnine. Do you think you could take this wagon into Afton and fetch back about thirty sacks of the stuff?"

The old man looked a little startled for a moment, then he bobbed his head.

"That's fine," Bender said. "Suppose you get right at it. Oh —and Jose! Better fetch a few hundred Colt and Winchester cartridges. Some of these coyotes we might have to kill by hand."

When the old man had taken himself off to catch the team up, Bender's eyes searched out Scar Face. He looked at him so long the man at last began to squirm. Then Bender said without preface: "You sleep all right last night?"

The bravo's face wrinkled up into an expression of puzzlement but the mismatched eyes clouded over and turned watchful. "Sure," he said. "All the time I sleep good—"

"Where?"

The fellow jerked a thumb toward the men's quarters back of him.

Bender shook his head. "Not last night you didn't."

"Oh—last night! No. I see my wife. In Columbus. She going to have the baby."

Gonzales spoke up. "He had my permission—"

"Nobody's talking to you." Bender watched Scar Face's eyes getting smaller and smaller, saw them drop to his waist and come up again, brightening.

"And yesterday, I suppose, you were watching the cattle."

Scar Face shrugged. "Every day I watch the cows."

The jingle and scrape of Bender's big-roweled spurs flung out bleak vibrations as he walked up to the man, crowding him away from the advantage of the wall, and forcing him to turn until he could not see Gonzales. "If there's one thing I never been able to abide it's a goddam belly-crawling sidewinding liar. You never went near Columbus last night!"

Out of the shocked stillness Gonzales' voice cried harshly: "How can you know where this man was?"

"Sheriff found me, didn't he?"

Don Leo peered at Bender incredulously. "Are you trying to tell me this man is a spy?"

"Do I have to?" Bender countered. "Hasn't it struck you as odd that pair should have arrived so opportunely at a moment when nothing else could have saved Block 10 for Deef Lasham? That they came with drawn guns and knew right where to find me?"

"But," declared Gonzales, "it was not Fentress who found you. It was this other one, this Red Hat, that told him who you were."

"And," Scar Face sneered, "it was after Esteban sent Eusebio—" He broke off abruptly, his whole look stiffening.

Bender's hard teeth gleamed behind tight lips.

The Mexican, knowing he was trapped, abruptly flung himself at Bender with a kill-crazy snarl. A knife flashed in his hand, its honed blade glinting wickedly. But the Texan, expecting this, ducked the murderous slash and put four knuckles hard against the fellow's chin.

The Mexican's head was slammed sideways. The knife fell out of his paralyzed fingers. For a moment he hung there, teetering wildly, falling suddenly backwards. His shoulders struck like a burst sack.

Bender stepped into the bunkhouse. He came out with a

bucket, splashed the contents over the prostrate man and watched him come spluttering up on an elbow.

"Get onto your feet!"

The man rolled his eyes like a stallion bronc. He levered his back up off of the ground, got a knee planted under him and went for his gun.

Bender stood blackly watching. He waited till the man had almost got the thing from leather then he brought down the bucket, breaking it without mercy on the man's unprotected head.

Breath sighed out of the staring crew.

Bender showed them a tough and thin-stretched smile till their eyes found something better to look at. Several crossed themselves, silently muttering, and the Texan, turning his head, saw that Blanca was standing, shoulders taut, beside her father.

She said in English, "Was that necessary?"

"Maybe you think I should have given him a medal."

"You should have used a little tact. Do you want them to hate you?"

"Should I care about that? I'm buildin' a crew that'll jump when I tell them." He gave her back a look as bleak as her own. "Any time I don't suit, your old man can fire me. Until he does, I'll do the job *my* way. *Agua!*" he snapped, and a man ran to fetch it.

He gave Blanca a knowledgeable grin and watched her eyes flash.

"You're as hateful a man as I have ever encountered," she said with her breath jerking in and out angrily. She turned her back and went over and stood beside the redheaded foreman.

The man who had gone for the water came back with it and, at Bender's nod, sloshed it over Lasham's agent. They got him onto his feet where he stood dripping and miserable, in his wet clothes looking like a half-drowned rat.

When his mismatched eyes swung blearily into focus, Bender said, "Pick up your belongings and go pack the rest of them."

THE crew stood around with expressionless faces while the discharged man threw his gear on a horse. When he came from the house with his bedroll Bender said to Gonzales, "Take a good look at him. He's the one you can thank for losing that grass."

"I hired him," Blanca frowned. "You don't need to blame Pete. He came up off the desert by the same trail you did."

Bender ignored her. The man got on his horse, not quite making it the first time, and rode through the gate. When they couldn't hear the horse any longer Don Leo said wearily, "He will tell that Lasham about this poison you are buying."

"I hope so," Bender nodded. He waved a hand at the men. "Better put on the feed bags. We've got a hard night before us."

He turned to the rancher. "Where's the nearest market? I'm going to round up your beef."

"The nearest market's Deming—but is this wise, do you think? A little later in the season—"

"A little later in the season you won't have anything to market. If *we* don't move them the sheep crowd will. I want that dough you got from Lasham."

Don Leo stood for a long while silent. When he spoke his voice was hardly more than a whisper. "I do not have that money."

"You don't have it!" Bender stared. "What the hell have you done with it?"

Gonzales said, "Coming back from Deming last night I was robbed."

10 | RED HAT

"WELL, isn't that just ducky!"

Gonzales' eyes swiveled away and he hurriedly put more ground between them as though half expecting the gringo to strike him.

Bender stared at the girl, then looked at her father, and it took all the will he had to keep silent. Small wonder the old man was losing his grip. He had known about this when they'd talked in the patio; it was why he had been so anxiously insistent that Bender write his own ticket for this deal. If they couldn't pay off they might not have any ranch!

"When does this money have to be paid back?"

The old man shrugged. He looked stupid.

"On the tenth," Blanca said.

Less than two weeks away!

"And what do you figure to pay it with—peanuts?"

"There are the cattle," she said, her eyes watching him anxiously.

"Yeah," Bender said, "the cattle," and swore. "Get the stuff on the table," he told her gruffly and, turning away from them, clanked into the passage and went scowling across the patio.

He strode into his room and buckled on his shell belt. Then he took out his gun, going over it thoroughly, cleaning it and oiling it and slipping in fresh cartridges. And all this while he kept thinking of Deef Lasham, turning over what he knew, considering other things suspected.

He hadn't any doubt but what Gonzales had been robbed. It was just the kind of stunt that bastard sheep crowd would have thought of. They'd tried it once before only this time they'd got the job done. Had they used Art again or was this some of Hazel's handiwork?

There wasn't much chance he could get it back even if he knew who had taken it, but any kind of chance was better than sitting here.

He picked up his hat and went out to the *comedor*. The food was on the table. Gonzales was drawing his chair up. Don Leo, already seated, was staring unseeingly into his plate and the girl was fixing a snack for her mother.

Bender flung down his hat and dropped into a chair. Hardly waiting for the old man to get done with the blessing, he said grimly to the foreman: "How many of them jumped you?"

"One," Gonzales said.

"Was it Red Hat?"

"How could I know? He wore only a flour sack with holes for his eyes."

"Well, he said something, didn't he? Wouldn't you recognize his voice?"

Gonzales shook his red head.

"Where'd he stop you?"

"In the town," Gonzales grunted. "He was in the mouth of that alley between the Aces Up and the Bottleneck Bar. He told me to drop the money and, when I did, he said 'Now hump it.' "

Pretty slick, Bender thought. A man had to admire its extreme simplicity. It was the kind of a deal that would appeal to Syd Hazel and it had Hazel's boldness.

When they shoved back their chairs and he an·l the foreman were shaping their smokes up, Don Leo, finally rousing himself, asked hesitantly, "Is there anything we can do?"

Bender scratched a match on the seam of his levis, got his cigarette going and scowled through the smoke. "There's probably a lot of things—if a fellow could think of them."

"I went back after awhile,". Gonzales said.

"Did you go into those dives?"

"Into both of them, yes. But I did·n't know who to look for.

I did not see this man of the red sombrero. A fat man was playing cards at a table with the sheriff and two others."

That fetched Bender's head around. Gonzales nodded. "It was the man who gave me the money. Lasham."

Bender stubbed out his smoke and picked up his hat. "Post two men at that shack. Take the rest of the crew and start rounding up cattle—round up everything wearing the Three Pines brand. I'll be back, like enough, before you've got the herd ready; but if I'm not, start the drive and keep your eye peeled for trouble."

"Where are you going?"

It was Blanca, coming back from the bedroom with her mother's empty dishes. She asked him again, and there was something in her look that made him—just a moment—wonder.

Then he shoved the thought aside. "I'm going after that money," he said, and departed.

It was ten fifteen by the fly speckled clock above O'Cleary's bar when Cash Fentress stepped through the green-painted batwings and, cutting a way through the crowd with his shoulders, dropped into a chair at an empty table that was placed one stride from the closed side door.

This table, its location and his own presence at it were familiar facets of the dive's nightly ritual. Blue smoke patterned the air beneath the hanging lanterns and a steady drone of talk made soothing background for the clack of chips and the chants of the housemen. This was the part of his day most enjoyed by the sheriff and he looked around with approval as he imagined the money rolling into O'Cleary's till. There were bottles on most of the tables, the bar was packed three deep and the games looked to be in a satisfactory state of progress.

These appearances put the lawman in a mellow frame of mind for he had this big Irishman right where he wanted him and the more the man made the bigger the take that was in it for Fentress. Silent partner was a role he played very well as others besides O'Cleary could have bitterly attested; and now he was about ready to move in on Red Hat.

He hadn't yet discovered what Syd Hazel was up to but it was certainly something crooked. Setting up a dummy to bid in Indian grass was a business sure to be frowned on if it were brought to the government's notice; and there was also that business of Bender. It all added up to what should be a sizeable profit soon as he learned enough of the background to understand where to put the squeeze. Perhaps he could get it hooked up tonight. The man should be dropping in pretty soon.

He glanced again at the clock and got out a cigar. He was biting the end off when the side door opened. He wasn't facing the door but he felt its brief draft and supposed this was Hazel.

Fellow'd certainly been in no lather to get here!

Fentress dug up a match without looking around, snapped a light on his thumbnail and waggled it in front of his smoke with much ceremony. Let the sonofabitch wait!

When the match was about finished he shook it out and looked up.

Instead of seeing the man he'd expected, he found Walt Bender standing over him. He did a quick double take and nearly choked with the shock of it.

Bender grinned toothily. "Push over," he said.

It went through Fentress' mind to start raising the roof but a second covert look at Bender's eyes derailed the impulse.

He got up as though hypnotized. "Not there," Bender growled. "Plunk your can down where you can look at the wall. You won't be so tempted to commit suicide that way."

Like a man on stilts the sheriff moved over and eased himself down like he was squatting on a time bomb.

Bender slid into the vacated chair.

During the following uncomfortable silence the walls, the room and its gabbling customers seemed to feather away like sun-cut mist, leaving only the table and that Texan's hard stare. Fentress' world wouldn't swing into proper focus. It just didn't make sense a guy wanted for murder could be such a fool as to come here and sit down with the man he'd just got away from.

"Kind of queer, ain't it?" Bender said conversationally—
"damn near as queer as you lettin' me get out of there. Only
that ain't queer to me. I savvy that part plenty."

He leaned abruptly forward, whispering weirdly, "Happens
sometimes like that to the best of us."

Fentress occasionally had nightmares, but nothing like this.
His throat was like cotton. He licked at his lips. He had to
lick them again before he could manage to say, "What does?"

The words came out in a hoarse kind of croak.

"Getting caught in a crack. Feelin' it closing in on you."

Bender's teeth gleamed again in a horrible grimace and
he signaled a waiter, ordering some beer—"In a bottle," he
specified.

The man came and fetched it and drifted away.

Bender said, reflective like, "I've seen critters do some queer
things in a trap . . . Some rats will gnaw their legs off. Snap
their bones in their teeth just like you'd snap a match stick.
Go crazy, I guess."

He poured some beer in his glass but made no move to
pick the glass up. "Reckon whatever they give you must have
looked just like gravy. It most generally does in a case of that
kind. No trouble, no fuss; a chunk to add to the nest egg. Only
when you lap gravy," he said, suddenly savage, "you want to
wipe off your mouth!"

The sheriff was a fish abruptly jerked out of water. He
gasped and he goggled.

"You're in a bad spot, Fentress." Bender eased the table
toward him, making himself more room behind it, letting his
right hand drop below its ledge out of sight. "You've got a
bear by the tail and now it's your move again."

The sheriff drew a long breath but it didn't thaw out the
cold lump in his larynx. He shook in his boots like a man with
the ague. It didn't help him to know that all this guy'd said
was a bunch of damned words, that nothing had changed but
his view of this business. Treacherous himself he expected
treachery in others and what Bender'd said rang a loud bell of
warning. He could call out for help—and he would probably

get it—but the both of them knew he wasn't about to. Not with that hand underneath the table.

Bender's eyes held the shine of old cinch rings. "You're a sittin' duck, Fentress. They've got you out in the cold and lonesome. You gave 'em the lever when you lugged me off to that foolproof jail and let me get loose."

"Hell's afire!" Fentress snarled. "Say what you mean an' quit beatin' the bushes. If—"

Bender's smile broke his words off. Bender's eyes, moving up and just a fraction away from him, were looking toward the door with the most pleased expression they had shown in a long while. "Come right in," he said heartily—"come right in and sit yourself down."

His hidden hand moved briefly, his left boot thrust a chair out. Fentress, goosey as a schoolgirl, twisted his head and saw Red Hat standing like a glowering bull behind him.

Hazel seemed to be having a little trouble with his breathing. The sheriff felt for him, but not very much. He said, "Yes. By *all* means. I've got a few things to say to you myself."

"Relax," Red Hat said, "he ain't goin' to kill no one." He swung the pushed-out chair around; sat down with its back in front of him. "What's stuck in *your* craw?" He flung the brusque words at Bender.

"A little matter," Bender said, "of forty-five hundred dollars."

"Do I look like a walkin' bank?" Hazel sneered.

Bender's hand made a movement underneath the table. "Cough up—an' quick."

His eyes were polished glass, without expression.

Hazel's burly shoulders rose in a shrug. "Always glad to help a friend," he drawled, grinning sourly, and thrust his left paw at his left hip pocket, at the same time lunging across the back of the chair in a forward dive that carried everything before it.

The table went over with a hell of a crash. Bender's gun went off and Fentress screamed like a hog.

11 | THE MUSCLE MEN

THERE wasn't anything wrong with him a drink wouldn't cure, but you'd have thought the way he lay there in that twichery heap he'd been salivated surely and was dying now by inches.

Bender, also on the floor, discovered that time could be elastic. With Fentress' uproar jerking at his nerves, it seemed to take forever to get himself untangled from the wreckage of that chair, to roll and come up on two knees and an elbow —even his pistol seemed to fire by slow motion.

Actually his movements had a speed little slower than lightning. He got in the first shot—even triggered a second at Red Hat crouched behind the overturned table before anyone else got a gun into action. Then he flung himself upright and lunged for the door.

Behind him everyone was shouting at once. Questions and orders and curses all were scrambled in a deafening racket and some damn fool was blasting the door full of peepholes, but he got the thing open and stumbled outside.

After that bright blaze of lights this alley looked dark as a stack of fresh-blacked stove lids. There was a very present danger he might trip and go down—about a five-to-three chance if you wanted the odds on it—but this wasn't any time to be worrying about intangibles. He tore through the murk like a bat out of Carlsbad, trying to get around the corner before that bunch came through the door.

He pretty nearly did it. He was within two strides of cutting it when the guns opened up behind him. He caught the thin whine of unseen bullets; in these narrow confines the re-

237

ports of those shots were like rocks coming down off a cliff in spring thaw. And then he was around the corner and the night was less black and he was safe for the moment.

He pulled a ragged breath deep into his lungs. His horse was still tethered under the branches of a tamarisk thirty feet away. The big dun was watching him nervously, fretful and alarmed by the continuing racket. Bender went over to him, murmuring soothingly, unknotted the reins and then paused, not quite decided. He was loath to go off without recovering that money.

He led the horse around and tied him back of the tamarisk. There were a bunch of beer and whisky kegs stacked up behind the back end of the building and a low shed roof coming out just above them. A hunch sent him toward them and in a matter of seconds he was on the shed roof, considering the second story's two black windows. He listened a moment, hearing nothing from the alley but a mutter of voices. On hands and knees he went up the roof's incline, rose carefully before the nearest window and tried it. The lower sash wasn't locked and he shoved it up quickly, mainly concerned with getting himself out of sight. As he thrust a leg over the sill he heard the sheriff's voice in the alley.

He swung himself through and quietly closed the window. He couldn't see a thing and he crouched there, breath jammed, while he strained his ears to catch other breathing. Satisfied he was alone, he stretched out his left hand until his fingers touched a wall. Moving slowly and cautiously he felt his way around it, coming finally to the door. He pressed an ear flat against it but he didn't hear any movement.

He tried to put himself in Red Hat's place, wondering what the man would do. It didn't seem at all likely Lasham's sheep boss would bother to do anything. The burden of action rested squarely on Fentress. To make things look right the sheriff would probably swear in a posse and go through the motions of making a search. At least, Bender hoped he would; and the bigger the posse the better he'd like it.

With all the stealth he could muster, Bender opened the door. The barroom sounds were much plainer now; he could even make out occasional snatches of talk. A flight of stairs led sharply down at his left. There was a door at the bottom with light splintering through the cracks in its panel. To Bender's right a narrow hall went to a window at the front; the blind was pulled down but light from the street came in around its edges, enough for him to see three other doors opening off the hall. There was light under the middle one; he didn't hear any voices.

He still hadn't figured how he would get hold of Hazel. Even if he dared lurk at that window a view of the street wouldn't be much good to him if Red Hat decided to depart via the alley. One of these other rooms might have a window on the alley but to watch that alley exclusively could hardly be any better and, if these rooms did not happen to be regularly occupied, there was the considerable risk he might be detected by whoever was in that room with the light.

He scowled through the gloom, bitterly considering a new thought. Hazel, if he hadn't already nipped off, might be planning to wait for the return of the sheriff.

There could be no profit in Bender waiting that long. If he was going to get out of here now was the time.

He started back into the room, abruptly stopped and looked back toward the room with the light. He had no damned reason for thinking such a thought but it was in his mind Deef Lasham might be in there and he was pulled toward it strongly. It would be a hell of a lot easier to get the money from Lasham than it would trying to take it away from Syd Hazel.

Just the thought of Deef Lasham was enough to stir sparks from the hot core of anger that was smoldering in Bender. He had the sheep king to thank for everything that had happened to him and he stepped back in the hall again, glaring at the crack of light that came from under that closed middle door. If this wasn't Lasham's room, or if the fat toad wasn't in there, the only alternative that crossed his mind—short of going back to Three Pines without accomplishing anything—was to go on downstairs and try another whack at Hazel.

Bender, grating his teeth, was starting toward the middle

door when light, with an uprush of sound from the barroom, fanned out across the ceiling and, with an equal abruptness, vanished. The stairs creaked under a heavy tread and Bender, smothering a bitter curse, again backed into the room he had come out of, flattening himself against the wall, not daring to shut the door lest it screak.

The boots reached the top of the stairs and stopped. Bender, holding his breath, could visualize the fellow warily eyeing that open door. The boots moved again, coming cautiously nearer. A hand reached out, the door swayed and groaned, and through the hinged crack he could see the black shape of the man's hatted head.

Bender's heart started knocking. The need to breathe was sheer torture. Every nerve pulled tight and trembled, and just as Bender felt he couldn't any longer stand it the head was withdrawn and the boots moved up the hall.

Mere air had never tasted one half as good. It was like some heady elixir, and Bender thought he never could gulp in enough of it but he forgot all about such abstractions as breathing when light targeted the man moving into that middle room.

Red Hat!

There was no doubt about it; the guy was Syd Hazel. Bender heard the muffled growl of his voice as the closing door blanked out the light.

Like a stalking cat he was out in the hall with his ear to that door before Hazel got seated—he even heard the chair scrape as the sheep boss dropped into it.

Now was the chance to overhear a little something that might give him a clue to what the sheep crowd was planning; but even as the thought went through his head Bender was reaching for the knob, knowing he didn't have the time.

He flung the door open and stepped in, gun in hand.

He'd guessed right about one thing; it was Lasham's room. The sheep king was seated beside a roll-top desk. His jowled face quivered around like an over heaped plate of jello. His mouth fell open and his eyes looked like they would roll off his cheekbones.

Bender, staring at the man, simply couldn't understand it. Ever since that day back in Texas when the sheep king had framed him with the killing of Toby Bronsen, he had never thought of anything he would like half so well as to get his two hands wrapped around this fat hog's neck. He had ridden a thousand miles with that picture, had dreamed a million times of just how he would do it—and now that, at last, he had come up with the bastard all he could feel was a nauseous contempt.

Why, the fool was half out of his mind with fright! He had built Bender into such a fire-breathing monster he had come to the point where he believed those lies himself.

Just looking at the fellow made him feel like puking. He said, "I'm not going to waste any time with you, Lasham. Your handyman here"—he jerked his gun snout at Hazel—"lifted forty-five hundred off Gonzales last night. I want it back. Right now."

The fat man's cheeks were gray as ashes. With shaking hands he peeled the bills off his roll.

"Now add another five thousand for that range you ruined for me."

More bills fell to increase the pile on the desk top.

"Dig out a clean sheet of paper. Get a pen and some ink." He kicked the door shut with his heel while he watched Deef Lasham do this. "Now put down what I tell you. To whom it may concern: I, Aaron Abijah Lasham, knowing that Toby Bronsen, the Texas senator, was about to tell his constituents I had been paying him large sums of money to put through legislation advantageous to sheep and particularly to the sheep pool with which I am connected, did wilfully and deliberately, on the occasion of the Labor Day rally at Kermit, put a forty-five slug between his eyes at close quarters. I make this confession for the good of my soul, which same may God take mercy on.

"Now sign it," Bender grated, "and get over against that wall."

Red Hat looked at his boss incredulously. "You're a fool if you give him a thing like that—tear it up!" he snarled.

But the fat man signed it, staggered out of his chair, put his belly against the wall and thrust both hands above his head.

Bender focused the gun on Lasham's gaping *segundo*. "I'll want your signature as witness—"

"You can go right on a-wantin'."

There was a cold hard watchfulness in the look Bender slanched at Hazel. "I'm not figuring to stand any foolishness from you. At the first sign of trouble I'm going to smash both your elbows. Now get out of that gun belt."

Red Hat looked at him toughly. "Take your dough an' git goin'—you ain't shootin' nobody. You know what'd happen if you let off that popgun. Half the boys in that bar would come poundin' up them stairs."

"They won't be much comfort to a busted arm. For the last time I'm telling you: Unbuckle that gun belt."

Red Hat settled himself like a millstone. His cat's yellow eyes loosed a glow of derision. "Hell with you," he said; and Bender squeezed the trigger.

THE sheriff, Cash Fentress, had a lot more wheels in his thinkbox than either side in this ruckus had given him credit for. His dive for the floor and subsequent howling was a fine bit of acting designed not only to keep the gunfire away from him but to lower his importance in the minds of those who witnessed it. He wasn't near as scared as he made himself out to be and when, after Bender's hurried exit, Syd Hazel's scathing words reminded him of his duties he put on another good show of shudderingly pulling himself together. When it was amply apparent Bender'd gotten away he went blustering out and swore in a posse. He put the town barber in charge of this outfit and told him to case all the trails leading north. "This feller's dangerous—don't take any chances. If you cut his sign send somebody after me. While you're gone I'll be combin' the town."

He didn't care what they thought; he wanted only to be rid of them. As soon as they'd climbed into saddles and gone, he got his own horse and rode off east of town into the region of shacks given over to section hands, teamsters and other personnel commonly employed by the railroad. He knew the place that he wanted but he spent several minutes angling cautiously around to make certain he wasn't followed. Finally convinced, he took off his badge and slipped it into his pocket, loosened the gun in his holster and, softly whistling the *Cowboy's Lament,* moved leisurely up to a decrepit unpainted shanty whose yard was cluttered with a bunch of chicken coops.

Several birds started squawking as he got out of the saddle. There were blankets over the windows and no sign of light. He knocked three times and growled, "I wanta buy some chickens," before he got any answer. Then a gruff voice grumbled, "Wait'll I git on my pants," and Fentress, scowling with impatience, snarled, "The girls don't wear pants where I come from."

The door was whisked open and he stepped inside.

"Don't you ever get tired of all this damn tomfoolery?" Art Chesseldine chuckled. "What you got on your mind?"

He had a round long jaw and ears that stuck out like handles. His bulging forehead was sheathed in sandy short cut hair and the big-jawed face was unlined and ruddy. He didn't look to be over twenty-two or twenty-three but was solidly built, heavily muscled and swell-chested, with a huge pair of hands that could have twisted bar iron. It was hard in the smoky light of that lantern to be sure of his expression but the sheriff wasn't letting that stand in the way of what he had come for.

"You know any guy named Bender—Walt Bender?"

"I've heard," Art said, "that he got out of your jail."

"He got out," Fentress growled, "because I was well paid to let him."

"I kind of figured that out. Pretty well heeled, eh?"

Fentress brushed that aside. "I found out most of this after it was over. A rough lookin' gent in a red hat come after me; said there was a guy at the auction that was wanted in Texas— wanted five hundred bucks worth; an escaped murderer, he tells me. So I pull the guy in. Then this Red Hat, later, slips me double the bounty to look the other way while this Bender gets loose."

"Must of taken some doin'."

"Some dame got him out. I want to know who she was."

"So now I'm a mind reader." Chesseldine grinned.

"You can tell me, all right. There's somethin' damn big gettin' ready to break here an' when it tears loose I want to be in on it."

"You better talk to this Red Hat—"

"Wait a minute," Fentress said, "I'm goin' to show you the angles. Yesterday Esteban, a guy with more debts than he's got buttons on his clothes, shows up at that auction and bids in a big bunch of land, payin' cash. At the time I show up, fetched by Red Hat, this Bender's outbid him on a block that joins Tres Pinos, a tamale outfit south of the Floridas. Red Hat calls the turn on Bender, I lug him off and the spik gets the land—that make any sense to you?"

Chesseldine shrugged.

The sheriff said, "I don't catch it right off. But when Red Hat slips me double the bounty to keep outa the way while this dame springs Bender, things begins to add up."

"You figure this bird put up the dough?"

"He's slipperier'n a basket of snakes, I'll say that much. He shows me a dodger an' gets action on Bender. My juggin' Bender lets that land go to Esteban. When the Mex gets the land our red-hatted friend should of been done with Bender, but instead he pays me double what I could of cashed the guy in for. Just to keep outa my office for awhile. Is this guy ackshully Bender or ain't he? If he is, why bail him out? Why bail him out *anyway?* And where's the girl fit into this? An' who the hell *is* she?"

Chesseldine considered the sheriff without comment. He rasped a hand across his jaw, got up and turned down the wick of the smoking lantern.

"An' here's another odd thing," Fentress growled. "Tonight I'm sittin' in the Aces Up, havin' my evenin' smoke like usual, when in walks Bender. He comes in that side door right alongside my table and sits himself down just as cool as a well chain. He feeds me some guff about bein' a settin' duck. Red Hat shows his mug about then an' Bender jumps him, tellin' him to shell out forty-five hundred. There's a ruckus, of course. Bender gets away—I'm supposed to be huntin' him now with a posse."

"Busy night," Art offered.

"That all you can say?"

"What'd you want me to say?"

Fentress, scowling, climbed out of his chair. He banged a fist down so hard on Chesseldine's table it made the dirty dishes jump. "I got a gold mine here if I can find the damn vein!"

"So I should turn cartwheels mebbe?"

"I need help," Fentress grumbled.

"So I rake in the chestnuts while you sit back an' eat 'em. No thanks."

Their eyes locked and held. The sheriff said, "I need your boys, Art. I'll take the bite off your rustlin' an' cut you in for half of every damn dollar we get out of this deal. Does that sound?"

"I can't hear it."

Fentress' cheeks turned dark with anger. "What the hell do you want?"

"You think my bunch is goin' to work at this for nothing? I want it split three ways—"

"Two for you, eh?"

"One for me, one for you, and one for the boys that'll be takin' the chances."

Fentress' twisted mouth showed the tumult inside him. Art Chesseldine's face was like the side of a mountain. Fentress said, voice tight with fury, "I let you in on—"

"You ain't lettin' me in on a goddam thing! I was workin' on this before you ever got wind of it."

"Says you!" Fentress sneered.

"You can take it or leave it."

Fentress had no real choice and he was smart enough to know it; he'd suspected all along that this damn rustler was in it someplace. "All right," he said finally, putting the best face he could on it, "we split the take three ways—now let's hear what you know."

"First," said Art, grinning, "I'll take my two-thirds of what you got from Hazel on Bender."

For a number of pregnant moments it looked as though Cash Fentress was about to burst his surcingle. But he got hold of himself, managing to keep the hot words jammed inside him, very probably helped by the knowledge implied in Chesseldine's use of Red Hat's name. With his eyes winnowed down to glittering slits he counted out the rustler's cut and flung the bills down on the table in silence.

"Bender's wanted, all right," Art said calmly. "I'm not sure just yet where he comes into this thing but I've had a man back in Texas and it seems Bender killed a senator called Bronsen. After Bender ducked out his cattle disappeared and Lasham sheeped off what was left of his range. This red-hatted Syd Hazel is Deef Lasham's sheep boss and the money Esteban used to bid in them lease lands probably come from Lasham."

"Bender was tryin' to get himself another start in the cow business, you think?"

Chesseldine shrugged. "I think he was bidding on Block 10 for Tres Pinos. I think Lasham's moving in here. Red Hat arranged with me to see that Lopez, who owns Three Pines, got to know about that auction. He's got his range overstocked and could use some extra grass, but he ain't got the cash to go bid at that auction. So I tell him where he can get it and Lasham loans him forty-five hundred. On a short term note."

Fentress considered this. "Never, of course, havin' any intention of lettin' Don Leo bid in that grass. What Lasham was after was a right-of-way through the old man's place. But how did Bender get into that biddin'? I wouldn't think he'd—"

"He's been holed up at Tres Pinos."

"The old man's been hidin' him?"

Chesseldine spat. "You could call it that, I reckon. He's been livin' in the house; gave him the room right next the girl."

Fentress looked at him carefully. "You must have got damn close to know that much."

"I had a man planted on 'em. A spik. In the outfit."

The sheriff looked interested. "What else have you learned?"

"They've made Bender manager, right over Gonzales' head. First thing he did was send a wagon after strychnine."

"They're goin' to fight Lasham then." Fentress swore. He said disgustedly, "Lasham's movin' in. He's fetchin' his sheep across that desert an' the shortest way to get them on this grass is through Three Pines." He scowled at the money he'd flung down beside the dishes.

Chesseldine nodded. "Nothing in that for us."

"You don't look disappointed enough. Kick in," Fentress scowled. "What's the rest of it?"

"Well, it looks like to me that that's about the size of it. It looks like the sheep crowd's tryin' to rub off some of Bender's rep on Lopez or—which amounts to the same thing —on his ranch. That's all he's got that I ever heard of. Figurin' they'll fight, Lasham's tryin' to use Bender to discredit 'em 'fore they get started. Then he'll call on you to keep order and allow him passage and, when you can't do it, he'll use Bender's presence as an excuse to call in the Cavalry."

Fentress chewed at his lip. "There's got to be somethin' else," he said doggedly, and Chesseldine nodded. "It just don't stand to reason," Fentress snarled, "that any tight-fisted skunk with the rep Lasham's got would be throwin' his money around like water if all he was after is a bunch of damn grass!"

Chesseldine said, "It's knowing Deef Lasham that sticks in my craw. I knew him over in Texas when he didn't have a pot and from all that I've heard he ain't changed any. There's two hundred thousand acres of Indian grass in them leases and, countin' Block 10, he didn't bid in more than half of it, probably figurin' to steal the rest. But—and this is the part I keep stumblin' over—it's the first time that bastard ever paid cash for anything! So why did he do it?"

"Let's consider what it gets him."

"No secret about that. It gets him the chance to spread his

damn sheep clean across the whole business. There ain't none of it fenced an' he'll claim he couldn't hold them."

"Sure," Fentress said, "but it gives him more reason for crossin' Tres Pinos. Just like the note he holds for that loan. With the note *and* them leases there ain't a court in the country would blame him for takin' his sheep through that ranch."

"Which brings us right back to Bender," Chesseldine grimaced. "Lasham *wanted* Bender loose. He *wanted* Blanca Lopez to spring him. He wants Bender publicly tied in with that outfit." •

"I'll buy that," Fentress nodded.

"Then it leaves us right smack out in the cold. Because, if that much is true, all Lasham's after is that grass."

"He could be after the land—"

"He's only got the land *leased*."

"I was thinkin' about Tres Pinos. . . ."

"Tres Pinos!" Chesseldine snorted. "There ain't enough grass on that spread to—"

"Maybe," Fentress scowled, "that's been our trouble. We keep thinkin' of grass but it could be somethin' else."

"Sure. A gold mine, mebbe."

But the sheriff wasn't laughing. He was staring intently into the flame of the smoky lantern, his thoughtfully narrowed eyes gone hours away from this confab. "There was a guy in the land office goin' through the records. . . ."

Chesseldine came off the bunk like a cat. He caught Fentress' shoulder, savagely shaking him. "When?"

"Couple of weeks ago. One mornin'. Early. Big sloppy jasper with a cud in one cheek an' a oversized belly—"

"My Gawd! Lasham!"

12 | ALARMS AND EXCURSIONS

Even as the jarring crash of that shot slammed against the walls and came racketing back, Bender knew with a nightmare sense of panic any chance he had left would have to hinge on split seconds.

There was no time to think, no time to do anything; yet he could not, would not, go without that paper which might be no good at all to him unless he could make Syd Hazel sign it.

Against the wall Lasham's shape was grotesque with shudders. Shock had twisted Red Hat's face and above the ghastly cheeks his eyes were wild with a murderous fury as Bender jerked him wickedly out of his chair and flung him with no care at all toward the desk. Hazel bared his teeth but, with the snout of Bender's gun staring at him, he bent over the desk and picked up Lasham's pen.

Bender tore the sixshooter out of his holster and flung it under the rumpled bed. "Down at the bottom write 'witness' and sign it."

Red Hat leaned with one hip braced against the soiled wood and, half crazed with pain, scrawled his name left-handed while shouts from below came up through the flooring and blood dripped redly into the carpet from the useless fingers of his numbed right hand.

He crouched there a moment, head canted and listening. Then, straightening, with a malicious grin he deliberately cascaded the stacked pile of currency onto the floor.

In a rage Bender struck him across the face with his pistol; but with that sound of pounding feet on the stairs he dared

249

waste no more time. Snatching up what he could he jerked open the window—there was no chance now of going back through the hall. Throwing a leg over the sill he stuffed the recovered bills into a pocket, thrust the pistol in leather and, bringing up the other leg, twisted over on his stomach.

Outside now, gripping the sill with only the tips of his fingers, he heard Lasham yell and bitterly let himself go.

There wasn't over a twelve-foot drop beneath his feet but the alley was littered with old cans and bottles. He struck hard and went over, landing flat on his back, and the force of the impact knocked all the breath out of him. Black shapes filled the window and his picture of these was laced with bright flashes and the sound of the guns was like hell with the hatch off.

Bender sprang to his feet with lead thudding all around him. He reached for his gun, thinking to drive them from the window, but the fall must have jarred it out of his holster. He took to his heels like an old cow in fly time, knowing they'd be after him now in grim earnest.

He got to the tamarisk barely in time to see Chucho, reins flying, make off into blackness.

Bender didn't have enough breath left to curse with. He saved what he had to keep himself going and plowed on through the trash with his heart pounding wildly. He had wrenched his left leg in that drop from the window and before he had reached the third building he was staggering. He had to reach a horse soon or concede he was done for; he hadn't a chance to elude a thorough search in this town and only along the lighted portions of the street would he be at all likely to get hold of a horse.

He cut down the next alley, each breath a raw agony, each new fall of his weight on that left foot sending splinters of pain jabbing through him like fire. Somehow he kept going. He came into the street, saw a tierack of horses hitched before a saloon, eyes guiding him unerringly to the best of the lot, a hammer-headed roan that had a lot of bottom to him.

He could still hear the uproar—even through the in-and-out wheeze of his breathing he could hear Lasham yelling like a prodded steer. He jerked loose the roan's reins and got a foot in the stirrup. When his hand touched the horn the damned bronc started pitching but he got aboard him anyway and wheeled him into the street. The horse got his head down, started bucking in earnest. In the midst of these gyrations Bender felt the horse wilt. He thought the hammer-headed fool was trying to fold up under him until he saw the blood spurting from the hole in its neck.

That was when he heard the rifle.

He drove in his gut hooks, felt the roan rock forward, but he knew in three strides the bronc was going to die under him and kicked his feet out of the oxbows, figuring to jump. The roan folded too quick and he went over its head.

Bender tried to land rolling but he took the full impact on the backs of his shoulders. Then his weight ground one side of his face in the dirt; his legs came down like the stick from the rocket and he caught at a sort of fuddled impression of having been over this same road before.

Dimly he heard the crazed brutes get under way, the clacking of horns, the shouting and swearing, the futile popping of cork-stopper guns as the hard-spurring hands made desperate efforts to head them. They couldn't do it, of course. He would like to have brained the fool who'd flapped that blanket. What a thunder they made as with increased tempo the wild run of those hoofs avalanched ever nearer. Like the roar of an express train crossing a trestle—and the dust! He could feel the grit of it under his teeth, the scorched stench of it seeping through the folds of his bandanna. In a kind of a panic he pushed himself over, got his head up a little and saw where he was.

He would have taken the stampede if he'd had any choice. His fall had thrown him within ten feet of the horse and tiny snakes' heads of dust were spurting up all about him, and it didn't seem possible with so much lead being thrown they hadn't shot him into doll rags.

He didn't wait for them to do it. With the front of that howling mob still twenty yards from being on top of him he rolled frantically for cover. He brought up behind the slaughtered horse and, dragging the Winchester off the saddle, he levered three slugs into the front of that bunch and saw them break like startled quail. He knocked one skinny guy flat on his kisser. Sent another doubling over like he'd caught a dose of colic. Three brace of horses at a hitchrack tore the top rail loose and went through the scattering crowd like a scythe through standing sorghum.

Bender didn't wait to see what else might happen. There were three nags still nervously fretting and pawing before the lighted windows of a place on the corner whose fresh-painted sign read TIGER LILY BAR—Jas. Bascomb, Prop.; and he stumbled to his feet, weaving drunkenly over the pot holes, desperately striving to reach those horses before they bolted.

He saw the largest go down like a poleaxed steer while he yet hadn't covered more than half the distance. Cursing, he whirled, savagely emptying the rifle, seeing one man come staggering out of a grog shop's doorway.

He let go of the useless saddle gun, shambling into a wheezing run, his wrenched leg commencing to act up again. He watched the whole middle drop out of a window—saw the place go black as those inside snuffed the lamps.

He still had a couple dozen strides to go and had just about decided which of the remaining pair he'd take when the horse of his choice went screaming up on hind legs and, with forefeet thrashing madly, fell thin-squealing over on its back. The unhit horse shied the length of its reins, snorting with terror, its eyes rolling crazily as gun-thrown lead kicked splinters off the tierail.

With a groan of despair Bender dived at the animal, was inches short of getting a hand on its cheekstrap when the soaped reins parted. The gelding's braced weight flung it back on its haunches and, before it could whirl, Bender's hand was in its mane. The frightened horse whirled anyway but Bender got one knee around the pommel and, as the bay broke into a headlong run, he clutched both arms around its neck and clung there.

The horse careened dizzily around the Tiger Lily's far corner, gathering fresh momentum with every stride it took. The guns were lost in the scream of the wind and not until the last of the lights were left behind did Bender pull himself into the saddle.

13 | THE BUSTED FLUSH

THE horse, plunging forward, had its nose pointed east and for a long five minutes after quitting the town Bender permitted it to run before reducing its speed to an easier lope designed to keep a few beans in the boiler. There was no sense at all in fooling himself; what had happened in that room had changed all the values and they would not now be saving him for anything. They'd prefer him dead, and the deader the better.

He wheeled the bay off the road, thankful there would be no moon for at least another hour. They wouldn't bother for a while with trying to pick up his tracks; they'd expect him to head south with that money and, if he went that way, they'd have him bottled between themselves and the sheriff's posse. For him to keep going east would be almost as bad for if they failed to turn him up this side of the Floridas they would guess right away that he had lined out for Crater intending to by-pass the mountains and drop south from there. Not until they still failed to find him would it occur to them he might have gotten cold feet and be trying to get out of the country. When they reached this thought they would head back to town for a look at his tracks. By then it ought to be daylight.

This should give him five hours, maybe six if he were lucky. In that length of time, swinging north to further confuse them and then bearing west to make trailing harder through the hills below Holy Cross, he should be entering

Columbus. From Columbus to Tres Pinos on a good fresh horse hadn't ought to take longer than another three hours.

Scanning these conclusions for faulty reasoning and not finding any beyond the natural complexities of human behavior, Bender pointed the gelding's nose into the north and let him break briefly into a gallop.

He wasn't underestimating Lasham. He knew very well if he fell into the sheep king's hands before morning he would be a cooked goose and no two ways about it.

The man would never feel safe so long as Bender was at large with that confession in his pocket, but by morning the sheep king's mind should be working with all its normal cunning. He would realize then he had to go at this careful. That confession in the wrong hands could get Deef Lasham lynched, and he had made too many enemies to relish taking needless chances. He wouldn't be throwing any honest law at Bender; he would send picked men that he could trust to keep their mouths shut.

But anyway, regardless of what Lasham did or did not do, Bender couldn't sidestep the knowledge that Tres Pinos had first call on him. Don Leo needed the money in Bender's pockets and there was Blanca to be thought of. Disquieting as he had found the girl—he was sure he didn't like one thing about her, including that carnal appeal to the senses—there was always the chance that Lasham, misinterpreting what she had done at the jail, would seek to reach Bender through striking at her.

Sand hummocks were lifting their gray shapes around him when he turned the horse west and pulled it down to a walk. He wasn't too happy about the gelding's action; it was much too inclined to shows of impatience to have any large amount of stamina, he thought. But he was stuck with it now and until he could get another he would have to conserve all he could of its strength.

He got to wondering how much of that money he'd come off with, and from this speculation his mind turned to Red Hat. At least he wouldn't have to be worrying about Hazel. That shattered elbow he had given the sheep boss would keep

Syd Hazel pretty well under wraps and, with him out of the running, Bender reckoned he could make it pretty goddam costly for anyone who tried to cross Tres Pinos with Lasham's sheep.

It was a comforting thought but it didn't last longer than a June frost in Texas. He was suddenly remembering that swift scratching of the pen as Hazel signed Deef Lasham's confession. It had been a natural thing, instinctive and without trouble, for the burly sheep boss to scrawl his name left-handed.

Bender cursed with a whole-hearted bitterness. The man was a southpaw! Instead of putting Syd Hazel on the sidelines for keeps that busted right arm was like to get Bender's neck broke. Nothing loomed surer than that Red Hat wouldn't rest until he'd evened the score plumb complete with compound interest.

FAR to the southeast the lights of Deming still showed faintly when Bender, anxious to get into the hills, finally turned the bay south. By this time, near as he was able to figure, Lasham's crew of drunks and barflies should have met up with Fentress' posse, discovered the fugitive hadn't cut south, and be lining out for Crater.

The terrain commenced to get more broken up. The greasewood thinned, there was a lot more yucca and the grass came in tufts, poking out of the drifts like fringe round the sides of a bald man's skull. For the last three-four miles he'd been traveling in cycles; walk awhile, jog awhile, strike a high gallop. They were in the walk now with the ground rising under them and everything someway seeming plainer than before. Abruptly jerking up his head Bender found suspicion verified. Beyond a black peak less than five miles distant, round and orange and very large, the moon was making its appearance.

He came out of his thinking, hauling the bay up sharply, with a faint impression of dust in his nostrils. For an unconscionable time he sat motionless, listening, but unable to catch any rumor of riders; and finally, snorting disgustedly, he relaxed his grip, the gelding resuming its head-nodding advance. *Getting jumpy,* Bender thought, not liking the notion.

A hundred yards later the bay dropped into a wash. This was a broad one, deep sided, more than sixty feet across with a thick growth of brush along the west rim where its course swung east around a ledge of uncovered sandstone. It was darker down here, the dry bottom glimmering with its myriad of mica.

Half way across this floor he smelled dust again and, this time, there wasn't any doubt of it. Riders had passed this way within minutes and a couple strides later he came onto their tracks. They were heading upstream, going south and going without sign of any obvious hurry. If they'd been traveling in the open he would have written them off for punchers ranchward bound from an evening in Holy Cross. As it was, they might be rustlers on their way to lift somebody's cattle.

With lips squeezed together he put the bay into motion, urging the animal toward the opposite bank.

He was on the way up when he heard them coming. One moment the wash loomed completely empty, in the next three riders suddenly bulged into sight.

Bender kept the bay climbing, looking over his shoulder. It didn't take those fellows very long to spot him. The one in the center yelled: "That you, Sim?"

Bender, not stopping, threw a grunt back for answer and the man called irritably, "Where the hell is that barber?"

Not risking an answer Bender flung a hand northward, but just as the bay got into the brush one of the men down below snarled, "That ain't Sim!" and Bender kicked in the hooks.

He heard the thin whine, the double crash of two rifles, and flung himself forward to get his shape off the skyline. He heard yells on both sides and before he could swerve, the bay with the bit in its teeth was rocketing full tilt into a group of stopped horsebackers.

Bender heard a scared curse. He saw the pale shrinking blobs of startled uptilted faces and kicked both booted feet free of the stirrups. The bunch tried to scatter but he was too soon into them, the bay careening headlong into a red dun's middle. Bender left its back in a flying tackle. One out-flung arm wrapped round a beard-framed face and, like blown chaff, this man was swept from the saddle. He commenced a frightened squawk but the ground thumped it out of him. Bender rolled clear, the squawker's gun in one fist, the squawker's reins in the other.

He triggered three shots into that milling confusion; through the shouts and yells he drove one more and watched a man spill backward off the rump of a rearing pinto. Flinging himself into the captured gray's saddle, Bender emptied the pistol and spurred into the brush.

This was the same stretch of brush he had so recently come out of, the brush that concealed the west rim's ragged lip. Breathing hard, Bender braced both feet in the stirrups and pulled the horse to a stop with its still skidding hoofs barely inches from the brink. In one blurred motion he was out of the saddle. In the next he had the stallion turned completely around and, crouching low, reached up and got a grip on its nostrils. The horse tried to shake loose but, using his grip like a twitch, Bender forced the big brute into a stance of utter quiet.

There wasn't one chance in ten this play could have fooled any man who had his wits about him. Bender was staking his life on the belief this bunch was too muddle-minded to know straight up from down—and he was right.

A guy with a bull-throated voice was bellowing, "After him, you pinheaded nitwits!"

"Where the hell did he go?"

"He went down in that wash—"

"Not while we was there," the one who'd yelled at Sim said. "We just come outa that wash an'—"

"That's when he done it. Just as you was comin' up. I seen his hat drop outa sight off't the right of that stunted cedar."

"Yeah," another voice backed this one up. "He was on Treeny's gray an' he was sure as hell headin' south—"

"He was headed *north!* He turned on the lip; I seen his shoulders comin' round—"

"You goddam fools," shouted Bull Throat, "git down there after him 'fore we lose him!"

"I don't see *you* bustin' your pants out t' git there!"

"What's Fentress want him for, anyway?" asked another; but nobody answered him.

Bull Throat said, "Dave you take three of these boys an' cut north up that wash. You take the other pair, Curly, an' cut south."

"An' what'll *you* be doin', Mister Godlemighty Jones?"

"I'll stay right where I'm at in case he tries to double back."

"That's a damn thoughty notion," one of the others pronounced approvingly. "Mebbe I better stay with you. Just in case you ain't able to stop him."

"Hell—come on," some one else growled disgustedly. "That feller's prob'ly halfway to Mexico by this time—or Canada."

Bender heard horses moving, the creak of leather, the tinkle of spur chains. Treeny's gray was getting tired of this and so, for that matter, was Bender's hand, not to mention the rest of his still-crouched anatomy. Time, that so precious commodity, was passing and the moon, cheese yellow, was getting higher and brighter.

Now the sound of breaking brush lifted two diverging lines of clatter. Bender longed, so covered, to let go of the stallion and reload Treeny's pistol but he knew, if he did, the damned horse would betray him.

There was the cold feel of sweat along the back of his neck and a mounting rage was burning away the controls of his caution as it became increasingly evident his inspired ingenuity was about to leave him in a first class jackpot.

Had he kept on going when he'd first wrapped his legs about the quivering gray he would have gotten clean away from this procrastinating outfit. Trying to play it smart had handicapped him intolerably and in another few moments they'd have him glued to this brush like a fly to gummed paper. Already that moon was too bright for his liking and if he clung to this place much longer and these birds ever got spread out on three sides of him . . .

He brought his back out of its cramp a little, minded to run for it while he still had a chance. Neither part of the split posse had yet got quite abreast of him and, with surprise in his favor, he could probably get into the wash. He had a terrible urge to make the try and only his remembrance of the thing restrained him. Common sense told him he could never get across sixty feet of deep sand fast enough to beat the bullets this pack would be sending after him.

He tightened his hold on the gray while he listened to the sound of the southmost group file past. While its noise was still close, their horses slithering down the bank, he pulled the stallion deeper into the concealment of dusty foliage, his idea being to get away from the edge where there was now too much chance of the horse being spotted by the men who'd just passed him.

He made the shift without discovery but the dust shaking down off the bushes almost strangled him. He had to fight for every breath and, to aggravate him further, the horse started pawing up a fresh cloud off the ground. Bender had to lean against the gray to keep it enough off balance to stop this.

"Hey, Treeny!" came an E-string whine from the wash. "That guy never come down here. Only tracks we kin find's our own. Outside of the ones he left goin' over."

"Hell, we seen him. Look again."

"We already hev."

"Then hunt his sign along the bank."

"We done that, too. I tell you that ranny's pulled a fast one someway. If you're wantin' *my* notion he never come outa that brush."

The dust got the best of him and Walt Bender sneezed.

14 | "START MAKIN' TRACKS!"

BENDER froze against the horse as stiff as any startled posseman, hardly daring even to breathe in the intensified ear-ringing silence. He felt like something chained in a vacuum until the fed-up gray tried to kick him. In his angered excitement Bender gave the brute too hard a shove and the off-balance horse fell into the brush like a wagonload of bricks dumped against a tin siding.

For an outraged instant Bender hung on the edge of braining the beast; then he heard Treeny's yell and shouts from the wash intermingled with hoofbeats tore through the petrified chaos of his emotions and, with a snarled curse, Bender sheathed the emptied pistol. He kicked the horse to his feet, slammed into the saddle and raked the gray's sides with the spiked wheels of his spurs.

The stallion took off like something hurled from a catapult. A pair of rifles cracked viciously from Treeny's position, flame licking pallidly across the bright moonlight, and then the big gray was out in the open, streaking south like the haze funneled up in a twister. He struck another patch of brush and ripped his way through it like a mill saw going through a twenty-foot plank. He had speed to burn and Bender used it, the sounds of the posse falling rapidly away in a fading whisper that was soon gone entirely, swallowed up in the night.

He was five miles into the tumbled hills when Bender caught the first rumor of another rider. The gray had latched onto its second wind and was running smoothly through the blues and silvers of the shadow-dappled range. Ahead in the distance, perhaps four hundred yards, there was a black stand of pine darkening the brow of a ridge, and Bender sent the gray toward this without slackening its gait.

They went into these fast, then Bender's knees slowed the horse and swung it left at right angles, holding it down to a lope as they paralleled the ridge just inside the belt of trees. In this direction the pines extended their cover a quarter mile and, just before they hit the open, Bender pulled the stallion up. He could hear the other's hoofbeats coming on at a pushing pace, reaching down from the north over ground the gray had covered.

He sat quiet, grimly listening, knowing his own dust wake must be guiding this unseen rider. Unquestionably this fellow was one of that left-behind posse, a man with a mount fully as good as his own; and with his lips pulled back off his teeth Bender lifted the Winchester from beneath his stirrup fender.

He got down and, tying the gray, sank onto a knee where he could watch the bright ridgeside and, almost at once, he saw the rider streak out of a fold in the hills and pound toward the place where he'd come into the trees.

Too far for good rifle range. Bender, knowing this, lowered the Winchester and got to his feet. No sense in warning him. Better to let him go and ride his wake or, better still, cut farther east and thus avoid any chance of an ambush. Any man who could track another by smell would be too canny to go far after losing the scent.

Then, just as he was about to go back to the gray, Bender saw the rider, now partway up the slope, pull his horse to a stop and twist his head this way and that. He looked like a puzzled dog sniffing air and, sure enough, after a moment he started cutting for sign. You could tell when he found it by the sharp way he stopped and sat there studying the trees.

This guy was too smart to have been with that posse. Bender's dodge in the brush wouldn't have fooled him a moment. Bender hadn't any notion of who he was, nor did he give a damn. This bird was too slick to do any messing around with.

He watched the man ease his horse into motion again, abruptly turn it east in a track paralleling the line of trees.

The fellow was too wary to come into these pines; he was going to skirt their edges and cut Bender's sign beyond them. If Bender let him.

Bender had no intention of letting him. Estimating by present progress the point at which horse and rider would pass nearest and, allowing for elevation, Bender again raised the rifle and, with narrowed eyes, waited. A hundred yards was duck soup with a saddle gun but, just as the man was about to ride into Bender's sights, something frightened him. He yanked the dun's head around, spurring him savagely. Bender knocked the horse sprawling before he'd taken three jumps.

HE rode into Columbus an hour after sunrise.

He took the big gray to a livery. He turned him over to the hostler with explicit instructions concerning bed and board. They went out and looked over what the guy had for sale, Bender finally parting with forty dollars for a mouse-colored gelding with one gotched ear. The animal had no real claim to beauty but at least it looked reasonably durable.

With the gray's gear hung up and with a secondhand rig on Don Quixote, Bender moved into the shine of the sun. He racked at a hash house where he treated himself to ham, eggs and coffee, battening this down with two slabs of apple pie. After which he once again climbed aboard his mouse-colored hack and struck out for the West Potrillos.

THE trip took four hours of damned weary riding.

He knew as soon as he sighted the house he wasn't going to be getting any sleep just yet. A strange horse was standing on dropped reins by the gallery and, at the far end of it, a number of *peones* with their straw hats in their hands were staring open-mouthed at a gesticulating *gringo* who appeared to think shouting was the key to translation. He didn't look to be making much headway but with a contemptuous flap of the hands he dismissed them, gave his gun belt a hitch, and went into the house.

Bender had no need to catch the flash of his shirt-front to know he had been looking at Cash Fentress, the sheriff. He had recognized the man about as soon as he had seen him. He let the *grulla* stop and sat awhile considering. Fentress obviously hadn't seen him. He could still back away and hang around out of sight until Lasham's bought law had departed.

He could, but he knew mighty well that he wouldn't for he never had been able to convince himself there was any real profit in postponing the inevitable.

Arrived at the gallery he stepped off his horse. Inside he could hear Fentress laying the law down. By his tell of it Don Leo was not only consorting with criminals but had actually gone so far as deliberately to employ one.

If the old man was in there he was keeping his mouth shut, something few Texans would have had the wit to do.

"Furthermore," Fentress snarled, "so long as there's a plaster on this haywire outfit, I don't wanta hear of you sellin' off any of them cattle—savvy? You tell them tamale-eatin' never-sweats of yourn to scatter that herd an' *leave* it scattered!"

Bender loosened the reloaded pistol in his holster, quietly crossed the gallery and stepped through the open door.

He saw the girl's lifted chin. He saw her father's frozen features and, over across the room, he saw the Three Pines ramrod intently engrossing himself with a hangnail.

Blanca was saying stiffly: "What we do with our cattle can be no concern of yours."

"I can damn well make it my concern," the sheriff snapped. Then his tone simmered down and a kind of leer crept into it. "I reckon you'd find me reasonable if you'd exert yourself a little."

Don Leo got angrily out of his chair but Blanca said with a deal of composure, "I suppose you mean if I would go to bed with you."

"Well, I wasn't figurin' to put it that plain—"

"You don't need to. I won't. I wouldn't wipe my feet on a *gringo* whore's son who would use his badge to steal a girl's virginity."

The sheriff's neck turned red. "You'll come beggin' for the chance to be nice to me, sister, before I git done with this damn greaser outfit! I ain't forgot you busted that crook outa jail an' for two cents, by Gawd, I'd—"

The sheriff's wind whistled out, his wide-eyed stare gone incredulously down to the pair of bright pennies which had just struck the floor within inches of his boots. These had come from behind him and Fentress, blanching, settled into his tracks like a squatting duck.

The girl's scathing laugh fetched his rage back, cheeks livid, spun him round like a cat and sent his hand slapping hipward. His muscles jammed, locked solid, as the spread fingers curled about the handle of his pistol, clamped there immovable, frozen by the fear of what he read in Bender's gaze.

"Don't drag that iron unless you're figurin' to use it!"

The sheriff stood rock still while the visible strain dug gaunter lines beneath his cheekbones. Some bitter thought laid its murderous track across the stare that couldn't quite conceal the sheriff's frightened indecision and, resorting to bluster, he caught his breath in a snarl. "You're under arrest! Hear me? Git your goddam hands up!"

"For what?" Bender said.

"For assault, for battery, for armed robbery and coercion, forced entry, breakin' jail, disturbin' the peace an' for the willful abduction of Jake Paintor's bay geldin'—"

Bender laughed in his face.

"You better come," the lawman spluttered. "You better not make your case no worse than it is. You got the best of me by a trick but don't think tricks'll git you out of this. There's a bunch of hard-ridin' posses combin' the brush for you right now an' if you ever expect to git to trial you better come with me an' you better come peaceful. I'll do what I—"

"Come up for air," Bender said derisively.

"There's a law in this land!" Fentress shouted; and Bender's eyes turned black with hate. He caught the sheriff by the slack of his shirt and hauled him forward with a savage tug, tripping him over an out-thrust boot. When the squawking putty-faced lawman stumbled Bender fastened a second savage hold on his belt and, carrying him that way, stepped through the door and heaved him into the hoof-tracked dust.

"Three Pines don't need your kind of law. If you ever show up on this ranch again I'll make it my business to see you're planted here permanent. Now get onto your hind legs and start makin' tracks!"

15 | POINT AND COUNTERPOINT

BENDER, rubbing his palms on the legs of his levis, came into the room and pinned a hard glance on the face of Gonzales.

"There's only one way to handle skunks, Pedrocito."

The foreman's look turned sullen with hatred. He got out of his chair with a desperate lunge when he saw the big Texan commence to start toward him. One fist dived into his sash and got hung there when Bender's iron grip flung him into the wall. "Is this the way you watch out for those cattle?"

He shoved the man roughly in the direction of the doorway, anger deepening the angles of his cheeks, eyes winter bright with an unforgiving fury. "When you ran this spread you did as you pleased. *I'm* running it now and you'll do what I say or I'll break every bone in your white-livered carcass. Now get out on that range and stay with that stock till you've got a buyer's check in your pocket—go on! Clear out of here now before I lose my temper."

There was no talk in the room until Gonzales' steps faded. The old man sat wrapped in a dismal kind of quiet and the girl's face was marble with no expression on it.

Then her head came around. Her glance locked with Bender's and he could read in her eyes the veiled disgust and suspicion his proximity seemed always to arouse in her. From the very first, even when she'd been working hardest to enlist his aid in behalf of Tres Pinos, antagonism had been the keynote of their relations. Flint against steel.

Bender's mouth corners tightened.

"I approved," she said, "the way you handled Cash Fentress, but you didn't waste very much thought on Gonzales—"

"He got all he had coming."

"That's a sample of your attitude. The ranch should come first no matter what you think of him—"

"I put the ranch first."

"You took a poor way of showing it. The man was following your orders. He put two men at the shack, he put the rest with the cattle. He rode in this morning to see about that poison—"

"Nobody asked him to see about that poison!"

They glared at each other, hate in both their faces. Blanca drew in her breath and let it out again carefully. "The man represents a vital portion of our resources—surely you can see that? With a little more tact you might have managed to retain his tolerance. Now he'll hate you—"

"I can stand it," Bender said.

"But the point you seem to have overlooked completely is that this hatred for you may undermine his whole outlook. His loyalty."

"That would be too bad—for Pete," Bender grunted. The heat of his anger still rode through his glance and the rage smouldering in him stared uncaringly out of it. "You hired me to save this ranch from Lasham's sheep. If you'll keep out of my hair long enough I may do it."

"I'm not sure," Blanca said, "that I care for your methods."

"They at least have the merit of getting results." He dug the roll of bills out of his pocket, clanked across the room and dropped it into Don Leo's lap. "Count out your forty-five hundred. If there's anything over it belongs to me."

The old man stared at the bills he was holding. It seemed to take a long time for their significance to reach him. Bender saw incredulous hope break through the gray mask of the rancher's indifference. His jaw started quivering. When he finally commenced to thumb through them he had to stop twice to still the shaking of his hands.

Bender grinned, feeling good, and went back to face Blanca, not expecting any thanks but certainly not prepared for the smile of cold scorn which flattened the lips across her teeth.

"Only an optimist, I suppose," she said, "could have expected anything different from a gun-hung drifter picked up off the desert."

"What's the matter?" he scowled. "I got what I went after —I got your dough back, didn't I?"

"But those lease lands are gone—of what good is this money? You stupid fool!" she cried bitterly. "Why didn't you fetch back the note we gave for it?"

A FAR piece of Bender's mind heard the old man get up and move across to the table. "Fifty-three hundred eighty dollars," he chuckled. *Dinero mucho.* The Blessed Virgin be praised. There will be no need to dispose of my cattle, no need to put that accursed poison . . . eh?"

Bender could feel Don Leo's puzzled stare, could sense the rancher's shrug. *"No le hace*—I will leave your money on this table, *amigo."*

The old man's boots tapped their heels toward the patio. Bender looked at Blanca while the stillness piled up and got quieter than silence and his thoughts tramped around the inescapable truth.

She was right. He had been seven kinds of a nitwitted nump to go risking his neck getting hold of that money when he might just as easily have demanded the note. He'd been ramming around like a chicken with its head off, and to about as much purpose. He'd got the money all right but, so far as the girl was concerned, all he had accomplished was to cut the cards back to where they'd been in the first place. A hell's smear of motion but no tangible results. Lasham still had the note. Tres Pinos was still mortgaged.

"When's that borrowed money due?"

"On the tenth. Twelve o'clock noon."

Seven days. One week. Around a hundred and sixty hours,

more or less. Bender scowled at his knuckles. With the money on hand that seemed like plenty of time to get the slate rubbed clean. And ordinarily it would be. Only he knew damned well they'd never get that note paid off so long as Lasham could prevent it. He would move heaven and earth to keep that note unpaid and, if it didn't get paid, he was going to move in here come hell or high water. A couple of hundred dead sheep weren't going to hold him back.

Blanca said with her eyes still hating him, "What have you got in mind to do next?—if I'm permitted to share your confidence."

"We've got to have more men."

"You've got thirteen now—"

"You can't run this ranch, move those cattle, hold off the sheep and get that money to Lasham with thirteen men! Out of the question."

"You'll be able to. Just put that magnificent brain to work—"

Bender scowled angrily. "If we're to save this spread we've got to all pull together—"

"You should have thought of that when you were bullying Pete."

All the unnatural restraints which Bender had been forcibly imposing on himself commenced to tear loose in a rush of fury. He caught hold of her wrist and they glared at each other in a fast-breathing silence. Cheeks white, she struggled to break his hold and, goaded anew by the look on her face, he took a perverse delight in piling on pressure until she suddenly cried out and then, ashamed, he let her go.

She got back away from him, rubbing her wrist, her eyes looking wild as a cougar's. "If you ever try that again I will kill you."

"Yeah? With kindness, I reckon!" Bender laughed without humor and strode into the patio.

Don Leo stood by the barrel with a little jar of insects he had captured among the shrubs. As Bender came up he could hear the old man clucking. Even a kid in three-cornered pants, he thought angrily, would have better judgment than to coddle a goddam snake—particularly one for whose bite there was no known antidote.

He said without preamble: "We've got to have more men. You know where I can get them?"

"Los bravos?"

"Men who know how to use a gun anyway. This is going to get rough and—"

"There are such men in Deming but with what would we pay them? All the money I have is that which you just gave me."

Bender chewed at his lip.

"What is it that you have in your mind, *amigo?* Perhaps my good friend Cuerna Vaca, at Tularosa—"

Bender shook his head. "We can't wait that long. What about these *peones,* these *mozos* you've got lollin' around?"

Don Leo smiled sadly. "They are as children, *senor*—"

"They can pull a trigger, can't they?"

"What would you wish them to do?"

"We've got to finish that roundup, get the herd off to market. You've got just seven days to pay off that note; we've got to spread that poison and we've got to have men ready to stand off those sheep—"

"But what need have we now to dispose of my cattle? Surely—"

"Need!" Bender shouted. "My God, Leo, do you honestly believe that wool-lovin' vinegarroon is going to throw in his hand just because we've got that money back? He'll hit you with everything he can get hold of!"

"But the cattle . . . I don't see—"

"Look," Bender growled. "He's comin' up from the desert. The only way he can get into Tres Pinos is by the trail that comes up past that shack on the bluffs, so between here and there is where we dump that poison. You don't want your cattle eatin' strychnine, do you?

"Now, to give him a legal excuse to go through here, he's got to be able to show he owns a chunk of this outfit; that's why he made you that loan on a short-term note an' got you to put up this spread for security. He's goin' to try to go through anyway, but if you pay off the note he won't have the courts back of him. Obviously then he's going to do all he can to make sure you can't pay it. One thing he can do is keep out of your way. While you're rampin' around with that money tryin' to find him you'll be a first-class target for robbery, won't you? Same way with those cattle—they represent a cash asset. Try to keep them here and he'll set Chesseldine onto 'em; try movin' them out an' Chesseldine's gang will make a play to stampede them. To fight that bunch off, whether we hold them here or move 'em, we're going to need every damn one of your cowboys. While they're engaged with the cattle Lasham brings in the sheep. Now do you see why we need more men?"

Time's furrows showed plainly in Don Leo's cheeks. He stared haggardly at Bender. "We have no chance at all?"

"We've got a chance, a mighty slim one. But I've got to have more men. We've got to use these *mozos;* I'd like to hire a few leather slappers—the hell of it is we haven't got much time."

They stared at each other. The old man said with touching faith, "I put myself in your hands. Tell me what I can do."

"You can organize these *mozos.* Give every man a rifle. Put a couple of them to work with a wagon shovelin' strychnine. Take the rest of them down to that shack on the bluffs and make a big show of guardin' that trail. You better stay right with them; that way, maybe, they won't break and run before we're ready to take over with our big artillery. Once Lasham understands you're intending to use force he'll probably sit tight until that note falls due. This much I'm sure of—his Yaquis won't move without he gives them the nod."

He was about to set off for the stables, intending if he could to catch Gonzales before he left and revise his instructions with regard to the roundup, when the old man hesitantly reached out a hand. "What do you think I should do about that money?"

Bender swung around. His eyes looked worried, undecided. "That's as tough a nut as we've got to crack. Anything you try is going to be damn risky." He glowered at the knuckles

of his left hand a moment. "Tell you what," he said finally—
"if you want to trust me to take care of it I'll see what I
can do."

Don Leo, obviously happier, thrust the money into his hand.

Bender stuffed it carelessly into a pocket. "You camp out
on that bluff until you see me again."

He went back through the house, caught up the reins of
his *grulla* and got into the saddle. About to line out for the
scene of the roundup he decided, inasmuch as he could not
hire any men short of one of the towns, to catch up a fresh
mount and turned, instead, toward the stables.

Going around the huge house he turned Don Quixote toward the gate which led into the *parada*. Engrossed with his
problems he'd put the gelding through the gate before the
sound of the girl's voice fully jerked him out of his thinking.
A saddled horse on dropped reins dozed not ten feet in front
of him and beyond its sorrel bulk Blanca was talking to
Gonzales who had not, it would seem, been in any great sweat
to get back to the cattle.

Bender's knees involuntarily put a brake on the *grulla*, but
he would have gone on immediately to apprise the foreman of
his latest intentions had the girl not said, "But that's silly—
you should know me better than to believe anything so stupid.
You *can't* quit us now!"

"I will not work for this pig of a *gringo*," Gonzales said
furiously. "Do you think I have no pride at all?"

"Would you let your pride—"

"It is not only that! I have seen the way you look at this
fellow—"

"Tres Pinos needs his gun and his experience. He knows
these people as we could never hope to know them; he has a
feud with this Lasham—"

"Do not tell me these lies. They have nothing to do with
the way you look at him. *Sangre de Cristo*—do you think I
am a fool?"

"You are beginning to convince me," she said coldly. Then,

softening: "How can you be so blind, Pedrocito? For this man I care nothing—"

"Is that why you let him put his mouth on your mouth?"

"Are you now to become my *duenna* also?"

"Por Dios, you need one," Gonzales growled huskily. Gravel grated harshly beneath the twist of a boot. Their shadows merged, clung and broke apart.

"There," she said with a breathless laugh. "Can you believe me now? Ah, *pobrecito,* do not look so fierce. That Yankee gossoon is but a means to an end, a thing to be used, fire against fire for the good of the *rancho*—"

"Querida . . . I love you so much I could kill you . . ."

Tight-lipped, Bender kneed his horse forward. Swinging into their orbit he got out of the saddle, tossed his reins at the girl and said to Gonzales, "How long will it take you to get the herd ready?"

Gonzales' eyes were suspicious. He growled sullenly in Spanish, "Perhaps three more days."

"Make it two. Add three more for the road and you should have it in Columbus this side of nightfall Thursday—"

"Columbus! I thought you meant to sell it in Deming—"

"Those plans have been changed. You'll take it to Columbus and keep your eyes skinned every step of the way. You'll have trouble with Chesseldine so, to make sure you get through, you will take the whole crew—"

"Then what of the ranch? What about those sheep?"

"We'll worry about that when they get here. Your job's the cattle. You have them in Columbus before the sun sets Thursday. I'll have a buyer waiting to take delivery at the stock yards."

AFTER the foreman had gone Blanca, realizing she held Bender's reins, threw them down. Her eyes looked as though she were going to curse him. "I'm not your *moza,*" she said on an indignant outrush of breath. "I understood from the first you were a mannerless barbarian, but I did not think you would stoop to plain spying."

Bender's ears grew hot under her scornful regard and the

knowledge that he was flushing was fresh fuel to his anger. "At least a Yankee gossoon would have more regard for the conventions than to let a half-breed paw—"

She struck him across the face, her eyes blazing.

Bender sneered. "I'm surprised, being a spik, you didn't go for a knife."

She said with biting contempt: "No matter how low a *gringo* gets he is always able to see himself as being infinitely better than—"

"You're goddam right! Your ol' man can see it, too! Why else would he have sent you to a *gringo* school an' be all the time aping us every way he knows how? He's got more sense than you'll ever have!"

Cold scorn bared her teeth and he said, determined to hurt her, "Bet you'd never catch *him* ruttin' around in a stableyard with—"

She did have a knife after all, he discovered. With a flash of white leg she tore it out of her garter. The wicked glitter of that blade was no less savage than her look. She sprang at him in a rush that came within an ace of skewering him.

He leaped back in quick alarm but she was after him like a wildcat. She seemed everywhere at once and that damned blade was like a snake's tongue. Three times it ticked him, slicing cloth, and it was all he could do to keep his legs under him as he went reeling backward, twisting and swerving in his desperate attempts to keep himself clear.

He began to sweat. He began to wonder if he was going to outlast it, tired as he was with all those hours in the saddle. He tried to grab her wrist and lost part of a shirtsleeve. Goose-flesh traveled up his spine like prickly heat as he threw himself aside, barely avoiding the jump of that blade again.

He was fighting for breath now. His legs felt like lead, and the left one he'd wrenched in that drop from the window wasn't going to be able to take much more of this. He made a swift feint and thrust a boot out to trip her but those kill-crazy eyes of hers took her around it with the grace of a boxer and he saw the shimmering gleam of that naked steel leap straight for his throat.

Too late to dodge he flung his right arm up. Pain ripped from wrist all the way to his elbow and, when he saw that welling pattern of blood, all else blurred away in a white blaze of anger.

Blanca's eyes, grown enormous, were suddenly pools of frightened horror, but Bender never noticed. All he saw was her shape through a red fog of fury as he turned on his heel and swung into the saddle.

16 | A MERCHANT IN GUNSMOKE

THE urge to smash his fists into something was almost beyond his power of containing when Bender whirled the tired horse through the gate and lifted it into a headlong run. His thoughts were a welter of conflicting emotions with Blanca holding the top spot as a target—it was God's own mercy he hadn't knocked her damn teeth out! Bad enough at a time like this to be cursed with the pain of a twisted ligament as well as half groggy from lack of rest without having his gun arm put out of commission.

Still keeping the *grulla* to a ground-eating gallop he unknotted the scarf from about his neck, gave it a couple of left-handed shakes and awkwardly wound it about his cut arm. Probably lousy with germs but he had to do something to get the blood stopped. He pressed the arm to his side and kept riding. There was an all-gone feeling squirming around through his guts by the time he came in sight of the shack but he forgot all about it in his rage at not finding any guards on the job.

He saw a pair of hitched horses dozing back of the lean-to and found the pair of *vaqueros* squatted down on the porch engaged in some kind of Mexican card game.

Bender scattered the cards hell west and crooked. Both men jumped up, their faces ludicrous with fright. Bender grabbed one fellow and spun him clear around. Snatched up a rifle. Shoved it into his hands. "Now get down in that brush along the edge of the bluff an' do what you been told to do! As for you," he said to the other one, "get the gear off this horse and put it on the best of that pair out back."

He went into the shack, stripping off his shirt. In the frame of mind he'd been in leaving Blanca he'd forgotten his intention of getting a fresh horse, but one of these would do well enough. He went over to the sink, dippering himself a cold drink from the bucket of well water standing there. Then, very gingerly, he peeled off the stuck neckerchief and swished his arm around in the bucket. Damn water stung but it got some of the caked blood off. He poked around in a cupboard, got hold of a bottle marked *oil of salt*, twisted off the cap and liberally dosed the again-bleeding gash.

He stuck his head out the door and called in the man he'd put to work with the horses. "Cut the back out of these red flannels," he told him, and when the fellow, with sundry mutterings, had done so, he had the man rip the cloth into strips and bind his arm. Then he picked up his shirt and threw it down in disgust. "I'm goin' to have to have yours. Climb out of it," he growled.

The man's look, which had been curious, now reshaped in sullen resentment but he didn't put any of that feeling into words. Bender got into the shirt. It was a kind of tight fit but it covered that wrapped-up arm, which was the main thing. He said to the scowling *vaquero*, "Until the *patron* comes you're the boss. Keep your eyes skinned."

HE was ten miles along the rutted trail to Columbus before he encountered any sign of another horseman. He was into a canyon by that time and the afternoon sun was well along toward the west. There had once been a rough kind of wagon road through here but now the tracks were almost hidden in weeds and to the right of this lane the solid trunks of pines rose tall and straight; the cut-over left side was a tangle of scrubby brush and live oak.

He was just coming off the crest of a rise, jogging along at an easy rack, when cowbirds wheeled up out of the brush and went winging off soundless toward the shadow-draped crags that rimmed the canyon's left wall. Bender kept his shape flexible but his eyes turned sharp and he was not surprised when a rider came out of the trees and pulled up, hooking one knee about the horn of his saddle.

"Spare the makin's?" he asked when Bender got near enough.

"Swap for a match." Bender tossed him his Durham which he'd thoughtfully removed from the shirt left behind.

While the man rolled his smoke they considered each other. Tile-green eyes stared at Bender around the bulge of a nose that had once been broken and very carelessly set. His ears were large and cupped forward like shelves built on to rest the brim of his battered old hat; this hard-used appearance extending clear down to the run-over heels of his brush-clawed boots. His teeth made a shine when he licked his cigarette, but his eyes stayed on Bender even when he bent to touch a match to his smoke.

He passed back the sack along with a couple of matches, glance drifting lightly over Bender's right arm. "Any jobs floatin' round through your part of the country?"

"Depends what you mean by jobs," Bender said.

"I wasn't lookin' for hard work."

"A little gun work, maybe?"

"I wouldn't turn it down if you'd get the price fed up enough."

Bender, needing gun hands, had the notion this fellow might be champing on the bit. He wouldn't put it above Deef Lasham to have steered a stake-out at them. He looked the man over coolly. "My name's Bender—Walt Bender."

Bat Ears nodded his round face indifferently. "Yeah. I'm Butch Stroad." He licked a pale tongue across tobacco-stained teeth. "Heard you was runnin' the Three Pines outfit—matter of fact, I was on my way over there. Kinda figured you might be toppin' the market."

"You've got your rope twisted, Butch."

"I could shake out the kinks."

"Three Pines don't run to that kind of jack."

"Looks to me like neck meat or nothin'. An' like to be nothin' if they don't git a move on."

"Yeah," Bender said, trying to think where he had seen this fellow before. He wasn't sure he had but there seemed something—

"I don't like sheep, either."

Bender shook his head. "They're scrapin' the bottom."

"Two hundred would get my name on the payroll."

"Two hundred on top of what you're drawin' from Lasham?"

Stroad showed his sour grin. "You gotta take some kinda chance in this world. That two hundred only keeps me a week but, the way I got this thing doped out, that oughta be long as you'll have any use fer me."

"Got it all down pat, eh?"

"I got enough to git on with," Stroad said, looking cagey. "I was outside the warehouse when the star lugged you off. I was back of the jail when you went off with the skirt an' I was in the Aces Up when you an' Red Hat pitched the table."

"So now you want a job?"

"You oughta be in line fer all the help you kin locate."

"You got plenty of gall, I'll say that for you."

"Stock in trade. I'm a businessman, Bender. I know without askin' Lasham wouldn't pay two hundred."

"There's a limit to what a man can know and stay healthy."

"So I been told." Stroad stubbed out his smoke on the heel of a palm, showing his yellow teeth in another tough grin. "You buyin' or ain't you?"

"Got a pencil on you?"

"It's cash on the barrelhead, Jack. With a poor risk like you I can't afford to take chances—"

"You'll get an order on Don Leo, the owner of Tres Pinos."

"Collectable when?"

"When you get to the ranch. Providin' you don't make any detours or any changes in the note."

Stroad dug up a pencil, tore a page from a dog-eared notebook, and handed them over. Bender scribbled the note and gave it to him. "Until I get back you'll stay with the crew we've got out watchin' for the sheep."

17 | OVERTURE TO
VIOLENCE

THOSE who weren't already eating were about to get ready to when Bender reached Columbus a couple of hours later. His arm was beginning to hurt like hell and, what was more disconcerting mentally, it was becoming a chore to move it. A fine shape to be in if he should run into trouble.

The nose bag could wait. He headed straight for the livery.

"Come after your nag?" the old hostler greeted.

"Right at this moment I'd like to find me a sawbones."

"Doc Slink's got a office up over the bank. Hurt yourself, did you?"

"Scratched my arm on some barb wire. You want to do something for me? Go over to the mercantile and get me a shirt and put this horse out of sight till I get back."

The doc was just about to go out for his supper. He clucked when he saw the look of Bender's arm. "Oil of salt," he snorted. "Well, you might have done worse." He cleansed the wound, swabbed medicine on it and was making ready to apply a heavy dressing when Bender said, "Somethin' flexible, Doc—"

"Now see here," said Slink sternly; "if you want that arm to get well you're going to have to take care of it."

Bender grinned without much mirth. "A guy that's as close

to the furniture as I am ain't going to be worried about no damn arm. What's more, I probably—wait a minute."

Bender chewed his lip, thinking. A derringer covered by two splints in bandage . . . but the doc would never go for it. "Oh, well," he growled, "go ahead. Wrap it up. But keep it as thin round the wrist as you can."

The doc's eyes narrowed. "Somebody gunning for you?"

"It could happen."

"I'd suggest, in that case, you keep under cover. This arm's in no condition for that kind of exercise."

Back at the livery the hostler handed him a parcel. "Only thing he had that looked big enough to fit you. Cost me—"

"Put it on the bill," Bender said, tearing open the paper. He pulled off the one he'd confiscated from the shack guard. "Who's buyin' cattle?"

"Your best bet's to wait till Bart Spurlock gits in—"

"I want to get shut of this herd in a hurry."

The old man's eyes widened. He took a good look around and lowered his voice. "Art Chesseldine's your man, then. Him or old Krantz. But you'd do better to—"

"Where'll I find Krantz?"

"I'll git word to him. How soon you want to sell 'em?"

"Thursday."

"I hope you know what you're doin'. That bugger'd skin a gnat for its hide an' taller."

"I'll worry about that when the time comes."

Shrugging into the blue shield-fronted shirt, Bender thrust in the tails and awkwardly buttoned it. Wool, by God! But at least the bandage didn't show; that was the main thing. He didn't need to look into any crystal ball to know what would happen if Lasham's crowd learned his arm had been crippled.

The hostler said, "I'm goin' to eat now. I'll have Krantz here before mornin'."

LEFT alone, Bender wearily climbed into the loft. He scooped out a bed in the darkest corner, pulled some hay down over him and tried after that to get himself a little rest, feeling more dragged out than he could ever remember.

But the wheels of his mind continued to churn. His wrenched leg ached. His arm throbbed distractingly, but with not enough distraction to put a brake on his thinking.

God, but he was pooped—and fed up, too. Lasham, in spite of everything, had got this deal sewed up. He'd bought the sheriff's star; he'd made some kind of pact with Chesseldine. And coming in with his sheep was that kill-hungry bunch of crazy Yaquis; Don Leo's *mozos* wouldn't last five minutes faced with those kind of *hombres*. No use kidding himself on that score, or of putting any hope in that slick-talking Stroad. If the guy was on the level he'd probably get cold feet.

There wasn't a chance in a thousand they'd ever get to pay that note off. There'd been little enough chance before Blanca'd carved him up. Now, with this crippled wing, he'd be the worst kind of fool if he went anywhere near Lasham.

The last thing he wanted was to think about Blanca. He thought about her anyway. She was still in his mind when sleep finally claimed him.

THE loft was blacker than a stove lid when Bender's jerked-open eyes became aware of somebody shaking him. "For Chrissake," came the hostler's aggravated tones—"you gonna pound your ear forever?"

Bender said with a groan, "What time is it?"

"What's time got to do with it? I got that feller waitin'."

Bender knuckled glued eyes and got to his feet. Every bone in his body felt as though it had been pounded but he followed the liveryman down the ladder. The man who stood waiting in the cobwebbed office was gaunt, stoop-shouldered and clad in scuffed range clothes with his face hid out behind a tangle of whiskers. "Understand you've got some cattle. How many, what breed and in what kind of condition?"

"Mixed herd. Longhorns. Around three thousand head. Pretty fair shape."

"And you'll have them here Thursday?"

"If the price is right. If it ain't I may swing 'em over to Cruces or go on to El Paso."

"If you was plannin' to do that you wouldn't have bothered

with me at all. I'll give you a dollar and a half a head, straight through, when they're tallied and in the yards here."

Without a word Bender wheeled and started for the door.

"Hold on," Krantz growled—"what's the matter with that?"

"I'm not offerin' you stolen cattle and I ain't takin' no rustler's price!"

Krantz's triangular eyes were like pieces of glass. "Then what the hell are you comin' to me for?"

"A quick sale," Bender said—"isn't that your specialty?"

"So now we get words!" Krantz's eyes smashed into the cringing hostler. "Did I ride thirty mile to get a mouth full of language?"

"He said he wanted to sell—"

"*Sell* is right." Bender shook his heavy shoulders together. "Make your bid or get off the pot."

"A tough guy we got." Krantz blew out his cheeks. "You got out-of-state cattle?"

"This stuff was raised right here."

"Well . . ." the man's tone turned dubious. He pawed at his whiskers. "I might go as high as maybe five dollars—"

"What'll you give for them right where they're at?"

"Where they're at I don't know—"

"They're within forty miles and held ready to trail."

In the light of the lantern Krantz looked at him carefully.

"There's something stinks about this or you wouldn't be tryin' . . ." Krantz let that trail off. Something fled through his stare and was gone and he said, "I notice you ain't put a name to the brand."

"I wasn't born yesterday. You ain't runnin' off with this herd till it's bought—"

"If it's bought on the ground I'll have to know where to find it."

"You'll know," Bender grinned, "after I've pocketed your money."

"You think," Krantz said angrily, "I pay out good money for a herd I ain't seen?"

"If you want this one you will. I'm givin' you a chance to beat the market; most the stuff in this country won't be

rounded up for sale for another four weeks. With the government leasing all these Indian lands there'll be a lot of new
contracts let out for beef. You could pay five dollars and
double your money—"

"It takes a crew to move cattle. And in country like this—"

"That won't bother you. There's nothin' whatever wrong
with this stock. It's a registered brand. You'll get a bonafide
bill of sale with the herd. Now put up or shut up. Do you
want them or don't you?"

"I'll give you four," Krantz scowled; and Bender took it.

LASHAM shoved away from the table. "That note falls due
Saturday morning at noon." His eyes slanched a look at the
scarfaced Mexican Bender had fired from the Tres Pinos
crew. "They'll try to pay it off—Don Leo or that dope of a
red-headed foreman. Your job's to see they don't get no chance
to. The forty-five hundred is yours if you stop 'em. That's
all. Beat it."

He waited till the man had shut the door behind him, listened till the steps had faded off down the street. "Your job,
Art, is to get rid of those cattle. Stampede 'em, steal 'em; I
don't care *what* you do just so you make sure they're gotten
off Tres Pinos and beyond any chance of that outfit gettin'
cash for 'em. Savvy?"

Chesseldine nodded and picked up his hat.

After he'd gone, Lasham said succinctly: "Syd, you're goin'
to loan Fentress here about three of your Yaquis—the best
shots you've got. You'll bring up the sheep and move them
onto Tres Pinos just as quick as the sheriff gets Bender arrested or, preferably, planted."

"What about that strychnine?"

"Bluff," Lasham sneered. "What cowman in his right mind's
goin' to scatter that stuff? However, Fentress here, when he
goes after Bender, can take a look around and, if the bastards
have put anything like that out, he can lug that don off to the
lockup, too. Of course, he may throw in with that murderin'
Texan—try to keep Fentress from arrestin' the man. In that
case, naturally, he'll be treated as an accomplice. In any civi-

lized society the law must be upheld and all infractions punished or you've got nothin' but anarchy. I trust," Lasham said, fixing cold eyes on Fentress, "we've a capable man here . . . a sheriff who knows his duty and can be depended on to do it."

Fentress looked from one to the other of them licking dry lips.

"Got a tongue in you, don't you?"

The sheriff's cheeks took on a tinge reminiscent of Roquefort cheese. He gulped a couple of times but managed to get his head nodded.

"It's not often," Lasham smiled, "that duty and inclination are able to go so well in hand. By the time you get back they'll have tried to pay that note off. You'll have to pick Enrico up for whatever he's done about it but, once his mouth has been permanently shut, it won't occur to me to ask what has happened to that money."

He let his teeth show more plainly. "I think we understand each other. You'll be wanting to get ready for your trip now, sheriff. Be back here ready to leave in ten minutes."

Hardly had the rasp of Fentress' boots dimmed away than Red Hat said, scowling, "If you think, by God, I'm goin' to—"

"You'll naturally insist on going with them. I could hardly confide all the details to Fentress; and while we've got that chiseling crook in the talking I may as well tell you we're going to have to get rid of him. We'll use his star to cover this deal an' Scar Face; you can rub him out then an' pocket that dinero. We may have to get rid of that rustler, too, but we can work that out later."

"You want me to destroy that confession?"

"Just fetch it back," Lasham said. "I'll take care of destroyin' it. Personal."

18 | THE LONG GUNS BARK

BLANCA, with a mist of old lace setting off the dark luster of hair held in place by a high-backed comb, stood irritably regarding the bullring posters that splashed a profusion of blues, reds and yellows across the blank side of the brown adobe which housed Deef Lasham's new office. Cream colored silk was about her shoulders and black taffeta molded her shapely hips in the dapples of lamplight crossing the street from the batwing doors and unshaded windows of the Caballo Colorado.

The calle de la Piedad off the plaza de la Virgen at this time of night was no kind of place for a girl unattended—certainly no place for the daughter of a don. She hadn't the faintest excuse for this loitering. The wagon was loaded. She could see how restive the team was becoming yet still she remained, moving into deep shadow, half frightened, excited and thoroughly determined.

She'd been ready to start for home when the mercantile closed two hours ago and had climbed to the seat, had the lines in her hands, when a chance remark had frozen her motionless. Two passing *vaqueros,* conversing about sheep, had mentioned Lasham and a *muy grande* office. Following this lead she had learned at the corner *botica* that the sheep king had indeed opened an office here and, armed with its address, she'd returned to her wagon.

In the gathering dusk she had driven past the place. One thought had led to another, more daring, and almost at once she had conceived this wild plan. Risky? Of course it was, but if she could get back that note. . . .

She'd left the wagon three doors down and walked back and slipped round to the rear of the establishment by way of the alley which ran between this building and the next, there discovering a grimed window which had not been bolted. About to push up the sash she was stopped by the sound of some inside movement. Returning to the street she had again passed the front, this time seeing light fanning out around drawn shades.

She'd come around to this side. Four men, singly, had gone into the building and, thus far, only three had come out. Two she had recognized, Enrico and Fentress, and sight of these had sent her hastening into the deepest shadows. Five minutes later she heard door sound again and impatiently listened to the departure of footsteps.

She drifted back to the corner. The lamp was still burning. She walked back to her wagon and spoke a few words to the restive team.

When she next passed the office the light was out.

She hurried around to the back and climbed in through the window.

Inside her eyes strained against the thick blackness. The smell of snuffed wick was an acrid presence; not even the tick of a clock broke the stillness. She could feel the battering pound of her heart and her breath seemed all to be hung up in her throat. She made herself go forward. With infinite care and hands outstretched she moved toward where the lamp smell was strongest until the front of her thighs came against unyielding wood. The touch of her hands discovered this was a desk, a rolltop and locked. She touched the still-warm base of the lamp on its top and only then remembered that she had no matches.

She closed her eyes and tried to think where she'd be most apt to find some; the room didn't appear quite so dark when she opened them. She could vaguely see the dim bulk of objects. Now, close by the desk, she saw a coat on a wall peg and snatched it down with feverish hands, ransacking its pockets; and her fingers uncovered three matches.

She let the coat drop and struck one, saw the gun belt

looped over the knob of a chair and the half of a knife sticking out of its sheath. This reminded her of Bender and a whole flood of memories tangled up her emotions till the flame of the match licked against her fingers.

Shocked out of her thinking she snuffed the match and, picking up the knife, moved back to the desk. The place seemed twice as dark now but she went grimly to work, occasionally pausing to lift her head and listen.

Abruptly the lock snapped back. The top slid up disclosing an untidy clutter of papers. She went through them hurriedly and then commenced sifting through the stuff in the pigeonholes, convinced before long the thing she sought was not there. She forced the drawers frantically; there was nothing resembling what she hunted in any of them. Did Lasham carry the note in his wallet?

Where *was* it? If not in Lasham's pocket it was pretty near bound to have to be in this desk unless—and she hoped not— he had put it in the bank. She felt through the litter of papers once more and a sense of panic rushed through her and her fists clenched at the bitter injustice of a fate which could allow her to take such risk with so little reward for her enterprise.

She felt through the drawers again without finding it. A growing conviction of disaster had hold of her, warning her, urging her to get out of this place, but she wouldn't give up while there still seemed a chance she might uncover the note.

She took her chin in her hand and thought for a bit, but the most likely place was obviously this desk. She pulled the center drawer out and ran her hands along the tracks without finding either crevice or roughness. She felt again through the pigeonholes, pressing and prying in the hope that somewhere she might release a secret drawer; with each passing moment she became more frantic.

She scratched the last match and, in its raveling flare, she went once more through that clutter of papers. She stood up and her eyes, darting round in despair, abruptly paused in grim focus on the gilt-framed chromo of a voluptuous blonde basking in nude splendor on the wall above the desk.

Her gaze narrowed.

She was reaching for the picture, convinced the note was back of it, when her match flickered out. And at that precise instant, bent forward, still reaching, she caught the sudden rasp of a key being turned. She crouched there, frozen, incapable of movement, while the opening door flicked the wall with brief radiance. She whirled, eyes enormous, as the door was eased shut, leaving her in darkness through which the key turned again. And then soft steps started toward her.

BENDER in the doorway of the Three Brothers Hotel stood applying the sharpened end of a matchstick to divers particles of recalcitrant ham while trying to decide if he should go on to Deming or hurry back to Tres Pinos.

The note would have to be paid to clear the ranch of Lasham's hold on it but they still had more time to give to that chore than they had to get ready for a number of other things; and Krantz had promised to take delivery tomorrow, reminding Bender if the tally proved short he would expect the return of a proportionate amount of what he'd paid for the herd. The man had gone to the bank with him less than an hour ago and Bender had opened a ranch account for Don Leo, putting every nickel of the sale price into it. Although tempted to include that forty-five hundred he had finally gone to breakfast with it still in his pocket.

Yes, he thought, he'd be smart right now to get back to the ranch for, in addition to the need of making sure the herd was ready, there was always the chance Hazel's rifle-packing Yaquis might try to move in the sheep ahead of the deadline.

He picked up his horse and set off with a nagging disquiet at the back of his mind. His right arm, though not stiff, was almighty painful and he didn't have to move it much to feel its sharp protest. This was another of the reasons he'd decided against Deming; he was certainly in no shape to have to draw against experts.

He struck up a fast lope and was ten miles out and at the fork of the trail which ran north toward Cambray and Deming, with Mt. Riley well hidden behind the crags of the Potrillos, when he briefly debated swinging north after all.

That goddam note was a burden on his mind; but common sense prevailed and he kept on toward Tres Pinos.

Since he hadn't yet freed the crew of that herd, and couldn't until Krantz arrived to take delivery, he thought it might be better if he had the herd fetched down and either concentrated in the canyon itself or bedded at the foot of the bluffs. This would make the crew available in case of trouble with the sheep, and that many head of bawling horn-tossing cattle could be employed as a wall against invasion should Red Hat's crew of Yaquis attempt immediate entrance. With three thousand cattle he could choke the trail plumb solid where it ran along the base of the cliff in its ascent toward Three Pines' headquarters.

As a defensive measure this looked better than strychnine. For as long, at any rate, as they still had the cattle. And after that he'd have the crew. With *vaqueros* and *mozos* blended into one outfit dug in among the pines where the trail pinched in as it climbed through the bluffs, he should be able to make quite a dent in any invasion.

The more he now considered it the less inclined he felt toward using that strychnine. Barbed wire entanglements snarled across the trail should prove even more effective, and wire wouldn't hurt the range. In fact, so far as that went, now that the expectation of poison had been so firmly planted in the minds of the sheep crowd, common flour scattered around should be just as efficacious.

He couldn't help but feel events might be taking a turn for the better. With the discovery of Krantz and the sale of the cattle he now had a fighing chance to beat Lasham, to keep him at least from overrunning Tres Pinos. The ranch and Don Leo were still up against it but the future didn't look quite as dark as he'd imagined it. He hadn't netted too much from the sale of that herd but what he'd got was better than having it stampeded or stolen. Only one thing could wreck that part of the set up—the appearance of Chesseldine in advance of Krantz's coming. That, he thought, scowling, would screw the works proper.

He raked a swift look around. They were now quartering

along the southern footslopes of the Potrillos and somewhere along about here, he remembered, was that little-used
trail he'd seen angling northeast. He didn't believe Syd Hazel
could have brought up the sheep yet but, in the event Syd
had, their presence, even if unchallenged, might very well
have closed the south trail to travel. He couldn't afford to risk
it if there were another way in. It might take him a little
longer to reach Tres Pinos through these mountains, but sometimes the longest way around was the shortest. Red Hat wasn't
the man to forget that smashed elbow or to overlook any
opportunities for ambush.

Bender found the dim trace and turned his mount into it.
He knew it might turn out to be nothing more than a rabbit
run, but if he'd calculated right and this was actually some
long-abandoned way through the mountains, it should bring
him out somewhere between the Lopez ranch headquarters
and the lake Don Leo had offered him before the loss of the
lease lands had cancelled that deal.

The terrain became increasingly more difficult to negotiate.
At times the route became completely impassable, choked and
lost in patch after patch of pear and chaparral; at other places
it was strewn with rock rubble and cut away by gullies. It was
a nightmare trail, if trail it ever had been, and when, still
climbing, he rode an hour later about the base of a towering
butte of red rock and found himself immobilized on the rim
of a precipice, he cursed in bitter outrage. He could see nothing in front of him but turquoise sky.

He got down off his horse with the wind flapping at him and,
dropping to hands and knees, peered over the edge. He almost
lost his breakfast. What looked to be the green of blobs of
brush far below him were unquestionably the tops of two-
hundred-foot pines. But this wasn't the sheer drop he had
first supposed it. A kind of natural ladder led down the face
of this fault. Great blocks of rock showed sunlit slants from
which gnarled junipers occasionally lifted and the pagan shapes
of flowering *sotol;* shattered cliffs and tangles of catclaw; talus
and shale and, far below in dreamlike splendor the octagonal

outline of a forgotten valley slumbering in the bosom of rolling sugarloaf hills.

Bender drew back to catch his breath and give his stomach time to right itself. It staggered belief to think that even a goat could find a way down, yet graven on the rock between his white-knuckled hands were the unmistakable marks of shod hoofs. And not all of these were old marks. There was one, streaked with metal, obviously made within the month. He knew then how Robinson Crusoe must have felt discovering his footstep.

When his heart quit thumping his gullet he peered over the brink again and, this time, saw Don Leo's *casa* like a tiny white box against a fold in the hills and, beyond it, dun and vast, the broad expanse of the desert. There was one lighter patch, a yellowish blaze, which he knew for dust and this, he concluded, was probably made by Lasham's sheep. By calculating the distance between the *casa* and the desert he estimated the sheep were still ten miles to the south of the bluffs.

He studied this dust patch carefully. It was no little flock Red Hat's Yaquis were moving. All the sheep Lasham owned must be under that dust and, if he willed it, the vanguard could be threatening Tres Pinos within a matter of hours; tomorrow night at the latest.

His guts turned cold and crawled at the thought of tackling the formidable descent to that valley, but time was suddenly become too precious to waste the span that would be required to go back. Clenching his jaws, he picked up the reins and stepped onto the two-foot ledge leading downward, narrowed eyes on his footing, a prayer in his heart.

At the ranch, Don Leo was opening the letter which Bender's hired gun hand had fetched with him from Deming. With Stroad left in charge of the trail-guarding *mozos* the old man had jogged up to the *casa* for lunch and now, having eaten, he'd remembered the thing, having carried it forgotten overnight in his pocket.

The name on the envelope lightened his spirits. Postmarked

Santa Fe, this had come from Don Ramon Eusebio de Vega, his good friend who was in politics and might conceivably therefore have some weight with Otero. Don Leo had written suggesting the removal of Cash Fentress from the shrievalty and felt a comfortable satisfaction in the prospect of his friend's enclosed assurances.

The letter, however, contained little beyond proof of Deef Lasham's vast influence. Don Ramon, it appeared, had lost the governor's ear. Strange forces were at work in the land, he reported, and corruption had its tentacles in every department. He'd be extraordinarily lucky to retain his own post for its normal duration. He was sorry but there was nothing he could do. Sheriff Fentress, for the present, was entirely beyond his reach.

WHEN Bender reached the valley floor he dropped exhausted in the sunlit sand and lay there shaking like a man with malaria. His face was white as paper. The blue shield-fronted shirt, reflecting the hazards of his experience, was glued to his back with sweat. And when he finally arose and looked back up he could hardly believe he had actually made it.

He climbed into the saddle, too bone-weary to do much more than hold the gelding to its course. Landmarks looked different from this perspective and he had considerable difficulty in picking out the things he had decided on to guide him, but he knew the general direction.

He rode quietly along, nursing his luck, and after about thirty minutes came into a region of scraggly looking brush, which struck him as odd because, when he had been looking this country over before that climb down the face of that bugger of a precipice, he had seen the glint of water and, according to the way those yonder hills were shaping up, it had ought to be somewhere right along about here.

He had, in fact, been rather counting on it. There was no water bag on his saddle and he was drier than jerked buffalo. The more he thought about it the drier he got; and then, coming over a low rise, he saw it, a short hundred yards ahead of him.

He thought it uncommon odd his horse didn't have his head up a-sniffing, was so indifferent as to have to be guided toward it. But the horse was smarter than he was, as he grudgingly admitted when he came to the pond's edge. No wonder nothing grew there. It was the stinkingest water he had ever got a look at; and one look was plenty. He didn't even bother getting out of the saddle. He wheeled his horse and headed straight for the hills.

He knew before he'd got over the first one he probably wasn't going to be able to make it in time. The sounds he had heard weren't made by any sheep and already the distant clatter of gunfire had become sporadic, sure indication of a running fight. He raked the big gelding's sides with his rowels, flinging him headlong through rocks and brush. A running fight could only mean one thing—that the herd was in motion.

And that meant Chesseldine.

19 | TOUCH AND GO

RUSTLERS, as a general rule, were prone to work under the cover of darkness, drifting off small jags of stock, seldom revealing the enterprise and brashness required to make off with an entire herd. That Chesseldine now should do so—and do it openly and boldly in the broad light of day—was practical proof of a tie-up with Lasham and, more significant, left little doubt but that the sheep king had abandoned all intention of further waiting.

Deef Lasham was a master of strategy. He always dovetailed his efforts with meticulous planning so that when he employed elements outside the law the goal was so nearly within his grasp that, when the smoke rolled away, there was no one left to tattle. Obviously then, timed to coincide with this minor coup which was pulling away the bulk of Three Pines' defenders, others in Lasham's employ would be rushing up the sheep to take advantage of this distraction.

No one man was going to head those cattle now; if Gonzales with the crew couldn't get the herd stopped there was nothing Bender's presence on the scene could hope to accomplish.

It was hard, bitter hard, to see his work with Krantz undone—to contemplate having to return Krantz's money, but this was out of his hands now, beyond his power to circumvent. And already he had made one howling blunder in jumping to the conclusion it was grass Lasham was after. Sure, the sheep king *was* after grass—no doubt about it; but the paramount goal of all his scheming had nothing whatever to do with grass. It depended primarily on his acquirement of Three Pines.

So why hadn't he sat back and waited a little longer? Why resort to open violence, which was bound to necessitate the addition of still further violence to cover it, when by waiting another four and a half more days, and making certain that note was still unpaid, he could have had the place lock, stock and barrel?

Bender slowed and abruptly stopped his horse. Obviously something must have changed Lasham's plans, something crucial, something dangerous, something incredibly alarming. Only fright could have pushed the man into taking such risks. Fright and a terrible need for haste.

That confession may have done it combined with the knowledge Don Leo now possessed the funds to pay himself out. Whatever it was, Lasham had laid himself wide open and, if they could stand off the sheep. . . .

Bender turned the horse southeast again and lifted him into a larruping run. He had just remembered where he'd seen that damned gunfighter. *Stroad was the man whose horse he'd shot down on that ridge below the pines the night Fentress' posse had been after him!*

HEADQUARTERS looked deserted when Bender pulled up beside the *casa's* long gallery. He found Josefa in the kitchen, asked for Don Leo and was told the *patron* was at the shack on the bluffs. Everyone was there, all the servants, except one, too old and crippled, who'd been left at the stables to take care of the horses. "Well, see if you can scrape me up something to eat," Bender said, and went into the patio, heading for the *parada*.

He found the old man cleaning stalls and sent him off on a horse to fetch back Don Leo and Jose Maria. "But Jose, *senor*, is cowboy. He will be with—"

"Have him bring someone else then and hurry it up."

Giving the barrel a wide berth he cut across to his room, hastily washed and went back to the kitchen. There was a big plate of beans and a stack of *tortillas* on the table together with a graniteware pot of black and very hot coffee. Bender lost no time in pulling up a chair.

All the time he was eating his thoughts kept busy. When he'd wiped his plate clean and finished the last of the coffee he got out the makings and shaped up a smoke, wishing to hell his damn arm would quit hurting. "The *senorita*—where is she?" he asked, stepping over to the stove for a handful of matches.

The old woman straightened up. She put a hand to her *reboso*. "You have not heard? She went yesterday to Deming with the wagon for supplies—"

"Where is she now?"

"Quien sabe? She has not returned."

"Not returned!" Bender stared, and cold fingers turned over the food in his stomach. "Are you sure?"

"Si." The woman crossed herself. "The *patron*—he is like the madman."

He had reason to be, Bender told himself bitterly. Few things in this world could have suited Lasham better than to get hold of Blanca. With her for a hostage. . . .

WITH his shattered right elbow encased in a cast, the ubiquitous Syd Hazel lacked considerable of looking as tough

as was his habit as he climbed the bluffs trail along with
Fentress and three hard-faced Yaquis cradling rifles across
their laps.

He'd encountered little difficulty in persuading the sheriff
to pin a badge on his shirt. The lawman was glad of all the
help he could get and he still looked like he was about set
to vomit. As they were reining their horses toward the trees
about the cabin Red Hat slanched a sideways look at the
bastard and twisted his lips in a grimace of contempt. That
goddam rep Lasham had hand-carved for Bender, plus the
fellow's recent warning, had so worked on the sheriff through
a long night of thinking that with the ghost of an excuse he
would have funked the whole deal.

"You've hit the end of the line, *compadres*. Just turn them
nags around now an' start back."

There was no one in sight but Hazel's narrowed eyes dis-
cerned the glint of several rifles. The sheriff had seen them
too and his cheeks had turned a fish-belly white. He shot a
scared look at Red Hat and stiffened enough to bluster: "You
can't stop people here—this is a public road!"

"Try it on an' we'll find out."

"You're talkin' to the sheriff of this county," Fentress
quavered.

A broken-nosed fellow with ears like a bat stepped out from
behind the bole of a pine. There was a battered old hat pushed
back off his forehead and a high-powered repeater in the
crook of one arm. With a twist of his mouth he loosed a
stream of tobacco juice. "This here's private property, gents,
an' I've just been give orders to keep it that way." He regarded
Fentress with a snaggle-toothed grin. "If you're a sure-enough
sheriff let's have a look at your warrant."

Red Hat, scowling, made a project of wrapping the reins
round his pommel. "Show it to him," he said; and half the
curious *mozos* got up and stood gawping, muskets loose-
hanging from pudgy brown fists. "Go ahead—let him read it.
He's got a passion fer papers."

Stroad said, "You know how far you'll git with this, Hazel."

"Hell, it's no skin off my nose. He's the boss—we're jest

deppities. Go ahead an' stop him if you think you got a right to."

Fentress, having no warrant, didn't grasp any part of this but, under the compulsion of Hazel's iron stare, he put a rummaging hand to his coat's inside pocket, finally withdrawing a folded paper which he held out toward Stroad.

"I don't know what you think this'll buy you," Stroad said, looking hard at the sheep boss.

Red Hat grinned smugly, commenced unwrapping his reins as though this business of the warrant was a cut-and-dried sequence whose conclusion was so assured he had no need even to watch it.

Stroad snorted and stepped forward to have his look at the sheriff's paper. Swift as the strike of a snake Red Hat's hand swung saddleward and levelled, spouting flame.

Bender's gunfighter probably never knew what struck him. He spun half around with his mouth wide open, shuddered once and collapsed.

For an eternity of moments Bender stood without movement, oppressed by an overwhelming sense of futility.

He'd been an inexcusable fool—and worse—ever to have let these people start hoping he might be able to help them. Any two-year-old in diapers should have had the wit to understand once Lasham's toils closed round you there was nothing left but squirming. The man had too much influence, too much fire power, too much cunning. Each new shuffle of the cards had but served to strengthen this inescapable conviction. And on top of everything else, by God, from the instant he'd got into this thing, every move he'd made had been slapped around and bludgeoned by this girl's continual interference.

He heaved a sigh and got moving. No matter how badly he might be needed right here to cope with Syd Hazel, the sheep and Syd's Yaquis, the paramount issue right now was Blanca. They might stand off the sheep, they might beat the damn Yaquis, but so long as Deef Lasham had Blanca they were licked.

He remembered the confession but realized it was worthless. It would only give Lasham a belly laugh should he presume to offer it in exchange for the girl. It had been a real threat when he'd made the sheep king sign it but he had scrapped every vestige of a chance to use it by returning to Tres Pinos. A deep and hard-fought knowledge of Lasham's methods convinced him that by now every trail leading out of this region would be closed. Very probably he wouldn't even be able to get to Deming, but he had to make the try.

It would require a stout horse and a fast one.

The supply had been depleted by the need of mounting the *mozos*. What were left would likely be culls, he thought, moving through the passage and into the *parada*. His glance swept the stalls, abruptly focused on a dun. He hurried forward. It was Chucho!

He caught up the nearest saddle, grabbed a bridle off a wall peg; he was hastening toward Chucho's stall when the sound of horses twisted his head and hung him there, moveless, until Don Leo's voice gave him back mobility.

He had barely got Chucho readied when the *ranchero*, followed by a pockmarked *mozo*, came bursting into the stable-yard. The don's face had aged ten years and anguish rode the flash of his stare, but it was Bender who got the first words out: "I know—I'm going after her. Put this fellow to work right away. Have him tangle barbed wire all across that trail where it comes up from the bluffs—"

"But we have already put out the poison—"

"Nothing but barbed wire's going to stop those sheep, and you've got to stop those Yaquis as well. Spread all the loose wire you've got down there and make sure it's well anchored along both sides. Post your *mozos* in cover and tell them to drop every Yaqui they see."

"But, *amigo*—"

"But—hell! You ain't goin' to hurt them snappin' a saddle blanket at them! You got to grind that soft stuff out of your system—you can't fight that kind with charity! You—" He pulled his head up, listening. "Was that a shot?"

TRES PINOS' servants, in terror of the red-hatted *gringo,* threw down their old-fashioned muskets with faces blanched to the color of putty. Several of the more devout hastily made the sign of the cross, others stood goggling; two, more hardy than the rank and file, would have bolted forthwith had not Hazel's gun suddenly swung to cover them.

"Round 'em up," he grunted, and the Yaquis got busy.

Inside of five minutes every *mozo* was bound and piled up like stove wood out of sight in the shack. Leaving one of his Yaquis to make sure they stayed put, the sheep boss and Fentress and the other pair pushed on.

They were almost in sight of the *casa* before the sheriff recovered his power of speech. After two or three stammering starts he blurted: "Hadn't we oughta made sure that feller was done for?"

Red Hat spat, not bothering to answer.

DON LEO shook his head. "I did not hear anything."

Bender listened a couple moments longer, then turned with a shrug and picked up Chucho's reins. He guessed he had better get started. He recalled Blanca saying that any shots at the shack were easily heard here, so perhaps after all he'd just imagined the sound; in any event it had not been repeated. If there'd been trouble at the bluffs it wouldn't have been wiped out with one bullet.

"I don't know what I'll be up against—I may not get through; but while I'm gone," he said bluntly, "you watch that trail as though your life depended on it. You," he told the *mozo,* "go scout up that wire—*andale. Pronto!*"

He watched the man go hurrying off.

"You can arrange with Josefa about the food. Have it sent down. String all the wire you can get hold of. Leave it tangled and loose but anchor it solid at the sides. Scatter your men around through those pines and see to it that everyone keeps his eyes skinned. At the first sign of trouble start blasting—don't hesitate. Understand?"

Don Leo nodded.

But he didn't, to Bender, appear sufficiently impressed. He

was too obviously engrossed with his worries about Blanca. In an effort to get through to him, Bender said, "You're up against a man who's playing for high stakes. It's this ranch he's after and—"

He let the rest go, glance abruptly remote, head canted in absorbed attention. He had thought to have caught the dim flutter of hoofs but, though his every faculty strained to recapture it, he heard nothing beyond the pawing of the impatient Chucho. A bot fly droned through the sunlit quiet and the restive animal snapped bared teeth. Then, as Bender would have spoken, the crash of a rifle locked his glance with Don Leo's.

One instant they stood, like robot figures hacked from clay, chained motionless by their thoughts. Both faces, whipping around then, grimly focused toward the gallery.

"Damn!" Bender swore: and both of them lunged for the passage. The old man, in spite of his age, managed to reach its entrance first. Crowding his heels Bender followed him into the patio and was halfway across it, rounding the bird bath, hurt arm cramped in a reach for his pistol, when a hoarse voice cried out back of them: *"Hold it!"*

20 | DEATH IN THE AFTERNOON

BENDER knew the full futility of all he'd tried to do here.

A sinking feeling that was like a physical weakness churned through his bowels as his bitter stare, back-flung across a shoulder, took in the ragged shape of the grinning Yaqui crouched in the passage behind a levelled Sharps. A thousand thoughts pounded through his head and he'd have probably gone on and dragged his own gun anyway but for the nearness of Don Leo and the booted clank of spurs now coming toward them from the house.

When he pulled his face around he saw Syd Hazel and the sheriff and let the piled-up breath spill out of him. He felt the sheep boss' eyes bite into him and stood slack-muscled as Hazel, followed by Fentress, both with pistols in their hands, stepped around the fountain.

Hazel, sneering, stopped less than two feet away from him. "Unbuckle your belt and drop it."

Had the sheriff, white-cheeked and patently scared enough to shoot at the least provocation, not been quite so close, he might have made an attempt to kick the gun from Hazel's fist. It wasn't consideration of any personal danger which made him discard the impulse, but the conviction that any resistance now would get Blanca's father killed out of hand. The old man had plenty of courage but he was certainly not fitted to cope with renegades of this stripe. He wasn't even armed.

So he let the belt fall, hearing above the thud of his pistol the audible sigh that came out of Cash Fentress. It was like the sound of a pricked balloon and showed how tight the man's nerves had been strung.

A hungry emptiness climbed into Bender's stomach.

He had heard that soldiers facing death were often brought face to face with visions from their pasts, that drowning men sometimes had the same experience; and he realized now how apt were those descriptions. For superimposed against the sun-lit yard upon the baleful malevolence of Red Hat's features he saw a brief montage of himself in a hundred actions; all the salient milestones of his life reeled past in the kaleidoscopic shuffle of a couple of heartbeats. And then the past was gone, sponged as figures from a slate, and he was facing Syd Hazel across a pounding silence.

In the sultry brilliance of the man's vengeful stare he could read the violent ultimate of the sheepman's berserk fury—invited it by prodding him with a cold disdainful grin.

With a strangled snarl Red Hat struck him across the face with his pistol—viciously, deliberately, with all the towering strength of his outrage.

Staggering backward, half blinded, Bender retained the wit through all the racketing roar of monstrous pain crashing over him to guide his stumbling feet till he could fall where he'd intended. He had no consciousness of striking ground. Blue sky advanced and receded in pulsating waves of nausea. Don Leo's shocked and angry protest was a faroff whisper floating through miles of rust-colored murk, yet he clung doggedly to the sound of it, refusing to allow himself the luxury of oblivion. He must, his brain kept telling him, retain at least this toehold on reality lest all their lives be forfeit. He could not, *dared* not, pass out now . . . he had to get to Blanca.

He heard Syd Hazel's raging tones, a gasp, the wheeze of panting breath; and found himself on hands and knees. The world around him reeled and rocked on changing patterns of light and shadow. He got one foot planted under him and with a savage wrench of muscle lurched upright.

He saw them now, gyrating shapes that writhed and twisted like flames in hell—only these were black, grotesquely tangled, the grappling, cursing figures of men entwined in murderous scuffle. Even while his eyes strained to focus, one queer lopsided shape spun free trailing a spume of foul invective. The words were a screech half strangled by rage but the voice that propelled them was unmistakably Hazel's. "Stand back, you fools, so I can spill out his guts!"

There was a flash, a roar, and Bender, knuckling blood and sweat from his eyes, saw Don Leo stagger out of the group and fall headlong. One limp outflung arm abruptly twitched and was still with its fingers dug into the sunlit sand. Hazel, the smoke still curling from the gun in his fist, looked around and found Bender. "I'll have that money now. *And* the paper!"

Bender stared at the man's reptilian eyes and knew why he wasn't being gunned out of hand. The sheep boss first had to make sure of that confession, had to see it and handle it before he dared let his rage have full play.

He came nearer, suspiciously watching Bender's hands go through his pockets. "Pitch 'em over," he growled from eight feet away.

Bender's vacuous gaze took in the other pair's placement. They had paused indecisively where Hazel had left them beyond the fountain, six feet back of Red Hat; closer to Bender's dropped shell belt than he was—too close for him to ever hope to get at it.

Yet he had one chance left, an exceedingly thin one, hardly the ghost of a chance really but the one he had angled for while taunting the sheepman into knocking him sprawling.

He creased the bills once again and with an aggravating slowness carefully folded the confession so the banknotes lay beneath it. There was no breeze blowing, though he felt the breath of one. The currency, of course, weighed more than the paper.

He started forward, hand out, and saw Hazel's gun shift. "You biddin' for a harp?"

The muzzle of the weapon looked big as a stovepipe.

Bender licked at his lips. "I thought you—"

"*Throw* it!" Red Hat snarled.

The edge of a smile flattened Bender's mouth for he had the man now exactly where he wanted him. The rest of this play was on the lap of the gods. He thought morosely of Don Leo and desperately of Blanca and a leaching chill crept into his blood; and then he made the throw. The banknotes landed at Red Hat's feet. The confession wabbled in the air and dropped, still twirling, into the barrel.

THE sheepman's eyes winnowed down to glittering slits. It seemed as though his swelling chest would burst in another instant. Then his breath came out in a rasping laugh that bore no relation to anything human. "Tricks again, eh? Tryin' to get at that barrel! Well, you're not foolin' *me!*"

He called up the Yaqui. "If he jiggles a finger put a slug through him—savvy?"

The black Indian showed his teeth in a grin.

Hazel, looking equally malevolent, moved to the barrel and, still watching Bender, laid his gun on the ground and reached for the paper.

His face went suddenly the color of wood ash. He sprang to his feet and peered into the barrel and his eyes looked like they would roll off his cheekbones. He stared at his hand with twisted cheeks while a terrible horror-filled scream tore out of him. Cash Fentress came dashing from back of the fountain. The Yaqui's head turned and Bender leaped.

A musket crashed from the kitchen doorway. The Indian staggered and Bender's hand scooped up Hazel's pistol. He and the sheriff fired almost in unison.

Fentress' shot whined over his head. Dust whacked out of the starpacker's coat and he took three backward lurching steps with his mouth stretched wide in a strangled yell. Bender's next shot knocked the Yaqui down. The rifle went clattering out of his grasp as Josefa, *rebozo* flapping across a wild eye, waddled toward the *patron* with her black skirts caught in a shaking hand.

Bender ran for the stableyard.

21 | ''I'LL BE SAYIN' GOODBYE NOW''

LAMPS were being lighted as Bender rode into the outskirts of Deming. He had no idea where he might discover Lasham. He was well aware of the risk he would run in showing himself at the Aces Up but could think of no alternative. He had to find Lasham before the sheep king learned what had happened at Tres Pinos.

That he would learn, and swiftly, Bender could not doubt. The appearance of Red Hat with the sheriff and those Yaquis made it more than amply evident his trail block had been breached; Stroad, after all, must have been in the sheepman's pay.

Hazel, probably, had fetched up the bulk of his fighting

Yaquis and Don Leo's *mozos*, in the face of such force and that damned Stroad's defection, had been too frightened to offer any resistance. Someone, already, was surely packing the news to Lasham and, once the sheep king understood that the girl was now owner of Three Pines Ranch, he would take steps at once to protect his interests. He would find some way to make her sign the place over; then she would simply disappear.

This wouldn't be the first time such things had happened.

Consumed though he was by this terrible impatience, Bender had the good judgment to pull Chucho down before he entered the town. Anxious as he was to come to grips with the sheep king, to get at the final showdown, he was cool enough to know that he would first have to find him. He wasn't going to find him if someone shot him out of the saddle.

This day had been months in coming. He could afford to exercise enough care to get there. He had lived this accounting a thousand times in the light of the flames from his lonely campfires, perfecting each detail, polishing his remarks, enjoying the fright he would see in those bloating features. During all those days he'd been steadily pushed westward by Lasham's pet marshal he'd found time to get used to the feel of his fingers clamped around Lasham's windpipe—to revel in it and long for it. In his mind he had cold-bloodedly killed Deef Lasham times without number and found it easy as wringing the neck of a chicken. He could do it, all right, and pretty soon he was going to. Lasham's business with Blanca had become the final straw.

And he was all through trying to fool himself on that score. In spite of her exasperating ways, her present danger had shown him beyond all his angered attempts to doubt it that whatever it was he felt toward her it certainly wasn't hate. But even if he was fool enough to actually admit he cared for her, that would have to be the end of it; he sure wasn't going to go blurting it out after what he'd discovered about Tres Pinos!

He pulled up by the tie rack in front of the hash house next door to the place where he had smashed Hazel's elbow and dourly regarded the gold squares of its windows. If he went in there now and got the dope he was after and got out again, in a matter of moments he might be facing Deef Lasham. But if he went in there and didn't get it, or got killed in the process, what about Blanca?

But it was almost as risky being seen in this street. He felt a quick, tense excitement. Any one of this procession of ambling townsmen might glance up and chance to remember his profile. There'd been a lot of guys engaged in that shooting the other night; there had been several horses killed and a lot of glass broken, and the owners of these weren't like to forget him. Nor the owner of that horse he had finally got off on.

He watched three conversing punchers go past, their spurs dragging sound from the planks of the walk. Midway of the block they swung right and went into the Drovers Hotel. Another couple came along, a man and a woman. A dancehall girl by the look of her apparel.

Bender nudged his horse deeper into the blackness and asked gruffly if they knew where he might find a man named Lasham.

"Don't know 'im," the man said, but the girl's arm, acting like an anchor, swung him round. "What's he in—tobacco or whiskies?"

"Neither," Bender said, "he's a sheepman," and could see the pale blob of her face peering up at him. Her companion snorted and tried to pull her along, but she got hold of the tie rail. "Wait a minute, Joe. I wanta talk to this john—"

"You don't want no truck with a—"

"He's no sheepman," she muttered, and the man's head came round.

Bender eased Chucho back a bit and the man suddenly growled on an upswing of interest, "By cripes, I—"

"Get your hand off that gun," intoned Bender. "All I'm huntin' is a little information. You know where I can locate him?"

"If you mean the fat slob—"

"That's the one." Bender said.

"Anyone could tell you. He's sure been rollin' it—settin'

'em up for folks all over town. Got a flossy office in the Plaza of the Virgin. Gold paint on the window—Potrillo Sheep & Land Development. Open day an' night. I can't see how you missed it. Go eight blocks west and—"

"Gracie, you dimwit! This is the—"

"Now Joe, honey, don't get yourself all worked up about it. You don't know this gent. You just stick to your lovin' an' . . ."

BENDER tied his horse half a block up the side street, tugged down his hat and sauntered back toward the plaza. Under the board awning of the Caballo Colorado he propped himself against a post and fetched out the makings while his eyes ransacked the piled-up shadows behind the tan adobe housing Lasham's place of business. Might be a window or two back there but if there was you could bet it was covered. Deef Lasham hadn't set this stage to help Don Leo. The lamplit front of that office with the blinds clean up to the ceiling was sucker bait—same way with the people moving round inside it.

Bender hadn't ridden past the front of that place but he had got near enough to admire Deef Lasham's handiwork. Anyone who didn't know the way that scheming devil's mind worked wouldn't hesitate a minute. It was a trap though just the same—a cunning deadfall rigged for murder.

There was a fellow carefully blended with the shadows flanking the hardware shop who'd been very likely put there to take care of Three Pines' payment.

This bird was directly across the plaza where he could get a good look at anyone who went over there, hard to pick out in the gloom where he loitered. Anyone undertaking to pay their bills at that office was going to get the works if they came from Tres Pinos.

Just across the calle de la Piedad from where Bender stood before the Caballo Colorado there was a dark house whose left side flanked the back of that lamplit office. The girl was probably imprisoned in that house, tied hand and foot or locked into some room she had no chance of getting out of.

Lasham, too, was probably in there, hidden someplace in the felted blackness, watching to see if his trap would be sprung.

Bender chewed on his lip. To get into that house he'd have to cross this street, and it was a cinch when he tried that guy was going to start firing.

He was standing there, debating, when he caught the dim mutter of hoofs and knew he dared wait no longer.

He pasted the unlighted smoke on his lip and stepped away from the post. That fellow off yonder was harder to see now; like enough he'd stepped back where the gloom was piled deeper. Bender's heart banged around like a chained canary. He felt the cold sweat creeping out along his collar but he held his advance to a snail's pace till he was certain he'd got clear away from the saloon and had nothing behind him but solid night.

Now, drawing his gun, he moved in swiftly while the hoof sound got louder and he expected any moment to feel the impact of lead.

But the fellow didn't fire. He didn't try to bolt, either. He turned out, when Bender neared him, to be nothing more alarming than a stoop-shouldered peddler still pottering around his little pushcart of fruit.

Bender, wheeling disgustedly, was smothering an oath when some sixth sense made him throw a glance upward. He was barely in time to miss the rush of the bullet that came racketing at him from the store's sloping roof. The peddler took to his heels. Bender, lunging sideways and dropping as he did so, hammered three slugs at a sky-shrouded shape. The last one did it. He saw flailing arms as the man quit the roof.

The staccato of hoofs climbed into crescendo. Bender, ducking his head, punched shells from his pistol and with frantic fingers plugged the holes with fresh cartridges. Light from the front of Lasham's office thrust golden lanes into the square's black shadows but, with that oncoming rider less than three blocks away, there was no time to lose.

Bender tore across the plaza, plunging into the alley to the left of Lasham's office. Stumbling and lurching through tin cans and bottles, he scrambled up an embankment and reached the clapboarded side of the dark house behind it. He had one last moment of desperate wonder when the paralyzing thought leaped fullblown through his mind that perhaps once again the sheep king had outslicked him by somehow hiding Blanca among the crowd in that office.

He tongued the unsmoked cigarette off his lip. He faced a terrible choice. The girl's life might be lost if he guessed wrong now—she might be spirited away while he was making his mind up. But if he went into this house and she wasn't there. . . . There simply wasn't time for him to look in both places and the sound of that horse thundering into the plaza decided him.

He turned left, cold with dread, and went up the back steps of the house. He hit the door hard with the point of his shoulder, took the splintered wood with him as he lunged into a blackness that was rank with the smell of recently burned tobacco. His knee struck a chair and sent it skittering through darkness. His left, outstretched hand came against the slick surface of a painted wall. He moved the hand along this and with cocked muscles followed it through an unseen opening into another room where the cigar smell was stronger and a faint sound of breathing suddenly stopped him in his tracks.

Somewhere in this impenetrable blackness another shape was also crouched, finger about trigger, eyes wide with staring, ears straining in the agony of pinning sound to source.

He imagined he was confused by lack of sight when, after holding himself completely doggo for many seconds, he still was not sure where that breathing was coming from. He would have sworn at first he'd caught the sound on his right, then began to think it was more nearly in front of him, winding up half convinced it was off to his left. No man, even bootless, could have shifted that rapidly without leaving evidence in creaking boards and, when he realized this, Bender had no choice but to conclude the room was packed.

One of these people might conceivably be Blanca but neither his eyes nor his ears could tell him which one. It was an intolerable situation, a deadlock which would only be resolved when someone's nerves could stand the strain longer and impelled him, or her, to suicidal movement.

And what if the first sound came from Blanca?

How could he know? How, indeed, dared he fire, *not* knowing.

The two matches Stroad had given him were still unused in the band of his hat and he turned this knowledge over while he wondered what had happened to the rider whose horse he had last heard entering the plaza. Where was that man now?

He remembered abruptly that the back door was open, splintered and sagging on twisted hinges. The night was too black for him to show up against it, but not too black for that mysterious rider to find the way in through its unguarded opening.

The thought brought its cold stir of air curling round him; and out of this pulsating nightmare of silence came the sibilant whisper of cloth brushing cloth.

Bender's heart started pounding and the stillness piled up and churned tighter and tighter. Like a lantern slide thrown on a sheet by projection he saw Toby Bronsen's white face as it had looked in that awful moment before buckling knees had dropped his dead flesh in the yellow dust. And then, through remembrance, through the brittle quiet of nerves stretched taut and the ghastly run of the dragging minutes, he caught the stealthy creep of movement.

No sound to put a name to. No scratch, no thump, no scrape or rustle. Not even enough to hold a hint of direction —a conviction rather. A presentiment of motion.

Bender held himself rigid, the sweat pouring out of him.

He couldn't maintain this position much longer. A muscle twitched in his jaw. His back felt as though it must snap any moment.

He put up his left hand to get hold of the matches. But a deep and hard-bought knowledge of danger warned him not to pull them out of the band. The rasp of their sticks against the felt of his hat would be all the sound needed to send hammers against cartridges. He pushed the hand higher and, with

infinite patience, worked the hat off his head and braced
s body to toss it.

He was like that, waiting in the stance of Discobolus, when
knuckles rapped loudly against the front door.

Muzzle light leaped across the blackness in front of him and
Bender, clapping on his hat, ripped a slug through it frantically and struck the floor, rolling, as another sixgun loosed a
livid flash from the left. He felt the shock of the bullets tearing through the thin planking. Somewhere in the pounding din
a man's lifted scream dropped away to a gurgle. The ex-
plosions' pulsations beat against the walls like sledges and he
fired three more times and jumped erect, coldly waiting
through that swirling stench of powder to throw in a final shot.

Lasham's cracked voice groaned, "I've got enough. Don't
fire—I'll throw my gun down."

Bender heard it thump the floor. He neither spoke nor
moved, just waited.

"I—I'll strike a light," Deef Lasham quavered.

A match flared in the sheep king's fist. His monstrous
shadow climbed the walls. Bender's glance flicked once to
Blanca's face then watched the fat man light a lamp and, when
its yellow glow spread round, saw the Yaqui's dead sprawled
shape six feet away and wondered how the man had passed
him. Not that it much mattered.

Weariness bowed his shoulders and reaction was like a cold
lump in his belly. He looked at the cowering hulk that was
Lasham and all he could feel was a tired contempt.

He dropped the gun in his holster. Gagged and lashed in a
chair by the splintered desk Blanca's eyes were like crazy.
Like usual, he reckoned, she was bursting to get in her two-
bits worth of talk and having a hemorrhage because he didn't
move faster.

He threw a glance round the room, noting the blanket
covered windows, the blanket-draped chair in the room's far
right corner, the dead Indian, the gross bulk of Deef Lasham
standing back of the desk.

There was something about the man's shaved-hog features
which seemed not quite in keeping with his air of resigned

deflation. But when he looked for and found the sheep kɪ
dropped pistol, shoved it off to one side and hazed him ba
from the desk, Bender felt free to give his mind to the giɪ

Now the danger was over he could think of Blanca morє
dispassionately and was able to persuade himself it was
probably just as well she hadn't guessed his true feelings.
They'd been too differently reared—would have clashed every
whipstitch. Bound to. They were opposites in everything,
with the additional barriers of race and temperament. Mexican
and Texican. The two just didn't go together.

Smothering a sigh he shook his head and moved toward her.

Her eyes wigwagged at him with frantic desperation; but it
was the glint he caught in Lasham's that wheeled him just as
gun's thunder jumped the flame of the lamp up. A second shot
crowded it so close as to be inseparable, and Chesseldine staggered from behind the draped chair, spun half around and
folded.

Stroad in his sockfeet, with a gun in his hand and a badge
on the front of his blood-stained shirt, came out of that dark
back room, toughly grinning.

Bender understood then. "Lasham's pet marshal!" he said,
and passed out.

WHEN he opened his eyes he found his head in Blanca's lap
and her white frightened face bending over his own. "Don't
die—please don't die," she said and Stroad, inelegantly, back
of them snorted.

"Never heard of anyone dyin' yet from a .44 slug goin'
through the wrong shoulder—that Art was a helluva shot," he
said critically. He came around and looked down. "Just hold
the bandage right where I put it till the doc gits back—that
was him you folks heard knockin'. He'll be round soon's he's
satisfied the fireworks is over."

Bender said, "Where's Lasham?" and in the same breath
allowed he felt able to sit up, but the marshal opined he'd
better let well enough alone.

"You're in good hands," he winked, "and I've got that fine
sheepman all taken care of. I'd already had me a talk with

nsen that mornin' afore he got knocked off; so when
sham come along, figurin' to buy himself a lawman, I acted
he underpaid public servant an' let him talk me into pushin'
you west'ard."

Stroad grinned. "Figured if I give the old goat enough rope
he'd save me a lot of trouble, an' he did. There's one thing
about crooks—they ain't never so slick as they make their-
selfs out to be.

"I hear the doc comin', so I'll let you tell Miz Blanca what
it was them birds was after. She knows about her Dad an'
about Gonzales savin' the cattle. Hazel's dead an'—he was
another rotten shot!—Cash Fentress will live to learn the error
of his ways. I got that confession. Likewise a bankroll; so
don't either of you get to frettin' about that note. I'll see it's
taken care of an', by this time tomorrer, I'll have them sheep
an' Lasham well on the way to Texas where that bustard will
be lucky if he don't git his neck broke. I'll be sayin' goodbye
now—you take care of that young lady."

Bender sighed and Blanca looked at him anxiously. He
could see she had been crying—probably worked up over her
father. Not knowing what else there was he could say, he told
her about Tres Pinos, about that pond in the valley he'd found
at the foot of the precipice. "There's oil under there. That's
what Lasham was after. You won't have to be worryin' about
payin' your hands off, or the cost of more range or anything
else now. You'll be richer than Croesus—"

"No!" Blanca said. "That land is yours. My father gave it
to you."

"That deal was called off—"

"By you, perhaps. Never by us. When we give to someone
something we do not take it back—ever." She turned her
face away stubbornly. "Do not anger my father's memory.
The land is yours."

"Very well," Bender said. "But after we get married—"

The change in her face was amazing.

"Oh—*querido!*" she cried and Stroad, softly chuckling,
tramped down the steps and departed.

Nelson Nye was born in Chicago, Illinois. He was educated in schools in Ohio and Massachusetts and attended the Cincinnati Art Academy. His early journalism experience was writing publicity releases and book reviews for the *Cincinnati Times-Star* and the *Buffalo Evening News*. In 1935 he began working as a ranch hand in Texas and California and became an expert on breeding quarter horses on his own ranch outside Tucson, Arizona. Much of this love for horses can be found in exceptional novels such as *Wild Horse Shorty* and *Blood of Kings*. He published his first Western short story in *Thrilling Western* and his first novel in 1936. He continued from then on to write prolifically, both under his own name and the bylines Drake C. Denver and Clem Colt. During the Second World War, he served with the U. S. Army Field Artillery. From 1949 to 1952, he worked as horse editor for *Texas Livestock Journal*. He was one of the founding members of the Western Writers of America in 1953 and served twice as its president. His first Golden Spur Award from the Western Writers of America came to him for best Western reviewer and critic in 1954. From 1958 to 1962, he was frontier fiction reviewer for the *New York Times Book Review*. His second Golden Spur came for his novel *Long Run*. His virtues as an author of Western fiction include a tremendous sense of authenticity, an ability to keep the pace of a story from ever lagging, and a fecund inventiveness for plot twists and situations. Some of his finest novels have had off-trail protagonists such as *The Barber Of Tubac,* and both *Not Grass Alone* and *Strawberry Roan* are notable for their outstanding female characters. His books have sold over 50,000,000 copies worldwide and have been translated into the principal European languages. The *Los Angeles Times* once praised him for his "marvelous lingo, salty humor, and real characters." Above all, a Nye Western possesses a vital energy that is both propulsive and persuasive.